Books by Ned Calmer

BEYOND THE STREET

WHEN NIGHT DESCENDS

THE STRANGE LAND

ALL THE SUMMER DAYS

THE ANCHORMAN

THE ANCHORMAN

The ANCHORMAN

NED CALMER

DOUBLEDAY & COMPANY, INC., GARDEN CITY, NEW YORK

1970

Library of Congress Catalog Card Number 72-105615

Copyright © 1970 by Ned Calmer

For C. Edmonds Allen

AUTHOR'S NOTE

The people of this story come not from the real world of broadcasting, but from the truer world of the novelist. As such they are all imaginary, and all true.

CONTENTS

I: MAKING IT

1

It was quite a building. Bigger than the vast Hilton Hotel a few blocks
down Sixth Avenue where he'd dropped off his suitcase on the way
from the airport, ten times as big as the Boston building where he'd
worked for the past nine and a half years of his life. In the elevator
you couldn't even feel the motion' as it shot upward, only the
polished steel panel noiselessly clicking off the floor numbers gave a
bearing in space, and the music issuing faintly from hidden vents
around him echoed more of the unreality he'd felt since yesterday.
For a moment he had an odd sensation of both security and helpless-
ness, as though on entering this anonymous moving box you cut
yourself off for good from everything you'd known before and volun-
tarily surrendered all responsibility to the invisible forces behind its
smooth and subtle power. The other occupants stood silent, as if
awed. Then he was nudged onto the thirty-ninth floor by an impatient passenger behind him, and he saw Hedley Johns standing
three feet away waiting for a down car.

The celebrated commentator looked tired and older than he
looked on the TV screen. The lonely nose was high in the air and
the eyes were focused somewhere far away. The young man staring
at him suddenly wanted to put out his hand, but didn't, and the
moment was lost. An elevator door opened and Hedley Johns moved
on.

A receptionist who evidently had her instructions led Lloyd Garner
through a noise of teleprinters and typewriters that he seemed
strangely to be hearing for the first time and left him in a cubicle
office with a staggering view of Manhattan. He was numbly looking out the window when a voice behind him drawled, "Coffee or
whatever?"

The voice was standing in the doorway, tall and slightly bloated and possibly twenty-eight, the accent matched the upper-class tailoring and the expression of permanent boredom. He added, with a trace of smile, "It's free."

"I'll skip it, thanks just the same."

The young man showed no disposition to be on his way. "New?" he said.

"Brand new."

He nodded. "This your office?"

"That's what the girl just told me."

"Then I'm your regular office boy. If you need anything—"

This was an office boy? Lloyd smiled watching him go. He wished he owned a suit like that. He was opening the drawers of his desk for want of something better to do when he had another visitor, this time a slender blond man somewhere in his forties. "Lloyd Garner, isn't it?" He offered his hand. "I'm Drew Stimson, I heard you were moving in today and I thought you might be free to have lunch. Or will you be going out with the brass?"

"The brass?" He laughed. "All I know is I'm supposed to meet Mr. Schonwald at three o'clock."

"Shall we?" said Drew Stimson. *His* clothes looked pretty good too.

"I think it's a fine idea."

They took the same car down that Hedley Johns had taken. For Lloyd there was a trace of his aura still in the air. "I saw Hedley Johns going out when I was coming in. I had an impulse to speak to him, but I thought I'd better not."

"He would have been pleased," Drew Stimson said and added with his easy smile, "I saw you talking to Bev."

"Bev?"

"Beveridge G. T. Hambleton the Fourth, our office assistant, as he's officially called."

"He looks like a character."

"We're all characters in this business, don't you think?"

Who was Drew Stimson, anyway? Not another office boy. "I guess I should know your name," Lloyd said, "but I don't."

"I'm not a broadcaster. I'm in the research end. Let's walk over to the Brasserie, it's a nice day."

The Brasserie was the kind of restaurant Boston didn't have and never would have. Europe must be like this. Drew Stimson introduced him to *choucroute garnie* and they drank delicious Alsatian beer. The quiet voice opposite was saying, "You're sort of a mystery man, you see. Everybody's curious about what you're going to do."

"I don't know myself," said Lloyd. "Honest I don't. All they told me in Boston was I was hired and to get down here as soon as I could. Who's Schonwald?"

"He produces the Hedley Johns show."

Lloyd showed his elation. "Maybe that means I'll be working for Schonwald."

"Maybe it does." The warm smile again, inviting friendly confidence. "Had you been angling for a job very long?"

He shook his head. "The funny part of it is they called me up right out of the blue. I didn't know anybody in New York even knew about me. I'd been doing radio mostly and filling in occasionally on our evening TV show. Then Milo Wilson—do you know him?—he came up to Boston last week to see me and we settled it in five minutes over a drink."

"Interesting," Drew Stimson said. He suggested the cheesecake and they split a third bottle of the beer. It was the best cheesecake Lloyd Garner had ever tasted.

"I'm still sort of stunned, if you know what I mean," he said between mouthfuls. "I can't quite believe yet it's happening. Like I've been walking around in a sort of a dream today."

Drew Stimson understood. "And Wilson didn't tell you how it all came about?"

"Listen," Lloyd smiled, "I wasn't asking him any questions. He offered me a network broadcasting job and I took it before he could change his mind. He said we'd work out the details in New York. That was fine with me."

"I know just how you feel," Drew Stimson said. He took the check.

Walking back down Park Avenue in the dazzling sunshine they met Bev, the office boy. He was just going into the Racquet & Tennis and he gave them a little smile.

"What's that place?" said Lloyd.

"It's a club."

Miss Valenti was still sitting in the little office when Lloyd Garner came back from his meetings with Buck Schonwald and Mr. Pollitt of the business department, which was on another floor. It had been a long, exciting afternoon and everything was wrapped up. "Hello, Mr. Garner," she said in her calm fashion and stood up beside her desk.

He looked at his watch. "It's after six."

"I know." She had a low, nice voice.

"Don't they let you people go home at a decent hour?"

"It's your first day," she said. "I didn't know if you might need me."

"What I really need is a stiff drink, Miss Valenti."

"That sounds perfectly reasonable. And by the way, since I'm going to be your secretary for the foreseeable future, I'd feel more comfortable if you'd call me Rita, Mr. Garner."

"That sounds perfectly reasonable." He mimicked her tone a little. "Do you always talk in that serious way?"

"I'm a serious girl."

Not a girl, not any longer. She was his age or older, possibly even thirty-three or thirty-four, nearly as tall as he was, black-haired and white-skinned and handsomely Italian, with long shapely legs and breasts almost as big as Fran's but obviously a lot firmer. He looked at her, smiling. "Where do they drink around here, Rita?"

"All kinds of places. What kind of a place do you like?"

"A place where they have bourbon whisky and little bottles of club soda." He hesitated and then added, "Will you lead the way to it?"

Her slow smile. "If you'd really like me to, I will."

"Why shouldn't I really like you to?"

"Well, I've heard Bostonians are very polite."

"Not that polite. Let's go, I'm thirsty."

The offices along the main hall were empty and darkening. The only activity apparent now came from behind them at the far end,

a distant confused clashing of voices and machines. He said to her,
"I like that sound."

"The newsroom? I'm so used to it I don't notice."

"You've been around awhile, eh?"

"Awhile."

"Is that why they assigned you to me?"

"Possibly."

"You're the breaker-inner."

"I'm versatile."

It was a medium-sized slightly shabby place with medium-bright
lighting a block away from the office, a busy bar as you came in
and tables in semi-alcoves at the back. The bartender looked up and
nodded at Rita Valenti. About half the tables were occupied.

"Would you like to sit at the bar, Mr. Garner? Or the tables
are less conspicuous."

"Less conspicuous?"

"It's better for you not to be seen drinking with a secretary. Of
course you can do as you please."

They were smiling at each other. "If you think I'm that important,
let's try a table."

She joined him in a bourbon and soda. "Anyway," she added,
"the network people rarely come in here. You'll be seeing all the
chic joints with the brass."

"I like it here." He glanced around and raised his glass. "Cheers,
Rita."

"Cheers, Mr. Garner."

The whisky buzzed pleasantly in his head and he felt the tensions
of the day begin to fall away from him. "That's better," he said.

"Of course it is." Her voice as she watched him had a soothing
quality he hadn't noticed before. "Tomorrow," she went on, as if
remembering something she had meant to tell him, "I'm having a
TV monitor put in across from your desk and we'll order some paper
with your name on it. Do you have any idea what hours you'd
like me to keep—what time you'll be working?"

"Well, the first few days I'll just be looking around. Schonwald
wants me to get acquainted with the plant."

"Why don't I come in at nine-thirty to start with? Nobody ever gets in till after ten, except for big fresh-breaking stories, of course."

"You talk like an old newshand, Rita."

"I told you, I've been around awhile."

"I'm going to need you to fill me in on a lot of things, so I won't look like too much of a yokel."

"You look all right," she said.

"Thanks, but up there it's a lot different from where I've been working."

"Really so different?"

"Lady, I was bogged down in a hick operation so long I gave up hoping I'd ever get out of it." Something crossed his mind like a shadow. "Will you promise not to run away while I phone?"

"I promise," she said.

He ordered two more drinks and went to the booth next to the door marked with a top hat and cane. He put a handful of change down on the ledge beside the phone, gave the number, deposited the coins and waited, hearing it ring seven times before Fran answered. He knew from the sullen sound of her hello that she was already over the hill. Immediately it spoiled everything.

"If you don't recognize my voice," he said harshly, "this is your husband."

"I recognize it," she said. She sounded much farther away than Boston.

"It took you so long to answer I thought there was nobody home. Were you on the john or something?"

"I guess I fell asleep," she said. "What time is it?"

"Too early to fall asleep. I'm in New York, Fran."

"I know that," she said and was silent again.

"Do you want to hear about it or don't you care?"

"Why you say that? Course I want to hear about it."

"You're stumbling," he said.

"Oh, for Chrissake, Lloyd."

"Look, I'll keep you just a minute, then you can go back to sleep again, okay?"

"I'm not going back to sleep again."

"Not before you've had another slug, you mean. Goddamn it, Fran, did you have to get drunk *today?*"

"What are you talking about?" she slurred. "I'm not drunk."

"All right, this is what I have to tell you. I've signed a contract and the job is all set."

There was a silence. Finally she said, as if with effort, "Well, great."

"I'll accept that as your final word. Now, listen carefully and try to remember it when you wake up again. I telephoned. I'm at the New York Hilton. I'll call you again tomorrow and we'll make some plans, right?"

"Right," she said.

"And for God's sake lay off the sauce!"

He went back to the table fighting down his anger and disappointment. He had wanted it to be a happy call. He had wanted her to laugh with him and then call Harvey and Stan and maybe some others at the station and tell them what Lloyd had pulled off in New York. Rita Valenti was smiling up at him and he tried to smile back. "That was the final business of the day," he said and gulped down half his bourbon. "Now we can relax."

"Boston?" she said.

"Yes, Boston."

"Your wife?"

"Yes, my wife."

"I'll bet she's feeling pleased right now."

"I'll bet," he said. "Rita, have you ever been married?"

She nodded half amusedly without speaking.

"To Mr. Valenti?"

"No, that's my father's name. My father was a *nice* man."

For a momemt he wished he could have said the same about his own father. Then he turned to motion to the waiter for another round and said to Rita Valenti, "Shall we change the subject?"

Waking, his head throbbing slightly and the taste of the Italian food and wine all through his body, he tried to remember where he was and then remembered. The bed was wide and long and warm and he had the impression of a high ceiling in a big

room. He stirred and turned, reaching to touch her with his finger-
tips. She lay on her back, her legs flat out and wide apart, her head
half buried with its burden of thick, soft hair in the pillow, her
body long and warm like the bed, her soft breathing redolent of
garlic and Chianti. "Hello, Mr. Garner," she said in her low voice
in the dark.

"I didn't mean to wake you."

"You didn't wake me."

He dropped his arm across her breasts, they were as hard and
smooth as marble. He kissed her cheek. "You've been good to me.
More than that."

"You were good to me too." She gave a little mock shudder that
went through her whole body. "Were you ever," she said, and
stretched luxuriously.

"I don't remember too well." He was talking with his mouth
against her throat. "We had a lot to drink."

"Just enough. You liked my little wop restaurant too."

"I just hope I can find it again. Where is it? In Greenwich
Village somewhere?"

"It's just around the corner from where you are now, Mr. Garner."
He could feel her smile in the dark. "Anyway, you've got to admit
this is better than sleeping all by yourself in the Hilton."

"I admit everything. I also want you to know I like you. I
like you very much."

"You made me know it," she said. And after a moment, "Do you
want to know something else, Mr. Garner?"

"Anything."

"You're not old enough to make love as well as you did to me."

"It was you, not me. Besides, how old do you have to be to make
love well?"

"Fifty, usually."

"You know so much," he said.

"You'll find out someday."

"I thought the old guys slowed up."

"Fifty isn't old, Mr. Garner. You're showing your ignorance."

"I've got a lot to learn."

"Some guys never slow up. Not till the day they die."

"You know so much."

"You'll find out. You're just a child. You've hardly started to live."

"Just tell me one thing. How could Mr. Valenti give you up?"

"I gave Mr. Valenti up."

"Was he with the network?"

Her smile again. "Nothing like it."

"You know," he said after a silence, "I got kind of a thrill being up there today. The big-time atmosphere. The conferences and all."

"They were taking you, Mr. Garner."

He raised his head. "Come again?"

"They take everybody new. Did you sign a contract today?"

"That's right."

"Was your agent with you?"

"My agent? I have no agent."

Her voice was soft. "That's course for the par. What are you going to do for them?"

"Do? General assignment. Spots on the Johns show. Some traveling, I think. I don't care. I'm in no hurry, now."

"You should care, Mr. Garner. You'll learn to care. I have a feeling about you and the network."

"What kind of a feeling?"

"Like they've got something up their sleeve about you."

"Like what?"

He felt her breasts rise under his arm as she drew a breath. "I don't know. You'll have to wait on that one. It's just the way they're doing this, somehow. Drew Stimson . . ."

"What about Drew Stimson?"

"I saw him sniffing around today. He doesn't interest himself in just anybody. The little sneak."

"We had lunch together. I like him."

"That's what he wanted you to do. He was trying to find out something. So he could run and tell somebody."

"Lots of luck," he said. "I didn't know anything."

"He could find out a lot just by looking at you and listening to you."

"Yes? What?"

"That you're somebody, and they've discovered it, and they're making plans."

He laughed and kissed her. She was exaggerating, of course, but it sounded good. In the silence she was caressing his body. "And what did *you* find out just by looking and listening?" he said.

"That you're a beautiful man who doesn't look like anybody else, with a smile that suddenly lights up the world. That you have a beautiful voice that doesn't sound like anybody else's. And that you were going to ask me to show you a place where we could have a drink together."

He lay there like a sultan, his hands clasped behind his head, while she touched him lightly and slowly. From outside the sounds of summer in the Village intimately entered the room. He was in New York. This was the big time. He was making it.

2

Several times that first week, remembering his small-hours talk with Rita, he tried to find out from Buck Schonwald just what his long-term work was going to be. The responses were vague and joshing, teacher to pupil, "Take it easy, fellow, time enough to discuss it after you look around a little, don't you like it here? Okay, so don't come on so strong, not yet awhile, right?" He also determined to get a professional agent's opinion of his contract but decided to wait until he knew a good professional agent. Twice he was on the point of dropping in on Drew Stimson and asking him for a name, but again he recalled Rita's comment on Drew Stimson and let it ride. It had sounded pretty wonderful when they talked about it in Pollitt's office and he put his signature on it—three hundred a week to start, with a raise of a hundred a week each year for five years. The contract was binding on him for the full five years, but the company had the right to cancel with a month's notice before the end of each year. They assured him that was in all the network's contracts. They also said they would pay his hotel and eating expenses for a month while he got settled in an apartment, but later Schonwald told him not to hurry it on the apartment, he might be doing some traveling before he settled down in New York. At worst, the deal was better than his wildest dreams in Boston, New York was exciting and glamorous and still untried. He told Fran not to plan to join him until he knew more about his immediate future. Meanwhile he would send her money regularly and get up to Boston when he could, he was not certain just when that would be. He suggested she get Grace Cassidy to move in with her and keep her company, Grace Cassidy being a good influence and his brother Phil, faithful Phil, being nearby to keep an eye on them both. But Fran would come down and do the town with him when he got

to know his way around a little better. He would check in by
phone each evening and give her a report on developments.

Developments right now were meeting the people in the newsroom mornings and watching Schonwald's staff put together the
Hedley Johns show afternoons. The basic routine he knew from
his own experience, but there was no real comparison with the
Boston operation; everything was bigger, faster, more efficient here,
from the moment the bulletin bell rang on a teleprinter to the
ultimate airing of the story with the backing of a world organization
of correspondents and the resources of a technical pool unsurpassed
anywhere. Writers, editors, reporter-contact men went into action,
film crews were called out at the nerve centers of reaction at home
and overseas, the research staff and film library were on the job in
minutes. The labs were ready when the story came through in
visual form, rushed from the airport by couriers to be developed and
passed on to the network news complex in midtown. Sometimes
a mobile lab was standing by for the plane to save the time of
transit across the city. Lloyd sat in with film cutters in the pro-
jection rooms, accompanied crews of reporters and cameramen on
New York area stories of interest to the network, watched each
aspect of the day's general coverage as it took shape all over the
country and abroad. But the real thrill was the Hedley Johns operation, the model for them all.

Johns himself was curiously aloof from it. He rarely left his
glass-enclosed office adjoining both the big news studio and the newsroom until a few minutes before air, questions of editorial content
were ironed out with Schonwald in presence usually of the chief
editor, Earl Greminger, and Lloyd met him only once, much like
a college student being introduced on a conducted tour, the great
man's handshake was no more than that. The staff seemed to
regard Johns with a mixture of awe and reverence. Especially
reverential was Harry Ferguson, the chief writer, a solemn man of
forty-odd who appeared to have Hedley's personal confidence and
sometimes was consulted directly on the copy. Beside Ferguson's
typewriter stood a framed quotation from Walter Lippmann that
read: *The news of the day is an incredible medley of fact, propaganda, rumor, suspicion, clues, hopes, and fears, and the task of*

selecting and ordering that news is one of the truly sacred and priestly offices in a democracy. The power to determine each day what shall seem important and what shall be neglected is a power unlike any that has been exercised since the Pope lost his hold on the secular mind.

Beyond the newsroom, surrounding it, cradling it, lay the outer world of technicians and clericals, of laboratories and expediters, each sector with its drones and gadflies, working at long desks under strange blue lights or hurrying down the network of endless corridors on their missions, all feeding ultimately to the TV screen. A closed world of feature producers and their staffs, some of them with projects scheduled a year ahead, of film and tape editors, directors and assistant directors, crowded in tiny rooms, no names on the doors, around machines that flashed or barked or quacked like Donald Duck, an array of electronic equipment specialized and sophisticated beyond understanding. These were the people who did the groundwork, they were multiple and anonymous, it was all you knew about them and all you dared to know. Their quarters, rarely visited by outsiders, looked like the control rooms of spaceships in science fiction drama and they talked a language from another planet, their messengers dressed like astronauts and roared through the city on motorcycles, helmeted and grim. And something else set these technicians apart. They had strong, belligerent and feared unions, you couldn't move a studio chair or touch a piece of apparatus without risking a strike or slowdown. On the editorial side, as Lloyd observed, a kind of intellectual elite moved in their own special sphere, a different breed entirely, and of these the brightest satellites decorated Hedley Johns's evening news strip, the network showpiece.

With Greminger and sometimes Schonwald as well, Ferguson put together the daily story line-up at a conference in early afternoon, then assigned to his three assistants the writing and research chores involved and the fitting of narrative text to news film where needed. By air time, the major part of the program and the opening and closing headline summaries had been written or rewritten by Ferguson himself. Everybody, from the control-room staff to the grips on the studio set, was good-naturedly tolerant of Lloyd; he kept out of the way and was particularly careful during the last hour before air when tensions were high. But he could say he was there, on the scene, "working with" a famous guy who had in turn worked with guys like Kaltenborn and Murrow and Elmer Davis back in the days when there was no TV, only radio, and he could tell Fran in his evening report, "You'll meet Hedley when you come to New York," implying the first-name basis.

Johns was one of the few big names to have made the transition from radio to TV successfully, like starting a brand-new career. For radio now was the weak sister, the obsolescent medium, and everybody got out of it if they could. Daily, Lloyd saw the network radio news staff grinding out their predigested crap from AP and UPI for the regular summaries, crouched over typewriters in their own humble corner of the newsroom. He found no difficulty sharing the contempt of his TV colleagues for radio's inferior status. He for one was never going back to radio as long as a camera was handy, never again. So far, he'd made no appearance on the network screen. Schonwald sent him to cover the hip scene in the Village, as well as assigning him to several documentaries, but he was just an observer. He found the network reporters affable but guarded, over drinks or a meal they tended to question him about his background and seemed mainly interested in fixing his status. They obviously didn't believe him when he said they knew as much about it as he did. Among themselves they spoke with respect of Buck Schonwald but had little for Walter Hacklin, the titular head for News who rarely showed up at the actual operation and had greeted Lloyd Garner only once, with a hearty handshake and a closed face. The reporters made reference occasionally and always carefully to the big boss on the floor above and the close check he kept on his favorite network department with a regular evening call to Hacklin, but Lloyd hadn't yet laid eyes on him. He took the cue and asked no questions.

What he really needed was a chum he could talk to, somebody like Harvey Lewin back in Boston who shared his life with you without reservation, but he figured that would come in due course, maybe somebody he hadn't even met yet. An early possibility had been Drew Stimson, but there were no more invitations to lunch

although always that big smile in the hall. Twice Lloyd had
seen him with Hedley Johns in the street outside the building, but
otherwise Stimson had no apparent pals in News and his research
unit was quiet and a little forbidding. Beveridge Hambleton the
Fourth on the other hand, for all his aristocratic background, was
open and friendly, in fact he took Lloyd to the Racquet & Tennis
for lunch, a great occasion, and in return Lloyd took him to 21 for
drinks, another great occasion. Standing at the bar, money in his
pocket and a new sports jacket on his back, Lloyd ventured to ask
him for the name of his tailor. He went there the next morning, a
somber upstairs place off Fifth Avenue which surprised him with
its simplicity, and ordered two suits while Bev stood by offering
advice. It occurred to him only afterward that one reason Bev was
glad to do it was to bolster his own battered credit standing with the
tailor. Later Bev brought him coffee as usual.

The evenings might have been lonesome if there hadn't been
Rita Valenti. He really wasn't seeing much of his room at the
Hilton, only to change a shirt or make his call to Boston, where the
domestic situation appeared quiet. Rita's place was an oasis after a
crowded day. First, steamed mussels or gnocchi or piccata di vitello
in the Italian restaurant, then espresso in one of the coffeehouses,
then the big high-ceilinged room with books lining all of one
wall, a kitchenette in the alcove and a huge bathroom where everything wheezed, creaked or cascaded like Niagara, with Rita's bras
and panties and stockings lined up on the shower rail. Making love
with Rita was relaxed, happy and, as he realized, educational.
Without sacrificing any of her intensity she always knew what she
was doing. She was the first woman he had ever had who made
love to him as much as he made love to her. Afterward, naked,
they sipped Vecchia Romagna and talked. He couldn't understand
why Rita Valenti didn't want her life to continue this way forever.

"I want to live in Europe, Mr. Garner, that's why."

"Suppose you get there and it isn't right."

"I've been there. I take my vacations there."

He smiled. "Alone?"

"Sometimes."

"You mean you go with another gal?"

"That's the last thing I'd do. That's no way to go to Europe."

"And when you went alone, you met people?"

"Sometimes." Lying on her side, facing him in the easy chair opposite, she looked like a Renaissance painting.

"Where do you like it best?"

"Rome, and some Italian hill places."

"Not Paris?"

"Well, it's beautiful, but it doesn't get to me right away, like Italy. It would take some knowing. I haven't been there long enough, I guess."

"You'd miss New York."

She shook her head and reached to sip the brandy. "Not for a minute."

"New York would miss you."

"That's sweet. Come over here and give me a kiss, Mr. Garner, and tell me about yourself."

He laughed and got up and kissed her, sitting on the edge of the bed with his arm around her. "Come on, you're in that office all day."

"What does Buck tell you?"

"Nothing, as usual. Everything is working out fine. I'm going away somewhere soon. Oh yes. He said today, you know how he looks at you with half-closed eyes, is Rita taking good care of you?" He looked down at her, waiting for a response.

"That's our Buck," is all she said.

"Is he—an intimate friend?"

"He has been."

"And other guys in the office?"

She was looking up at him calmly. "Yes."

"I see."

He turned his head away and she reached up with both hands and turned it back toward her. "Mr. Garner, darling," she said softly, "a very, very nice thing about us has been that you don't ask, and I don't tell. Don't you agree that that's a very nice thing?"

He said after a moment, "I guess so," and smiled.

"That's better. Now tell me where you're going for Buck."

"I wish I knew."

"Do you want me to tell you?"

He sat straight and stared down at her. "What?"

"I said do you want me to tell you?"

"Wait a minute, how the hell do *you* know?"

"Buck's secretary told me this afternoon."

He gripped her shoulders. "All right, Miss Valenti, spill it."

"You're hurting me. You don't know your own strength."

"Spill it."

"Washington."

"Washington! What's the job?"

She was smiling. "That's all I know, honest. Bonnie overheard him on the phone."

"You rat, why didn't you tell me right away?"

"And have you pestering me with questions all evening? I had something better in mind than that."

He grinned and relaxed. "So you did."

"And I was right, wasn't I?"

"Were you not, baby, were you not."

Schonwald called him in the next morning and told him about it. He was to follow the work of the Washington bureau just as he'd been doing in New York, duration of stay indefinite for the moment. "Am I going to get a chance to broadcast?" Lloyd said.

Buck Schonwald smiled his bland, benevolent smile. "Here we go again, I told you to take it easy, there's lots of time."

"I haven't been on the air since I left Boston."

"You'll have your chance." He got up from behind his desk and put a hand on his shoulder. "And keep it to yourself around here, fellow. Everything comes to him etcetera. Now go see your wife in Boston and tell her not to talk about it either. When there's anything further you'll hear about it, from me."

"Okay, Buck."

"One other thing. While you're in Washington we're going to set up a pilot taping, just you alone reading some news items off a Teleprompter, okay? We've never seen you actually reading some of our type of stuff. Then we'll have our speech expert give it a listen and you can have a little conference with her, Jo Ellison, a great girl."

"Speech expert?"

"You've got some regional traces, it's understandable. Mostly your a's, that's all I've really noticed. You see on the network we try to rub away anything regional, then the viewers like you better, you can see how they would, nothing to prejudice them. With your ear, you'll have no trouble getting rid of those a's, I've noticed an improvement even since you came to New York."

"That just may be true, I've always reacted like a chameleon."

"What did I tell you?" He seemed very pleased. "Well, that's it for now, Lloyd. Give me a call from Washington." He pressed a button and spoke into a box, "Tell Greminger to come in here, will you?" The interview was over, Schonwald was not going to say one more word about anything than he had already said. Just be a good boy and do what we tell you and don't ask any questions, that was still the message.

He walked back to his office highly satisfied with the world, avoiding the short cut across the newsroom. Bev Hambleton was standing at Rita's desk talking to her and Lloyd said to him, "Outside, son, we've got work to do." Then he closed the door and sat down at his desk and couldn't resist saying to his secretary, "Him too?"

"Don't be rude, Mr. Garner, just because you've got stars in your eyes."

He laughed. "Have I? Then I'm not leaving here till I look normal again." He told her what Schonwald had said and she was not in the least surprised by any of it.

"Remember?" she said. "I told you the first day. Do you want to talk to your wife now and tell her you're coming?"

It was raining hard when the plane landed at Logan. Coming out of the tunnel into the mean streets of the city, it looked dreary and sad, you could smell fall in the early evening air and lights were on in buildings and shops along the way. Odd how everything looked a little smaller than when he had left it, such a short time ago. The yakking cabdriver's Boston accent annoyed him. It was hard to focus again, and there was no joy in coming home.

The old elevator shook when he dropped his suitcase on the floor and pressed the button. As the car ground upward the whole building stank with its permanent odor of corned beef and cabbage, and a whiff of whisky fumes greeted him from the other side of the apartment door even before Fran opened it to his first ring. Some things didn't change.

"Hi, sweetie!" she was saying, in her best dress. She had a glass in one hand and a cigarette in the other but she managed to put her arms around him and give him a wet kiss on the cheek. Phil was standing in the middle of the room looking awkward and Grace Cassidy was sitting in the chair by the window, his old chair. She had a glass too. His brother seemed to think the occasion called for a handshake. Grace called, "I like your jacket!" Fran stood back and said, "Let's get a good look at you, why, I think you're thinner, Lloyd."

He put down his bag and said, "If this is a celebration, I want a drink too," and Phil said, almost apologetically, with a glance at Grace, "We all joined in, after all it's a special occasion, isn't it? I'm taking Grace out to dinner in a minute so you two can powwow, right, Grace?" He bustled into the kitchen for another glass.

"We had to have just one in honor of the great commentator," Grace said. "Washington, after all!"

Lloyd was smiling at his wife. "I wish I could take you with me, honey."

"Why, Lloyd, naturally not, you're just beginning with them," Fran said. Her voice seemed unnecessarily loud but she was quite sober, for a moment he thought all this might have been easier if she was drunk.

"We've watched the network every night, both shows," Phil said, handing him his drink, "but we haven't caught you yet." He shifted on his shabby shoes.

"No, I haven't been on yet."

In the silence Phil said, still nervous, "Well, Grace, old dear, let's go and leave these two." Old dear, his mother used to say that; Lloyd felt a quick stab of nostalgia.

Fran was saying, "I've got the biggest steak you ever saw, Lloyd, you hungry after the trip? I can put it right on."

"No hurry, honey." He watched Grace Cassidy lifting her big can out of the chair and crossing the room to the door while Phil got their raincoats out of the bedroom. "I don't have to come back tonight, you know," Grace said coyly, "if you and the madam would rather be alone."

"I have to go in the morning," Lloyd said, and Fran said, "She's got all her things here, Lloyd, she's been sleeping on the couch, so we'll look for you later, Grace."

"Sure?" Grace said.

"Definitely," Lloyd said. His brother stopped in the doorway after her and turned back, smiling his frightened smile.

"Well, Lloyd. Well, good luck if I don't see you."

"Do something for me? Call Harvey at the station tomorrow and tell him I didn't have time, I'll call him from Washington."

"He'll understand," said Phil.

They were gone. Fran said, "She's always had a thing for you, Lloyd. Like all the girls."

He laughed. "That'd work out fine. Phil likes you."

"Oh he does not."

"He'd marry you tomorrow."

"Oh, Lloyd."

He took her hand and they walked over and sat down on the couch. Would anybody marry her now? The large round blue eyes with the Irish smudge of black in them were veined with red and her skin was puffy and coarser. He might be thinner but Fran was getting heavier all the time. As though there wasn't a good reason for it. "How's New York?" she said more quietly, and he was ashamed to feel superior and sorry for her.

"Well, quite a lot of work, just getting used to it, but I'll survive." He smiled and squeezed her hand. "Been lonesome, honey?"

"It's different with you away, but I don't mind it too much. Grace and I *laugh* . . ."

"You been feeling okay?"

Her eyes flickered away. "Don't worry about me, Lloyd, I'm going to be fine."

"I talked tough a few times on the phone. I'm sorry."

She put her other hand over his hand. "Lloyd, that's all right, I know you get upset. I'm sorry too."

"It's only for your sake." *Frances Agnes Delaney Garner, the woman I'm married to, you're blowsy and scared and pitiful and something has to be done.* "You had any more insomnia, honey?"

"Oh no, Lloyd, I've been fine."

"Phil said he persuaded you to go to Stapleton, what did he have to say?"

She looked at him vaguely. "Nothing much, he gave me some pills." She was trying to change the subject now. "I didn't know how long you're staying or anything, or I could have asked Stan or Harvey to stop by maybe after dinner. I thought you might like to see—"

"I mean what did Stapleton say about the drinking?"

"Oh that." She laughed with some effort. "He said I ought to cut down, so I did." She stood up, making a joke of it. "Speaking of that, you need a refill yourself," and she started for the kitchen.

"Not right now. Sit down, Fran, let me say something, just while we're here alone, eh?" He caught her arm and went back to the sofa with her, noticing a recent cigarette burn in the cushion behind him, taking the glass out of her hands and putting it on the end table. "Try to tell me the truth," he said. "How many have you had today?"

"You mean drinks? Why, nothing, except one before you came and this one."

"Does Grace drink along with you?"

Her forced laugh. "You know she doesn't drink, Lloyd."

"Look"—he was trying to be patient, he was trying to be gentle— "look, Fran, I was hoping while I had to be away you'd make a special effort, I mean at least till I could come back and see about us, about the future, now that I have this new job—"

"You drink as much as I do," she said harshly. She jerked her arm away from his hand and lit another cigarette. "I don't need a lecture from you, Lloyd Garner."

"It isn't how much you drink, Fran, or how much I drink, haven't you figured that out by now? It isn't that at all. It's how much

can you take. And you can't take as much as you used to, it's
that simple." She was listening watchfully. "I mean, why?" he
was saying. "It can't be just because you're bored being alone, or
with Grace, you were drinking just as much before I went to
New York, when we were here together—"

"You like a drink," she said, "so do I, what's wrong with liking
a drink?" Her voice broke and the tears came, he tried to take
her in his arms but she pulled away again and turned her head
against the back of the sofa, the sobs shaking her body. "Oh,
Lloyd, I'm sorry, I'm *sorry*, can't we leave it at that and talk
about something else?" She let him take the cigarette out of her
hand and give her his handkerchief. "I wanted you to have a
nice homecoming and now it's all spoiled."

"Nothing's spoiled, honey." And he wondered if she knew now
as he did that maybe there was nothing much left to spoil anyway;
it was just the way it was. He would talk to Stapleton in the
morning without telling her and get his advice. "I'm sorry I made
you cry, I was only trying to help, you know that, don't you?"
She nodded, still sniffling. "Do you know what I'd like you to do
now? I'd like you to get us two fresh drinks and put that steak on.
I've been hungry for a decent home-cooked meal."

"I'll get you a drink but I don't want one," she said, "not
another drop."

He laughed and comforted her, "Don't be childish, I said two
drinks, if you don't have one I won't, but let's eat, shall we?"

She was sitting up and trying to smile, her face red and puffy,
the pouches under her eyes more pronounced. "You're a nice man,
and you've got a no-good wife."

"I'd put it the other way around," he said.

"No, it's true, I realize it."

He laughed. "Come on now, two drinks or nothing." When she
got up to go into the kitchen he patted her behind.

"That feels good, Lloyd. Remember when you used to say I had
the prettiest little ass in Boston? Not any more."

"It looks good to me."

She called from the kitchen. "You notice something? I splurged and bought Old Forester for tonight, it's a celebration. We can afford it now, can't we?"

"We certainly can."

His drink in his hand, he stood in the kitchen doorway and watched her doing something she knew how to do well, and he knew she would pour herself another drink and then another while she was cooking the meal. He knew that when the food was on the table in the little alcove she would make a pretense of eating something and then stop to pour another drink for herself and urge him to have another, holding out the bottle to him with slightly trembling hands. He would do the talking and she would ask no more questions, sometimes seeming not even to listen, and there would be no real talk about his job, or the future, or their future together, which was all he had on his mind. Once he tried to imagine what it would be like living in New York with Fran but he couldn't picture it. But already he knew, he had known since he walked back into this apartment tonight and saw Fran and Phil and Grace Cassidy waiting for him; he would never live here again or any place like it, he was through with people like Grace and Phil, he was past them. He was heading upward, he didn't know how far yet, but nothing, not even Fran, was going to get in the way.

"Steak's just right," he heard her say.

"Great."

He was feeling a little drunk now. They would both be sleepy early, but Fran wouldn't be too sleepy to want him to make love to her, and he knew he would manage to do it. Then he could sleep too.

3

It wasn't until the taxi stopped in front of network headquarters in Washington that Lloyd remembered he didn't even know who to contact there. Then he smiled and shrugged, the network would provide. He was in their hands, as usual. He regretted only that he hadn't had a chance to see Harvey Lewin in Boston. Alone of the station people he had worked with so long, Harvey was a pal. They had never neglected each other. As a link to the past, such as it was, Lloyd didn't want to lose Harvey Lewin. Looking back to the fun times, the laughs, Harvey was always in the picture, consolation for the routine drudgery that never changed, the escape to understanding and sympathy. One of these days he'd get Harvey a job in New York, that was it.

Now, swinging briskly through the glass doors, Lloyd Garner held his head high and looked around him with new eyes, with the feeling of holding the future in his own two hands. He gave the receptionist his name and she said immediately, "Hi, Mr. Garner, Mr. Thorpe's expecting you, he's the second office on the left, go right on in." The drawl reminded him he was in the South now, and why did her accent, the taxi driver's, the hotel people, all seem somehow familiar despite the fact he'd only been in Washington once in his life? Because maybe when you got past the solemn buildings, the red tape of the federal establishment, the people were as small-town as Boston, from the President down. The hall he was passing through smelled as provincial as Vermont. He glanced at the rows of pictures of the local broadcasting celebrities looking down at him and grinned; he'd been there before.

Hal Thorpe sounded Texan and looked it. Lloyd had heard of him every day during his stretch with the Hedley Johns show; he was in charge of the Washington news operation and Schonwald's daily telephone contact from New York. Thorpe rose to his considerable height and extended a big, rawboned hand across his desk. "You come down this morning, Lloyd? We'll have to find you a place to live."

"No, I'm all set, thanks, in the Statler, my secretary fixed it."

"Then we can get right down to business. Jerry Lacey's going to take you around, just sing out if you want to know anything special."

"Sounds fine." Gerald Lacey did occasional spots for the Johns show and Lloyd liked his work.

"Oh, and I'm setting up that taping for you in our studio here," Thorpe was saying, "will tomorrow suit?"

"Sounds fine."

"Buck sent your script down, you'll have plenty of time to look it over before we tape." He took Lloyd into the newsroom, Boston again, and left him with Lacey, young and red-haired with an easy smile. They went over the newsroom setup together, Lloyd aware of the curiosity he was arousing among the staff. With a little thrill he noticed an office door giving onto the room with a name on it, *Mr. Ward.* Kent Ward was the chief Washington correspondent for the network; Kent Ward was big time. "Well," Jerry Lacey said, "we might as well start at the top, shall we go over to the White House?"

Lacey had credentials for him, waved them at the gate and passed him through. Already, from their chat in the taxi, the chief pre-occupation of the President and practically everybody else in Washington had become apparent. Lloyd could feel it almost physically, an intangible ever-presence in the very air, the Vietnam War. Its invisible pressures were beating on the walls of this place like strong winds. For a moment Lloyd had an image of the lonely man in the middle who was getting in deeper every day and every night that passed and was powerless to help himself for all the power he had, or once had. Lacey was explaining as they went in that because of the President's impulsive decisions to call news conferences at any hour, the network's White House man, Tad Armbruster, had to live around the clock with his job. Armbruster, thin-faced and studi-ous, left a huddle of his colleagues to greet Lloyd cordially and show him around the executive offices with the casual informality of an old hand. He could not, he regretted, arrange a fixed meeting with the President, not these days, but stick around enough and a handshake could be achieved after one of those conferences.

"So I can tell my grandchildren?" Lloyd smiled. "Thanks, Tad, but don't let it worry you. Buck just wants me to get the feel or soak up the atmosphere or something like that."

Again the curiosity in the other's eyes, what are they going to do with this one? Lloyd was just leaving with Lacey when the short, round figure of Kent Ward blocked their way at the door. Ward acknowledged the passing introduction with a brief smile and then stopped and turned back to them. "Lloyd Garner," he said. "I know that name, but how and where?"

His look was as sharp as the famous voice. Lloyd said, "I'm flattered, Mr. Ward, but I couldn't say, unless you heard me or maybe saw me up in Boston."

"Boston. No, not Boston." Kent Ward was ruminating and Jerry Lacey was watching him with fascination. "So you're from Boston, are you? Somebody was saying something about you the other day, now, just what was it? Ah yes." He smiled suddenly. "You're the mystery man, Mr. Garner."

"Am I?"

The probing eyes were not unfriendly, Ward seemed amused at some private knowledge of his own. "Don't you know whether you are or not?"

"The mystery man? Maybe Buck Schonwald mentioned—" He remembered then that Drew Stimson had used the same phrase in New York.

Ward was still amused. "No, not Buck. You've been working with Buck, isn't that it?"

"That's it."

"And now you're with us for a bit?"

"So they tell me."

He nodded and then, whatever it was that tickled him, Kent Ward was dismissing it. He looked as if he had begun to think of something more important. "Have fun," he said, almost absent-mindedly, and went on past them. Jerry Lacey said at Lloyd's arm, "What about going over to the Hill next, both houses are in session today."

Jerry Lacey, like Tad Armbruster, wasn't asking any questions. Neither was Lloyd Garner.

Two cameras pointed at him in the darkened studio; behind them the cameramen stood alert and poised. Hal Thorpe was beside him at the desk, a raised table with a tiny monitor sunk in one side of it and a kind of lectern for his script. It was a routine script, at first glance just the news of any recent day thrown together, but Lloyd had noticed reading it over that the items were cleverly slected for contrast and change of mood. It was designed by a craftsman to give the reader full range. Nobody in Boston could have assembled it, that was sure.

"Whenever you're ready," Hal Thorpe said at his side.

"Any time," Lloyd said. Was this going to be the test on which final decisions were made? If it was, he was as ready as he ever would be, clothes, make-up, hair, voice and manner. There was also, and he was suddenly aware of it as the camera's red light winked on and he began to read from Teleprompter, the cumulative feeling of weeks of waiting. He had wondered last night, waking from the jumble of a troubled dream, whether he was going to be nervous about it. Now, hearing his own voice reverberate strong and serene around him, the buried anxieties of those weeks that had risen in his dream retreated to the back of his mind in a series of faint flashes and were gone with the sound of Fran's sobs, the dazzle of New York and Washington. Kent Ward's mystery man was doing the job he was made for and trained for, there was nothing mysterious about that. What he was doing was as natural to him as steady breathing. His hands held the script without a tremor as he glanced down from Teleprompter at just the right intervals. It all went well.

He knew it before he was halfway through, he knew it before he signed off and the lights went up and the "Tape okay" came through. Hal Thorpe came out of the control room beaming. "Yes," he said, and again, "Yes." Lloyd suddenly felt so tired he turned away to conceal it and drank from the glass of water on the table.

"We'll send this up to New York today," Thorpe was saying, with something in his voice Lloyd hadn't heard before. "You'll be hearing from Buck about it. And by the way, how about you come on over to the Press Club for lunch?"

"I'm willing," said Lloyd. He could use a drink.

For the first time, standing with Thorpe at the bar, he felt he belonged in the big time, had his finger on the pulse of it. These men around him in the long smoky room belonged. You could hear it in the wry, measured talk of the veterans, most of them years older than he was, in the no-bullshit stares and the cynical laughter. They knew the score all right, and more of it than they could tell. Thorpe introduced him to the Washington *Post* man standing at his right, who set down his glass, appraised him and spoke past him to Thorpe, "One of the recruits from New York, did you say, Hal? I thought he looked pretty smooth to be mingling with us bumpkins."

"He didn't get all his make-up off," Thorpe laughed.

"Before the cameras, were you? Garner was the name? I don't think I've seen you, but then I don't watch the TV much. I'm a holdout."

"You'll come around," said Thorpe.

"Any kin of Cactus Jack, down in Hal's home state?"

"Not that I know of, sir."

The *Post* man grinned. "Thank you for that sir, I just wondered if Hal here was pulling a little nepotism over at the studio. Have another drink, son."

"Thank you for that son," said Lloyd, "but I think I'll stay with this one."

Over lunch, though, he had another with Thorpe and listened to a salty recital of bureau problems. Schonwald, it seemed, came up with last-minute ideas for the show under the illusion that you could snag anybody in Washington for live comment on half an hour's notice. "There isn't a man on my staff can't tell the story better than some bumbling congressman anyway."

"I met Kent Ward at the White House yesterday," Lloyd said. "He called me a mystery man."

"The hell he did." Thorpe laughed. "But I reckon I can see why."

He was cutting carefully into his lamb chop. "You know," he said after a moment, studying the chop, "that audition you did this morning was good, Lloyd."

"Well, thanks, I mean I really appreciate that, from you."

"But that wasn't all, it was different. We do these things every so often, of course, but you, this one today had something extra, I guess I'd call it individuality, that's the hardest thing in the world to find."

"Thank you, Hal." He waited.

"New York doesn't tell me much, I don't know any more'n you do what they're going to assign you to, but I'll say this; I wouldn't turn you down for my shop, I would not."

"You think they have a job in mind for me here?"

He shook his head. "Nothing was said about it, nothing whatever."

The second bourbon was sitting well and Lloyd went ahead. "I'm disobeying Buck's instructions even talking about this, but I wish there wasn't this, sort of, secrecy involved. Like when Kent Ward acted like he knew things about me I didn't know. I'm getting a little fed up, not knowing anything. Would you blame me?"

The other man shook his head. "I don't think I would." He smiled and added, "Buck did ask me to keep it quiet while you're here, but I can see you're a pretty discreet young fellow, you won't need any help on that."

"Well then," sensing it was a friend talking, "off the record, Hal, what's up?"

Hal Thorpe leaned forward. "If I knew, I think I'd tell you, and the hell with that bunch in New York. But whatever it is, I don't think you have to worry about a thing, Lloyd, not from here on in."

It was entirely to Lloyd's surprise, four days later, that Kent Ward invited him to a cocktail party. He had barely seen Ward in the office after meeting him that first day and assumed he had been dismissed from Ward's mind as the mystery man he had joked about in a White House hallway and then forgotten. The invitation was characteristically abrupt and apparently only an impulse. They had met as both were leaving the building for the day and Ward said casually, "If you've nothing better to do, come along and have a drink with me."

"I'd like that very much."

At first he thought it would be the Press Club or the Metropolitan. He knew about the Metropolitan by now. But Ward drove him to his house in Georgetown. He would live there, Lloyd knew about Georgetown too. The house was small and elegant on a small, elegant street. A colored man in a white jacket opened the door to them and said, "Nobody arrived yet, Mr. Ward." So there were going to be others. The man served them a drink in the narrow book-lined living room that gave onto a little, lighted garden, still green and fresh beyond the glass doors. "Gee, this is a nice place," Lloyd said.

"Bought with the ill-gotten gains of electronic journalism," Kent Ward said. "I used to be a starving newspaperman, weren't you?"

"I can't claim that, practically all my working life has been in radio."

"You're the new breed, Garner."

"I guess I am, at that."

"A mysterious breed, to me."

Lloyd laughed. "Is that what you meant the other day in the White House?"

"Huh?" He remembered. "Not precisely, now that you mention it."

"I don't know what exactly you did mean," said Lloyd.

"Let's just say I'm amused sometimes the way the people who run this organization try to disguise their ultimate purposes, even before they've decided what their ultimate purposes are. Do I make myself clear? I doubt it." He smiled and moved up a chair. "Sit down, fellow entertainer." Ward lounged into a deep chair opposite. "Our leaders," he went on in his half-bantering tone, "are well-intentioned businessmen according to the lights of businessmen, which are not exactly altruistic, and if they were running a traditional kind of company they'd know how to proceed in a straightforward manner. The trouble is that after twenty years of it they still don't know how to deal with the problems of this tremendous machine they've got hold of, this monster, commercial television. So they duck and stall and prevaricate through situations they haven't learned to handle yet while they try to make up their minds. Oh, I sympathize, a little. There's never been anything like it before, this bastard offspring of corporate finance, show biz and, occasionally, when somebody remembers or feels embarrassed, public service. Only it's supposed to belong to everybody; it can't be owned, so it's more than just an advertising project dedicated to the profit motive for the benefit of the stockholders. So many other annoying elements are involved —the regulatory rights of government, the influence of the political parties, the church, the pressure groups—all demanding a share, everything pulling against everything else. It's not surprising that what comes out of it all is the lowest common denominator of compromise. Actually the company's position is much stronger than it thinks, or pretends to think, in terms of real power. But when the chips are down it always backs away. The byword is caution even when it hurts the till, and that's so un-American it's really surprising."

Lloyd listened, motionless. It was like listening to one of Kent Ward's pieces on the air. Ward grinned. "If I sound like I'm talking seriously, I probably am. Of course the News end of this extraordinary enterprise is just as much of a grab bag as the rest of the industry, and because of the unusual elements in its make-up, nothing functions smoothly. We've had a whole generation to do it in but we're still firming up the rules. We haven't even got a respectable morgue yet, we have to go to the newspapers for that. We're still growing so fast and so big we can't find enough suitable people, and the woods are full of attractive young men like yourself trying to fit themselves into this complex profession that requires a brand-new mixture of talents. Some of you should rightfully be reporters, but others would do better, much better, as actors, or teachers, or bank tellers, or barbers, or chasing ambulances." He smiled again. "But you all want the same thing. You want to be famous. You want to be loved."

The watchful colored man was serving them another drink. "I don't quite see myself cutting somebody's hair," Lloyd said.

Ward laughed. "I didn't have anyone in particular in mind. I'm just saying an original TV reporter, born and trained to the job of real news gathering, is about the rarest bird around, and yet network television now exerts so much influence it should be the main journalistic force in this country. Instead it's just a glamour factory turning out wire service headlines read off Teleprompters by pretty people who don't know a news story from a hole in the ground." He raised a hand. "No, don't let me exaggerate, it's not all as bad as that. There *are* some good people, when they're allowed to be. There *are* bright spots, by fits and starts. But the general run of coverage, I'm sorry to say, is entirely inadequate, and the outlook is not for much improvement."

He paused and sipped his drink. "God knows we've got models to work from. Ed Murrow, a really heroic figure, used TV news as it should be used. But there's no Ed Murrow around today, we're in the don't rock the boat era, and if you stay in network news, Garner, you're going to learn there are limits imposed on what you can say on the air. Some people try, take Hedley Johns for example. He believes with Mr. Justice Holmes," said Kent Ward, "that as life is action and passion, a man should share the passion and action of his time at peril of being judged not to have lived." He smiled. "Translating that, Hedley's constantly in trouble with the White House, the Pentagon, with the self-appointed censors in New York, including the sales department, the minute he says something that makes real sense of the situations these people want us to avoid. They don't want to suppress the news. Oh no, but they don't want it explained too much either, in a way that the little guy watching, when he bothers to watch, can make some sense of it for himself, for his own life, for the future of his family. Sure, they'll accept courageous reporting of an event, like a war or a race riot, but they want to see it presented in unrelated segments, in haphazard glimpses of the surface, so to speak, and they *don't* want you to go deeper and tie it into the total meaning. To ask, for instance, *why* the Vietnam War, or any war, especially if they fear the wrath of some archbishop, or some sponsor, or J. Edgar Hoover, for God's sake." His smile flashed. "They call this being fair to both sides. Garner, sometimes I find myself leaning so far over backwards to be fair to both sides that what I'm trying to say just gets lost. Of course I'm only a character part in this production, I've got more leeway. Hedley Johns is in a quite different position up there in New York—he's a star. They don't want Hedley to be a reporter, they want him to be a father figure. And I suspect he's going to have to choose one of these days between his conscience and his job."

They sat facing each other in silence. Lloyd felt the older man's appraising look on him again as he had at the White House, and he wondered how much of that long speech was intended personally for Lloyd Garner. But there was to be no time for questions. Suddenly there were people at the door, laughter and women's voices among others. Kent Ward sighed and stood up. "Well, back to the revels." He smiled and went to welcome his guests.

Everybody was arriving at once, in ten minutes the room was full. There might have been twenty-five people crowded into the small space, all of them seemed to be talking at the same time. Lloyd wished he could have been alone longer with Ward, there was so much he wanted to ask him, but like Lloyd, the host was trapped in the babble around him. There had been no time for introductions and he didn't recognize a single face. He just drifted from one conversation to another and listened to the Washington gossip for as much as he could make of it, which wasn't much. The colored man kept an eye on his needs; he was given a third drink, then a fourth, trying to follow the strands of talk but bewildered mostly until a slim-shouldered handsome woman with close-cut dark hair moved up to him through the crowd. She was very smartly dressed and held a cocktail in one bejeweled hand. "I don't know your name," she said abruptly, "mine's Alix Weddern."

"Lloyd Garner, Miss Weddern."

"Mrs. Weddern," she said, "but I'm divorced," and she added, "Are you?"

"Why, no, as a matter of fact."

"Not even once? You look like a man who's either had several wives or was smart enough never to get married."

"Give me time, Mrs. Weddern, I'm still young."

"Not that young." Her smile was insolent and he liked it. "I'll bet you're older than I am."

"Oh, that. I'm sure I am."

"How old am I?"

He looked at her, laughing. "I couldn't begin to guess, maybe twenty-five or six."

"You're lying, Lloyd Garner, we'll change the subject. Are you Washington or just dropping in? I know I haven't seen you anywhere."

"Just dropping in, I work in New York. How about yourself, Mrs. Weddern?"

"For heaven's sake call me Alix, I'm New York, too, mostly."

"And what do you work at?"

"Work?" She laughed. "Never did an hour's work in my life, not even in school, what could I do?"

"You could certainly model," he said.

"Can't, my ass is too big."

He laughed again and glanced at it. "Looks like just the right size to me, Alix."

"I like your laugh and I like your voice. Let me guess, you're in TV, along with Kent."

"I think I'm about to be," he said.

"You're overdue, Lloyd Garner."

"Just call me Lloyd."

She smiled and jiggled her almost empty glass. "Shall we try to find another drink?"

They found it and found themselves in the hall. "My very best to you." He raised his glass.

"I have to go back to the man I'm with or he'll object," said Alix Weddern. "Shall I see you in New York?"

"I think that's just a great idea."

"You and your wife come in for a cocktail."

"May I come alone?" he said.

"Sure. I'm in the book, the only one."

"You certainly are."

She laughed and pressed his arm and he watched her move back into the crowd. She was the world of station and success. In the moment, more than anything else, he wanted to belong to it.

The call came two days after Kent Ward's party. It was a Friday morning, Lloyd was to understand later why the call came on

Friday. Right now, picking up the phone in his hotel room just as he was about to go out the door, he knew the voice but couldn't place it immediately. "Lloyd Garner?" it rolled across the wire full of authority and assurance, "this is Walter Hacklin."

"Oh. Yes, sir."

"How's everything going, Lloyd?"

"Why, fine. Fine, thanks."

"I'm with Milo Wilson, Lloyd, you remember the man you talked with in Boston before you joined us?"

"Of course. Yes indeed."

"We'd like to have a word with you, could you make it right away?"

"Why, sure, just the time it'll take to fly up there, Mr. Hacklin, I ought to tell Hal Thorpe I—"

A suave chuckle interrupted. "No, we're in Washington, Lloyd, right here in the Statler, just got here, although you had no reason to know that. In fact the bureau doesn't know it and I don't want them to know it." The chuckle again. It sounded somehow mechanical. "If Thorpe finds out, I'll be stuck here the whole day with his problems, you can see that, and I have to get right back to New York."

"I can see that," Lloyd said. "Are you in the lobby?"

"In 1213, Lloyd, can you come down now?"

"I'll be right down, Mr. Hacklin."

"Oh, call me Walter, Lloyd, it saves time." He chuckled once more and hung up.

Room 1213 was the network's permanent suite in the Statler. Lloyd hadn't been in it but he'd heard it talked about. Going down in the elevator he looked at his watch and thought they must have taken a pretty early plane from New York, maybe a company plane. He also realized that if the vice-president in charge of News had come to Washington only to see him, then the wheels must be turning somewhere up above, and Kent Ward's words about network reasoning flashed through his mind. He didn't have time to think anything else. The door to 1213 stood open and Milo Wilson stood just inside, drinking a cup of coffee. Across the spacious green-gray room Hacklin was standing by the windows. For some reason the whole picture was unreal as a dream.

Milo Wilson said in his careful voice, "Come in, Lloyd," and Hacklin, heartily, "Like a cup of coffee?" He motioned to the portable table the waiter had left and Lloyd helped himself while they waited in silence. Then Hacklin smiled out of his moon face and pushed up a big period chair for him. The other two sat down on the long plush settee on the other side of the room. When Hacklin spoke his voice seemed to come from a long way off. "We have some other business to do before we go back, Lloyd, but I did want to see you while I was here."

Lloyd nodded, waiting, the coffee balanced on his knee.

"We've been very pleased by the way you've shaped up, Lloyd."

"Thank you."

"We think you're ready to do a job for us."

He ventured a smile. "I hope I won't disappoint you."

"We know you won't." Hacklin was doing all the talking. "That was evident from the tape you made, we saw it in New York. We think you're ready for exposure."

He wanted to say something, anything, but his mouth was dry.

"To be specific," Hacklin rolled on, "we have the Hedley Johns show in mind. It isn't set yet—I want to make clear that our talk today is just tentative, involving a possibility only, you understand, but we wanted to explore your willingness to do the job."

"What kind," he heard himself saying, "what kind of job would it be?"

"Anchorman, the Hedley Johns spot."

In the pause Lloyd waited for him to continue. The hand holding the coffee on his knee was trembling and he reached back and put the cup and saucer on the table. He turned back. Both men were looking at him intently. Hacklin said with his mechanical smile, "We want to know if that's agreeable to you and if you think you could handle it if called on."

"Agreeable to me?" He repeated the phrase and heard himself like another man speaking. "If you think I could do it, I'm sure I could, yes."

Hacklin was nodding solemnly. "We are entirely confident in you, Lloyd. Our intelligence on you is entirely satisfactory. If it happened, if you did take over the job, you might be a bit nervous

at first, we would understand that. But we believe you have the
natural, well, poise to do it, to feel perfectly comfortable after a few
days, am I right in assuming that?"

He swallowed before replying. "Why, yes, sure. Only I'm surprised. With all the other people who—"

Hacklin overrode him with genial finality. "You would be the
choice, Lloyd. The only thing I can't tell you, yet, is when it
might start. But I want to caution you that it could be very soon,
maybe as early as next Monday night. That will depend on some,
er, conversations with Johns now in progress." His brief chilly laugh.
"And then again I may just call you and tell you to forget we ever
had this talk. Oh, we'd find something else, something good, don't
worry about that. We signed a contract with you because we respect
your talents, you have a place with the network in any event."

Lloyd murmured, "Thanks," and Hacklin said, "Of course I could
fib to you and say Hedley's considering a vacation or a leave of
absence or something of the sort, but I'm giving it to you straight,
that's the way I prefer to deal with you, now and in the future.
That's my reputation, as Milo here will attest." Wilson nodded
vigorously. "If Johns goes, you go in, and when you go in you stay
in, it's the only way to fill a job like that. You can't run a string of
anchormen and ask the viewers for their opinions." Wilson was still
nodding, definitely not that. "Well, that's all I wanted to say, Lloyd.
If you have any doubts about your own ability to take it on, let's
hear them now."

He shook his head and heard himself say, "None. None at all."

"Good, then here's what we think best for you to do. Don't
go into the bureau today, just pack your bag and check out of
here and go back to New York." He stood up and Lloyd stood
up too. "Don't even call anybody here, and don't say a word to
anybody about me or our talk."

"I was supposed to go over to the State Department this morning
with Jerry Lacey, he—"

Walter Hacklin had an arm around his shoulders. "Conscientious,
eh, Milo?" He smiled. "Forget about the State Department, the
State Department can take care of itself. I hope to God," he added,
and Wilson laughed dutifully. "Milo will call Thorpe and fix it.

When you get to New York *don't* go to the office, just check in somewhere and let Schonwald know where he can reach you during the weekend, right?"

They walked to the door together, Hacklin still had his arm around his shoulders. "You understand, Lloyd, this is all confidential, so keep it strictly to yourself until you get the word."

"You can count on me," Lloyd said, and left them.

He reached the airport just in time to make the shuttle flight. It wasn't until they took off that he remembered he had nothing in his stomach but three sips of coffee. He must be returning to normal. But beneath the surface calm a fierce elation still gripped him. He wanted to *tell* someone, he wanted to shout it to the whole airplane. The stewardess found some cookies left over from another flight and he sat there munching them trying to regain control. Once he laughed aloud at Hacklin's mysterious tactics; it was hocus-pocus as usual at the network. Suddenly he wanted to talk it over with Kent Ward, sitting together as they had sat the other night in Georgetown. Something big was going on about Hedley Johns behind the scenes, that was obvious now. Was it linked with what Ward had said about censorship trouble? He went back in his mind over the Johns programs he'd seen these last few nights on the TV in his hotel room but he couldn't remember anything Johns had said that sounded unusual unless it was that new commentary piece he was putting at the end of each show. He was lost in speculation when they landed at La Guardia, and the first thing he did was drink two bourbons and eat two hamburgers before he took a taxi to the Hilton. It was midafternoon when he picked up the phone in his room and called Buck Schonwald.

Bonnie, the secretary, answered. "Sorry, he's got people with him, can he call you back?"

"I was supposed to call him, I'm in New York."

"Maybe he won't be long, you in your office, Lloyd?"

She might be calling him Mr. Garner soon. He said, "Just do this, Bonnie, put my name on a piece of paper and hand it to him, I'll wait."

He was grinning. He'd learn hocus-pocus with the best of them before he was through. Almost immediately she said, "Here he is," and Schonwald came on.

"I had an unexpected visitor in Washington this morning, Buck."

"Uh-huh."

"He told me to tell you I'm in 1741 at the Hilton, that's 1741."

"Got it."

"Can I talk to my own secretary, Buck?"

"No."

"Okay, Buck, you know where to reach me."

"Stay there."

"Okay, Buck." The other man hung up. He had sounded not quite himself. Lloyd threw himself down on the bed and thought about it. If even the unflappable Schonwald was upset there must be quite a drama on. *And Lloyd Garner, boy reporter, was waiting in the wings.* It made him want to laugh. If he could really believe what was happening to him he would laugh these walls down in a wild glee. But this was no time to laugh; these people were dead serious at their game and he was in it now with them. It could go on like this for days.

The room was too quiet. He got up and switched on the little radio cabinet in the night table and stood there listening, grateful for the tinkling music. Then he went to the window and looked out over the city, gray clouds darkening over New Jersey. The confused distant roar of traffic from the streets below had a mournful sound. He had never felt so alone, he needed somebody to talk to, about anything, just to keep his mind off what was happening, but he was afraid to use the phone in case they called him. Finally he used it long enough to order a bourbon and soda. He had a sudden ridiculous urge to tell the waiter all about it when he brought the drink. Afterward he switched off the radio and turned on the TV, but the dreary succession of soap-opera scenes depressed him and he turned it off again, lay down once more and closed his eyes. He couldn't think about anything any more. He was tired, the tension was too much for him, the hell with all of them, Johns, Schonwald, Hacklin! Dimly, insistently, the ringing phone pierced his consciousness and he reached for it, knocking it off the stand,

groping in a dark room. "Just a minute," he heard his own voice
saying thickly, to anybody, and picked up the receiver on the floor.

"Lloyd? Can you hear me? Buck Schonwald."

"Sorry, I fell asleep. Dark in here. What time is it?"

"After eight. I'm waiting for you in my office. Hedley Johns has
resigned."

4

All the papers had the story the next day but the *Times* was the most complete and probably the most accurate. Lloyd bought the Late City edition at a newstand at 3 A.M. on his way back to the hotel after the meeting with Buck Schonwald, which had lasted nearly six hours. Walter Hacklin had taken part at the beginning, then clapped Lloyd on the back and cheerily departed. Milo Wilson had looked in for a moment later, to congratulate him, and afterward Lloyd said to Schonwald, "That guy hired me but I still don't know what his job is," and the producer had smiled and answered, "He's only Hacklin's liaison with the sales department, and when you know that, you know he's second in line to God around here." Except for the night skeleton crew, the newsroom like the offices was deserted when Lloyd arrived from the hotel. He felt like a ghost walking through the hall. Every man in the newsroom looked up at him. It was nine o'clock, too early for the reporters from the papers to have had time to arrive, but they'd all been on the phone to Schonwald since the press associations carried the brief network announcement, which didn't mention a successor to Hedley Johns. Schonwald said that announcement would be made tomorrow. The grapevine was working, though, and those men in the newsroom knew all right. Lloyd looked into his own office on the way out and found a note slipped under the door. It said: *I look forward to working with you,* and it was signed Drew Stimson. Talk about a mystery man. Hedley Johns himself had made no immediate statement but Schonwald had remarked to Hacklin that Johns was undoubtedly talking to Jack Gould and might make a formal statement later. Schonwald didn't want to talk about Johns at all to Lloyd. "You and I've got an awful lot of work to do before Monday night."

There were things in the *Times* story that Lloyd had never known. It said the network had begun objecting to Johns's attitude as long ago as the first big civil rights disorders, with frequent disagreements erupting over what Johns himself had added to reports from the scene. The southern affiliates had been protesting ever since, but even more bitter editorial quarrels had developed as the Vietnam War moved to a stalemate and antiwar feeling increased throughout the country. Johns's decision to add a closing commentary to the daily program had apparently been the final straw. He had twice refused to go on the air in the past month unless it was passed as written. At the end of the Friday program, while Lloyd slept in his hotel room, Walter Hacklin was waiting for Johns in Schonwald's office. The vice-president told Johns it had been decided to drop the closing commentary immediately. Johns then sat down at Schonwald's typewriter and wrote out and signed his resignation to take effect at once. The resignation was accepted.

The *Times* didn't speculate about a successor. They had evidently put their information together just before the deadline for the last Late City edition, but there was a hint that the decision to get rid of Johns had been taken some time ago and management had waited until after the week's programs had all been broadcast before putting its decision into effect. That served to prevent Johns from possibly ad-libbing any sort of closing blast at his employers on the air, and also gave Schonwald a weekend to prepare the new man before the next show went on. It was going to be a frantic weekend, with dry runs of the program's regular format Saturday and Sunday night including typical taped inserts, commercials and all, to familiarize the new anchorman with his job, and full crews working overtime.

Standing in the empty Hilton lobby reading the story Lloyd shook his head in wonder. They'd had it all figured out, they knew what they were doing from the first step to the last. Then he started at the voice behind him, "Lloyd, you rascal," and turned and saw Beveridge Hambleton the Fourth standing there smiling.

"For God's sake, Bev, you scared me."

"Didn't mean to do that, old boy." He was quite drunk and as might be expected was holding it well.

"What are you doing around here at this hour of the night?"

"Heard you were here, Lloyd. Been to rather a late party."

"But how'd you know I was in New York?"

Solemnly, "If you don't give me away, Bonnie told Rita you were back and Rita told me."

"They told you where I was staying?"

"Sure. But I didn't tell anybody. By the way, great friend of yours sends you all the best."

"Great friend of mine?"

The owlish grin. "Come on, Lloyd. Alix."

"Oh, you know Alix, do you?"

"Come on, she was married to my uncle. Nice fella. High goal, you know."

Lloyd was shaking his head. "Try and keep a secret around here. I had a good luck note tonight from Drew Stimson, he seems to know just about everything."

"Sure, why not? CIA."

"CIA! You're kidding, how would you know that?"

"Cousin of mine in Washington told me. Absolute fact."

Suddenly he laughed, helplessly, his tensions fell away and things began to look real again. Bev was holding himself together stiffly and surveying him. "Like that suit you're wearing, Lloyd."

"You helped me buy it."

"Thought so. Say, you got a nightcap for me in your room?"

Lloyd took his arm and steered him toward the elevators. "I sure have." The enormity of the weekend he faced was dwindling and he knew now you had to take it in stride or you'd never make it. A couple of bourbons with his old friend and office boy and he could even sleep.

The ad, carried in the Sunday papers of all cities that saw the Hedley Johns show, described Lloyd Garner as a veteran reporter who had seen service with the network in New York and Washington. It didn't mention his career in Boston. The audacity of that "seen service" was too much, Lloyd heard his own incredulous laughter. On an impulse he picked up the phone and had the

network operator put him through to Kent Ward's house on the
Washington tie line. "I didn't wake you up, Kent?"

"I've been up for hours." He chuckled. "Reading the ads."

"Tell me," Lloyd said. "Nobody else will. What really happened?"

"Where are you?"

"In bed, alone. You can talk."

"I don't know anything, Lloyd. I don't really. But I can give you
an educated guess. What they wanted first was to censor Hedley or
get rid of him. The White House has been kicking for some time,
you know. I suspect the President finally got to the big boss. By the
way, where *is* Hedley?"

"I don't think they know. Schonwald won't talk about him. But
Kent, why me for Hedley Johns?"

"As I see it they wanted to replace him with an entirely new
face. Unconnected, uncommitted, with no past, only future. Little
Father gives way to Big Brother, something like that. They needed
somebody with reasonable intelligence and, above all, youth. The
accent's on youth now. And of course with looks, voice and hair,
each equally important."

"Hair?"

Kent Ward laughed. "Hedley resolutely refused to wear a toop,
you know. Maybe a humble reporter here and there is allowed to
be bald, Lloyd, a network anchorman never. And they want an
anchorman, not a political correspondent. A news reader, not an
editorial spokesman. They want somebody to spiel what's written for
him by Harry Ferguson and edited for him by Earl Greminger, not
a thinker or the chairman of a panel of analysts, you follow?"

"I follow, but I've got a lot to learn."

"Why? As an anchorman you're not expected to *know* anything,
you just look personable and sound authoritative. They'll teach you
what they want you to learn. It isn't what you can learn, anyway,
it's what you were born with, star quality, that they want. You're
there to please as well as impress, Lloyd. You're there to appeal to
women as well as men. It's all aimed at creating a devoted following
of viewers who tune in primarily because they want to watch a
beloved object at the same hour every day. The viewers don't care
as much about what he says as how he looks and sounds when he

says it, I suspect a lot of them don't really listen at all, except to the commercials. And that ultimately is what you're doing, selling the product, bringing in the advertising buck."

"Kent, you're better than the ad."

"Haven't I heard Milo Wilson tell Walter Hacklin a hundred times?"

"But how did they *find* me?"

"If I ever discover that I'll let you know, some talent scout we've never heard of, probably."

"I feel funny," Lloyd said. "I'm floating on air and scared at the same time. It's just not happening."

"That won't last. In a month you'll be so self-important you'll begin to believe you're invulnerable."

"Now you sound serious, Kent. Are you warning me?"

He laughed. "We'll see if I'm right. Good luck, *Mister* Garner."

Still holding the newspaper, he got out of bed and went into the bathroom and looked at himself for a long time in the mirror. This was Lloyd Garner, remember him? He shook his head, no, he was crazy, it was a mocking dream. In a day, in an hour, he'd wake up again in that little apartment in Boston, the battered old alarm clock clicking away on the dresser, Fran asleep beside him, both of them trapped together and helpless, hopeless. A sudden disgust clutched him like nausea. He never wanted to think about that part of his life again. But somewhere far down under the layers of his new success a gnawing guilt began, the feeling he was leaving Fran behind, deserting her. Fran was in trouble; he would have to do something about it, something definite, but he didn't want to think about that either. He would when he had time, but it didn't look as if he'd have much of that for a while. He stared into the mirror. Fran could wait. The man she knew as her husband was about to belong to the whole country. But would she understand? He hadn't asked for this; it had simply happened. Was it his fault it had brought him to the top of the world, suddenly, unbelievably, without her? Was it his fault her drinking had turned their marriage into a life of strangers? A surging sadness swept over him, surprised him, poor old gal, poor old Fran. He'd call her, he'd call her as soon as he'd bathed and shaved.

For right now nobody could call him. Lloyd Garner was on ice, as effectively concealed from public view as when he spent that long Friday afternoon in this room. During the Saturday dry run newspaper and magazine people had been kept out of the studio and Lloyd was instructed to refuse all interviews. They had, of course, found out he was staying at the Hilton. The man from *Time* warned him from the other side of the locked door that he would write his story about the absurdity of such mysterious tactics and then tramped angrily back to the elevator. Schonwald thought that was just fine. There had been a long picture-taking session in the studio after the dry run was over; photographs would be released for the Monday papers along with a biography worked out with Jay Weiss, the department's public relations man. Weiss had already had half a dozen calls from Boston. Today, Sunday, Lloyd Garner would appear on a closed-circuit broadcast to the affiliate stations at his most charming. There would be a second dry run of the whole program in the evening and a brief talk, he mustn't get tired, with Jo Ellison about accent. First interviews would be granted immediately after the show went back on the air Monday night, and Weiss was lining up a series of guest appearances for him later in the week on other network shows, giving him all possible TV exposure at the beginning. "Just keep your cool," Schonwald had said to him last night, "and it'll be a breeze."

The phone rang and Lloyd came out of the bathroom to answer it. "I thought I better tell you about this one," the hotel operator said, "it's Boston calling, the lady says she's your wife."

"I'll take it," he said, and Fran was on, "Lloyd? *Lloyd!*" She sounded excited and fearful and very, very impressed. "I've just seen an ad in the—"

"I was just going to call you, honey, I'm sorry I couldn't before, they wouldn't let me."

"I tried to reach you all day yesterday, they said you didn't answer your room and your office phone just rang and rang."

"I've been working in the studio, honey."

"Oh, Lloyd, *Lloyd*, I almost dropped dead just now when I saw the paper."

"How about that? I'll give you all the details Monday night after the first show, we can't talk about it till then."

"Harvey called," she said, "he thought I knew it already."

"Nobody knew it, I didn't know myself till late Friday night. Listen, are *you* okay?"

"I'm feeling fine, I really am."

"That's what I want to hear, girl. Look, I have to cut this short now and get back to the studio, don't worry if I don't call you till tomorrow night late, right?"

He could hear her weeping a little. "I just think it's so *wonderful*."

He took off his pajamas and went back into the bathroom and turned on the shower, soaping himself under the warm streaming water he felt his whole body shaking with a sudden exuberance and he laughed aloud, like a child with a secret. New vistas were opening, he was going to be a Name. Just once he thought of Hedley Johns and dismissed him from his mind. Every dog has his day, thought Lloyd Garner in the shower.

"The important thing is get a good night's sleep," Buck Schonwald said to him, "you've got nothing more to worry about now." They were winding up in Hedley Johns's office after the final dry run, the first time they had been alone together since the session two nights ago that had lasted into the predawn hours. Outside, the studio was dark and empty again, only the Sunday skeleton staff was on duty in the newsroom. Schonwald was still talking but the words drifted out of Lloyd's mind and away, his gaze was traveling over the office that was his now but still full of Hedley Johns's trophies and mementos, certificates of Peabody Awards on the walls with the pictures—Johns with H. V. Kaltenborn, Johns with Murrow and Elmer Davis, with Huntley and Brinkley, with William Shirer and Quincy Howe, with Ed Newman and Don Hollenbeck, with David Schoenbrun and Sevareid, Johns with a camera team in Korea, grim with Omar Bradley in World War II, smiling with Hammerskjold at the U.N. Standing there Lloyd Garner felt again the strange, triumphant disbelief, this had to be happening to somebody else, not him. Schonwald's voice came back. "You did good with Jo Ellison," the producer was saying, "she says just remember about

those a's and you'll be right on the beam. And you can thank
Earl Greminger and Teleprompter for your success on the closed
circuit, the affiliates liked you fine."

"Did the big boss like me?"

The grin faded. "If he didn't, you wouldn't be here, fellow.
Don't worry about him. Leave that to the people who do, okay?"

"Okay."

The producer was looking at him closely. For the first time Lloyd
felt a kind of hostility in the look. "You and I have a lot to talk
about, Lloyd. It was different with Hedley, he'd been up so high
for so long he wasn't listening to anybody any more, and that's
what happened to him, you dig?"

"I dig."

"You're not Hedley Johns and you never will be. Among other
things that means you won't write a line for this show, understand?
Every word written for you will be checked with Greminger before
you go on the air and he's the best editor in the business, you won't
have to fret about that. Harry Ferguson is also the best news writer
money can buy and the whole staff is the envy of their profession."
He paused. "If you want this job, you leave everything to them."

"I want the job, Buck."

"Naturally you're going to get a new contract, we're not going to
be cheap with you about anything. You'll be going into that with
the business end later in the week. You've got one problem that
comes first, only one. Be at your best tomorrow night, that's what
matters right now."

They walked down the empty hall together toward the elevators.
"Buck," Lloyd said, "were you sorry to see Hedley go?"

He couldn't see his face in the dim light but Schonwald slowed
his step a moment. "How would I answer that?" he said tiredly.
"I'd say yes and no." And after a moment, "There's something
you ought to get clear. In this setup, you're Talent and I'm Executive, we're not in the same boat. Hedley's mixed up about that, he
always was."

They were stepping into the elevator. "What's he going to do?"
Lloyd said. "I mean Hedley Johns."

The other man shrugged and spoke almost harshly, "I wouldn't know, he hasn't communicated with me."

"I can't help feeling strange about him, after his great career and all that, and here I am."

"Shut up and forget it, that's the last thing you should be worrying about, fellow." They stepped into the lobby and Schonwald gave him a bleak smile. "Now *sleep,* take a pill if you have to, lie around in the morning, eat a good lunch and then don't eat anything until you're off the air tomorrow night. I don't want to see you before two."

"Okay, Buck."

The big man raised his arm and strode off, Lloyd watched him disappear through the swinging doors into the city night. His machine was tuned up and ready to start. Tomorrow he would push the buttons.

A little before ten o'clock in the morning, still lying in bed and contentedly full of a room service breakfast, Lloyd put aside the *Times* and called Rita Valenti at the office. When she answered he said, "Where the hell have you been since Friday?"

"They told me not to come in, Mr. Garner."

"I needed you. Aren't you the best and only secretary I ever had?"

"For the moment, yes," she said.

"How come for the moment?"

"Because you're moving into Hedley Johns's office and you're going to have a different secretary, not his. I don't know what they'll do with her but they certainly won't let her stay on in that job."

"But I want you to be my secretary in Hedley Johns's office."

Her voice was somehow wistful. "Do you mean that, Mr. Garner?"

"I never meant anything more."

She seemed to hesitate. "I'd like to but I can't."

"How come you can't?"

"I've decided to quit."

"You're teasing."

He could see her solemn way of saying it. "I'm going to Europe, Mr. Garner, I'm going to Rome."

"You mean to stay, to live there."

"Exactly."

"Your dream is coming true."

She laughed a little. "I figured if I don't do it now I probably never will."

"Just when I need you most."

"You don't need me, Mr. Garner, the network has other secretaries just as competent."

"Look, if you really mean this, can't you at least start calling me Lloyd?"

"Lloyd," she said. "Lloyd. I kind of like it."

"All right, now listen. You aren't only my secretary, you're my friend. I don't want any other secretaries just as competent, I want you. I'd have told you that three days ago but they wouldn't let me talk to you."

"Isn't it just like them," she said. "Oh, by the way, congratulations, Mr.— Lloyd."

"You're the first friend I ever had at the network, you don't think I'm going to let you go now."

Another slight pause. "It was nice, wasn't it?"

"It was more than that and you know it. I owe you a big debt of gratitude, Rita, you gave me some very good advice when I needed it. I still need it."

"Not you," she said. "You don't need me or anybody now."

"What are you doing for lunch?" he said.

Her little laugh again, "Today? This is your big day, you haven't got time to have lunch with me."

"You'd be surprised how much time I have, Buck doesn't want to see my face around there till two o'clock. I'll meet you at our old place in the Village at twelve-thirty."

"No, you'll drink too much and I don't want you to drink today."

"Not even a glass of wine?" he said.

"I guess a glass of wine would be all right, but no whisky."

"I love the way you have my interests at heart."

"I always will," she said.

She was there before he was, just to make sure, she told him, that he didn't sneak in a couple of bourbons before she arrived. "What do you think I am, some kind of a drunk?" he said and kissed her.

"You can't just kiss girls like that in restaurants, not any more," she said with her grave smile. The proprietor made a fuss over him as they sat down and then retired bowing. "You see? He saw your picture in the *News* this morning."

"I saw the one in the *Times.*"

"So did I," she said. "Didn't they make anything better than that?"

He was laughing. "They took about a thousand, I thought it was a pretty good likeness."

"Have you got yourself an agent yet, Lloyd?"

"How about you taking me on?"

"Seriously. They're giving you a new contract, aren't they?"

"Buck mentioned it."

"You'd be crazy to negotiate yourself, don't even appear, just let your agent do it all."

"But who?" he said. "I thought I might ask Drew Stimson, the CIA man, if he knows anyone."

"CIA?" She looked bewildered.

"That's what I've been told."

"Oh. Well, it wouldn't surprise me if that was one of his little side lines."

"Maybe *you* know a good agent."

She thought a moment and then smiled. "I can tell you the name of the one that gives them the most trouble, he represents a few of the big guys."

"He's the one for me, then."

She wrote Sime Sussman's name on a piece of paper and gave it to him. "If I were you, Lloyd, I'd just turn over my career to him, he'll get you a better contract than you'll ever get yourself." She was looking at him reflectively. "I don't think you realize how important you've suddenly become."

"It hasn't hit me yet, Rita."

"You'll find out eventually."

"But *why?* Why *me?*"

"First they used you as a warning to Hedley. He called their bluff. But you don't call the bluff when it's the big boss. And that was all for Hedley Johns."

"So you think it was the big boss."

"I'm sure of it. He invented you, Lloyd Garner. You should be grateful."

They shared a half bottle of wine over their bistecca fiorentina. The place was quiet and only half filled at lunchtime. "You know," he said, "you're a handsome girl and you live just around the corner from here and I'd like to take you there right now and give you a good fucking the way I used to do."

"And have no voice left for your first broadcast."

He was laughing. "You really believe that old wives' tale?"

"When I'm no longer living just around the corner from here," she said, "plenty of other girls will be available to help out. And then there's your wife, what about your wife?"

"She's not coming to New York right away."

She smiled. "Alone in New York and on top of the merry-go-round. They'll be waiting in line to take care of you."

"I've often wondered if Buck Schonwald ordered you to take care of me. As part of the treatment for budding stars."

"Seriously," she said, "you've got a career to think about now. A place to settle down, one of those town houses in the East Sixties, like Milo Wilson's, where you'll have dinner parties for the brass and other biggies. Those are the people you're going to spend your time with from now on."

"Do I have to?"

She turned to the waiter and said, "We want the check, please."

"Are we going to your house?"

"We're going to the office. Now."

He laughed and put his arm around her. "Rita," he said. "What would I do without you?"

"Camera 2 looks okay now," a voice said. In the darkened control room, eleven men crouching before a panel gleaming with tiny lights, it was hard to tell which had spoken. One of a dozen

telephones ranged along the table before them buzzed sharply and
another voice said, "Washington on 7, can you break it momentarily?"
while on the big illuminated clock above their heads the black hand
jerked one more minute toward the hour and the red hand ticked
off the seconds without arresting its smooth sweep. Either side of the
clock stretched a row of television screens, some blank, some with
images from the three networks and New York local stations, one
for color pattern. Out of an unseen speaker a voice barked, "You're
giving color to studio, right?" and another said querulously, "Go
ahead, go ahead, now look at output." "A little higher, Jerry," a new
voice said, and still another, "Narration is on sixteen-five but the
voice-over on this one is too sibilant, start it about twenty seconds
in." A patient droning came from the other end of the row of heads
and crouching bodies, "Go back . . . counter . . . a little more . . .
hold it there . . ." and an earlier voice, "Cameramen on cans, please."
Somebody said, "Got your SP yet?" and somebody else, "Newark
audio on number 10." The chatter of teleprinters heard dimly on
one of the speakers was suddenly magnified and from somewhere a
voice rasped, "Still want a bloop on thirty-five four?" "How about
the remote?" an insistent monotone was repeating, "give us the
remote." "We're not synchronized," snapped a speaker. Blank until
now, the large central screen under the clock lighted up, wavered,
then swam to clarity, showing the head and shoulders of Lloyd
Garner with part of a world map outlined behind him. Two small
hands, not his own, were applying make-up to his eyelids. The
profile, glimpsed for a moment as he turned, was strong and
young, the hair, now under ministration of deft swift touches with a
paintbrush, was rich black, thick and real. "We don't have SL Five
yet," complained a voice. "Control . . . Control . . . this is thirty-
six!"

A dead, flat, white sound filled the control room. "We're feeding
tone," announced a speaker, and a man sitting just below it remarked,
"Anacin is in color." Next to him, leaning forward beside the
vacant chair in the center of the row, a nervous, youthful man cracked
his knuckles and watched the clock. On the central screen the deft
feminine hands had finished their work. The subject, smiling and
nodding tensely at some unregistered comment, lifted his head to

glance warily once at the still blank Teleprompter, then looked
down again at his script. "He's real scared," observed a voice in
the control room. "Wouldn't you be?" said the voice next to him.
"Just for the preem," said a third voice, "tomorrow he'll be too busy
to think about it." "Yeah," commented a fourth, "too busy counting
his money," and a snicker ran along the row of heads.

The man they were talking about sat before the studio camera,
waiting. Always before he had been the spectator, even during that
period in New York when day after day he'd watched at first
hand while the Hedley Johns unit put the show together. Now
they would call it the Lloyd Garner show, and never until today,
not even during the two dry runs he had done himself, had he
really felt himself part of it, personally responsible, personally involved in the incredible operation that would now somehow culmi-
nate in the finished program on the air. Writers, editors, reporters,
technicians, here in the New York news complex and beyond to
the other side of the earth, God knew how many of them, were
girding for the effort of which he would be the spearhead. And
waiting were the unseen millions upon millions who would sit in
judgment on the result. Today in his glass-enclosed office, looking
out on the newsroom at one end and studio at the other, he felt
the tension like the beating of invisible wings. He had to struggle
with himself to concentrate on the script being assembled page by
page on his desk. At least it had been a routine news day. So far,
there was no world-shaking crisis or sudden disaster to disrupt the
delicate machinery of preparation. Two Vietnam film spots, remotes from Chicago and Newark, a congressional hearing and a
Kent Ward political report were scheduled in the half hour, all of
them securely in hand, but he shivered at the thought you could
never know when something might break right in the middle of the
show that would throw the line-up off and leave the rest up to luck,
and skill. That was the one thing the staff couldn't prepare him for,
everything else was anticipated and set down to the last timed
second. He looked up again at the clock in the studio, six minutes to
air, and at Buck Schonwald's burly shoulders bending over the
editors' desk, and suddenly he felt a surge of gratitude to them all.
In these past three days of backbreaking rehearsal not one had given

a sign that the departure of Hedley Johns was a cause for resenting Lloyd Garner. Today they had all, from stagehands on the news set to Bob Lentz the director, wished him the best for his first performance. He became aware that the phone on his desk was ringing insistently and picked it up.

"This is Ward in Washington with the word for tonight. The word is relax."

"The condemned man is about to mount the scaffold, Kent."

"I know how you're feeling, that's show biz." The voice was warm and casual.

"If I could pray I'd be praying right now."

"Take a slug of whisky three minutes before air, Ed Murrow used to."

He was laughing. "I can get along without, tonight. I think."

Earl Greminger came in with the last page of the script. It was marked at the top, 23: *Bufferin*, 35/1, 27:15, and under that, 24: *Garner, live close*, 40. The editor held the watch while Lloyd timed out the closing headlines, then Schonwald was beckoning from the studio and Lloyd picked up the script and took it to the broadcast desk as the two cameras moved into position in front of him. The make-up girl was waiting to give him the final touches. He leaned back in the swivel chair and surrendered himself to her hands while Bob Lentz hurried out of the control room and checked his script with Lloyd's page by page. "It's a good show," he muttered finally, "we're off to a good start." "Two minutes, Bob," said the AD on the control room speaker. Lentz grunted and waddled back across the studio. Schonwald leaned across the desk and smiled at him before he followed Lentz into the control room. The man sitting before the cameras was alone.

Around him the studio clatter fell to a sudden, terrible hush. He was conscious now only of the tyrant clock and its inexorable red hand, its face inscrutable as the faces in the outer dark, every one silent and every one watching him. He did not look toward them. Of the others beyond, the millions, he could not think. He cleared his throat with a loud, shocking sound and ran his tongue over his lips, breathing deeply to quiet the clamor of his heart. Then he smiled very slightly and looked the camera in the eye. He would never be as frightened again.

In the control room Bob Lentz was settling his broad buttocks into the vacant seat in the center of the row. Above him the face on the central screen blurred out, was lost, wavered in again, then out. "Normal opening," Lentz said tersely, "super up first." "*One minute!*" and the young man next to him cracked his knuckles again. "Coming out to Two," said Lentz, "lead him a little." The camera's eye focused with deliberation and the image came back to the screen. "*Thirty seconds!*" said the young man. He began to speak rapidly now and all the others were silent. "*Ready black. Go to black. Punch! Swing into One. End super. Ready to dissolve. Ten seconds. Five seconds . . .*" The face on the central screen was alert and lively, with a sudden-flashing smile, but the voice was grave and vibrant and deep. "*A very good evening to you all!*" it said to an estimated sixteen million viewers from coast to coast. Lloyd Garner was on the air.

5

Sime Sussman finished reading Lloyd's old contract and put it down on his desk, the little man's laugh was a croak. "They murdered you with that one, we'll keep it for a curiosity. They talked money to you yet?"

"Buck Schonwald said they wouldn't be cheap, that's all."

The round black eyes were snapping behind the heavy glasses. "Schonwald has no say on this. You haven't seen anybody on the business side?"

"Only Pollitt when I signed that."

"You won't be dealing with Pollitt any more, he's for the mugs. You'll get Max Gross this time, I mean *I'll* get him, and believe me, Lloyd, it'll be a real pleasure. Tell me this, what kind of a reaction to last night?"

"They told me this morning there were thirty-three phone calls from viewers and most of them were asking where was Hedley Johns. Seventeen telegrams, some saying they liked me and the rest protesting about Johns."

He croaked again. "They'll forget about Johns, you'd be surprised how fast they forget. Remember, the ones that phoned and wired are only the tiny minority of viewers anyway, the mob out there is going to like you better than they ever did Johns." He chain-lit another cigarette. "You saw the notices, the *Times* was kind of spiteful but he couldn't really fault you, I happen to know *Variety* is going to give you a good one. In six months you'll be pulling more mail than Johns ever did, believe me."

Lloyd said, "I'd like to believe you."

"You can," Sime Sussman said, "I saw the show. Say, where did they get you?"

"Boston. I've been doing radio and occasional TV there for nine years."

"Wife and kids?"

"Wife, no kids."

"And whose brainstorm were you?"

"Who picked me? That's one thing I haven't found out."

"It doesn't matter, Lloyd, you're in now and you're staying."

"That's what Walter Hacklin said too."

A hoarse cackle. "That nebbish, he's just a dummy for the big boss."

"I'd like to meet the big boss sometime, I've never even seen him."

"You may never see him, but he's the one has to like you, and as long as he does you can ignore the rest of them over there." He was making some quick figures on a memo pad and talking in his rapid semi-stutter. "They'll probably offer you a guaranteed thousand in the new contract, I'll set the figure at two and come down to fifteen hundred with regular raises. Maybe we can tie it into ratings as well as commercial fees, lately the show's been in trouble with ratings."

So that was another reason they got rid of Hedley Johns. "Did I understand you to say fifteen hundred a *week?*" Lloyd said.

He looked up. "Yeah, and fifteen per cent for this office. We'll bank your checks for you and watch their accounting and take care of your tax problem, that's your main headache." He slapped the contract on the desk and laughed his unpleasant laugh. "We'll also get some new features put into this, they're overdue in all their contracts, in your case they can't refuse."

"Fifteen hundred a week," Lloyd said, and felt dizzy.

"It's a beginning," said Sime Sussman, and added, "You and I will have a contract of our own, of course. By the way, who suggested you come to me?"

"You're famous, Sime."

"So don't tell me." The little man stood up and offered his hand. "I'll send it over to you this afternoon, meantime refer any contract talk to me, don't sign anything whatever, insurance, pension, nothing, just send it all to me. They'll tell you you can do better without an agent, just be polite and say it's already decided. Call me if there's the slightest trouble with anybody, understand? You're an artiste, Lloyd, you can't be bothered, you've got the *news* to think about, you've got an agent now."

"It certainly looks like it," Lloyd said, and laughed. Going out he thought warmly of Rita Valenti who had steered him to Sussman. Bev Hambleton was sitting on the edge of Rita's desk when Lloyd arrived at his office. "You two are always together," he said as he came in, "you got a secret?"

Bev slid casually off the desk. "What about *your* secret? You disappeared last night."

"I was tired, I turned my phone off."

"Had a little party all arranged," Bev said. "Just close friends."

"That was nice of you, Bev."

"We missed you," Rita said, "but we don't blame you."

"I had one drink with Buck and the unit, I talked ten seconds to Walter Hacklin, then I telephoned my wife and went to bed."

"And you didn't even know Rita and I were in the control room for the whole show, special permission of Bob Lentz," Bev said. "Well, c'est la TV." He smiled from the doorway. "Coffee?"

"Go," said Lloyd. They watched him saunter into the newsroom. "I'm very fond of that guy," he said. "What's he doing in that menial job?"

"So am I. He wants to be a reporter someday."

He looked down at her. "Have you ever slept with him?"

She shrugged. "If I have I'm not going to tell you and you shouldn't ask anyway."

"Rita, I'm sorry! What did you think of the show?"

"It was good and you know it."

"Let me tell you something interesting, I've just signed up with Sime Sussman, thanks to you. The contract will be coming over so be on the lookout for it."

"Somebody else will be on the lookout beginning tomorrow, Lloyd."

He felt a sharp pang of dismay. "You're not walking out on me?"

"It's my last day, I'm sailing Friday night on the *Michelangelo.*" She sat straight and calm, looking up at him.

"I won't let you, goddamn it."

"They were nice about it, gave me an immediate release with my severance and told me I could come back when I get tired of Rome."

"I give you three months, make it six."

She was smiling now and shaking her head. "Come and see me sometime."

"You really are going," he said. "What am I going to do? What's *everybody* going to do?"

"Now ask me who's going to break in the budding stars."

He laughed tenderly. "You'll never forget that crack, will you? I was only teasing, honest. There isn't anybody I respect more than you, Rita."

"It's mutual, you know."

"Okay, we've forgotten I ever said it. Can I come and see you off on the boat?"

"Why, Lloyd, that would be nice!"

His face clouded. "Friday night, no, I can't. My wife's coming from Boston for the weekend. Can we have lunch, though? Like today?" Again he stopped and shook his head. "No, Schonwald set up lunch with him and Hacklin."

"It's right here on your pad," she said, "but you were sweet to think of me."

"Oh hell."

She gave him her grave smile. "You may as well get used to it, Mr. Garner, that's the way it's going to be from now on."

And it was. The build-up was underway. In his first week a different lunch was arranged each day, culminating on Friday with a network occasion at 21 to meet the program's current and prospective sponsors and their agency representatives. Jay Weiss had appearances set up for him on the daytime entertainment shows and he gave a series of interviews to the local and trade press including *Variety*, which as Sime Sussman had predicted gave him a solid send-off in its review. *Variety* found him vigorous, savvy, with the pro touch, and so on in its own vein. *Time* sneered at lack of sufficient experience, regretted Hedley Johns's departure, deplored censorship, but to *Newsweek* he was fresh and likable, uninclined to preach

like his predecessor but serious and sound in his approach. Viewer
mail began to pile up in front of his new secretary, Gaby Berman,
much of it from women, much of it favorable after the early burst
of protest from Johns's admirers. (Johns himself was at a friend's
house in Arizona, giving no interviews.) Taxi drivers cocked their
heads back at him and said, Say, don't I know you from somewhere?
and he was asked for his autograph in restaurants and stared at
perplexedly in the street. Meanwhile Sussman was deeply involved
with Max Gross in negotiations for the new contract, "haggling
like a couple of Algerian rug merchants," as Buck Schonwald
described it. Buck had called Lloyd in and said, as foretold by Sime
at their first meeting, "Fellow, I think you're making a mistake
tying up with that guy, why didn't you speak to one of us first?"

The weekend would bring a lull, then everything would start
all over again Monday, next week's lunches were already booked.
Meanwhile the shows were getting easier to do each night, he felt
more himself, more relaxed and warmer each time. Jo Ellison was
watching his accent but could only catch him in a few pronunciation
faults which he immediately corrected. It hadn't mattered in Boston,
but he couldn't say *Dee Gaulle* any more, or Moscow like cow, it had
to be Mosco. The first time he had Quincy, Illinois, he called it
Quinzy, a natural error for a Massachusetts boy, but there would
always be place-name errors, like pronouncing it Biloxi, as written,
instead of *Biluxi*, until Jo's daily memo came to his desk.

The tricks that life could play! For ten years he had worked
hard for long hours, six or seven days a week for little money,
now he was earning ten times as much and more for five short
working days with hardly any effort at all except the performance
of what someone else had worked to prepare for him. Did men
like Earl Greminger and Harry Ferguson resent the fact they were
paid so much less than he was? He guessed they did. Never before
had he passed a shop window and been able to stop and buy something just because it pleased him, without the guilt feeling that he
couldn't afford it or didn't need it. Now for the first time in his life
he had no financial obligation of any kind that he wasn't going to
be able to meet. Queerest of all was his new feeling about Fran.
She had been a part of his life for so long that she seemed insep-

arable from everything he did, but here in New York he missed
her not at all. The Boston years began to seem unreal, as though
they'd been lived by somebody else, not Lloyd Garner, not *this*
Lloyd Garner anyway. And that Friday night, meeting Fran in
his hotel room after the show, she seemed suddenly to be a stranger,
he felt somehow shy or irritated or both. She had intruded.

"Hello, honey," he heard himself say. He put his arms around
her and felt the tension in her body, maybe he seemed like a stranger
to her too. "Stand over there by the lamp and let me look at you."

She was wearing a dress he hadn't seen before, something she
must have bought with the weekly salary checks he'd had sent to
her while he was living on his expense account. It was a little tight
for her. He was disappointed that she hadn't seemed to lose any
weight. She was smiling, still tense. "You like?" she said and turned
around once.

"I like fine, I wish you could have come to the studio but it
was better not, not this first week."

"Oh, I know that, Lloyd, much better not."

"You got the show all right on this TV?"

"It was marvelous! *Think* of you, the whole country watching."

"I'm getting the feel of it. I guess tonight was my best show so
far."

"Those poor guys in Vietnam," she said, "I think that dying
marine was the saddest thing I've ever seen."

He wasn't worrying about the Marines. He was looking at the
bottle of bourbon and the glasses on the table. "I see you've had a
drink."

"Why, sure." She opened her eyes wide and smiled. "Right after
I got here from the airport, wasn't that all right?"

He nodded. "Good flight?"

"Lovely flight." She came to him and put her arms around him.
"It was all right to have one little drink, wasn't it? I'm not drunk
or anything."

"You're fine."

"Lloyd, you haven't kissed me yet."

"How's this?"

"Mm, that's more like."

He broke away laughing a little. "You've got a real head of steam up."

"I've only seen you once in five weeks, after *all*."

"Well, we've got plenty of time this weekend."

She was pouting half seriously. "I can remember when you used to throw me down and lay me if you'd only been away for one night."

"Honey, we're old married folks!" He caught her hands and smiled. "And I'm pooped, do you know what a week it's been?"

"I know, I do know."

"So how about we have a drink and talk about dinner, I'm hungry."

She took his arm and led him to the window. "The hotel is gorgeous," she whispered, her head against his shoulder. "Look at that out there, New York! I was so thrilled seeing it from the plane, the Empire State and all."

"It's a great sight, isn't it?"

Suddenly he knew how tired he was at the end of the biggest week of his life. If he didn't stand up right now and keep moving he was going to collapse. "Where would you like to have dinner?" He forced the lightness into his tone. "Someplace French? Italian?"

"Someplace glamorous," she said.

Her kind of glamorous. "What about the Rainbow Room?"

"Oh, Lloyd," she breathed, "could we? I've always wanted to go there."

So they went there, and Fran exclaimed some more over the view, and they had two drinks each, waiting for the steak which came overdone. To Fran's astonishment he ordered a bottle of champagne. "After all this is a big night, isn't it?" watching her drink it bravely without liking it. She was tight by the time they finished the bottle and so was he, in a dispirited sort of way, but Fran declined his offer of a second bottle and they went back to bourbon. She had launched into a long excited monologue about his brother and Grace Cassidy. They really should get married, he ought to tell Phil to stop stalling, and he half listened to all of it, fighting the desire just to shut his eyes and sleep sitting up. Once Fran said, interrupting herself, "Lloyd, you're not *talking*," and once he thought, picking up their fourth bourbon, "This is a hell of a way to help an alcoholic,"

but by that time they were both beyond any reasonable talk and the
dance music had started. They'd been in the place for hours. Fran
wanted to dance, of course, but he laughed and told her he was lucky
if he could stand up. She put her arm around his waist going out and
he told her she could have the beaver coat she'd wanted for so many
years and she kissed him in the elevator and looked proudly at the
other people going down with them. She saw they had recognized
her husband. Walking back to the hotel, Fran still wanted to go
somewhere dancing, he promised they'd do it tomorrow night after
the theater. Did she know what he'd gone through to get tickets for
Mame? They were passing Toots Shor's, she just wanted to peek inside, just peek, no more drinking, but they ended up sitting at the
bar and having another Old Forester and then a nightcap. Back at
the hotel they just managed to get undressed before they made it to
the bed and passed out.

It was his bleakest awakening in New York. He lay there
beside her trying to open his eyes, Saturday and Sunday stretched
ahead like wilderness. Fran slept stertorously; he turned his head
away from her whisky breath. He had no idea what time it was
and couldn't remember details of anything they'd done or said
after reaching Shor's. While he was soaking his throbbing head in
the bathroom he heard her call him and went back to find her
cheerful and talkative all over again.

"Jesus, we put it away last night," he said.

"I feel fine. Lloyd, I had a *marvelous* time." She sat up and
the covers fell away from her breasts. Didn't she know they weren't
beautiful any more as they once were? She held out her arms to
him, blear-eyed and smiling, and for a while he lay beside her motionless, staring up at the ceiling and wishing he was alone. "Hung
over, baby?" she was whispering to him. "We know how to fix
that, don't we?" The bed reeked of whisky fumes. She was touching
him, squeezing him with her fingers, and he thought, That was
what I used to love so much, just like that. "You're cute," he managed
to say, "you're trying to drive me up the wall, aren't you?" It was
what he used to say when she was doing this. He responded to it
at last, struggling up and covering her with his body, his eyes
closed, the long steady hangover thrusts shaking the bed. *"That's*

my boy," Fran whispered, tightening her arms around his shoulders, "*I missed my boy, I missed him,*" but when she turned her face up for his kiss he turned his head away and buried it deep in the pillow, loving without joy.

He wondered afterward if she had known. Standing in front of the mirror, shaving, he looked down at her lying full length in the big tub and saw her smile back at him.

"Was it good, honey?"

"You know it was good," she said, "but was it good for you too?"

He laughed. "It's always good."

"With me?"

"Of course with you, who else?"

"Some of these New York girls, maybe."

"Don't be silly."

The day was overcast but sunlight was beginning to break through. They walked up toward the Park, where he was going to take her to lunch at the Tavern on the Green. "I've just got to see the Fifth Avenue shops," she said, and he promised they'd do it after lunch. Once in the Park Fran saw the zoo sign and jumped up and down like a little girl, clamoring to see it. The sun was out full now, crowds were streaming into the zoo and children were everywhere. They spent an hour there, wandering from cage to cage. It was only as they were leaving to walk across the Meadow to the restaurant that he realized Fran had not been looking at the animals, she had been watching the children and her eyes were full of tears. "Hey, what's the matter with *you?*" he laughed, as if he didn't know, and she averted her eyes and said, "I want a drink, don't you?"

He was still feeling ashamed that he'd let her drink so much last night. "Okay, but let's take it easy today, shall we?"

She didn't reply and he felt again what he had felt after they'd made love this morning. She had drawn away from him, not very far but a little, into a troubled awareness. Maybe it was just her hangover. In the restaurant he was glad they didn't meet anyone from the office. Fran said suddenly, suspiciously, "What are you thinking about?" Goddamn women and their intuitions.

"I guess the beer's making me sleepy."

"You had such a faraway look on your face, Lloyd."

"Faraway? Knocked out, you mean."

He was so weary after they'd walked back across the Park that she said, "I'm going to see the stores and you're going back to the hotel and take a nap."

"I'm going with you."

"You're not going with me."

"All right, I'm not going with you."

He left her at Fifth and Fifty-ninth. "Just promise me you won't start drinking anything before you come back to the hotel, honey."

"That's ridiculous, of course I won't drink anything."

He flagged down a cab and she smiled and waved good-by. The driver had stared at him and as they drove off he saw a conversation begin between them, the driver would be asking if that wasn't Lloyd Garner and Fran would be saying yes, yes that was Lloyd Garner, and I'm his wife. He could hear them.

In the dream Fran was tightening the stirrup of his horse while he looked down at her from the saddle and Rita Valenti called out to him astride another horse on the other side of the brook, warning him to hurry. It was somewhere out West, but he had never been there before. He loved it there. Fran said, shaking him awake, "It's nearly seven, Lloyd, you've just got to wake up if we're going to the show." And he sat up, realizing he'd fallen asleep with all his clothes on, even his jacket. He frowned and then grinned up at her. "Why didn't you wake me earlier?"

"I couldn't bear it, you were so tired and peaceful."

"I didn't hear you come in."

She laughed. "Listen, an earthquake wouldn't wake you, Lloyd Garner." When she laughed he smelled the liquor on her breath.

"I thought you weren't going to drink anything."

"But I didn't!" She turned abruptly and said the rest of it with her back turned, moving away. "Not till I came in, I had one drink while I was waiting for you to wake up." She was in the bathroom starting his shower. "Come on," she called over the sound of the water, "get out of those clothes and fresh up!"

They hurried through dinner in the Place Lautrec room in the hotel. Fran was determined not to be late for the theater, then found they had twenty minutes more to wait after they reached their seats. "Third row on the aisle!" she whispered to him in her delight, looking around for celebrities in the audience. He said he thought probably all the celebrities had seen *Mame* by now and she called him a party poop. During the intermission a woman came up to them in the lobby and earnestly asked him for his autograph. Fran said when she went away, "And you told me there were no celebrities here tonight!" happily squeezing his arm. He wished he could be as gay about everything, for her sake, but the brash, noisy musical left him cold and he wondered if it was Fran's suburban housewife attitude that was depressing him. He welcomed the drinks at Sardi's after the show; Fran was agog at the actor types loitering at the bar. The liquor began to lift him after that and they pushed and shoved their way through the Saturday night crowds on a ritual tour of Times Square, ending up at the Cheetah which Fran absolutely *had* to see and where they danced and danced. For Fran it was like the old days. They used to go dancing a lot in Boston, in the wild din of rhythm she whirled away from him, imitating the mob around them, circling and lunging and shouting with laughter, but he only wanted to get out of the place. He was hot and sweating when they left, trying to keep the irritation out of his voice, but Fran was high now and wanted to go on. Couldn't they have spent this weekend some other way? But it was all Fran had ever wanted or cared about, to drink and dance and lie around the house, and for so long it had seemed enough. It was her weekend, he would do his best through the last day.

At Jimmy Ryan's they sat at the bar and listened to jazz until closing time, drinking three or four more bourbons, and finally there was no place else to go. Neither spoke on the walk to the hotel, not even looking at each other. They undressed in silence, in bed she turned her face to the wall without a good-night and fell asleep immediately. But he couldn't sleep. He lay there staring into the dark, reliving his week and the parade of faces, Sussman, Schonwald, Greminger, Ferguson, Rita Valenti's good-by, the nightmare of that first broadcast. But the nightmare was real, the camera's red light winked on, grew larger, exploded like a sun, frantic voices were shouting in the control room, "Go ahead, Garner! *go ahead!*" but he was frozen in his terror, frenziedly looking for the script that held the only words he knew, the Teleprompter was blank and the studio filled with mocking laughter. He sat up in bed with the fresh sweat breaking out on his body. What time was it? Gray daylight was pushing through the window. He got up then and dressed, still shaky from his dream, went down to the lobby and got the Sunday papers and read them sitting in the chair until Fran woke up. It was nearly ten.

"Hi, how you feel?" he said across the room.

She gave him a sleepy smile. "Terrible," she said.

"Want some breakfast?"

She shook her head and looked at the bottle of bourbon and the glasses. "I want a drink."

"That's just too bad, honey, because you're not getting one."

"I thought you'd say that."

"I've been a bad husband, Fran."

"Why?"

"You know why. We've been drinking all weekend just like it didn't matter, and it does matter, from now on."

"Don't fight," she said.

He got up and sat down beside her, looking down at her. "I'm not fighting, I'm just thinking about you."

"You drank just as much as I did."

"I know. I'm ashamed. I'm not doing it again."

She was toying with his tie. "You're all dressed."

"I went down for the papers, that's all."

"Then get undressed again and come back to bed."

He laughed. "All right, I will."

The same old drill. He lay beside her and let her arouse him, kissed her and touched her against his will. When he was ready he began, methodically, mechanically, hoping she wouldn't know what he didn't feel, but she did know, he was sure she knew, and the knowledge of what she felt and what he didn't feel took the heart out of it for him. He was trying. Suddenly, for a moment, he thought he could make it, and then he knew he wasn't going to make it, and knew she knew. His body's movement slowed and stopped. He forced a little laugh. "No use, honey. Guess I drank too much." Leaving her there silent, not looking at her, he got up and went into the bathroom and took a shower. When he came back into the room she was standing naked beside the table pouring whisky into a glass.

"No," he said and jerked her arm away. The glass struck the wall as she staggered back off balance and the bottle fell on its side, the whisky poured out onto the floor. *"Lloyd, you damn fool!"* She grabbed at the bottle and he threw her back roughly, *"No, I said!"* She stood there glaring at him in fury and astonishment, then turned and dropped face down on the bed, her shoulders shaken with deep sobs. "I'm sorry," he said and picked up the glass and stood up the empty bottle. He stood waiting by the window until she stopped crying. He had never heard her cry with such hurt and hopelessness. "Please," he said. "Please, Fran. Let's get dressed and go out, there isn't much time before you have to go back."

The streets were empty and cold with a city Sunday morning desolation when they left the hotel. She shivered and turned up the collar of her coat. "Shall we find some breakfast somewhere?" he said, but she shook her head. She hadn't spoken since she stopped crying but he knew it was not just because of the fight over the drink; there was more to it than that. For a time they walked east. The neighborhood changed suddenly from hotels and office buildings to quiet town houses near the river, and here she began to look around her. She spoke at last, "It's nice over this way. If I lived in New York this is where I'd like to live."

They had reached Beekman Place, a chilly wind was blowing over them off the river. He stopped and put his hands on her shoulders and she looked up at him. "Are you still mad at me, Fran? I told you I was sorry."

She was looking at him as if she saw the end of their marriage in his eyes.

II: LEARNING IT

6

He had expected Fran to call from Boston to apologize, to chat, to say anything, just to put them back on the track again, but she didn't call. He let it go for several days; he was a busy man. Finally he called himself, it was Grace Cassidy who answered, friendly but cautious, a new respect in her voice he'd never heard there, but then it figured, didn't it? No, Fran wasn't in, she was out having her hair done. She'd said she had a wonderful time in New York and talked about nothing else. Was there any particular message? Of course, he was just checking in. Grace would tell her, and bye-bye for now.

He felt relieved. He'd done his duty. Actually it was up to Fran now; he was damned if he'd call again before she did. Hadn't he done his best to entertain her? Hadn't he apologized for their quarrel? What more did she want, for now? The more he thought about it, when he did think about it, the more her attitude annoyed him. Any husband can fail occasionally, even on a honeymoon, for Christ's sake, was she going to hold that over his head? As if it hadn't happened before!

No, let her get in touch with him when she had something to say. If anything went really wrong Phil would tell him. Phil knew how it was with Lloyd Garner, he wouldn't burden him with anything unnecessary these first weeks in his new job, he knew how important it was to leave a man alone, he knew how to show respect. Professionally, that's what Lloyd Garner got from every-body now, respect and even adulation. He enjoyed it, sometimes it even seemed necessary to his feeling of well-being, like the habit of daily exposure on the tube. Vast audiences watched and listened to the show every day, wherever he was he was usually the center of attention. It was now the rule rather than the exception when he was recognized in public; he found himself surprised and even a little resentful when he was not. In a studio all eyes were on him, all efforts directed to his needs first. Stagehands adjusted his chair, lighting men studied his profile like artists concentrating on a painting, cameramen and soundmen followed his movements and inflections with doting care. He took a sensual pleasure in the ministrations of the make-up people, especially if it was a girl. Operation Studio was rather like lying back in a barber's chair with masseur, manicurist and bootblack all laboring over you at once. The taste of luxury, he liked it. And he liked the deference of executives treating him with the special courtesy reserved for hot company properties, and of course the news staff was ready to show concern if he raised an eyebrow. Even the tough guy, even Buck Schonwald.

Buck Schonwald, a television animal. He lived for it, he was it. Somewhere back there he'd got his start in radio, but as soon as TV was out of the experimental stage and regular programing began he switched to the new medium and survived its chaotic period of growing pains. He told Lloyd the story in random glimpses of the past during afternoon coffee breaks in the network lunchroom, the only occasions except one dinner at Schonwald's the producer ever took time to talk about anything but the Lloyd Garner show. Even the dinner in the Schonwald apartment on West End Avenue was interrupted repeatedly by phone calls from Hacklin, who had had his evening call from the big boss and was ready for post-mortem discussion of the day's program. Lloyd said, feeling slightly high on Pilsner Urquell and smiling across the remains of a solid German-Jewish meal, "Tell me, Buck, how do I get to meet him?"

He knew what was meant but said, "Meet who?"

"The big boss."

"Are you on that again? How the hell do I know? Ask Hacklin."

"Suppose I bypass Hacklin and just ask for an appointment."

He seemed seriously affected by the thought. "He wouldn't like it."

"Who, Hacklin or the big boss?"

"Neither. I wouldn't do it, fellow."

"Who found me, Buck?"

"Found you? I don't know. I never knew."

"Come on, you don't expect me to believe that."

Large, somber and placidly unobtrusive, Schonwald's wife was taking the dishes off the table. "If and when the big boss wants to see Lloyd Garner," her husband said, "it'll be arranged."

"Milo Wilson would know, he hired me."

"Then ask Milo Wilson."

"I couldn't believe him, either."

They were both laughing. Schonwald got up and put an arm around his shoulders. "What's eating you? You're in and you're going great. They're already starting to imitate that way you have of leaning on the end of a sentence." Over the coffee in the big, gloomy living room he changed the subject and went back to his memories of Cedric Taylor, generally regarded as the creator of television news. "Seemed like even at his drunkest C.T. could think faster and clearer than anybody in the business, and toward the end he was drunkest *all* the time. Came the night when he was so drunk Hacklin wouldn't let him into the studio, we had one studio then and one daily show, so C.T. stormed back to the elevator declaring he would see the big boss about that. Only Hacklin, for once, was ahead of him, and when C.T. waved his arms and shouted to the operator, *'Up!'* the elevator went *down*, to the street floor and out."

Sometimes described by his employees as a petty tyrant with a heart of gold, Taylor was given to venomous rages but seldom held a grudge or fired a man once the man had proved himself competent. As one of a number of impish foibles he kept a growing collection of fluffs by news broadcasters with which he would regale his visitors on occasion, roaring with as much glee as if he'd heard them for the first time. His Rome correspondent, for instance, had once quoted the Pope deploring the fact that "immorality is rife and sax is lax." Another of his boys, reporting from the Far East, had cited a high hource in Panmunjom for his story, and then there was the reference to Sir Stifford Crapps, an unfortunate spoonerism from London, which had caused Sir Stafford Cripps some embarrassment but given Winston Churchill his best laugh of the day. C.T.'s favorite was one from a Washington reporter who in describing some Roosevelt inauguration festivities said cheerfully, "Both the presidential balls are in full swing at this hour."

Those were the days when Cedric Taylor did his hiring and firing sitting at a desk with a bottle of Scotch standing in front of him, and there was lot of hiring and firing because he was inventing television news technique as he went along and some people learned how to use it and some didn't, but nobody knew anything until they learned it from Cedric Taylor. He'd made his early fame with newspapers and wartime radio. He dictated the first manual of TV news operation from that same desk and he ended his network career with characteristic bravura by passing out while making a speech at an affiliates banquet. He was carried from the room and seven months later died of cirrhosis of the liver.

It was fitting that Cedric Taylor departed when he did, because television news had gone big time and required a different breed of executive, a Walter Hacklin, to deal with its economic and political complexities, to settle the News and Public Relations departments into the burgeoning corporate structure and to front for the big boss's personal interest in this aspect of the company's operations. Hacklin knew how to delegate authority and dodge responsibility for mistakes, as Buck Schonwald told it, and it was left to Schonwald to develop the evening news show as the prime achievement of his department. Although Hacklin was in title overseer of the morning and afternoon news shows as well as the big evening production, he preferred the public relations end and spent much of his time conferring with the network's Washington lobbyists, grappling with issues like equal time for dissenters, coddling the FCC, which was easily coddled, and heading off recurrent threats in Congress and elsewhere to the broadcasting establishment. He also had to deal with perennial problems involving the affiliate stations and their sometimes anti-network news departments, particularly where race conflict was concerned. Thus it was Schonwald who rode herd on program content and talent while concentrating on building Hedley Johns into the industry's outstanding TV news broadcaster. But TV news grew fast, and eventually grew even bigger than Hedley Johns, the last of the pioneers. The other networks caught up, and by the time Johns departed it had evidently been decided that news programs were now bigger than the names of their anchormen.

Schonwald was as evasive about the Hedley Johns blowup as he was aloof in his relations with all the men on his staff, including Lloyd Garner, and the staff took the cue from their chief. In this shop, Lloyd was quick to observe, the key words were caution and mistrust, suspicion and vigilance; it was dog eat dog in the competition for the next step up from whatever level. Gossip was crafty and guarded but the rumor mill ground nonstop. From Hacklin down, you didn't put your confidence in anybody, personal loyalty wasn't being practiced around here. As far as Lloyd could see there were few out-of-office friendships, especially at his level. When you were up this far you were alone. Everybody was scared, even on weekends at home. You lasted as long as the machine needed you and there was always another man conniving for your job.

Among the broadcasters the three daily anchormen were in the most coveted and therefore the most precarious spots, then came the foreign correspondents, then the domestic bureau chiefs and then the field reporters. Editors and writers, in that order, had a hierarchy of their own, intense and harried competition prevailed. At the bottom level was Bev Hambleton's category, the purveyors of coffee and sandwiches, dreaming and hoping for the future in their copy-boy hearts.

Lon Carey and Weldon Duff, anchormen on the morning and afternoon shows, were theoretically Lloyd's equals in the talent scale, but both showed him a special respect that failed to conceal entirely their resentment at his success in the prime spot. They'd been around quite a while before Lloyd Garner was ever heard of, and evidently felt they'd deserved the chance given so unexpectedly to an outsider. At the same time they accepted the situation as just another of the sudden spectacular mysteries characteristic of the game, probably no one would ever know the reason, or all the reasons, why it happened. Lloyd noticed that Carey and Duff shared an occupational obsession, worrying about their program ratings as they fluctuated on the listener charts, Carey perhaps more so than the younger Duff. Lon was getting up toward fifty in a business where you could be considered old at thirty-five, he was wearing a hairpiece and showing signs of nervousness about his age. In the lunchroom he insisted on holding to caste distinctions, he welcomed Schonwald or Lloyd to his table but nobody of lesser rank, and

harped on a favorite complaint that his writers couldn't adapt to
his speaking style. Recently his vocal delivery seemed to have grown
thinner and higher, with a vaguely audible gurgle to it, so that some
of the announcers referred to him privately as Old Adenoids.
Weldon Duff, who doubled as the network's moonshot expert, was
something else again. An undersized man with an oversized voice,
he'd been on the air for so many years he was still on even when he
was off. He always took a beat between sentences, and every phrase
was a broadcast. Even his gait in the hall had a deliberate, modulated
quality, like his gestures, which never were wider than the width
of the lens. But Duff was not one to hang around and worry with
his colleagues. He almost always left the building immediately after
his show and headed for Michael's Pub, where he drank steadily
and chatted with anybody until time to catch his train for Mt. Kisco.
Walter Hacklin, of course, lunched in the executive dining room if
he wasn't at 21, and never was seen in the news department
lunchroom.

It was Bev Hambleton who kept Lloyd apprised of these and other
aspects of the staff social life, including the exploits of a fellow
copyboy, Jake Lumb, whose announced project for the year was to
lay every secretary in the department and had already scored thirteen times.

"Did you say knocked up?"

"Said notched up, Uncle Lloyd, but it's true there were two
pregnancies and Jake had to take out a bank loan."

Bev was special, a veteran of Lloyd Garner's first day at the network. And it wasn't in Bev to be obsequious to anyone. He came
from that world of gentlemen Lloyd knew too little about, of which
his manners, his clothes and the Racquet & Tennis Club were
symbols, and he moved on easy terms with people like Alix Weddern. One of these days Lloyd would get back to Alix Weddern, but
first things first, he was just hitting his stride, everything would
come his way in the end. Later, soon, he and Alix Weddern would
resume where they left off that evening at Kent Ward's in Washington. Kent Ward, who had drawled his congratulations after Lloyd's
first show and added dryly, amusedly, "Look out, you're making more
money now than Buck Schonwald."

"You mean Buck resents it?"

"Wouldn't you?"

Tonight in his Washington spot Kent Ward was noting the beginning of a new phase in the nation's life that would bring sweeping and dangerous political consequences. Robert McNamara was leaving the Pentagon and Eugene McCarthy had challenged the White House by declaring himself a candiate for the Democratic presidential nomination. Both events could be seen as linked, said Ward, as symbols of growing opposition to Administration policy in the Vietnam War reaching all the way down to the grass roots; both could be read as signs of the growing unpopularity of the President himself. Congressmen were hearing from angry constituents about rising American casualties and the Senate Foreign Relations Committee was restive, the Secretary of State wasn't allowed to come over to the Hill even for an executive session. Undertones of Negro inequality unrest provided ominous parallel. By next summer if not sooner there would be a domestic problem of utmost gravity and antiwar demonstrations all over the country that would make the recent march in New York look like a Sunday-school picnic.

Listening to the measured tones from Washington, waiting for his cue for headline summary and sign-off, Hedley Johns's successor reflected that more and more the show was concentrating on those areas to the exclusion of almost everything else. The battle footage from Vietnam was getting bloodier all the time, the Saigon bureaus of the TV networks were in competition to produce the highest percentage of firefights per week. Interviews with bereaved parents on the shows were heartbreaking, and Negro militants in the situation at home were protesting so violently that Walter Hacklin had ordered them kept off the air until the spots were submitted to him for approval. *"Kent Ward in the capital,"* concluded the quiet voice from the screen, and Lloyd remembered Schonwald's instruction, "Always make it a *cheerful* good night."

The producer was sitting at Lloyd's desk at the phone when he walked in, the script still in his hand. "I know all that, Kent," he was saying unhappily, "but did you have to say Rusk wasn't *allowed* to testify? That puts it right in Johnson's office, for God's sake." He listened, nodded wearily. "Sure, but it's straight guesswork about McNamara's reasons, after all he didn't *say* they disagreed on Vietnam. Honest, fellow—" He glanced up morosely at Lloyd. "Anyway things are bad enough already without you talking grim about what's *going* to happen, will you try to watch it? We don't want another call from the White House." He hung up shaking his head.

Lloyd grinned at him. "How was my good night, boss? Cheerful? Or do we wait for the word? I assume Walter called."

"He called all right."

"Big Daddy's watching pretty close these days, eh?"

"Never mind that, I want to talk to you."

"Me too?"

"Not about the show, the show was good, except for Kent's piece. This is something else, namely the union. You're a member, naturally."

"Doesn't the network say I have to be? I think Sussman said it's in the company contract with the union."

"Sussman, Sussman. Do we have to bring Sussman into this? He's right, of course."

Lloyd laughed. "Why do you hate him, Buck? Yes, I signed up in Boston years ago, not that they ever did anything for me but collect my dues. I guess they'll up the ante now that I'm making more money, but I haven't heard from them yet."

"You'll hear from them, but not about dues." His voice was grave. "They're about to call a strike."

"Strike?" He felt a sudden sinking sensation of dismay. "Come on, Buck, this union hasn't called a strike since it came into existence."

"A strike was authorized by membership vote the first time the negotiations bogged down."

"But that's just a routine bargaining move. It happened before I came to work here."

"Negotiations deadlocked last night and Hacklin told me this morning the company's not going to budge."

"So?"

"The union negotiators walked out tonight saying we can expect a strike any time. AP just ran their statement on the wires."

There was a silence. Schonwald puffed his pipe and looked at him. Lloyd said, "What's the issue?"

"A number of issues, but mainly impossible money demands and broader duties for announcers in the new contract."

"Okay, let the announcers strike, I'm not an announcer."

"You belong to the union, Lloyd. In case of a strike it's the same thing."

His heart was beating faster and his breath felt short. "How come nobody's told me about this before? How does the membership feel?"

"It's not up to the membership any more, not since the strike vote. The negotiators are professional union officials, they run the union and they can call the strike any time they decide."

"But surely they'll hold a final vote!"

"They don't have to."

Lloyd looked at him. "Maybe the company *wants* the strike."

"No, the company doesn't want the strike, but if it comes we're going to take it and sit tight. You have Hacklin's word for it, Lloyd, that's final."

There was another pause. The producer of the Lloyd Garner show refilled his pipe and then said, "Well?"

"Well, what?"

"What do you think, Lloyd?"

What did he think? That he was being trapped into a strike against the company that had given him his big chance. He said instead, "It looks as if what I think doesn't matter a damn."

"Walter said it would be too bad," Buck Schonwald said, "to have to replace you just as you were getting started and all. Of course we can keep the show going, and all the other news shows, with executive personnel. We can do that as long as we have to, make no mistake about it, we've done it before in strikes by the technicians unions."

"I know."

"We already have assurances that some of those unions are going to cross your picket lines."

"My picket lines." Lloyd laughed shortly. "For God's sake, Buck, do you think I want to go on strike for a bunch of announcers? And what are these impossible money demands? I haven't heard anybody complaining about money."

"There are raises in the proposed contract for the people who asked for them," Schonwald said. "As much as the company can afford. But every time the union came back to us they asked for more. If you want my opinion the *negotiators* want the strike, not the company and not the members, not a majority anyway. It's a power play, pure and simple."

"But why?"

The big man shrugged. "I can't see any reason for it but arrogance. They've rejected the best deal in the industry."

In the new silence Lloyd looked at him and looked away. "Suppose," he said slowly, "suppose they call the strike and the members, some members, refuse to walk out. Just refuse. What can the union do to them?"

"The union can try to penalize them. And"—he leaned forward over the desk, his voice softer—"the company can protect them."

Lloyd drew a long breath. "Maybe it's all a bluff, maybe there won't be any strike."

"Maybe," Buck Schonwald said. "Hacklin just wanted you to know how things really are. If they do strike, it looks like a long one."

Calling Sime Sussman from his office afterward, he could see the worried little huddles in the newsroom and feel the tension suddenly injected into the atmosphere by the AP bulletin. "Yeah," Sussman said, "I was just going to call you, Lloyd. What have you decided to do?"

"What have I decided to do?" He exploded in anger and exasperation. "What do I pay *you* for?"

A rasping chuckle. "The network's on the spot in this one. They bargained people like you into the union originally in exchange for something else they wanted at the time and now they're stuck with it."

"You think they'll call the strike, Sime?"

"If they do they're nuts. From what I know they were near enough on the money issue to go ahead and sign."

"Then Schonwald was right, it's just a test of strength. And we're the guinea pigs."

The cackle again. "For Schonwald read Walter Hacklin. And for Hacklin read the big boss."

"He didn't come right out and say so, but he was obviously advising me to stay on the job."

"Hoping others would follow your lead. Sure, they'd like to break the union, what company wouldn't?"

"What are your other clients doing, Sime?"

"What do *you* think, they're throwing fits, they don't give a screw about the union, they're afraid they might lose a few fees."

He could hear the frustration in his own voice. "Just when everything's going for me this has to happen."

"I know, I know. But you still got to decide how you feel about the solidarity bit. With some people it's a personal thing, Lloyd. You either stay with the union or you cut the traces. You got any feelings about that?"

"Sime, I don't owe anybody anything. The union never did anything for me."

"Well, then, you answered yourself, didn't you?"

He said slowly, "Maybe I did. What's *your* answer?"

"What can I tell you? It's a personal thing. This one is your decision."

His decision. He sat there staring at the wall. Then he called Kent Ward in Georgetown. There were voices in the background. "I'm sorry, I guess you've got people there, Kent."

"Hello, Lloyd. It doesn't matter, they can take care of themselves."

"Do you know about this strike thing?"

"Thorpe called and read me the AP story, yes."

"Does it involve you people in Washington?"

"Yes, just like New York, didn't you know that?"

"And if the strike comes, Kent, what will you do?"

He sounded a little surprised at the question. "Stay home, of course."

"Buck says the union's making an idiotic move."

"I'm not up on the last stage of the negotiations but I wouldn't be surprised if it is. I don't think anybody really expected this, they've always gotten together before."

"I'm told it would be a long strike."

He chuckled. "Then I can catch up on my reading, it might be rather nice."

"But Kent—"

"That's how it is," Kent Ward said and went back to his guests.

Alone in his glass-enclosed office Lloyd looked out into the empty studio. Everybody had left right after the show as usual. The AP bulletin must have come in too late for them or Earl Greminger would have been still in there worrying his head off. Ferguson was a good family man who had dinner at home every night if he could make it. Bob Lentz caught a train to Princeton. Through the other door, looking into the newsroom, the little groups were still huddling, occasionally one man or another looked in Lloyd's direction and looked away again. He had a sudden impulse to go out there and talk to these guys, find out what they were saying about this. But something else in him said no, you're Lloyd Garner. If anybody wanted to talk to Lloyd Garner about it they could come to him, and that included the union.

He took his coat and hat and went out through the studio, avoiding the newsroom. In the hall, a few feet along, he almost bumped into Drew Stimson. The research director was just leaving his office. "*Hel*-lo, Lloyd!" Always the big smile.

"Heard about the strike threat, Drew?"

"I have, yes." They were walking side by side toward the elevator.

"Looks pretty serious, eh?"

"I'm afraid so, Lloyd."

"Does it affect your staff at all?"

"We're just about the only ones, with the writers, who aren't involved."

And lucky to be out of it. "You're not a union man, Drew?"

"Just not eligible. Of course I've been keeping track of developments in the talks."

They were stepping into the elevator. "Got time to stop for a drink?" Lloyd said.

"Wish I could. Have to catch a plane."

"Washington?"

"Why, that's right, yes."

"Get down there very often?"

"Every now and then." He was talking looking away from him.

"You mean for the network," Lloyd said.

The eyes returned swiftly. "Sure, what else?"

"Sorry you won't have time for a drink, I'd like to hear about the negotiations."

"I'm sorry too," Drew Stimson said. The elevator doors opened and he moved into the lobby, walking fast.

Lloyd watched his retreating back, then left the building by the side street entrance and went into the first bar on the block. He had ordered his bourbon and soda and perched up on a stool when he noticed that Bev Hambleton was smiling at him in the mirror from the next stool. "You, here?" Bev Hambleton said.

"I might ask you the same question."

"I like the prices."

Lloyd laughed. "I visualize you at the Racquet Club."

"Not till I pay my bill, unfortunately."

"Let me lend you the money, Bev."

"You're very polite, but couldn't consider it."

"Then let me buy you a drink."

"Accept with pleasure."

It was a nondescript little place, almost empty at this hour, a tiny radio spluttered feebly at the other end of the bar. Lloyd said, "I'm glad I wandered in here, now I'll have company for dinner."

The idea seemed to amuse Bev Hambleton. "Should think you'd have to fight people off for dinner."

"Not every night."

"The broadcasters going to strike, Lloyd?"

"I wish I knew."

They sat there in silence through a second drink and then a third. Lloyd had the impression it was about the seventh for Bev Hambleton but there was no way of telling except a certain stiffness in his bearing. Finally he spoke, "Something's annoying you, Uncle."

"The strike thing. I don't know why I feel shook about it,

they may not call it at all. But if they do I'll have to make a decision."

The younger man laughed and seemed to understand very well. "Toss a coin," he said.

"I may at that. I've been trying to figure why it bothers me so much. For some reason it seems to go way back, maybe to something I can't remember, I don't know what."

"In the meantime," said Bev Hambleton, "shall we have another drink?"

"We certainly shall." And with the fourth one he felt definitely better. He turned from the mirror and said, "I like you, Bev. I always have."

"Like you too."

"It's not because we're the same kind of people, it's because we're so different."

"Don't know about that."

"Oh, yes you do. I've been sitting here going over the early years of my life, Bev, and they weren't like yours. Remembering my mother going out to jobs and getting laid off. Remembering some days we literally didn't know where the next meal was coming from." He stared at his drink. "The three of us would eat out of a couple of cans of spaghetti and that was it. Phil, my brother Phil, and I would get after-school jobs if we could. I worked in a jewelry store for a while, wiping off silver and stuff like that. The old guy followed me around and kept after me every second complaining, sneering. Weekends we worked the bowling alleys, pinboys. I can remember running up to where they'd been bowling after they left and grabbing pieces of sandwiches they'd bitten out of that were still on their plates and checking out the empty beer bottles for a mouthful at the bottom, half starved. Sometimes there was one guy, just one, that gave a tip, a quarter for each of us. I liked those guys." He turned to look at his listener. "Where were you when this was going on? Groton? St. Paul's?"

"Several places," Bev Hambleton said. "They never kept me anywhere very long."

"Money looked so big, Bev. But other people always had it, not us." He heard his own small laugh. "And now I've got some, for the first time, and it's like somebody's about to take it away from me, do you understand? Like somebody's about to take it away from me, and drop me back to where I was, long ago but not forgotten, in the boarding houses with the bedbugs, skipping to beat the rent, back to that bowling alley. Just when I've landed the big job, just when I'm on top of the world. And I want to stay there. I don't want anything to trip me up, not for a minute. Not any lousy strike, not anything. I'm in the money, Bev. I'm staying there."

"Money's not so big," Bev Hambleton said.

"How would you know?" He rapped on the bar and motioned to their drinks. "For me money was the thing that stood for happiness, it meant, I guess it meant what it would have meant for my mother, not having to be snubbed any more, a decent place to live, decent clothes." His hand tightened on the fresh glass. "I was so *ashamed* when I was a kid, ashamed that my father had left us, ashamed for my mother working behind counters in stores where I had to go to get lunch money she'd borrowed for me, or wait for her there on payday, sometimes I heard the way customers talked to her, the women. Sometimes she had to pretend I wasn't her son because some little bastard of a floorwalker was watching her." He shook his head slowly, looking at the glass. "I lived for years on hand-me-downs from a family we knew, friends of my mother's, the only *nice* people we knew, who had a good house on a good street. They had a boy a year older than I was and I got his clothes when he couldn't wear them any more. Bev, the only thing in those jackets that wasn't ready to throw away was the Brooks Brothers label. I can remember like it was yesterday morning one day when I went to school with a pair of his pants on, practically rags by that time, and when I was called to show something on the blackboard I tried to stand so they wouldn't see the seat of my pants coming through, but a kid in the front row was grinning and pointing at me." He turned again. "Where were you going to school that year?"

"My memory's not as good as yours, Lloyd."

"Nobody ever helped me," he was saying, almost to himself, "but I got somewhere, call it luck, call it what you like, just when I thought I was going to be nobody like everybody else, a news reader in the boondocks, a dime a hundred. And now some power-hungry union guy looking for more status wants me to step aside and give him room to scream awhile."

"Isn't only you. Lot of others would be striking."

"And living to regret the day. Believe me, Bev, I bucked this issue in Boston once, they want you to put your whole future in doubt for a few lousy bucks a week more than you're getting. Look at the strikes here in New York that have closed down big newspapers forever, and for why? Because of a lot of unrealistic demands that would put a company out of business that tried to meet them, and where are the poor jerks now that had jobs on those papers?" He put his hand over his eyes, he was feeling drunk. "This thing could drag on for months and end with all of us out of our jobs for good."

The younger man grinned faintly. "We'd survive."

"Sure. You can say that. You have nothing to gain even when you win. You've got it all already, security, position. I've got everything to lose if I don't win, but you wouldn't understand that. I'm playing to win, Bev, *I'm playing to win.*"

They both looked up. The bartender was standing in front of them, both hands on the bar. "You boys from the television, right?"

"That's right," Bev Hambleton said.

"I guess we won't be seeing you for a while, huh? I just heard it on the radio."

"You just heard what on the radio?" Lloyd said.

"The strike. It's called for midnight. But I guess you know that."

7

His head was pounding and his mouth was dry when he woke, the room still dark. What time was it? He fumbled for his watch and couldn't find it, then got up and went to the window, pulling open the curtains. Gray daylight hurt his eyes, he went back and switched on the TV, sitting on the edge of the bed to watch it, rubbing his forehead.

The morning news was on and the familiar face of Lon Carey was absent. A stranger was reading the script, badly, some executive he'd never seen before. *So it had started.* He watched, fascinated.

"This is William Herndon substituting for Lon Carey," the stranger said at the end. There was no further explanation, a canned situation comedy followed a set of commercials. He got up again and took in the *Times* from outside his door. They'd front-paged it, of course, a two-column headline at the bottom. He read it and felt a kind of fear tightening in his belly. Just then the phone rang, Schonwald in a rage. "For God's sake!" the voice explored, "where you been all night?"

"Right here, Buck."

"The hell you have, you still weren't answering at four o'clock."

He remembered then going to some place on the East Side with Bev where they ate and drank until it closed. "I never heard the phone. But never mind that, I just want to know who's out and who's still on the job."

"They're all out, all the broadcasters that is, but some of the writers are in."

"Some of them are staying out?"

"Yeah, including Harry Ferguson, even though their union says they can cross the picket line."

"So there's a picket line."

"Of course there's a picket line, what the hell did you expect?"
He was still seething.

"I just didn't believe they'd do it, Buck."

"They did it. And they want everybody on that line, Lloyd,
especially you. Have you been in touch with the union?"

"No, I haven't been in touch with the union."

"Well?" The word had a savage edge. "What are you going to
tell me?"

"I haven't made up my mind."

"It's been damn near twelve hours since we talked about it."

"I'm sorry. I've been thinking it over."

"And how long's that going to take?"

"As long as necessary, I guess."

"Just who do you think you are?"

"Buck, calm yourself. I'm trying."

"If we'd been able to announce last night that you were refusing
to go out we could have got some others to stay, you know that.
Where the hell were you anyway?"

"I told you I was sleeping."

"In some broad's apartment, no doubt." He was really sore. "I'm
telling you, Lloyd, I thought you'd run out on us."

"Calm down, Buck, you can save the cracks."

"Well?" he came back, "what are you going to do?"

He hesitated. "I don't know. We've got a little time—"

"No. I want you in here by two o'clock if you're coming in,
otherwise I've got to line up your substitute."

"Listen, Buck, have you talked to Kent Ward?"

"Why should I? The whole Washington line-up is out, Thorpe
told me that at nine o'clock. We're not begging anybody to work.
It's up to them. They're going to regret it, but it's up to them."

"Didn't you talk to anybody?"

"Hacklin saw some of them late last night. If you'd been standing beside him it would have made the difference, they sure as hell
didn't *want* to go out, I can tell you that."

"Why didn't they tell the union, then?"

"I understand they are telling the union. There's one hell of a row between the fat cats and the rookies, from what I hear. The announcers are split right down the middle over this."

He felt the helpless anger rising. "Then why didn't they speak up before?"

"Look, fellow," his tone was finally calmer, "it's too late to argue. The strike is on and the union's not backing down. The only question is how soon the defections begin, and that's where *you* could strike the big blow. If Lloyd Garner is on the air as usual tonight it'll be the beginning of the end, you can be goddamn sure of that. I'm hanging up now, Lloyd, I've got things to do. I can't make up your mind for you, but for Christ's sake try to be sensible, will you?" He clicked off.

The room seemed strangely silent, shut away from the real world, leaving him in a world of memory. He stood staring at the receiver still in his hand but he was back in Boston again, a long-ago day, and he saw Fay Habersham's oily smile and heard his menacing laugh. Lloyd Garner had laid it on the line that day in the boss's office with all his buddies listening to him, and his buddies let him down in the end. If that was the price of courage then he'd been right to take the other way and play it safe from there on out. He was on the other side of the fence now, he'd come a long way since that day, farther than he'd dreamed. Was he going to throw it all away with the wrong decision?

He put the receiver down and walked over to the window. As always the city stared back at him, hostile and bleak, giving no answers.

In Washington, Kent Ward was out. If Hedley Johns had been doing the show, would he be out too?

A couple of blocks from here there was a picket line, he could see their faces, he knew them all.

He went into the bathroom and turned on the shower.

They were there all right, he saw them and then quickly looked away from them as he got out of the taxi at the corner, some of them carrying strike placards in the cold wind, two cops standing at the main entrance, a little crowd of lingering passers-by. But though the pickets saw him just as he walked up, making it a point not to hurry his step but avoiding their eyes, not one of them spoke or jeered. Above him the great building seemed to open protective, mothering arms, anonymous and safe. Inside the lobby the press was ready for him; he'd forgotten about the press. There was a brief flurry of movement around him, flash bulbs flared, then he was in the elevator and it was over.

"Hello, Janey," he said to the pert little receptionist when he strode past her. He heard the surprise in her voice, "Oh. Hello, Mr. Garner."

In the studio Schonwald was talking to Earl Greminger, the editor looked nervous, for a moment Lloyd thought Greminger was going to shake hands with him. He noticed Harry Ferguson was not at his desk, the assistant writers would be doing the script. Everybody else seemed to be on the job as usual. He felt himself smile automatically and walked on into his office. "No outside calls," he said to his secretary. After that, it was easy.

He went through the afternoon as though watching a stranger, himself. Everything he did seemed like another man doing it. Once he knocked off for a little while to eat a roast beef sandwich and drink some soup Gaby ordered for him, and once Schonwald came in to say it had been decided he should cover the strike late in the show without comment of any kind and without reference to his own position. He added, "The reporters are here, of course, Earl's working out something for you to say to them after the show. And the union's been calling me because they can't reach you, it was John Carney, I told him I was sure you'd get back to him, okay?"

"Okay."

An hour before air the executive phone rang and Gaby said, "Mr. Hacklin."

"Yes, Walter."

"I just wanted to say how pleased we all are up here that you're taking a stand, Lloyd. *All* of us."

"Thank you."

"The company won't forget this. How do you feel?"

"I'm okay."

"I'm sure you are, your voice sounds good, Lloyd. Just do your usual fine job."

"I'll try."

"You always do, Lloyd. After you get rid of the reporters, you'll have to see them briefly, we'll have a company car waiting at the back of the building, it might be best that way."

"Whatever you say."

"We'll be watching, Lloyd."

He hung up and said to Gaby, "Has Kent Ward called me today?" She shook her head. "He's out, too, you know."

"I know."

Shortly before air Gaby put a late edition of the *Post* on his desk. The story had no indication of dissension within the union but no other unions had joined the walkout. There was a shot of Lloyd Garner crossing the picket line. A few minutes later Bev Hambleton stuck his head in the newsroom door, grinned at him and vanished again.

Bob Lentz came in to check script with him, looked at him sharply and said, "You feeling okay?" and the somebody else who was doing Lloyd Garner's job answered with a brief smile, "I'm feeling okay, are *you* feeling okay?"

"Usual staff working in the control room."

Lentz was like everybody who'd spoken to him today, no blame and no praise. They were all on the side lines in this, it was his problem, not theirs. Then Schonwald signaled him, he took his place before the cameras, and the show went without a hitch. There was no big national story to worry about. The pickups were all film from overseas. He had thought he would be nervous, but with this other fellow subbing for Lloyd Garner it was a breeze.

Half a dozen reporters were waiting for him in Schonwald's office with Jay Weiss. The show behind him, confident and relaxed, he felt a strange sense of elation, like an actor walking on stage in a familiar role. He had Greminger's typed statement in his hand as he faced them. "I'll read this, if you don't mind," he said, and read it slowly and deliberately. *"In my opinion this strike is unwise and unnecessary and I cannot support it. I believe a majority of the union membership does not want the strike. It was called hastily without giving the membership a chance to vote again on the ques-*

tion. I believe in union solidarity, but personal conscience must come first." He looked up, unsmiling. "That's all."

Several voices started to speak at once and Jay Weiss held up his hand. "Take it easy, boys, you wanted a statement of Lloyd's position and you've got it. He'll answer any reasonable questions."

"Why do you think the strike's unwise, Mr. Garner?"

"Because I believe the proposed contract is fair."

"Do you expect the union to expel you or penalize you?"

He shrugged slightly. "I have no idea what they'll do."

"Did you attend any of the bargaining sessions or union meetings yourself?"

Jay Weiss said, "Look, he wasn't even working here when the negotiations began."

A sardonic voice in the rear, "Let him speak for himself, will you? Suppose the strike lasts a long time, indefinitely, will you continue to broadcast?"

"As of now I intend to continue working."

"And how much money do you earn, Mr. Garner?"

"Whoa!" Buck Schonwald said, "What's that got to do with it?" but the somebody else who was Lloyd Garner at the moment smiled and said, "I'd be glad to tell you if I knew myself, you see we're paid on the basis of commercial fees and they vary."

The same voice, "You don't have any view about scabbing?"

"Now, just a minute," Weiss began, but Lloyd said, "It's all right, Jay, I've already said this is a matter of individual conscience."

He waited, there were no more questions. He felt them watching him, silent, contemptuous, above all envious. He didn't meet their eyes but he knew how they felt about him. He was one of their own kind and he'd betrayed them twice, by leaving them and then making it big. He would not be forgiven. Schonwald said, "That's it, then. If there's anything further from the network, Jay will have it. And I think Jay wants to buy you all a drink, right, Jay? Good night, boys." They filed out.

Alone with Lloyd he said, "You handled that like you'd done it all your life, fellow. Now watch the boys start coming home!" But Lloyd thought he heard a kind of contempt behind the praise and turned away.

"Walter said he'd have a car for me."

"It's waiting, take the back elevator. And if I were you I'd stay off the the town tonight. You want somebody to go along with you?"

"No."

Gaby had the phone in her hand when he came back to his office. "Mrs. Weddern, she says it's urgent."

"Alix! This is a nice surprise."

"I'm not even going to tell you I've been cross with you," the cool, level voice said. "You never called me, you know. I just want to say I know how much courage it took for you to broadcast tonight and I'm proud to know you."

He laughed and felt the real Lloyd Garner beginning to materialize again. "You happen to be the first person who's said anything like that, Alix. Where are you?"

"At home and I can offer you a drink, I'm sure you need one."

"I do and I'm accepting the offer, how's that?"

Gaby watched him hang up and write down the address. "You all right?" she said.

"Never better. Same time tomorrow."

He walked to the back elevator through an empty hall and found it waiting for him. As the night guard, wordless, swung open the street door he could see the limousine just across the sidewalk waiting in the shadows of the dim lit avenue, a burly driver somnolent at the wheel, and as he stepped onto the pavement a man hidden somewhere in the darkness beside the building sprang across the shaft of light from the doorway and struck at him, catching him hard at the side of his head. Dazed under the blow he staggered once and heard the hatred in the breathless muttered words, *"You prick!"* and the soft rush of footsteps away from him, down the block. Up at the other corner under a street light two sentry cops had seen it and started running toward him. There was a whistle blowing shrilly, repeatedly, the driver was out of the car fast and looming over him, holding him under both arms. The night guard joined them in the pool of light from the door saying, "You hurt, Mr. Garner?" The cops ran heavily past and the driver said, "There was two of them ran away, I didn' see them waiting for you." His head was clearing, his jaw stung and he worked it gingerly and felt it with his fingers. There was no blood. "Thanks, I'm all right," he said, pushing past the driver, "I want to get in the car." The guard came to the door of the car while the driver was getting back behind the wheel and said, "They all ran around the corner up there." "It's all right," Lloyd repeated, sitting up stiffly, "tell Mr. Schonwald about it, I'll call him later." And he gave the driver Alix Weddern's address.

By the time they drew up in front of the apartment house he had recovered from the dazed, scared feeling and was breathing normally again. Who were they? The union, probably, although he doubted they could have got one of the broadcasters to do it. Or, who knows, maybe just a couple of nuts, maybe the union didn't even know it happened. Whoever the guy was he'd hit him hard, but some instinctive movement of his head had deflected the full force of the blow; he'd been lucky. In the lobby he glanced at his face in the mirror, a little pale but not a mark on it.

Alix was not alone. An aging maid showed him through a marble foyer beyond which voices were happily engaged with cocktails. It was a large and beautiful room filled with period furniture and people who belonged in the setting. Alix was standing in the doorway talking to a man she introduced as Kenyon Spencer. He smiled affably at Lloyd with no sign of recognition. "He's famous, Kenyon dear," she said, "but you wouldn't know him."

"I *am* sorry," Kenyon Spencer said, more affable than ever, "can you forgive me for not knowing you, Mr. Garner?"

"I'm sure it's a relief for him," Alix said, and a butler appeared at Lloyd's elbow bearing a drink on a tray. "Double size for the occasion," she said, and Lloyd smiled at the thought of his jaw. She guided him to a corner. "I'm not going to try to introduce you, most of them wouldn't mean anything to you anyway. It's a safe bet they haven't looked at a news program on the TV in at least a month. I suppose some of them do watch the movies."

He laughed. "I'm conscious of a few well-bred stares."

"They're just wondering if you're my new thing, that's all. I had them come later than usual tonight so I could watch the Lloyd

Garner program before they came, to see if Lloyd Garner was going to be on it."

"And he was."

"I drank to you, my dear. I think it's *brave*. When I saw the news in the paper this morning I wondered if you would, of course I know nothing about the background."

"You know a lot more about a lot of things than you admit."

She smiled up at him with brilliant eyes. "How do your colleagues feel about you?"

"A bunch of reporters asked me the same question not half an hour ago. The fact is I haven't talked to any of them yet, but I doubt if they'll want to talk to me, now."

"They're envying your guts and wishing they'd had the courage to do the same thing."

"That's what the network brass is hoping."

"It's about time somebody in your position stood up to the unions," she said.

"Alix, you're talking like a member of the capitalist ruling class."

"But I am," she said, "and so are you."

They laughed together. The butler brought her another drink and looked politely at Lloyd's glass. "Not yet, but soon," Lloyd said to him. He glanced around the room. "You live in state, Alix."

"The opulence, you mean? This is my mother's apartment but she lives in Florida most of the year."

A highly groomed young man moved up to them, glass in hand, and spoke to Alix. "May I meet Lloyd Garner? I watch him almost every night."

"Seward Pratt," she said, "one of the few people in this room who knows anything about anything."

He was smiling at Lloyd. "Alix is being a little hard on her friends, but then she always is. I'm grateful for the flattering remark about me, though."

Lloyd liked him. "What do you do?" he said.

Alix was looking at Seward Pratt and laughing. "He doesn't do anything, and most of these other people are in the same business."

"Isn't there a strike on?" the young man said. "I think I read—"

"Alix and I were just talking about it. She's impressed by the fact that I refused to join in."

"I'm sure you had very good reasons, Mr. Garner."

"I think so."

"I know so," Alix said.

"You have a loyal supporter there, Mr. Garner." He said his good night to Alix and left them. Lloyd's glass was empty, but not for long. Others were saying good night now. Alix moved back to the doorway. "Promise you'll stay till they've all gone?"

He nodded. "Is there a phone handy?"

She motioned to a room off the foyer and he went in and shut the door against the sounds of departing guests. He got through to Schonwald right away. "You okay?" the producer said.

"I'm very okay. Did they pick up those people?"

"No. Have you talked to anybody about it?"

"Not a soul, why?"

"Walter says it's better to keep it quiet if there's no harm done, it just calls attention, you know?"

"I understand."

"We can do something about it later, if it's necessary. The cops are co-operating."

"Don't they always?" He laughed, remembering Boston.

"You sound okay, Lloyd, glad you didn't get hurt."

"It was nothing. I'd like to know the bastards who did it, though."

"We'll find out. And we'll use it if we need it."

"See you tomorrow, Buck."

He sat there and finished his drink. His jaw felt normal again and he decided he didn't care whether they found the guys or not, the hell with them. He could hear Alix's voice outside in the foyer, then he heard the elevator door close and got up and went back into the big room. She was giving some instructions to the butler, who bowed slightly to him and left them. Alix said, smiling brightly, "Business all accomplished? Or were you talking to your wife?"

"My wife's in Boston, no, I wasn't talking to my wife. Would you like to go out for some dinner, Alix?"

"I thought you might like a bite here, so I told Houghton to find us something."

"Better and better," he said. She fixed two drinks while he looked at the room. "That's quite a picture, the big one there."

"A Corot," she said without turning around, "one of the good ones. Actually mother's taste is very old-fashioned, she never got beyond Childe Hassam and that sort of thing."

"And your father?"

"He's been dead seventeen, no, eighteen years."

"And no brothers and sisters?"

"Jay was killed in that bobsled accident in Switzerland, maybe you read about it, he was on the Olympic team, Jay Ansel."

"I know that name, all right." Ansel Brothers, one of the biggest investment firms in the world.

"Got the biography all worked out now?" She gave him a sudden impish smile. "What's *your* family like?"

"Not as interesting as yours, I'm afraid."

"I can't control my curiosity about your wife, Lloyd. Who was she?"

"You say that as if you expect her to be a Mayflower descendant."

"Do I? I can't help it, just habit."

"Will this place her for you? Her father was a fireman."

In the pause her eyes were very bright. "I like your honesty. What about your own father?"

"Like they say, he left home. I was five years old at the time. Now you have the whole story."

"Is the marriage in good shape?"

"Not especially."

"You're separated?"

"No, I just haven't seen her much lately."

"While you've been rushing around," she said, "is that it? I must say you TV people rush around a lot, of course I've never known one of you at all well except Kent Ward, I mean I've met Chet and David and Walter and that handsome Howard K. Smith, except I don't much agree with Howard K. except on Vietnam."

"How about Hedley Johns, have you met Hedley Johns?"

"My dear, Hedley Johns doesn't go to cocktail parties, at least I've never seen him at one."

"Obviously you go to a lot of them."

"Is there anything else, in Washington?"

They were sitting side by side, surrounded by the faint scent of her perfume, which like everything else about her probably cost a hundred dollars a quarter-ounce. It occurred to him that he'd never been as close to anything as expensive as Alix Weddern. "Tell me why you spoke to me at Kent's party, Alix."

"Well, I saw you," she said. "And there was something a little bit hurt about your smile."

"Nobody ever said that before."

"But it's what makes it different, don't you see?"

Over another drink she told him briefly about her life, a New Yorker who always seemed to be somewhere else, went to school in Switzerland, two husbands, both nice and both impossible, divorced from Clay Weddern in Reno three years ago, never regretted a damn thing she'd ever done and was enjoying being alive, wasn't he?

"I think I'm beginning to."

They dined by candlelight in a long high-ceilinged room. A bottle of delicious white wine accompanied the creamed chicken and asparagus, the wine made him feel pleasantly drunk. Houghton moved noiselessly around them in and out of the kitchen, wearing white gloves. "You have a French chef out there," Lloyd said.

"For goodness sake, my Annie?"

"I like it here."

"I'm glad."

"I suppose you'll be busy over Christmas."

"I'm usually in Florida with mother, why?"

"I'd like to take you out to dinner."

"Can't we meet again when I come back?"

"I'll hold you to that."

They smiled at each other in the perfect room, and he thought of Fran and her voice and her clothes and the apartment in Boston.

Harry Ferguson's message had been waiting for him at the hotel when he got back from Alix's near midnight. He wanted Lloyd to have lunch with him, would call in the morning to confirm it. Now, sitting across the table from Ferguson in Gallagher's, it occurred to him that he'd never really talked with him before. The man had been his chief writer in the hectic weeks since the Lloyd Garner show began and had developed uncanny skill in writing for Lloyd's natural speech cadences, had become a kind of alter ego in the office, but it was the first time they'd had a meal or even a drink alone. Looking at him Lloyd thought, he's awkward and fat and he's got a high voice. He must hate me every time he writes a sentence for me to speak, knowing he should be there in front of that camera instead of me, knowing I get paid so much more than he does for the words he puts in my mouth.

"I'm glad you could make it, Lloyd."

"Why the hell not?" He grinned at him. "You think I can't take an occasional punch in the teeth?"

The other man looked puzzled. "Punch in the teeth?"

"Come on, Harry, you know about it. Don't tell me your pals in the newsroom didn't call. Or was it your pals at the union?"

"What the *hell* are you talking about?" Harry Ferguson said. "What's this about a punch in the teeth?"

Maybe he didn't know, maybe the grapevine hadn't reached Ferguson yet. "Okay," Lloyd said, "somebody threw a left hook at me last night when I was going out the back door and I thought that's what you meant when you said you were glad I could make it here today."

He looked genuinely startled. "And you don't know who it was?"

"There were two, apparently. The cops chased them around the corner but they got away. I never did get a look at the one that hit me, he came from behind, then he ran."

"He didn't say anything?"

"Just called me a pretty name. I assume the union put him up to it, whoever he was."

Harry Ferguson flushed. "I don't believe that, Lloyd. I don't believe that for a moment. There isn't an officer of that union who'd countenance anything like that, I can assure you. My own union wouldn't either. It would be defying union discipline."

"But you'll be back, I hope, as soon as this crazy thing's over."

The heavy eyebrows worked a little. "I don't get that. I just don't get your calling it a crazy thing."

"Well, isn't it? The only people who wanted it were a couple of professional union men and a few announcers. The news broadcasters don't want it, all but a few who envy the others the money they make, right?"

"You're talking like Buck Schonwald, Lloyd. You're talking like management."

"I'm talking for myself."

"But it's a question of *principle*," Harry Ferguson said. "And if the union loses this strike it could destroy the union."

"But your own union is having no part of it."

"And they're wrong, Lloyd, because the day will come when they need the broadcasters and the broadcasters won't be there to help them."

Lloyd signaled for the menu. "It's a risk you run. How come all the other writers didn't walk out with you, Harry?"

"Half the newsroom is out, or didn't you know? There's another caucus this afternoon, maybe they'll all be out by tonight."

"And how about the announcers? Are they caucusing too?"

"Last night." He shook his head sadly. "There's a faction that wants to surrender and accept the contract as proposed."

"And the broadcasters?"

"Some of them seem to be having second thoughts, partly because of you, Lloyd."

He laughed again and pointed to the hamburger on the menu. The waiter, hovering respectfully, said, "Yes, sir, Mr. Garner," and Ferguson muttered, "The same for me, whatever it is." Lloyd sat back in his chair and looked at him. "You seem to be pretty well up on the maneuvers, Harry. Did somebody send you around to change my mind for me?"

The jowly, sapient face was flushing. "Not exactly. I've been over there to see John Carney, he says you won't answer his phone calls. Why don't you have a talk with him, Lloyd? At least he can explain why the union did this—"

"It's plain to me why they did it, they did it just to show they *could* do it, and where's everybody now except out on their ass?"

"Some pretty good men are out on their ass, Lloyd, because they believe in union discipline, as I do."

"Oh, I'm all for union discipline if the reason is justified. In this particular instance I just don't think it is."

There was a silence. Lloyd wanted a second drink and decided against it. Harry Ferguson was drinking water. He said finally, his eyes grave and searching, "You know, Lloyd, we've been working together every day for quite a while now, but I really don't know a hell of a lot about how you think, I mean where you stand on things in general, your politics—"

Lloyd was smiling. "I'm glad you asked that question, as they say in our business. I guess I'm just not what you'd call a dedicated man, Harry. I'm sure you must regret the passing of Hedley Johns, but there it is, you're stuck with Lloyd Garner."

"No, Lloyd, I like you, don't get me wrong."

"And you'd like to guide me back into the true path, isn't that it? Anyway, I don't look at my work like some kind of a crusade. I've got a job passing along information to the people that want it, I work for a good news organization that gets it together, like you, and gives it to me to report. As I see it, that's where my job ends. You asked about my politics. I'm cynical about politics, I guess, and about politicians. I saw too many of them on the local and state level in Boston. I sat in the Senate and House not so long ago and watched them in Washington. Now tell me, Harry, is there anything much to admire in most of those people? You know damn well there isn't. Not enough to make me a registered Democrat or Republican. And not enough dedication in me to make me a registered anything else. Sure, I'm in favor of dedicated people. I guess I admired old Hedley, and I certainly admire a man like Kent Ward. But I think professional politicians are mostly full of shit, and their daily actions just about prove it."

The waiter brought their food and they sat there eating it, not speaking any longer, but Lloyd felt relaxed and relieved somehow, the better for having said what he'd said. So Harry Ferguson had asked him to face himself and he had done it. This was the way he felt, the way he was. It was only afterward, nodding good-bye on the street and watching Ferguson walk away, defeat in his back,

that he felt the tremor like shame again. This time he took a cab
to the back door of the building. There were no pickets around.
A guard greeted him with a knowing, friendly smile. A cop was
standing a little way down the block.

In the office he said, "Gaby, get me Kent Ward at home," but
there was difficulty. Finally he picked up the phone himself. "This
is Lloyd Garner."

"Yes?" Ward's secretary said. Lloyd recognized her voice.

"I want to speak to Mr. Ward, isn't he there?"

She seemed to hesitate. "Yes, he's here, Mr. Garner."

"Put him on."

He could hear the click while she conferred, then her voice again,
"Mr. Ward can't come to the phone, Mr. Garner."

"How soon can he call me back?"

Another pause. "Mr. Ward says he will not be calling you back,
Mr. Garner."

Gaby was still on the other extension. She looked at him and
put down her phone, then went back to her typing. "I guess,"
Lloyd said to her, "I've had it with Kent Ward," but she didn't
look up again.

It was as Harry Ferguson had said, some of the broadcasters
were having second thoughts. Two days later, with the strike not
yet five days old and Christmas a week away, Will Kenny and Paul
McIntosh, two of the network reporters, crossed their own picket
line and went back to work, asserting that the union had had time
enough to reach agreement with the companies and calling a further
walkout unjustified. The union promptly announced that Kenny and
McIntosh, as well as Lloyd Garner, would face drastic penalties, but
the next day union negotiators went back into session with the
network and on the Friday morning, on his way to the studio, Lloyd
heard on his taxi radio that agreement had been reached on a
new contract. The terms were not immediately disclosed but it was
obvious that the concessions had had to come from the union. The
taxi driver, a gnarled little man with a wild fringe of hair around
his baldpate, heard the bulletin without comment, but for a moment
Lloyd found himself wishing he had been recognized and maybe

congratulated for his stand. He said to the little man, "That's good news for the viewers," and the little man said with a contemptuous wave of his hand, "I never watch it," gesturing so sharply that the car almost hit a truck.

"What did I tell you, fellow?" Buck Schonwald grinned at him comfortably over a pipe.

"You were lucky," Lloyd said. "But what about me? What's the union going to do about me and the other guys who came back before the strike was over?"

"Relax. That was all settled before the announcement was made. We made it a condition of the agreement there would be no penalties."

Lloyd shook his head incredulously. "And they went along? They must have needed that agreement."

"They had no choice, they were already hurt enough. You know something, Lloyd? That union is broken so far as broadcasters are concerned, in fact a movement's started for you guys to have a union of your own, and some of your best-known colleagues from the other nets are leading the way."

"I haven't seen any rush to make me a hero."

"What do you want, blood? A few may be a little resentful for a while, but in this business they forget easy, believe me, there's no time to remember."

"Kent Ward's not speaking to me socially."

The big man laughed. "You two people need each other, he'll come around."

"I hope so." He shook his head and walked slowly back to his office. Why did it matter to him whether Kent Ward dropped him or not? Kent Ward couldn't hurt him. He didn't need Kent Ward. And he remembered Rita Valenti's words, *"You don't need anybody, now."* Once you got what you wanted in this business you went it alone, nobody was going to help you, it was the first lesson you learned when you reached the big time. But the feeling like sadness, like shame, still troubled him. Kent Ward had been a friend.

Gaby was waiting for him, a telephone in her hand. "I just had Boston, Lloyd, your brother's been calling. He sounded a little, like upset. Maybe you better get back to him right away."

8

He stood at Gaby's desk while she put through the call, afraid it was Fran again, knowing it must be Fran. Gaby handed him the phone and got up and left the office. "Lloyd?" The quiet voice was somber. "I've been waiting for your call."

"We're very busy here, Phil. I got in late today. What's on your mind?"

"It's Fran."

The old familiar dread. "Go on."

"Can you get away this weekend and come up here? Maybe you can do something with her. I tried."

"Look, Phil, just tell me."

"She started pretty soon after she came back from New York, I don't know exactly when, you know how hard it is to know sometimes."

"Just tell me."

"Not only on the whisky but pills too. I found some Tuesday in the bedroom, she claimed they belonged to Grace."

"Has she been drinking with Grace?"

"Alone. Grace says she was hiding the whisky in an old detergent bottle under the kitchen sink."

In the pause Lloyd drew a breath. "Where is she now?"

"Home, I guess. She was still sleeping when I stopped there this morning. Grace said she passed out about midnight, she couldn't—"

He felt a sudden helpless rage. "What the hell good is Grace anyway?"

"She's been doing her best, Lloyd, even when Fran yells at her. She almost gave up the whole thing a couple of times but I persuaded her to stay on till you could do something, we knew about the strike down there. I know you must have had a lot on your mind, Lloyd, I appreciate that, but now it's settled, isn't that right?"

"Phil," he was trying to keep his voice down, "how did she look when you saw her this morning?"

"She looked bad. Don't you think you better—"

"But hasn't Stapleton seen her again? Haven't you told Stapleton about this?"

"Of course I called him. That was last week. He came over to see her. But he can't do much with her, apparently. He asked about you, Lloyd. He said I better call you and ask you to come up here as soon as you can. He wanted to know where she got the prescription for the pills, they're from some drugstore not around here—"

His anger surged again. "Couldn't I trust anybody, even you, to keep her straight?"

His brother spoke quietly. "She's your wife, Lloyd, not mine."

He noticed he had been crumbling an unlighted cigarette in his fingers, the debris lay on the floor by the desk. The distant staccato of the news tickers suddenly sounded nearer. Then he was aware of his brother's voice in his ear again, frightened and patient, "Hello, Lloyd, are you still there, Lloyd?"

"Yes," he said, "I'm still here. I'll call Dr. Stapleton, Phil. I'll be up there tonight."

He didn't try to talk to Fran or Grace before he arrived. He didn't even know whether Phil would forewarn them he was coming. Right after the show he took a plane from La Guardia. Coming in from the airport he remembered lost Christmases of his childhood, Boston seemed almost gay with lights and the smell of snow in the air. There had been a Christmas once, he could have been five or six years old, when he and Phil had hitched their sled to a truck and ridden along joyously behind it through a blizzard until the truck stopped somewhere near Faneuil Hall and they were hopelessly lost. He could still see the dirty drifts at the side of the street and taste the softly falling, blowing snow in his mouth. Somebody had come for them to a police station to take them home, was it his father or was he still with them then? He couldn't remember. He would ask Phil if he remembered, Phil was older. Fran was a little girl then, who would grow up to love Lloyd Garner and be loved by him as much as he was capable of loving anybody, which was perhaps not enough.

Lights were shining in the apartment windows when he got out of the cab, but it was Phil who met him at the door, Grace Cassidy hovering behind him. "Fran's asleep," Phil said in a grave voice, "I didn't tell her you were coming, I didn't tell Grace either till I came over after work."

He put down his new pigskin bag and took off his coat. "You mean she's been asleep all day?"

Grace looked ready to cry. She shook her head. "She was up about noon, this afternoon she said she saw a marmoset on her hand, she was playing with it."

He felt a chill flicker down his spine. "She's been giving you a rough time, Phil told me."

"I don't mind, Lloyd. You know I'd do anything for the both of you, you know I would."

"I know you would. And you too, Phil." He looked at his brother. "I'm sorry I got mad on the phone, none of it's your fault, or Grace's either."

"Think nothing of it." His eyes were full of tears.

"For heaven's sake, Phil. Is this a wake or something?" He forced a little laugh. "It's like a funeral home around here, cut it out, you two, and get me a drink, I mean if there's anything left in the bottle."

Grace gave a semihysterical sob and went into the kitchen stuffing a handkerchief in her mouth. Phil said, "Did you talk to Dr. Stapleton?"

"I've arranged to see him tomorrow, whatever good that'll do. Jesus, you'd think we had a case of terminal cancer on our hands."

"She'll be all right now you're here," Phil said. Grace came back with a drink, sniffling and smiling.

"I mixed it already," she said. "You want me to stay tonight, Lloyd? I can sleep on the couch."

He shook his head. "Both of you go home and get a good night's rest, but I'd appreciate it if you come back tomorrow, Grace, just to stay with her until I get back from seeing Stapleton, the appointment is eleven. About those pills, she hasn't got any more of those, has she?"

"Not unless she's got some hidden."

"Christ, it's like a soap opera," he said and then remembered that Grace Cassidy took her soap operas seriously.

He let them go before he went into the bedroom, standing in the doorway for several minutes to accustom his eyes to the dim light. The room smelled faintly of stale bourbon. He went over and opened the window, fresh snow was falling into the alley below. Fran was lying on her back in the middle of the bed fully dressed except for her shoes. He moved closer and looked down at her face, softly outlined against the dark disheveled hair on the pillow. She looked in the dimness as she had looked in the first years of their marriage, vulnerable and sweet, and he felt the pity in his heart. It was a moment before he realized that her eyes were open and she was looking at him. Her lips moved in a tiny smile, her words were whispered. "Daddy came home," she said.

Dr. Claudius Stapleton was small, middle-aged, neat and old Boston. You had to wait quite a while to see him but once you were sitting opposite his desk he was in no hurry. "I'm glad you came alone, Mr. Garner, it's much better this way." The kind eyes were sharp behind the pince-nez glasses. "Your wife is in serious trouble. The difficulty in cases of this sort is that she refuses to believe it and the family doesn't understand what is happening."

"I probably don't understand either, Doctor, but I want to."

"That's half the battle, Mr. Garner. When I say Mrs. Garner refuses to believe what's wrong I don't mean she actually refuses. That is just a way of putting it. In reality she knows, all right. She can tell by the way she feels. But the peculiarity of her disease is that she is unwilling to face the truth and tries to hide it from herself, as it were, subconsciously, as well as from everybody else, including me." There was a faint trace of humor in the precise Beacon Hill accent. "Of course, I am not a psychiatrist, but I still have to know the answers to a few basic questions. She won't be frank with me, sir, even about her medical history, which is another symptom of what ails her. I am sure you will."

"I'll tell you as much as I know."

"For example, there is a history of miscarriage, is there not? She made a rather vague allusion to it, that was all."

"She's had three miscarriages, in the first three or four years after we were married." My God how long ago it seemed. "She was pregnant when we got married, I—"

Dr. Stapleton interrupted politely. "The miscarriages were not induced in any instance?"

"If you mean abortions, no. We wanted a child, I guess she still does. But she hasn't been pregnant since that last miscarriage, the other— Dr. Kenny over at General doubts that she can have a child now, not any more."

He was nodding, the bright sunlight glinted on his glasses. "It was Dr. Kenny who suggested to your brother that Mrs. Garner come to me. Tell me, sir, approximately how long has your wife been drinking heavily?"

"I guess it depends on what you mean by heavily. We both, she and I both drink, social drinking I suppose you'd call it, we always have, even before we were married." He paused, somehow this was tougher than expected. "I've never thought of either one of us as, as alcoholics. What would *you* call heavy drinking, Doctor?"

"What does Mrs. Garner drink in the course of a day, a normal day?"

"Well, that, of course, I can't be sure," he said rather painfully, "I'm not trying to hold back anything, I just suspect she drinks a lot more than she tells me. Before I went to New York, I have a new job there, she usually was, well, more or less intoxicated by the time I came home before dinner, and after that, well maybe she drank as much as a pint of bourbon, maybe more, before bed. Sometimes, just from noticing little things, you know, evidence, she might get up in the night and take a drink, or in the morning early, she was, well, sort of fuzzy, I think you know what I mean, Doctor, not remembering anything."

"And how long had this been going on, that is, drinking to this extent?"

He felt the palms of his hands sweating and clasped them. "Quite a while, I suppose. It was all so gradual that at first I guess I didn't really notice it much."

"A year or two?"

"It might have been, over a period, gradually."

Dr. Stapleton nodded and went on conversationally, "Would you call your marriage a happy marriage, Mr. Garner?"

The simple question startled him. He said after a moment, "I guess not, not any more. You asked me to be frank."

"Your wife feels about the same about that as you do?"

"I just don't know."

"But you still have sexual relations?"

"Well, sort of. I mean not often. Not lately." He knew he was flushing at his own awkwardness. He wished this interview was over, then he waited. Dr. Stapleton was thinking, his eyes on the green cover of his desk.

"Mr. Garner, there are two approaches to this problem. Your wife can go to a clinic, call it a rest home, which specializes in treatment of these cases. The old-fashioned word is cure. I would like to see her spared that, if it can possibly be avoided. The other way is analysis. It is longer, it is a more gradual thing, but in the end the results could be much more successful, if she tries, if she will try. Either treatment will be expensive. Your brother says you can afford it."

"Oh yes. Yes."

"There is a man in Boston who is as good as anyone in the country at this. I can give you his name." The blue eyes glinted cheerfully. "Why don't you persuade her to go to him? Do you think she would?"

"I'm sure she would." Suddenly he felt a deep sense of relief, everything was going to be all right now, for a moment he had stopped listening as the quiet, precise voice went on.

"—but if not, the consequences can be nothing short of disastrous. Irreversible damage to her liver, to her nervous system. She can ruin her life, Mr. Garner."

"I realize that."

"Try to make her realize it too. Then she will be on the road to a full recovery."

Shaking hands he was aware he had tears in his eyes. He laughed at himself. "Doctor, do you know what I feel like right now? A good, stiff drink."

"I prescribe it," said Dr. Claudius Stapleton.

Grace let him in. "Still asleep?" he said.

She shook her head. "She woke up a little while after you left. She's in there taking a bath."

"How was she?"

She smiled a little. "You wouldn't believe it but she's like perfectly normal. That's the way it is with these things, I guess. But she didn't remember you were here."

"What? She woke up and spoke to me last night before she went back to sleep."

Grace shrugged, she looked tired and still tense. "What can I tell you?"

"Hi," Fran said. They both turned, startled. She was standing in the bedroom doorway dressed in a skirt and sweater, the heavy layer of lipstick accented her pallor but she was smiling.

"Hey!" he heard himself say. "You okay, Fran?"

"Fine, just fine. Grace said you've been to see Dr. Stapleton."

"Well, yes."

She was still smiling. "Am I hopeless yet?"

"Of course not." He forced a laugh. "We just had a chat, that's all."

"I understand."

"I gotta go," Grace was saying, a little hurriedly. She picked up her coat from the chair by the door and looked back at them. "Call you later, Franny?"

"Thanks," Fran said to her.

"Thanks for everything," Lloyd said.

"You know there's nothing I wouldn't do for the two of you." The door closed behind her.

In the silence Fran crossed the room and sat down on the sofa. He started to follow her there, then went instead to his own chair by the window. Something about her composure made him feel at a disadvantage somehow. He waited until she spoke first.

"So what did little Claudius say today?" she said.

"He thinks you should go to a psychiatrist."

She opened her eyes wider, sitting there almost demurely with her hands in her lap. "Psychiatrist?"

"He gave me a name."

She nodded slightly but didn't speak. She was watching him. "I think we should take his advice, Fran. Don't you?"

A faint shrug. "All right. If you want me to."

He leaned forward. "Look, Fran, we might as well face it. You're a sick girl. You need help."

"I can take care of myself," she said.

He tried to keep the exasperation out of his voice. "You sound like you don't care whether you, whether you get well or not."

"I wouldn't say that."

"Well then, what *would* you say?"

There was a blankness in her eyes, as though she was thinking of nothing, and he wished he was out of this shabby little room and back in New York, back at his job, suddenly this was all nightmare. Fran was speaking again, tonelessly. "I'll do whatever you think is best, Lloyd."

"It's the doctor who thinks it's best, he knows more about you than I do."

"That's for sure," she said.

He stiffened. "And just what do you mean by that?"

"I mean I guess you're right. Aren't you always right?"

"Come on, Fran." His voice rose. "Say what you really think and stop sparring. We're not going to get anywhere if you ask me a question every time I ask you a question."

"Where is there to get?"

"There you go again." He fought to keep his voice down. "God-damn it, you know what I'm talking about, I'm talking about the future."

"Oh, that."

"Don't you care anything about the future?"

"I've been thinking about getting a job maybe."

"I mean the future of you and me, Fran. Why do you think I came up here to see about you? Right in the middle of trying to do a new job, a big job."

"I know," she said, almost wearily. "You're an important man now, right?"

"Fran, please. Don't joke about it. Try to be reasonable, that's what I'm trying to do. We have to reach an understanding. Or are you so full of alcohol and God knows what else that it's no use talking any more at all?"

"I'm reasonable," she said. Again he was astonished at the calm that was so unlike her. She went on, evenly, "If there's any understanding to be reached, maybe you better tell me what you have in mind."

He wanted her to say it first. "Don't *you* have anything in mind?"

"I told you, I'm thinking about getting a job."

In the long silence her eyes never left his eyes. Her mouth looked grim and defiant. He stood up then and went to the sofa and looked down at her, his voice quiet again. "Fran, whatever you're thinking, whatever I'm thinking, let's cut this dodging and talk it out like civilized people, both of us. Ever since that weekend in New York we've been strangers to each other. Was it because I failed you sexually that time? Is that what's eating you?"

"No," she said in a low voice, "things changed as soon as you went to New York to work. I don't have to tell you, you knew it."

"You were drinking, hard, long before that, Fran."

"I'm not blaming you for anything," she said, not looking at him any more. "You haven't failed me, sexually or any other way. I've failed you." For the first time her voice had trembled and her eyes filled with tears. "It isn't my fault, either. It just happened, it just happens to people, we aren't the only ones."

He turned and went back to the window, looking down into the desolate city noon. Across the way two women were gossiping on a stoop, a boy rode his bike aimlessly along the sidewalk. "You're saying," he spoke with his back turned to her, "we shouldn't be together any more." She made no rejoinder to that and he stood there with his back to her while a series of dull, automatic pictures moved across his mind: Fran returning to her mother's little frame house in South Boston, or taking a place with Grace Cassidy, maybe bringing Grace in to live with her here, what to do first about the divorce, and who to see, and what kind of settlement would be fair. But his mind blurred with sudden anguish and he could feel his heart racing, he hated thinking about any of it, he hated doing it. When he looked back at her at last she hadn't moved, her hands were quiet in her lap and she was staring at the opposite wall. "Well," he heard himself say, finally, "well, I have to be getting back."

She got up and went past him into the kitchen. "You better have something to eat before you go. I've got some of those little sausages you like."

"Fran," he said after her, he didn't know whether she heard him, he didn't even know why he said it, "Fran, I love you, I always will."

The ordeal was over, the rest of it couldn't be any worse than this. And strange how this last time was not at all what he would have predicted, no storms, no tears, just silence. He stood there by the window with his mind repeating it, this was the end of the story of Fran and Lloyd Garner, and where would he go from here to his next woman, his next wife? Because there would be a wife, the right wife, who could make the grade, who could keep up with him. She would be another step. He had made his way professionally, he was on top when he was in front of that camera. Now he would have to fill the rest of his day. In a couple of weeks he would be thirty-three, time was awasting. He had the name and the bread, the giddy rewards of success, but those things weren't the end-all, they couldn't be. Already he took them for granted, like his job. Rita Valenti was right, more was needed, to make it solid. He had the background to think of, he couldn't do it all alone. In his position the right wife was a must. He had a career now.

9

"They're calling us the handout medium," said Walter Hacklin. "It isn't fair." He tossed a sheaf of recent press clippings across the desk. "I've been collecting these. Something ought to be done. Something really ought to be done."

Lloyd glanced through the headlines. It was the first time he had been alone in Hacklin's office with Hacklin. He must be acquiring real status in the company. "Yes," he said, handing the clippings back, "I've seen some of these."

"The working principle of this network," intoned the vice-president for News, "has been to show both sides of an issue and then trust the public to make up its own mind. In the nine years I've been in this position that has always been satisfactory to all concerned. Americans know who the good guys are, Lloyd, if they have a chance to see them. They can recognize the bad guys too. Look what television did to Joe McCarthy."

Lloyd smiled at him across the vast, almost empty desk with the delicate leather facing on the green pad and the gold pen and pencil set. "I'm not about to disagree with you," he said. "I don't ache to give my opinions on the air, I don't change a line of the copy they give me to read, and I don't tell the correspondents what to say, either."

The genial laugh. "You're the least of our worries, Lloyd. What burns me is these jerk columnists getting on to us because we *don't* editorialize. Christ, what do they want? We give them the Vietnam action right down to the last drop of blood. We give them the riots, and there isn't a black nationalist in the country who hasn't had his turn on that screen." He waved his hand toward the huge TV image on his wall where a soap opera was agonizing silently toward climax. "But we're in business, Lloyd, we have to survive. We can't fill prime time with documentaries every night in the week and we can't preempt half a million dollars in commercials to devote seven straight hours to the U.N. Security Council, we wouldn't have a viewer left, or a stockholder either. No, I think we ought to fight back a little, and I think you can help."

"Me?"

He smiled. "Buck tells me you're talking to the high school editors Thursday. Earl Greminger's been working on a rebuttal piece for all this press criticism and it occurred to me that might be the best way to release it."

So it was that on Thursday morning, before a raptly listening young audience of six hundred from all over the country, Lloyd Garner stated the case for impartiality. "We have to ask ourselves what journalism really is, what it should be," he said from Greminger's text. "Shall we conceive its highest purpose as crusaders, with the aim of persuading or converting our fellow Americans to some specific cause, or as reporters, dedicated to the truth and nothing but the truth? Can we better serve the reader, the listener, the viewer, by grinding political and social axes or simply by refusing to take sides? Surely we will be more widely believed and followed if our audience knows that we're not advocating support of either side of any issue, knows that we're being strictly objective, strictly impartial, in every story we tell. I would say this is more than being merely effective journalists, I would call this a moral responsibility, a responsibility we owe to our brothers in the democratic society in which we live. Let us give them the facts, no less, no more, and the truth will set them free."

Solid applause rang through the college auditorium. He looked across the lectern at their faces and saw them alight with the vision he had imparted. There was a long, eager line for his autograph afterward. The youthful professor who had introduced him thanked him for coming and added, not smiling, "I can't say I agree personally with the basics of what you told them, in fact I'm disappointed that you think this way yourself, but they certainly got a thrill out of meeting Lloyd Garner."

"Call on me any time, Professor." The other man's steady eyes regarded him gravely, waiting for some kind of response, but Lloyd

let it go at that and turned away. He didn't have time to discuss
network news policy with him even if he'd wanted to, he had a busy
day ahead.

For the chores incumbent on being Lloyd Garner were increasing
in proportion to his rapidly growing popularity. He inherited Hedley
Johns's daily radio program, which Johns had written himself but
was now written by George Sowerby, star writer of the radio
news department, and in the first days of the new year he became
a featured panelist on a network quiz show, "Come On Along."
He also was selected as narrator of a sponsored documentary series,
"Sea Probe," which was set for at least twenty-six weeks in prime
time. The sliding scale of compensation in his contract increased
his earnings to a rate now close to a hundred thousand dollars
a year. At the same time, for prestige or commercial tie-in reasons,
he was required to make more frequent public appearances at the
network's pleasure, not only for meetings with affiliate station officials
and sponsors but for speeches before such gatherings as the high
school editors and for bows, smiles and repartee at store openings,
parades, beauty contests and state or municipal ceremonies. To make
things easier for him Jay Weiss became his personal PR man and
accompanied him on all public appearances.

He was in demand now as a speaker and two minor western
colleges had written offering honorary degrees and proposing an
address at their June commencement, but Sime Sussman nixed
them both. "Small stuff," the agent said. "We'll wait till you get
one from like Harvard or Columbia." The volume of his fan mail
continued to grow steadily, so he was assigned an extra secretary,
sometimes two, to handle it along with the daily requests for his
help, appeals from charity auctioneers and professional autograph
hunters seeking personal mementos, such as monogrammed handkerchiefs, neckties and autographed letters. Sussman was insistent on his
commitment to these obligations. "Don't ever forget, son, your real
strength is in the number of people who watch you." And he
likewise refused to accept Lloyd's indifferent attitude toward radio.
"It's gonna be around longer than you think."

"But they're such ratty little bastards, Sime."

"It figures." He pointed out that network radio executives were the small-time types of the industry who had failed to make the grade to television and gravitated into the poorer-paid jobs of the obsolescent medium. There, inevitably, they had created a protective maze of petty politics, a penny-pinching, back-biting, ass-kissing bureaucracy in which each reigned jealously over his own bailiwick, guarding it with the vanity of fear. The particular fief which handled Lloyd's new radio stint was ruled by a man named Jules Steiner. "Know him, Sime?"

"Pompous little guy with a foghorn voice? Yeah, he's got dreams of moving over to the talent payroll, so naturally he'll resent you."

Sime was full of advice on how to be a celebrity. For many of his clients life was a simple question of getting renewed after each thirteen-week sponsor's cycle. Lloyd Garner's problem was a longer-term challenge. Sussman put him under instructions to set up charge accounts everywhere he dealt for any purpose, to acquire all the major credit cards, and to pay expenses whenever possible with the cards or drafts on his checking account so as to record future tax deductions. Also, you never rejected a social or official invitation received in your office. You told your secretary to accept cordially even if you had no slightest intention of attending. "That way," Sime said, "they understand something could come up at the last minute with your job and you get the advance publicity." Likewise you joined all organizations which might lend prestige to your Who's Who biography, whether you ever bothered to appear at a meeting, and you gave your endorsement freely to noncontroversial causes, Sussman to be the judge of what was noncontroversial. Charity donations selected by the agent were to be modest but numerous, ranging from CARE to the Navajos, with a view to a wide tax deduction base, and it was to be remembered that many of these charities bought magazine ads that featured prominent contributors. As for investment, Sime's advice included purchase of real estate in foreign year-round resort areas which you then rented for steady income. Right now he was high on Portugal as an appreciation value.

Fan mail was no longer the problem it had been in the first weeks when he had tried to read every letter himself. Now the secretaries handled all but the most unusual ones, which Gaby

passed on to Lloyd who in turn consulted with Greminger or
Ferguson if he needed advice on the answer. One such letter, to
Gaby's giggling amusement, was all but an offer to go to bed
and contained a snapshot of a well-built young woman in a bikini.
She said she would be in New York a few days with her husband
on their way back to St. Louis from the Caribbean and suggested
that Lloyd phone her at the hotel during the day when her husband
would be elsewhere. Lloyd laughed off the letter but remembered
the name, and the next morning with the scent of danger spicing
up his mood called her and proposed that she come to his hotel.
They spent an hour together naked and though she was neither
beautiful nor interesting the background of the encounter gave him
a curious sense of excitement and power. There must be hundreds of
women he would never meet willing to offer him the same star-struck
homage. Most fan mail fell into one of a number of categories for
which Lloyd and Harry Ferguson had worked out brief but cordial
standard replies. All the secretaries had to do was check the
category number scrawled by Gaby on the letter. If the writer was
insistently specific on some idea or issue, the reply would open
with the sentence, "You may be right," and then go on with a stock
thank-you-for-writing message.

Lloyd had given Gaby a strictly personal list, letters not to be
opened unless Lloyd had okayed it. The list included notes from
Sime Sussman, copies of all communications from the bank and
Lloyd's newly opened brokerage account, which Sussman was
handling, and occasional letters from Dr. Nathan Charles, the
psychiatrist, who was keeping Lloyd informed of Fran's progress.
The reports were good; Fran's mood was submissively acquiescent,
but Dr. Charles advised against the possibly unsettling effect of
direct communication between husband and wife at this stage of
the treatment. Divorce proceedings, he suggested, could be instituted
in due course.

He had told no one about Fran, not even Sussman, who would
know about it soon enough when Lloyd put together his medical
expenses for the spring tax return. A couple of times Buck Schonwald had asked Lloyd casually about his wife, wondering perhaps
why she hadn't moved to New York yet. But people here were

different from Boston people in these matters; nobody pursued his curiosity too far. It seemed you could live for years in a New York apartment house without even speaking to your neighbors in the elevator. Nor had Alix Weddern been around to ask inquisitive questions. Her mother was ailing and she was staying on in Florida, Bev Hambleton said. He had shared a quiet Christmas dinner with Bev at the Plaza, two untroubled bachelors, and gotten comfortably drunk before going just as quietly to bed.

There was no more talk about the strike. Buck Schonwald had been right about the other broadcasters, outwardly at least they were as cordial as they'd ever been and Lloyd had simply ignored the union membership meeting at which some of the strikers had denounced the agreement to rescind the proposed penalties against Garner, McIntosh and Kenny. Schonwald had been right, but not about Kent Ward; he was still avoiding any phone talk with Lloyd.

Tonight, sitting in Schonwald's office, Lloyd watched the State of the Union address with the producer, an oddly subdued and dispirited appearance by the President, a Congress politely attentive but not showing its feelings at all. Once Lynda Bird, in the gallery, turned and stared somehow defiantly at the cameras. In his comment afterward Kent Ward did a mood piece quoting a report by the National Committee for an Effective Congress: *"America has experienced two great internal crises in her history, the Civil War and the economic depression of the 1930s. The country may now be on the brink of a third trauma, a depression of the national spirit. Malaise, frustration, alienation, identity, are now becoming part of the professional political vocabulary. At all levels of American life, people share similar fears, insecurities and gnawing doubts to such an intense degree that the country may in fact be suffering from a kind of national nervous breakdown."* A forthcoming Gallup survey, Ward went on, will show the nation is confused, disillusioned and cynical in the wake of the Vietnam War, due mainly to the inadequacy of our leadership to the problems of Vietnam, race conflict, inflation, and crime, associated in the public mind with riots. And Ward concluded with a sonorous reading from Yeats: *"Things fall apart; the center cannot hold; Mere anarchy is loosed upon the world."*

"Well?" Lloyd grinned. "Aren't you going to pick up that phone and call Washington?"

"Washington can wait." Schonwald leaned back in his chair and packed his pipe. "How'd you like to take a look at the war?"

Lloyd sat staring at him. "Come again?"

"I'm talking about a little trip to Vietnam. It's been suggested that maybe it doesn't look too good for our star broadcaster to sit around New York all the time while other American boys are fighting and dying for his show."

"Suggested? By the big boss?"

The producer laughed evasively and lit his pipe. "The big boss happens to be in White Sulphur for the moment, since you asked. Nobody in particular suggested it. Jay Weiss thinks it's a good idea."

"Jay Weiss wouldn't know a good idea if it kicked him in the face."

"All right, all right. Matter of fact I like the idea myself, don't you?"

He was still startled and uneasy. "Why, sure. It's just a little unexpected."

"Naturally you and Jay wouldn't have time to stay very long."

"Me and *Jay?*"

"Come on, Lloyd. Call it ten days, including the traveling, just long enough to get the feel of it, on the scene."

"Just long enough to say I'd been there, right?"

He frowned and put down the pipe. "Look, fellow, you can see a lot out there in a very short time. You don't have to miss a lot of shows here, we wouldn't want that. Of course we couldn't allow you to get shot at, nothing like that. But, you know, a chat with Westmoreland, a bird's-eye by helicopter, meet some of the grunts at a base, that sort of thing. We can set it all up in advance with Staley in Saigon, say you leave here Friday night, you're in Vietnam Monday, leave there the following Friday and you're back in time to go on the air Monday as usual."

"You mean leave this Friday?"

"Why not? You can get the shots you need right here in the building, no problem."

"Who'd do the show while I'm away?"

"I thought I'd bring Jack Milhouse on from Chicago. He's done it before, for Hedley."

"Who's Milhouse?"

"He's our big local voice in Chicago, not ideal for your spot but it's only for a week."

"Well—"

"I'll have Bonnie set up the shots with the nurse. It won't be too new for you. Weren't you Army?"

"I did my stint in the PIO office at Fort Devens, if that's what you mean."

"You qualify." The big man was grinning at him with those half-closed eyes. "We'll talk some more before you go."

The jolt was beginning to wear off. Vietnam. The real thing. Flying out over the Pacific. Yes, he wanted to do it. There was only one angle that worried him a little, this guy Milhouse. He didn't want him to look too good substituting for Lloyd Garner.

Gaby was putting on her coat. "Your friend from Boston, Mr. Lewin, he called from the airport while you were on the air. He said he'll meet you at the apartment."

"I'll go right over."

It was a two-room furnished place three blocks from the office that Bev had found for him on a month-to-month rental, now that Sime Sussman's new contract terms were in effect the network was no longer paying his living expenses except when he traveled on company business. He had time to get his make-up off and pour himself a drink before Harvey rang the bell. "Come in, old friend, it's glad I am to see you."

He stood in the doorway holding a cheap canvas overnight bag, prematurely balding and solidly built with a pleasant, ugly face. "This the new pad you mentioned on the phone? Not bad, not bad at all." He saw the bottles on the table. "Four Roses, you remembered."

"If you don't drink it somebody else will."

"Hah." He dropped his bag on the floor and opened the bottle. "The bastards tried to postpone the trip for a week at the last minute, wouldn't you know."

"They never fail."

"I told them to go fuck, and they can have the job if they want it."

"You're my boy. Want a job in New York, Harvey?"

He blinked over his glass. "With the network?"

"I can fix it."

"How *about* that?"

Lloyd laughed and punched his shoulder. "I can see Habersham's face when you tell him."

"I can see all their faces," Harvey Lewin said.

"Do you know the son of a bitch never even called up, never even wrote me a note?"

"If his station was an affiliate, he'd have had to write you something. He just couldn't stand it."

"He's the only man I ever really hated, Harvey."

"He's crummy, his whole outfit is, they don't know how to act any different."

"They'll never kick *me* around again. You say the word, kid, and I'll start it rolling for you right away."

The other man laughed, a little shortly. "Everything's rolling for you now, right?"

"Harvey, I made it. By the way, I'm going out to Vietnam for a week. Leaving Friday."

"Just like that."

"Sure. Why not?"

There was a pause. Harvey Lewin poured another straight shot, gulping it down. "What about Fran?" he said.

"What about her?"

"I hear she's going to a psychiatrist."

"Well, that. I don't know whether you know, Harvey, I just haven't had time to tell you. She's been hitting the bottle a little too hard. She's a pretty sick girl."

"Yeah?"

"She may be in analysis quite a while."

"Yeah?"

"Claudius Stapleton recommended this guy, Nathan Charles. He's the best."

"Yeah?"

Lloyd looked at him. "What's the matter, Harvey? Didn't I do right? It's costing me a fortune."

"I believe it."

"She's doing great, Harvey. So, so when she winds up all better she comes to New York, right?" Why was he lying to Harvey, of all people? He poured himself another drink and felt Harvey's eyes on him.

"Get that suit."

"Made to measure, like it?"

"The new Lloyd Garner," Harvey Lewin said.

"Listen, kid, what's the sarcasm? I have a certain kind of job now, I can't walk around looking like, well—"

"Like a small-time jerk, like your old buddies."

In the pause Lloyd looked at him closely again, then laughed. "You don't understand. Forget it."

Harvey Lewin grinned his sudden airedale grin. "Let's eat, I'm hungry."

"Steak?"

"Anything, but let's go."

He took him to Chandler's, not because he'd ever been there before but because Harvey had heard of it. They had another drink after ordering and Harvey remarked, "The waiter seems to know you."

"He can't quite place the face, I get that all the time now."

"You naturally would."

"Or they say, ain't you Chet Huntley? Or ain't you Walter Cronkite?"

"Yeah."

"Anyway, it's like they owned you, I don't like that much."

"I want to buy us a drink, Lloyd."

"I told you the whole trip's on me, didn't I?"

"I said I want to buy us a drink."

"Okay, okay. You're touchy tonight, kid."

Harvey tore into the steak, proclaiming it the best he ever tasted. Afterward they pub-crawled Third Avenue in a blaze of lights and holiday decorations. The sidewalks were crowded and between 55th and 49th they were solicited twice by rough trade in tight pants and leather jackets. They made Clarke's, Moriarty's, O'Hara's, the bar in Manny Wolf's and finally Tim Costello's, which they were going to pass when Harvey remembered he'd heard of it. The Thurber drawings on the walls he wanted to see were almost obliterated by neglect and the place was almost empty but Harvey liked it the best of the evening.

"Remind you of Boston?" Lloyd said.

He shook his head, he was well loaded by now. "Reminds me of Tim Costello's. Listen, Lloyd, I want to tell you something. I been thinking about that job with the network."

"Say the word, old buddy."

"Don't call me old buddy, how can we be old buddies?"

"What the hell are you talking about?"

He spoke painfully. "Look, suppose I came to New York and you got me the network job and all that, we couldn't be buddies."

"For Christ sake why not?"

"Because I'd still be a small-time jerk in the newsroom, and you're Lloyd Garner."

"You're out of your mind, Lewin, that wouldn't make any difference to me."

He was still shaking his head. "But it would to me."

"Another drink, Mr. Garner?" said the bartender. "This one on the house."

"He know you?" Harvey said.

"I told you I've never been in the place before."

"That's what I mean," said Harvey Lewin, "that's what I mean."

"Goddamn it, you're my best friend."

"Not any more, Lloyd, not any more." Tears coursed suddenly down his cheeks.

"You're drunk, Lewin, you've got a crying jag on."

"Don't talk to me, you scab."

He heard the quick bitterness in his own voice and felt the stab of remembering. "Who the Christ are you to call me a scab? Did you stick when the chips were down with Fay Habersham? Sure, all he had to do was look at you that day in his office and you collapsed and ran with the rest."

Harvey Lewin lifted wounded eyes. "We got a union out of it, didn' we?"

"Don't take any credit for that, Lewin. And I got no thanks for it, either. Fuck 'em all, that was my motto from then on. And I'm not about to find a new one, not for a drunk like you."

"If I wasn't drunk I wouldn't tell you the truth."

"What truth, you nut?"

"You changed, Lloyd."

"You're crazy, how have I changed?"

"What's Fran doing going to that headshrinker, my sweet Fran. If she was with you she'd be okay, what you trying to do, put her away?"

"They'll put you away next." He tried to laugh and put his arm around his shoulders but Harvey jerked back and almost fell off the stool. Neither said any more. A little later, after the drink on the house, they started to walk back to the apartment but they were both too unsteady on their feet and Lloyd hailed a cab. They arrived without speaking further and went to sleep immediately in the twin beds. In the morning when Lloyd woke up Harvey was gone without leaving a note, and so was his canvas bag.

10

The MAC-V charter from San Francisco put down to refuel in Hawaii long enough for a glorious swim at Waikiki in happy holiday sunshine and cooling breezes. It was more like a vacation trip than going to a war. For the last lap of the flight a new crew took over and one of the stewardesses served him a drink. She was a lithe girl with a fresh country face and a midwest twang. "You been to Vietnam before, Mr. Garner?"

"My first trip."

"I had a kid brother out here with the Marines."

"They've done a great job."

"He was killed," she said. She turned her head away from the front of the plane and he realized she was crying. "I'm sorry," she was saying in a different voice. She had found a little handkerchief and wiped her eyes. "I know it's un-American to feel like this, I should be proud he died serving his country, I really am proud of him, the whole family is."

"Yes," he said, he stood up awkwardly beside her.

She turned back and forced a smile, she was a stewardess again. "Please sit down, Mr. Garner, please excuse that, I'm all right now. Sometimes I just can't help it, I hadn't ought to of mentioned Mike." Her lips were still trembling. He pressed her hand and watched her go quickly forward and into the cockpit. He had just sat down again, staring out the window across a sea of cloud, when the brigadier general who had been sitting up front with an aide touched his arm, smiled, and sat down beside him. He had joined the flight in Hawaii and was the highest ranking officer among the dozen or so aboard. "Jake Handley, Mr. Garner, cigarette?"

"Thanks, I will."

"Staying long?"

"In Vietnam? Just a few days, I have to get back to my job. Are you stationed out here, General?"

He shook his head. "I'm in Washington but I get out fairly frequently on inspection. You'll be seeing General Westmoreland, I hope."

"I believe it's set up, yes."

The cool grey eyes looked back at him. "Nothing like going to the top source. Too many of your colleagues go for rumor and conjecture these days. It tends to give a false overall picture."

"I thought there was voluntary censorship."

"It's not the ideal system, Mr. Garner."

"I guess there isn't any ideal system."

The general had no comment on that. He said instead, "Get down to Washington much? I suppose your broadcasts keep you pretty well tied up in New York."

"Well, they do, yes."

"We'd like you to get to know us better, Mr. Garner. Matter of fact a superior of mine mentioned it just the other day, he'll be interested to hear I talked with you. Ever been in the Pentagon?"

"I'm sorry to say I haven't."

"Interesting place. A lot going on you should know about. Some of it not for publication, of course." His clipped smile.

"I realize that."

"I'll be back stateside in about ten days, why don't I give you a ring and set up a meeting? You'd find it worth your while."

"I'm sure I would."

The pilot came on the speaker, they were starting the descent to Tansonhut airport. General Handley shifted himself into the aisle and smiled down at him. "Don't believe everything you hear till you check it out with us," he said. "See you in Washington, Mr. Garner."

The two stewardesses smiled brightly as their passengers filed into the blinding day and one of them, the un-American one, leaned forward when Lloyd Garner passed and said hurriedly, "Please don't mention about me to anybody, my bosses wouldn't like it."

He was shaking her hand. "Of course not."

Outside the air-conditioned plane it was like walking into a furnace, a damp, smothering, consuming heat like nothing he'd ever known. The dead blast took the breath out of his lungs and little Jay Weiss almost staggered walking across the tarmac. "Jesus!" Weiss said to the Marine officer walking between them, "is it always this hot?"

The officer winked at Lloyd. "It's cooler in the highlands. You going up that way, Mr. Garner?"

"Maybe we better," Jay Weiss said.

"Well, luck to you," the officer said.

"You'll probably need it more than we will," said Lloyd.

Burt Staley was waiting to check them through, a calm, stocky young man wearing khakis like the military swarming around them. He hadn't met the Saigon bureau chief but Staley knew Jay Weiss.

"I've got a stomach ache," Weiss said. He looked green.

"Jay wasn't feeling very good on the plane, something he et in Hawaii."

"Isn't that Hawaii something?" Staley said, ignoring the PR man's stomach ache.

"The most beautiful place I ever saw," Lloyd said. "I just wanted to stay there."

"We got an air-conditioned hotel?" Weiss said. "I can't take much of this heat."

"Sure," Staley said. "You can go to bed and stay there, Jay."

Saigon had a beauty of its own. You'd never know there was a war on to look at this. Driving through the clamorous traffic in Staley's Renault, Jay Weiss hunched unhappily in the back seat, Lloyd saw the charm of it everywhere, the broad, shaded streets like Paris boulevards, the tropical languor of the countryside beyond, shuttered villas like houses in a Far East movie, exotic roadside shops and strange odors. Ahead of them and crowding their car were hundreds of bicycles coursing toward the center of the city, their riders all chattering to one another, the men in shorts and flimsy shirts with gleaming frowns or smiles, the girls wearing their national uniform of lampshade hats and white pajamas, pedaling away in their tiny straw sandals. Taken en masse they were the prettiest girls he had ever seen, and the smallest. What did good-looking people like this, living in their lovely city, want with a war?

He said it aloud, "And the best they can hope for is getting blown up and mangled one of these days."

Staley said, glancing at him from the wheel, "They've learned to live with it."

"Everybody in this country looks fourteen years old."

"You've noticed that, yes. But they're very grown-up people, believe me."

"I suppose you've got a girl."

Staley laughed. "I suppose I have."

"How do you take this heat, Burt?"

"You get used to it."

They left the heat behind in the Caravelle, Saigon's most modern hotel and the one favored by the press corps. The air conditioning was icy after the blazing late afternoon sun in the streets, Lloyd almost expected a vapor to rise off his body. "I'll be upstairs in the bar after you've had a bath and a change," Staley said. "No hurry."

Dressing in his new khakis after the shower he looked out the window onto the square now dimming toward dusk, watched the ridiculous taxis dodging in and out of military traffic, the little police and Vietnamese soldiers, the dainty girls passing, but it was all in silence. The window was sealed and cold air hissed through a vent overhead. He'd come halfway across the world in less than twenty-four hours flying time, New York to Southeast Asia, and the room he was in looked no different from a hotel room half a block from Times Square. Except maybe for the copy of *Stars and Stripes* lying on the table with its headline, ENEMY INCREASING PRESSURE ON KHESANH, but even the headline was right out of a newspaper back home. He laughed and went upstairs to the bar.

The décor was oriental but the faces were the same he'd seen at the Press Club in Washington, only younger. The room was crowded and full of cigarette smoke. The little Vietnamese hostess flashed him her smile as he came in. Staley stood up at a table behind her and introduced the youthful, thin-faced man sitting beside him, "Lloyd, I don't think you've met Bill Moran yet." He didn't need to add the *legendary* Bill Moran, at twenty-two as famous

for his bravery as for his reporting. "Bill just got back from up
north, you'll be glad to hear we're putting his footage on the
satellite, it's that good."

"Hello, Garner." He said it without getting up and without
smiling.

Lloyd reached to shake his hand and their fingers brushed briefly.
"Buck Schonwald told me to give you his special regards if I saw you,
Bill."

"That's nice," Bill Moran said, his face still blank and somber.

"What'll it be, Lloyd?" Staley said.

He had his bourbon and soda while the other two drank another
martini. Staley said, "We're still waiting on the general to set a day
to see you, Lloyd. It's always the way, but he'll get around to it
before you leave, it's Friday, right? The Embassy briefing's already
set for Wednesday, I think I told you that."

"You're not staying around very long," Bill Moran said.

Lloyd grinned at him. "I'm doing what they tell me to do, don't
you?"

His short laugh was mirthless. "That's just what I *don't* do,
Garner. And if they don't like it in New York I guess I can
probably find a job with somebody else."

"I guess you probably can," Lloyd said. "We're certainly proud
of the spots you've done for the show, far and away the best stuff
coming out of here."

"Gee, isn't that great?" Bill Moran said tonelessly. "It sure makes
me feel good to hear something like that. Especially from you,
Garner."

Staley laughed, sounding a little nervous now. "Bill's been here
eleven months without a leave," he said. "They want him back in
New York for a while but he won't go." He took the subject off
Bill Moran. "I've set up some chopper hitchhikes for you tomorrow,
Lloyd. You'll see part of the Delta and Bienhoa and a couple of
other places, give you the feel of it."

"It's the congressmen's tour," Bill Moran said, "everything very
quiet and very safe. With luck you might get shot at, in a casual
sort of way. Then you could tell the folks at home what it's really
like. You know."

"Where do *you* suggest I go, Bill?"

The somber eyes glinted. "You might start with an FAC mission." He looked at Staley and almost smiled. "I could make you a little list, Garner, but you won't be here long enough to check it out."

There was a silence, then Staley said, "By the way, Lloyd, Weiss won't be joining us for dinner."

"Who's Weiss?" Moran said.

"A PR guy from the network traveling with Lloyd."

This time he laughed outright. "Is that all? Doesn't he have a man to hold his cue cards too?" He stood up. "I've decided not to go with you, Burt, too tired." He went out without saying good night.

Staley said apologetically, "He needs a rest, Lloyd."

"Does he climb on everybody like that?"

"When he's in Saigon, yes. He only seems to be happy in the field."

"I meant what I said, Burt, I'd be glad to check out some hot spots."

The bureau manager was shaking his head. "You want to give Weiss a heart attack on top of his bellyache? Anyway, lately the brass here have been trying to keep the TV people away from the firefights, they don't like pictures of American losses. And with a celebrity like you, well."

"The safe treatment, like for congressmen."

They were both laughing a little. "Shall we eat?" Staley said.

Outside as they walked to the restaurant the tropic night hung low over the city, the sky studded with big stars, the streets cooler after the overwhelming day. It was a French place but most of the customers were Americans, with a few Vietnamese faces here and there at the tables. Staley pointed out two who were high-level black marketeers. "I don't know what these people were before the war," he said, "but they've become a nation of thieves. Even the ones supposedly working for us."

"They look nice enough."

"Of course the corruption's partly our fault. But you wouldn't believe what goes on. They've pulled guns on us more than once. Correspondents aren't allowed to carry weapons, but I know some who do anyway. Just the other day a couple of G.I.'s happened to walk into a black market meeting, accidentally, right here in Saigon. They were both shot down before they knew what hit them."

"I didn't see that story."

"It was hushed up. Public relations." He shrugged. "Yeah, life's pretty cheap in this part of the world right now. It's who shoots first, that's the only question."

He went on to outline Lloyd's tour. "You ought to be back from your trip tomorrow by late afternoon. Try to catch the briefing at the Mission press center, it's at five. Then meet me at the Continental about seven and we'll have dinner."

"Will we have the pleasure of Bill Moran's company?"

Staley's slow grin. "Bill will be back in Danang, I'm afraid. I know you're disappointed to hear that."

"I can't say I blame him for feeling this way about the fat cat from New York, counting casualties in an air-conditioned studio."

"What can I tell you?" said Burt Staley. "He's a combat correspondent."

The correspondents called it the Five O'Clock Follies, Staley had said, but it wasn't all that entertaining. As Lloyd came into the big bare room, thirsty and dusty from his drive in from the copter base, the briefing was already underway. Some thirty reporters were listening in varying attitudes of boredom, a few taking notes, while an officer holding a sheaf of papers droned at dictation speed through the day's statistics on air and ground action in the North and South. Outside somewhere was the war. Lloyd had looked for it but not found it in the green jungles and along the sparkling rivers he had crisscrossed today in the air. He hadn't heard a shot fired, and here in the briefing room the words were as remote from that reality as a botany lecture in a sleepy classroom. A correspondent interrupted the officer, "Any change in the situation around Khesanh?" The reply was negative, the lesson continued. A desultory thumping in an adjacent room was probably a Telex beating out a message to Tokyo or Washington or Cam Ranh. Lloyd could picture Burt Staley in the network office nearby, chalking up something on the assignment board and erasing something else, mission accomplished. He liked Staley. He wished he could like Bill Moran. Was Bill Moran at this briefing? Lloyd looked around and didn't see him, but then a press center was hardly in Bill Moran's line. By now he would be back in the North with his buddies, sweating out some horror pit with the Marines and waiting for the bullet or grenade or mortar shell that was bound to reach him eventually.

Bill Moran was a long way from home and liked it, and could have it. For the first time since taking off from Kennedy after the show Friday night Lloyd began to miss America. What time was it there on that other planet? He felt again the unreality of being here. Suddenly he was homesick for everything he was used to, homesick even for Boston, yet he'd been gone less than five days. What about these reporters sitting around him who'd been here for months? And the combat-weary GI faces he'd seen on his tour today, grinning and wistful as they watched him come and go; they had to put in a year of it at least. He was a visitor from civilization, free to move, safe out of the trap that held them all. He didn't want to think about those faces or remember their eyes following him, humble, respectful of the big shot, some of them had even asked for his autograph, to send home! and he felt shamed, embarrassed, writing his name for them; he only wanted to get away. Most of all he was haunted by the refugee children, silent, ragged, some crippled by wounds; he couldn't look back at their faces.

He left the briefing before it ended and went back to the Caravelle. He found Jay Weiss sitting up in bed, well enough to take a little chicken soup but still feeling miserable. He didn't want to get up yet, thank God.

Staley was late. Lloyd was on his third drink when he finally made it, smiling his apologies.

"Look, you're the working stiff, not me, Burt. I'm just a visiting congressman, remember?"

"Anyway it's a good place to soak up the local color, don't you think?"

"I'm enthralled. This is more like what I expected."

The mixed crowd was part American, part leftover French, who could be spotted usually by their resentful expression, and part Vietnamese. The Vietnamese girls were lovely. Staley said, "By the way, I just talked to Schonwald." He grinned. "He had a message for you, along with a couple of rockets for me. Positively no combat sectors for Lloyd Garner. He wants you back there on time and all in one piece."

"And what did you say?"

"I told him I'd do what I could."

"So what else is new?" Lloyd smiled.

"There's a report the North Koreans captured an American warship, it was just coming through while Schonwald was on the line." He laughed. "I hope it's true, it'll take the heat off us for a few days."

"You mean it might start up the Korean business again?"

He shrugged. "We've had signs Hanoi would like to wake up some other pressure points along with the big drive we're expecting in the North."

"For when?"

"Soon. Any day now. We've been moving a lot of stuff north in preparation for it."

"Does that leave Saigon unprotected?"

Staley laughed again. "Nothing ever happens in Saigon, not any more."

Sitting across the massive desk from the Embassy spokesman, Lloyd listened to the pleasant, courteous voice patiently outlining the military and economic situation. Burt Staley was sitting respectfully silent a few feet away, hearing what he'd heard a dozen times before in the same room. As the spokesman explained it, the VC was steadily losing strength, the ARVN was steadily getting stronger, the pacification program was making steady progress, and victory was just a matter of time, for time was on our side, etcetera. The diplomat expressed his belief that the enemy would publicly respect the Tet holiday about to begin, as it had in the past, while using it for infiltration from the North and a new build-up. But this time, he noted, the Allies were not being fooled by a long truce and their own observance of the holiday would be brief. Soon after Tet he expected the enemy to start an all-out drive around Khesanh in an attempt to achieve a little Dien Bien Phu, for even if the enemy were successful that's all it would be, etcetera, and there was no analogy, no real analogy, with the French defeat. We knew his plans for the drive in the North and we were ready for him.

"He makes it look pretty good," Lloyd said as they left the Embassy.

"He's an optimist. It's expected of him."

"But how do *you* see it?"

Staley chuckled. "I always get a belt from that victory line. Nobody wins a war, this one least of all."

"He said it's just a matter of time."

"Yeah, just a matter of time till the Communists take over the South, one way or another."

"And then good-by to the democratic life for all these pretty little people."

"They don't know what democracy is, Lloyd. Neither do the rotten politicians that run their government."

"Then what are we fighting for?"

"Sometimes I have the feeling," Staley said, "that we don't know why we're in here any more and don't know how to get out, it's all out of hand somehow. Of course you'd know more about that than I do, back there with the poop from the Washington boys."

Lloyd smiled. "Do we know *what* we want? That's what I wonder."

"The kids doing the fighting know. They know they want out."

He remembered the stewardess on the plane. "And how are the rest of us supposed to feel about it?"

The fine eyes were thoughtful. "We don't know what to feel," Burt Staley said, "because there's nobody to tell us." He swallowed his drink and changed the subject. "It looks as though you won't see the general, he's been alerted for a trip to Washington."

"I guess I can get along without the general if he can get along without me."

"You'll get your briefing from his Number Two, okay?"

"Okay, and then back to New York, Burt. You coming home soon?"

"Hell, no, I don't want to come home. I like it here. It's my own operation and I don't have to check in every day with some birdbrain executive for second guessing."

"Well, take a message from me to Bill Moran, will you? Tell him I'm not as chicken as I sound. I'm disappointed he didn't give me the danger list, but I'll have one for him when he comes back to New York. Beginning with the Black Panthers."

A likable grin lit up the chunky face. "I'll tell him."

Lying on his bed at the Caravelle he was suddenly drained and exhausted. The long flight had caught up with him, and there was also this feeling, a kind of anger mixed with compassion, about the men he'd seen in rest camp today. What was in their eyes as they looked back at him, watched him climb aboard the copter so carefully escorted by the spit-and-polish young West Pointer who'd earnestly and respectfully taken him on the VIP tour? A hopelessness, a longing, as they watched him go back to what they might never see again, and a bitterness born of battle they would never lose.

He stirred unhappily and reached for the *Stars and Stripes* on the bed table. JOHNSON SEEKS ACTION ON *Pueblo* IN SECURITY COUNCIL. JOHNSON CALLS UP 15,000 AIR RESERVISTS IN CRISIS. RUSSIA REJECTS MEDIATION. He didn't read any further, he was thinking now about that stewardess on the plane from Hawaii and her brother, the Marine. He was thinking about the refugee kids and their heartbreak of innocence.

The air conditioner was hissing softly, drowning a distant sound of turmoil, blanking out the world of headlines and diplomats and governments. And he closed his eyes, there was no war and no Vietnam; he was aboard a luxury airliner, heading for the French Riviera. The stewardess smiled down at him, the West Pointer slept at his side, somewhere he heard children laughing. Softly the jets hissed on. The newspaper slipped from his hand and fell to the floor.

11

Just one day after Lloyd Garner resumed his regular broadcasts from New York the Viet Cong launched the Tet offensive, a triumph of strategic deception that very nearly resulted in enemy occupation of the U. S. Embassy in Saigon. On the days immediately following it became apparent that the whole pacification program had suffered a grievous setback and any timetable for "victory" in Vietnam could be thrown out the window. In a series of filmed reports from embattled Hue, Bill Moran declared that the balance of power in Vietnam no longer favored the Americans, if it ever had, and from Washington Kent Ward called the new developments the biggest political minus in the Administration record. Lloyd's interview with the confident Embassy and his optimistic briefing by Saigon head-quarters, written by Staley and reported in Lloyd's first broadcast from New York, served to reinforce the impression that the government's major diplomatic and military spokesmen either didn't know or didn't want to know what they were talking about. It was an unhappy week for the U.S. command, the State Department and the White House.

It was also an unhappy week for Walter Hacklin and Buck Schonwald, whose budget estimates were shattered by the unexpected expense of emergency coverage. And for Lloyd himself, whose trip to the war zone had brought a deluge of requests for lecture appearances as an expert on the current situation. To most of these he could say no, using Sime Sussman as the buffer. Sussman had advised him not to accept any lecture dates for the present, no matter how lucrative, but to concentrate on building up his network image. Some of these offers were hard to turn down, providing for about an hour's work a fee five times what he used to earn in Boston in a week. But he couldn't reject suggestions from Hacklin

or Schonwald for appearances in which network prestige or the
insistence of an important affiliate station were involved, the suggestion amounted to a command. As likely as not the big boss himself
was behind it, as Sussman pointed out, it was too early in the game
for any prima donna refusals. Thus in that first week after returning
from Saigon he spent his mornings answering questions from the
trade press and his evenings after the broadcast addressing a series
of meetings arranged by Hacklin's office for sponsors, advertising
executives and other powerful network connections at such gathering places as the Union League and the Harvard Club. On these
occasions he stuck close to what he had learned from Burt Staley
and wryly pointed out the dangers of listening too hard to ambassadors and generals.

It was surprising, he told himself, how gullible these people were
about situations outside their own field of action. A few days in
Vietnam, just being there, endowed him with a kind of charisma,
gave him an insight they couldn't possibly hope to acquire themselves,
though God knows everybody and his brother from Bob Hope down
made the trip these days as simply as flying to Chicago or Dallas.
So they were content to drink the network's scotch and eat the
network's steak and settle back with the network's cigars and listen to
Lloyd Garner tell them what the network's correspondents had just
told him on the evening news show, following with answers to a
few polite questions about the outlook. For this he used Burt Staley's
comment, "There's still no light at the end of the tunnel." It was
safe enough, it satisfied them all. They sat there full of beef and
whisky, wreathed in their own smoke like an aura of success, and
accepted him as one of themselves, balanced and sensible and established. He had his thing and they had theirs. Vietnam was in
hand, more or less. The country was in hand, more or less. All things
considered it would be a good year, despite some trouble in the
streets, of course, despite those war casualties. Elections were coming
up and it looked like Nixon this time, which could be a hell of a
lot worse. Lloyd Garner was reserved on the campaign prediction
bit, "Anything can happen, it's just too early to say."

Lloyd had been curious about Jack Milhouse, who had replaced
him during his week in Vietnam, but Milhouse had already returned

to Chicago when he got back. Lloyd said to Schonwald, "I'm sorry I missed him, how did he do?" and the producer shrugged, "I told you he's not ideal for the show but there were no problems, he's a pro."

"I've never even seen a picture of him."

"Why don't you take a look at one of the shows?"

They reran the Friday night show for him while he sat alone in a viewing room. Milhouse was rangy and lean, with a challenging quality in his tone that made the words seem sharper than they were. Lloyd thought he could see the reason for his popularity in Chicago, he had the blunt midwestern you-show-me approach and a young cowboy kind of looks. "Isn't he ambitious to go network?" he asked Schonwald afterward.

Again the shrug. "He can make more money where he is."

"But doesn't he want a bigger audience?"

Schonwald was laughing. "He's not after your job, fellow, if that's what's worrying you."

"It's not worrying me." But it was, not only Milhouse but anybody that might conceivably one day take Lloyd Garner's place. For the first time, he had turned his program over to somebody else and discovered the uneasiness that went with doing it. Now he knew why Lon Carey and Weldon Duff seemed reluctant even to take a vacation or stay away from their programs for more than a few days at a time. He wondered if Hedley Johns had ever felt this way, and decided he was above it. He hoped his predecessor was happy doing his weekly stint for NET. Johns was receiving frequent critical acclaim for his outspoken liberal broadcasts, but of course the great rewards of money and audience were gone. Johns would have to do without them now.

For they were the great rewards, why not admit it? The fame that could make you a household word, the income that could change your life. Since long ago in the radio age Hedley Johns had had all that. Millions of listening Americans had grown up with him, had made him a rich man, and he had carried on until he chose to give it all up over an editorial difference with his employers, or was it just because fashions changed and Hedley Johns had outlived his own career? Whatever it was, he was set for the rest of his days, he could retire and never work again. But Lloyd Garner was just beginning, and he wanted it all.

Bev Hambleton, bringing him midafternoon coffee, had the news. As usual, it was done on a Friday. "Lon Carey was fired after his show today."

That little chill you had when you heard something like this, and that instant feeling, There but for the grace of God. And the question that came just afterward, "Who's replacing him?"

"Nobody seems to know. Buck could tell you."

"But what's the reason? I hadn't heard a thing about Lon lately."

"Well, he had another fight with his writers, but that's nothing new, is it?"

"They must have used it as the pretext, he's been fighting with his writers for years."

Buck would have the whole story, of course, but wouldn't tell it. And you didn't run and ask him to either. Before he laid eyes on Schonwald that afternoon the announcement had already crossed his desk. After fifteen years with the morning news program Lon Carey was regrettably resigning and would disclose his future plans after a vacation trip around the world. He would be succeeded by Jack Milhouse, long Chicago's leading newscaster, who would take over immediately. The announcement, signed by Walter Hacklin, concluded with the ritual good luck to Carey and a warm welcome to Milhouse. Though Chicago's loss was the network's gain, his thousands of admirers in that city would continue to see their favorite every day on the affiliate station, and of course his knowledge of Chicago would greatly enhance network coverage of the Democratic Convention in August.

Weldon Duff rang him right after finishing the afternoon news. The timbre was false-hearty cheerful. "Got time for a drink, sport?"

"I don't think I can get out. You going to see Lon?"

"Hell, no. He scampered right after they told him." The words covered a curious mixture of fear and satisfaction in his voice. "Who knows where he is now."

"What happened, anyway?"

"As usual, Lon was the last to know. I heard the rumor a couple months ago they'd decided he was getting a little old for the spot."

"*Old*, for Christ's sake."

"Yeah, even with that hairpiece." He sounded as if he'd had a couple of shots already, just for his nerves.

"Well, that means you and I are in out of the rain, Weldon."

"For now, anyway. This Milhouse is the coming boy. Watch him, Lloyd, watch him."

Schonwald was in the studio a couple of hours before air and Lloyd said casually, "What's the story on Lon Carey, Buck?"

"He had it coming. Lon just couldn't learn to read what we wrote for him and leave it alone."

"It says here he resigned."

"Yeah, they decided to put it that way."

He grinned. "Buck, just who are *they*?"

It amused the producer. "If you ever find out, let *me* know, will you?"

"Did you pick Milhouse?"

He was still smiling his deceptive smile. "I never decide anything, Lloyd, you know that. But Jack's the kid to bring the ratings up."

"I thought you said he didn't want to go network."

"Maybe he changed his mind after he got a taste of doing your show."

"That's what he'll want next, Buck."

The flicker of challenge in his eyes. "Not as long as Milo Wilson's around."

So Milo Wilson was in it. "Is there some question of Milo leaving?"

The big man threw back his head and had a good laugh. "You never know," he said.

You never knew. You could just about make that the motto for this outfit. And he remembered Kent Ward saying, how long ago it was already, that Lloyd would feel invulnerable after a while. But Kent Ward was wrong, was the great Hedley Johns invulnerable? They had wanted to tame Johns and he had refused to be tamed, and look at him now. Poor Carey hadn't even been trying to pull a Hedley Johns. Duff said he'd only started complaining again that his copy wasn't written for his speaking style, but that had given them all they needed.

From now on Lloyd Garner was keeping an extra pair of eyes in the back of his head.

The farewell party took place in an upstairs dining room at Cavanagh's, which was just about the right status level for Lon Carey. It was not an official party paid for by the network. That was evidently impossible under the circumstances of his departure, but when Carey's friends in the company decided there should be some kind of observance to honor his long service, Walter Hacklin let it be known that any financial deficit would come out of budget. In addition to the five free loaders who turned up for the festivities, there were thirty-one contributors at five dollars each, collected by Jake Lumb, the office cocksman, on several tours of the department during which he also made contact with several new secretaries. The proceeds bought the parting guest a not very expensive but dependable Omega watch, with appropriate inscription, and almost sufficed to cover the large number of drinks consumed by the free loaders plus Weldon Duff, who as master of ceremonies was first to arrive and last to leave and missed his usual train to Mount Kisco out of respect for the occasion.

Management, represented by Milo Wilson and Buck Schonwald, arrived early, planned to leave immediately after the presentation speech, and stayed together, talking other business in undertones. As they were there incognito under the rules of protocol, they confined their social activity to smiles and nods and to shaking hands with Lon Carey and his wife, a plump woman looking nervously defiant and wearing a huge orchid corsage offered by Lon's secretary and the two girls who worked for him as program assistants. Walter Hacklin, who had personally dismissed Carey, was not present, and neither was Sy Levin, the writer said to have been most often involved in the disputes over copy. But his two other writers after due consideration reportedly decided it was only fair to put in an appearance, and the rest of the morning news staff were all on hand, as were delegates from the afternoon and evening shows including Lloyd Garner, who attended out of morbid curiosity. Jack

Milhouse, who had already taken over the morning news and received flattering press reviews, did not attend. Carey himself, Bev Hambleton told Lloyd, had been reluctant to approve any observance at all, but was finally persuaded to come by his wife. After a couple of drinks she lost her defiant look, developed a very pink neck and forgot to keep an eye on her husband, who was circulating freely with a small, cynical smile and appeared to be quite rapidly getting drunk.

Apparently nobody had ever seen him that way before, and everybody except his wife was watching him, Milo Wilson with particular care, obviously because he didn't want an incident that would leak into the papers. The chief delegate from management looked grateful when Weldon Duff moved to the center of the smoky room and called for attention, which was quickly forthcoming from everyone except the guest of honor. Carey had worked his way to a position close to the bartender and was still talking when those nearest gently turned him around to hear the speech of presentation. Duff had probably had more to drink so far than anybody at the party but he was holding it well and had to pause only twice to clear his throat in delivering what sounded like a carefully memorized eulogy of the man and his work. Toward the end, after summarizing the history of the morning show and citing Lon Carey's notable attendance record, the past three years without even taking a vacation, the speaker lapsed into apparent ad-lib and concluded by declaring, "You may be gone, pal, but you'll never be forgotten by all those who labored with you in high times and low times, and they want you to accept this little token for *all* times of the day and night." He had momentary difficulty getting the box out of his pocket, then held it out to the recipient amid a burst of hand clapping. This was followed by silence. Lon Carey wore his small, fixed smile and didn't move. Somebody whispered, "Go ahead, Lon!" but it was the master of ceremonies who went ahead. He took three steps forward and thrust the box into Carey's hand. "*Vour pous*," he said. Laughter and applause.

"Well, thank you," said Lon Carey finally, putting the box into his own pocket without looking at it, "thank you all for your gift and for coming to the funeral service." The familiar clear and positive

syllables were oddly muffled or subdued, but the look in the eyes
was dangerous and Schonwald shifted uneasily on his feet. "I suppose," the honored guest continued, "I have to respond to those
comments by my esteemed colleague. Weldon, I never knew till
now you esteemed me so much." Duff appeared to be trying to grin.
"I know, Weldon, you think I'm drunk or I wouldn't be talking
like this. Well, I am drunk, and I'm not used to it, the way you are,
but there's one good thing about getting drunk, you say what you
believe, not that crap you were giving us a minute ago. I don't
blame you, Weldon. Somebody had to do it, and you probably got
some pleasure out of it, to which you're welcome. Who knows, maybe
I can do the same thing for you someday." Another long pause,
broken only by a nervous titter from one of the girl program assistants. The bartender was listening with a baffled expression.
"Weldon Duff and I"—Lon turned a glassy gaze slowly around
the room—"were both members of this outfit when it was still
small enough to be a human organization, when every other face
you saw in the hall wasn't the face of a stranger, and when executive decisions were made by people, not computers." He seemed
now to be addressing himself to Schonwald and Wilson. "Of course
I've never held with the ratings system, especially for news programs.
Maybe you can use it to measure, very approximately, the number
of boobs watching Bob Hope or the late late movie, so you know,
or you guess you know, who's buying how much toothpaste. But the
people who watch a news program regularly, and really *watch* it,
not just have it on, should be counted in terms of quality, not
numbers, and the extent to which this affects public opinion should
be appraised accordingly, if you can do it at all, and depending on
what you think public opinion is, other than the division of votes
in an election."

Bev Hambleton, Lloyd noticed, was staring at the speaker in a
kind of incredulous admiration, and so were others around him.
"There was a time in this country," Lon Carey was saying, "when
a news broadcaster could be listened to for what he said, whether
or not he had a deep voice and good looks and a head of hair.
It didn't matter whether he was thirty or forty or fifty, he was an
individual, even when you couldn't see him, not an automaton

giving you the headlines cut off every minute and a half for a singing commercial or a picture of a clothesline with two women telling you lies over it. If you didn't like him you had a choice of half a dozen others, or more, from left to right. You could even get mad at him and still stay tuned, the network thought that was all right too. But not any more. The sponsors don't want people to get mad. That's controversial. That's disturbing." He gave something like a sigh before he went on. "Well, I suppose I was lucky to last as long as I did, and I guess I ought to feel grateful for as much time as I had. I was certainly overpaid for it, considering the insignificance of what I was allowed to say. But in bowing out"—and his voice rose a little, his eyes panned the spectators for the last time—"I do have a final word for the people who decided for their own strange reasons that my usefulness is at an end. And, believe me, I'm going to feel good about this for the rest of my life."

With a gesture so sudden and swift that for a moment Lloyd didn't realize what he had done, Lon Carey ripped the hairpiece from his head and threw it in the direction of Schonwald and Wilson. There was a collective gasp, most of those present had never seen Lon Carey bald, but he looked now as though he thoroughly enjoyed being that way. Then he turned to his wife, still standing frozen and openmouthed watching him.

"All right, Helen," he said, "I'm ready to go home."

He had met Jack Milhouse once, the day the man from Chicago took over Lon Carey's show. Buck Schonwald introduced them casually in the newsroom and they always smiled and nodded in the hall and that was that. Then a few days after Carey's farewell party, standing in the studio just after coming off the air, Lloyd saw Milhouse emerge from the control room with Bob Lentz, wave good night to the director and disappear toward the elevators. "I didn't know we had a visitor," Lloyd said to Lentz.

"Who, Jack? He's been in several times lately, didn't you know?"

"How would I know? Nobody told me and I can't see the control room."

Lentz grinned. "You have any objections? After all he did your show for you while you were in Vietnam."

He was irritated. "What's that got to do with it? I'm surprised he didn't come out and say hello."

"You know these western types. Breezy." He waved an arm. "Got to run for my train, see you tomorrow."

Evidently the word got back. Milhouse was sitting at Lloyd's desk watching the monitor after the next day's show. He stood up. "Good tonight," he said. "*Damn* good."

"Well, thanks." The guy had just walked into his office and sat down at his desk.

"I've been watching a few times in the control room, just to warm up."

"Bob told me."

"It's the best show on the air, Lloyd."

And you want it. "How's your own show coming? I can't watch it because I'm asleep at that hour, of course."

The taut smile. "Nobody watches it, I mean compared to *your* audience. But it's building, so Buck tells me. I'll get it up."

"That's what they want around here. Carey had it way down."

"Yeah. You know, Lloyd, I never met the guy? One day they call me in Chicago, the next day he's out."

"Nothing new about that. It's the way I got my job."

Jack Milhouse laughed. There was something tense and wary in his laugh. "You got better hours than I did."

"You'll be used to it when you've done the show as long as Lon did." Try that on, Milhouse. "When do you sleep?"

"I don't sleep, never did." It figured. "I don't seem to need it, you know? Three or four hours is plenty."

"You don't miss Chicago?"

He waved a hand in contempt. "They all told me I would but they don't know me. I can work anywhere, all the same place to me."

"Your family like New York?"

He looked blank a moment. "No family problem, not any more. I tried that. How about yours, Lloyd?"

"Same report, for the present."

"In that case, how about we have a drink right now?"

They went to the place across the street and going in Lloyd said, "Not at the bar, that guy eats my ear off."

"Yeah? He fills me in a lot." That figured too.

The bartender began polishing a place for them but they went past and Lloyd looked away from the hurt face. In the corner, sitting at a table, he said, "What do you do with your long day, Jack?"

"Hang around my office, usually. Get to talk to Buck as much as I can. He's the best boss I ever had, Lloyd. I've told him so."

"No doubt about that."

"The best in the business, bar none. I told him I'd do some general assignment, you know, just to keep busy, like some shots for *your* show maybe, but he's not in favor, not right now."

"You're out of that category, Jack, like me."

"But why? That's crazy. I used to do it for my own show in Chicago, tapes or anything else they wanted."

"That was Chicago." He forced a grin. "You're in the big time now."

"Big time, shmig time, I want work, twenty-four hours a day if I can get it. I took a sacrifice when I came here and they haven't made it up to me yet."

"They will, Jack."

"They better." He called the waiter for a third drink but Lloyd signaled just one to him. "What's with that *one,* fellow?" He was already imitating Schonwald.

"Didn't I mention it? Got a dinner date," he lied.

"A broad?"

"Yeah, and she hasn't got a friend."

Again the contemptuous wave. "Who needs broads?"

Lloyd stood up. "Can I drop you anywhere?"

"Naw, I'll move to the bar."

With his friend. "Take it easy, Jack."

"You too."

He felt the steel eyes in his back. The bartender didn't look at him as he went out, he was smiling in the direction of Jack Milhouse. He knew a comer when he saw one.

12

"Walter and I fought it right to the top," Buck Schonwald said, "but no dice. Beginning Monday you're introducing all film commercials by mentioning the brand name yourself, Lloyd."

"In other words I'm doing the commercials. I thought that was against policy."

"It was, but it isn't any longer."

"Just one more little surrender to Milo Wilson, right?"

It was the first time he'd ever seen Buck Schonwald look sheepish. "Listen, you won't believe this. It's a new cigarette called New, and Sales wants you to say, 'Now here's the News story of the day.' Naturally we couldn't do that."

"Naturally."

"So we compromised. You say, 'Here's the story from News.' Period."

Lloyd was laughing at him. "That's a compromise? We're already burying plane accidents for the airlines, among a few other small concessions to Milo and his boys. Are we the editorial department or the sales department?"

"Don't ask embarrassing questions."

"I wonder what Hedley Johns would have done?"

"Quit, probably."

"And you'd have let him go, of course."

The producer wasn't smiling. "Are you going to do it or not, Lloyd? I have to know now."

He thought of Jack Milhouse and said, "Of course I'm going to do it, it's more money, isn't it?"

Now he grinned. "I figured you'd see it that way."

"Let's just say I'm learning, Buck."

The stranger was sitting on the visitors' couch, reading a copy of

Look that had been on the desk, when Lloyd went back to his office. He didn't recognize the man and since nobody outside the company would have been permitted to sit down without his okay Lloyd assumed this was somebody from another department. But the guy looked a little old and a little shabby for that, and his overcoat was on the couch beside him. Lloyd stopped and turned a puzzled glance toward Gaby, who nodded without expression and immediately left the room. The visitor had put aside the magazine and was standing up. "Don't you know your own father?" he said.

Actually he had recognized him at the same instant the man began to speak, not the voice, he couldn't recall that, but something in the way he was standing there, a kind of arrogance. The voice itself was harsh and tired. Lloyd said, feeling a stab of long-ago hurt and fear, "For God's sake."

"Aren't you going to shake hands?" Richard Garner, not smiling, was holding out a hand that trembled slightly and Lloyd took it and then dropped it.

"This is a surprise," was all he could find to say.

"If you don't mind I'll hang up my coat." There was indignation in his look as he hung it on the rack, as if his son had violated the rules of hospitality. A scene came back to Lloyd of his father hitting him when he'd accidentally broken a light bulb, he might have been four years old, suddenly the shame and hatred were as fresh as yesterday.

"Sit down," he heard himself saying, "I think I have some cigarettes somewhere," and he fumbled in his desk drawer.

"I don't smoke. I never did, don't you remember that?"

"I don't, no. After all, it's been a long time."

"Twenty-eight years, Lloyd. Your mother's been dead thirteen years."

"I do happen to remember that, but I didn't know you knew it."

The tops of his shoes were cracked. "I knew it. I would have come to her funeral, Lloyd, but I was a long way off and I didn't have the fare."

"Nobody knew where you were." He lit a cigarette. "Nobody ever knew where you were after you left us. You never wrote to any of us in all those years."

Richard Garner said irritably, "Don't smoke, son. Stop before it's too late."

"I wish I could," Lloyd said and waited.

In the pause the news tickers throbbed hesitantly beyond the door. Then Richard Garner said, "How's Philip?"

"Fine. He lives in Boston."

"Is he married?"

"No."

"Are you married, Lloyd?"

"Yes."

"Children?"

"No."

There was something hungry and angry about his eyes. He looked prematurely old, prematurely worn out. He looked as if he'd forgotten how to laugh or even smile. He said, "I often wondered if I had any grandchildren. I'd like to meet your wife, Lloyd."

"I don't think so," Lloyd said.

"How do you mean that?"

"I mean I don't think it will be possible. Tell me something, why did you come to see me?"

Again the look of arrogance, as though resenting a question that should not have been asked. "I'm your father."

"Did it take you twenty-eight years to realize that? Or is it just because you saw me on TV and found out where I was?"

"I'm your father," he said again.

"What do you want?"

"Lloyd," the visitor said, "you're not friendly."

"Why did you leave your family? Was that friendly?"

He shook his head, patiently, wearily, like a man trying to explain something to a child. "Your mother must have talked to you about that."

"Yes. She said you deserted her, and us. She said you were no good."

The shadow of a smile twitched at his lips, or was it just a tic? "Is that all she said?"

"You left her. You left two small children. What do *you* say?"

He spoke after another silence. "I have nothing to say to you about that, Lloyd."

"I want to hear what you have to say. I've been waiting a long time to hear it. I didn't know till you walked in here whether you were dead or alive."

"No," his father said. Anger quavered suddenly in the shaking voice, as at an impertinent question. "I won't talk about that."

The phone rang twice and stopped just as Lloyd reached for it. Gaby was taking the calls on another extension. He turned back to his visitor. "All right," he said, "what *do* you want to talk about? I've got to get back to work pretty soon."

"You're a busy man, I realize that." The words had an odd note of bitterness. "You're a big man, Lloyd. You've made a big success."

They sat facing each other, motionless. "What were you doing all those years?" Lloyd said. "What do you do for a living? Are you in New York?"

He didn't answer any of the questions. He said, "I can get a job in New Orleans, somebody I know there, but I haven't got the money for the ticket."

"Can you get to New Orleans for a hundred dollars?"

"Yes, I can."

"Here it is." Deliberately he took his check book out of the desk drawer and wrote a check for a hundred dollars and handed it across to him. "Why didn't you tell me right away you only came to put the touch on me? You could have saved us both some time."

The other man stood up again and took his overcoat from the rack, then faced him. "How dare you speak that way to your father?"

"They'll tell you out by the elevators where the cashier is, you can cash it there."

"Lloyd, I want Philip's address."

"It's in the Boston phone book. But don't ask him for money, he hasn't got any."

"How dare you speak that way to me?"

"I'll warn Phil. And I'm warning you now, don't come back to me for more. I don't want to hear from you again, is that understood? So far as I'm concerned you're not my father and you never were."

For a moment longer they faced each other without speaking, then the older man turned, still holding his overcoat, and went through the doorway into the hall. He looked proud, defiant and pitiful, and Lloyd Garner felt no pity for him. He was thinking then of his dead mother for whom he felt pity and love, he hoped she would have been pleased with him today.

The phone rang again, startling him, and he reached for it savagely. "Lloyd Garner."

"Oh dear," said Alix Weddern. "You're in a rage about something, I can tell."

"Alix! It's good to hear your voice, when did you get back?"

"A couple of days ago. I'll call later if you like, or you can call me."

"No. Everything's under control, now. You're right, I was having a bad moment."

"Nothing too serious, I hope."

He laughed. "Far from it. You're a welcome relief, Alix."

"I've never been called that," she said, "but I suppose it's the best I can get. From a man who said he'd call me in Florida and never did."

"You said you were going to write, remember?"

"Did I? But I don't know how to write anything except thank-you notes, I guess I could have done that."

"Let's call it a draw. I've been running around a bit while you were away."

"With whom, may I ask?"

"I mean Vietnam, that sort of thing."

"My dear, didn't I know. We watch you constantly, you know. Mother says I'm in love with you."

"Well, aren't you?"

He liked her laugh. "I haven't made up my mind about that. But we do seem to have fun together, don't we?"

"As nearly as I can recall, yes."

"You beast, can I see you tonight after your broadcast?"

"I'm taking you to dinner. You name the place."

"Call for me, dear. I'll think of something."

He hung up feeling suddenly cheerful. The little talk had steadied him, he could forget about his father now. By the time Greminger

and Ferguson came in for the line-up conference he was back in
harness and ready to work. Greminger wanted to cut three minutes
out of the George Wallace interview so they could put in film from
India on Mia Farrow's visit to the Maharishi.

"Earl, you can't do it," Ferguson said. "We've got to show the
evil of this guy. Give him enough rope and he'll hang himself."

"He's not evil. He's an old-fashioned southern demagogue."

"Earl, you can't do it." He seemed close to tears.

"I'm doing it. Three minutes of Wallace is out. Mia Farrow's in."

The dance music was on again. They got up and found their
way to the floor. He'd never been to El Morocco but it was a
favorite of Alix's. He was conscious of the looks that followed them.
People at several tables had called to Alix. "You know just about
everybody, don't you?" he said.

"They're jealous because I'm with you."

"These people? I don't believe it."

"You just don't know how good-looking you are."

"That's right. But I do know I'm with the best-looking woman in
New York."

She was in his arms looking up at him. "That's what you say to all
the girls."

"I gather Bev Hambleton comes here."

"Frequently."

"He's a nice guy. And a good friend."

"He's a souse, like his father, but at least he's working at something. For the moment."

It was the first time he had enjoyed dancing for longer than he
could remember. He felt drunk and gay. She said to him on the
crowded floor, "When you gonna sock it to me, baby?"

"In your accent that's the funniest thing I ever heard."

"But when?" She said it as if she really meant it.

"Tonight?" he joked.

"Okay," she said, "let's go home right now."

"And leave that bottle of champagne half full? Not a chance."

"The waiter will drink it, don't worry."

"But I don't want him to drink it, I want us to drink it, especially me."

"You're just like all the men, drinking comes first."

"But, Alix, think for a minute about that wine. It came so far, and it cost so much."

"Oh, all right then." She moved back from him and went into a series of expert teen-age twists and jerks.

"You didn't learn that at any school in Switzerland."

"You turn me on, baby."

He discovered at Morocco that a reputation for chic seldom guarantees first-class food, but the supper was elaborate and well served and Alix had made sure the second bottle of champagne came off the rack and not out of a refrigerator before it was put in the bucket. They were both up there when they left. In the taxi Alix said, wrapping herself in her sable coat, "How's your wife?"

"Fine."

"You never mention her unless I ask."

"It isn't interesting."

"When did you see her last?"

"Quite a while ago, to tell you the truth."

"I don't even know what she looks like."

"Handsome girl, big blue eyes, but she's gone a little buxom."

"And are you two kids going to get a divorce?"

He didn't answer immediately. "I wouldn't be surprised."

"Of course it's none of my business, dear, but I think it's stupid to let these things drag unhappily on."

"You're probably right about that."

In the dimness of the taxi she turned to him and smiled. "Anyone would think the way I talk I want to marry you myself. I haven't said that."

"I know you haven't."

"Kiss me, please."

The kiss lasted a long time and only mildly excited him. Maybe it was because he was drunk, but it should have been better than that. Alix said, finally drawing away from him, "Let's go to Nassau. Tomorrow. There's a place I borrow down there."

He was laughing. "You think I can walk out just like that?"

"Certainly, why not?"

"You make it sound so easy."

"It is. They can't refuse Lloyd Garner."

"Alix, try to understand. Right now my job is the most important thing. I haven't been doing it long enough just to take off like that. Let's plan something for later, for the spring, maybe. I'll feel much better about it by then." He smiled at her. "Where could we go?"

"Quince Barony's lovely till about May."

"What in the world is Quince Barony?"

"It's a shooting place of my uncle's in Georgia. One of the smaller ones, fourteen or fifteen thousand acres."

"But I don't shoot, and I'm probably too old to learn."

"Pooh," she said, "I'm a lousy shot myself, but we could follow the dogs around and watch somebody else shoot. There isn't much shooting, really. It's mostly drinking juleps and sitting in the sun, and lunching on quail in the woods, and eating ham dinners served by the slaves by firelight."

"It sounds absolutely wonderful, Alix, let's do it sometime, could we really?"

"Oh, we can think of lots of things to do," said Alix, "but nothing as good as what we're going to do tonight."

They had coffee in the big room where the cocktail party had been the night of the strike broadcast, and he declined the tray of liqueurs; he was feeling just right for whatever came next. Afterward she said, "Now I want to show you where *I* live," and took him down a narrow hall that opened off the foyer. It was a miniature apartment with lower ceilings. He followed her into a sitting room suffused with yellow light from a single lamp and the scent of her perfume, a bedroom in shadow beyond. She smiled and switched off the little ivory telephone on the escritoire. "For once," she murmured, "I don't want to talk, even to you, Lloyd Garner. Wait for me in there."

He knew she meant it now, so he was sitting naked on the edge of the bed when she came out of her dressing room wearing something frail and transparent and blue. "You don't waste any time, do you?" she whispered.

"I thought you weren't talking," he said and stood up to take her in his arms.

"I can't help it." She was looking at him as if fascinated. "You're such a big boy."

"Take that beautiful thing off," he said.

And he knew after a very little while that he was the best lover she had ever had, feeling her wonder turning to joy as though she had known nothing so prolonged and so complete. He was on trial with her, he was proving himself. Twice and a third time she trembled and lifted against him, once she tried to speak and could find no words, but he knew what she wanted to tell him. Taking her, he mastered the men she had had before him, and in this moment of possession knew that he was holding a world of which she was the center only, taking her body now was less the need of love than pride of mastery. He had entered her world in triumph and claimed it for his own.

After that night he saw Alix Weddern when he could, which was fairly often during the post-Tet lull in the news. They did all the things he'd read about and never done, the opera, the ballet, intimate cocktail parties in East Side apartments at which Bev Hambleton frequently turned up, private membership night clubs where Bev also frequently appeared, lunches and dinners at La Grenouille, La Côte Basque, Lutèce. Today, a Saturday in late February, they were driving out to lunch at Alix's Long Island club in her mother's chauffeured car. They had left the city traffic behind, the parkway stream of cars around them was thinner and swifter in the bright late morning light. "It's nice getting out of New York," he said.

"Purely selfish on my part." She laughed. "I want to show you off to my North Shore friends."

"It sounds pretty glamorous. Are you sure I'll know how to behave?"

"Just give them that smile. That'll be glamour enough."

"You're glamorous, the most glamorous girl I know."

"Among many."

He put his hand over her hand. "When do I get time to know a lot of girls?"

"When you're not with me, that's when."

"You haven't the slightest idea what I do so I'm going to tell you. Most of the time a network brass hat named Milo Wilson leads me around by the nose to meet prospective sponsors, make dull speeches and eat rubber chicken."

"Why do you bother with it?"

"Because it's the way I earn my living. I'm not rich and indolent like you, lolling in the back seat of a Lincoln Continental." He smiled. "By the way, what do *you* do when *I'm* not around?"

"I cuddle up by the phone and hope Lloyd Garner will call me."

"I can see you." She smiled and stretched her legs. "I don't like that smile, don't you believe me?"

"Of course I don't believe you. You've got a secret life. All men have."

"You seem to be resigned to it."

"Of course I am. I just don't want to hear the details."

They reached the club in ample time for three cocktails before lunch. It was his first experience of a place like this and he was grateful for the calming effect of the drinks. He noticed almost immediately that though everybody recognized him nobody looked at him unless Alix introduced him. Everybody knew everybody else, of course, and whole families seemed to be there, but even within themselves rigidly separated into age groups who occupied acceptedly separate sections of the club. He also noticed the formality of the children with adults, everyone except Mummy and Daddy was Mr. or Mrs. A solemn handshake, plus a quick curtsy from the little girls, went with the introductions. The youngest were watched over by nurses in uniform, their sub-teen brothers and sisters ran in packs, all boys or all girls, but from there up the two sexes mingled, but again in age groups. Around him Lloyd heard the familiar cocktail party accents in the snatches of talk, *stort* for start, learned came out something like *leerned*, somebody was happy as a clam in her new house, and had somebody else brought the wee ones today? The good life, Alix's untroubled world, he looked around him and found it more and more to his liking. The club itself was a life and a world. You grew up in it, played with your nurse on the terrace, trooped with your age pack, giggled with the group at junior dances, went

away to school and came back for the golden college summers,
brought your bride and, later, your children, and, still observing all
the rules as you always had, polite above all, proper above all, grew
very gradually old like these gracious old men sitting around him
now, serene in the security of a lifetime.

13

Suddenly the news woke up. At home, Eugene McCarthy won the New Hampshire primary and Bobby Kennedy thereupon decided to enter the race. Overseas, a new run on gold upset the financial markets and put the dollar under pressure again. On both fronts, what had looked like a routine, apathetic year changed abruptly to the prospect of domestic political excitement and imminent international danger, with nothing in sight for Vietnam but more escalation and Lyndon Johnson in the deepest trouble of his career. Policy issues were forced at last into the open, Dean Rusk's long feud with the Senate Foreign Relations Committee came to the showdown on nationwide TV. For the networks this meant commercial program pre-emptions and high losses. Walter Hacklin studied schedules and moped unhappily at his desk with one eye on the Senate hearings; wouldn't they *ever* adjourn and get off the air?

Then the President took a hand, announcing he would not be a candidate to succeed himself and would de-escalate the bombing of North Vietnam.

Buck Schonwald said, "Fasten your seat belt, Lloyd, it's going to be one of those years."

The reaction to Johnson's decision to quit politics (if he really meant it) and make a major military concession in a new effort to end the war (if the Communists really wanted to end the war) was swift and staggering. The country seemed to breathe a collective sigh of relief; the stock market rebounded with its biggest trading day since the crash of 1929. No less dramatic were the political consequences, projecting Hubert Humphrey into key position for the Democratic nomination and bringing Bobby Kennedy to the White House on the run for an interview with his old enemy. To compound the confusion, Gene McCarthy won the Wisconsin primary and vowed he'd fight all the way to the Convention without a deal. But the sharpest shock of all was still to come. Three days after the President made his announcement, Hanoi was revealed to be willing to talk peace.

Schonwald put the whole staff on standby for immediate call to the studio, nobody was to be more than a quick taxi away if another big break should come. Lloyd had to stick even closer. The prospect of negotiations with Hanoi put him back in the spotlight as a recent observer in the war zone, and he found himself once more in demand for a series of dinner meetings with Milo Wilson and friends of the network as well as a panel discussion at the Overseas Press Club—the subject, Possibilities for Peace. But he no longer worried much about occasions like this, the trick was to keep your cool no matter what was said and read your *Times* carefully for the background. He had learned that just being named Lloyd Garner went a long way toward carrying the audience. Others on the panel might be sharper on the problems under scrutiny but at this stage none of them knew any better than he did whether peace would come out of these proposed negotiations; it was still guesswork. His self-assurance in rolling out sonorous answers to all questions about the warfronts no longer surprised him. The assurance was what counted, and besides, hadn't he been there more recently than the others?

Afterward, as usual, there was a line to shake hands with this newly famous TV presence. And in the club bar later, his opposite numbers on the other networks, Tom Hardwick and Graham Gordon, drank genially with him; they were meeting for the first time. There was no mention of strikes or picket lines, though they had both expressed sympathy with the strikers at the time, and he remembered Buck Schonwald's comment that in this business it didn't take long to forget practically anything. Sitting there Lloyd wished that were true of Kent Ward. The Washington correspondent gave no sign of lifting his boycott of Lloyd Garner. Well, what the hell, you couldn't win 'em all.

Hardwick was saying, "I'm going to give you a ring, Lloyd, Hilary and I want to get you up to Pawling for a weekend as soon as the weather gets better."

"I'd like that, Tom."

"You'd like our place in Westport," Gordon said, "and there's always the boat."

"Say, that would be just great, Graham, I guess it's a little early for the boat, eh?"

"It won't be long now. We practically live aboard when we get started."

"I sure envy you that."

"Did you keep a boat up in New England?"

"Look, I had enough trouble finding the money to buy groceries up in New England."

They laughed along with him. The modest origins bit was always effective with colleagues, about the equivalent of telling a reporter I used to be a newspaperman myself. After a second drink Hardwick insisted they drop in at the Players for a nightcap. "What, you mean you've never seen the Players, Lloyd? That settles it."

On the way across town they dropped Gordon off at Grand Central, then turned south to Gramercy Park. "I stay here sometimes when I'm in town," Hardwick said, "it's a real hideaway for somebody like you and me."

Lloyd smiled in the half dark of the taxi. Tom Hardwick had said somebody like you and me. Hardwick was telling him about the difference between the Players, the Lambs and the Friars. "The Players is a club for gentlemen trying to be actors, the Lambs is a club for actors trying to be gentlemen, and the members of the Friars are neither actors nor gentlemen."

Club talk, more of the big time.

Two gas lamps, authentic old New York, flickered beside the massive doorway, above them the Stanford White façade gazed majestically across the park. It was mellow and cozy inside. Before they went downstairs to the bar Hardwick escorted him on a brief tour of the upper floors, leading him along portrait-studded halls past showcases of historic stage properties to the room where Edwin Booth died, the office where Actors' Equity was born, the library with its Shakespeare folios, Sargent's portrait of Booth in the lounge, and a paneled dining room decorated with playbills of the early English theater. Below the street was a long, low-ceilinged, quiet room with a billiard table at one end and a bar at the other. Hardwick introduced him casually to the group playing bridge at a corner table and they resumed their bourbons on a scarred wooden bench against the wall. "You thought of joining a club now you're settled in New York, Lloyd?"

"Not really. The only one I've seen so far is the Racquet & Tennis."

"Oh. Yes." He sounded impressed. "I think you should consider joining here. The club needs more people like you."

He felt a little burst of elation. "That's a very generous thought, Tom, but would the Players have me?"

"No problem. Let me start the ball rolling." He laughed. "You married, Lloyd?"

"Yeah, but what's that got to do with it?"

"Only that some wives object to clubs. You know, just one more thing they can't share."

"Do they have to share everything?"

"That's exactly what I tell Hilary." And they looked at each other with a look of tolerant understanding, successful men in a sanctuary of ease and leisure which not even their wives could penetrate. Yes, a club was a good idea. You added it to your acquisitions, like the twenty-five extra shares of IBM Sime Sussman had bought for him when the market started up again. He would ask Alix what her friends were buying at the moment, they would know.

Lloyd Garner, man of property, soon to be a member of the Players.

He and Hardwick were the last in the bar over their final drink, then they said good night and Hardwick went up in the tiny, creaking elevator to bed. It was quite an elevator, and like everything in the Players had its story. When John Drew was president of the club he got stuck in that elevator one night with Sarah Bernhardt and was nearly asphyxiated by the emanations from his guest, who hadn't had a bath in forty years. Still smiling at Hardwick's closing anecdote, Lloyd stepped into the frosty night. Alix was expecting him but he was going to disappoint her. Not tonight, Alix. He went to his own apartment and found a letter from his brother. No, Richard Garner hadn't turned up in Boston, he would be on his guard if he did, but Phil thought he ought to see him at least, after all he *was* their father. How typical of Phil. As to Fran, she seemed to be feeling much better since she started going to the psychiatrist, he wrote. Grace Cassidy was living with her now and keeping things steady. More than that, Dr. Stapleton had found a job for her in another doctor's office as a receptionist, a Dr. Wilford. She'd been working for a week now. She liked it, or said she did. You never could be sure with Fran.

He called her there in the morning. "Doctor's office," the voice professionally bright and cool.

Almost involuntarily he said, "It doesn't sound like you at all, Fran."

"Doctor's office," she said again, and just afterward the tone went a little cooler, "Lloyd?"

"The same. Have you a moment to talk?"

"Well, just a moment, yes."

"I want to congratulate you. I think it's just great you're working and feeling better."

"What's on your mind, Lloyd?"

"What's on my mind?" Her abruptness startled him. "Why, nothing. I mean, aren't you pleased with yourself? And Phil says Grace moved in to stay, I think that's a fine idea."

"Lloyd, there are patients waiting in the next room. Is that all you wanted to say?"

Suddenly he was annoyed. "Aren't you being a little snippy this morning? I'm not trying to sell you a vacuum cleaner, Fran, I'm still your husband, you know."

"Oh," she said, "you're calling about the divorce. Why didn't you say so?"

"Look, Fran, I wasn't even thinking about the divorce, anyway there's no hurry about that, I only called to say I was glad to hear you're, you're staying with it."

"I talked to a lawyer yesterday," she went on as if she hadn't heard him, "he wants to know who to get in touch with on your side."

"Why, sure. I haven't done anything about it yet, I'll have my

business manager take care of it right away, he'll know somebody."
The words sounded awkward and lame, as if she'd caught him trying
to deceive her in some way. He felt a surge of anger.

"Is there anything else you want to tell me?" Fran was saying,
"I'm very busy, Lloyd."

"Well, I think you might consider being a little less snotty the next
time, just to see how it sounds. You know."

"Snotty?" she said. "I wasn't aware of it. You'll have to excuse me."
Her tone hadn't changed.

"I mean we're not enemies, Fran, after all."

But they were, of course. Why hadn't he realized it before?
There's nothing as dead as a dead marriage. "I'll expect to hear from
your lawyer, Lloyd," she said, and hung up.

The bells that signal bulletins on press association teleprinters are
not particularly loud or distinctive. Amid the competitive clacking of
tickers pounding out seventy-eight words a minute in a newsroom
already crowded with typewriters and talk, and especially if no
breaking story is in progress, a stranger to this business might not
even notice the little warning noise. But a bulletin bell to a working
reporter has a peculiar insistence, no matter what may or may not
have happened in the course of the passing day, setting off reactions
that lie buried deep in his experience. Thus Lloyd Garner automatically glanced up from the copy on his desk when the bells drifted
through the open office door, and with a look for the moment no
more than curiosity watched Bev Hambleton put aside the New
York *Post*, slide lazily off his chair and amble over to the battery of
machines to read the message coming up letter by letter in pale gray
type. Then the bored gaze changed. Lloyd saw him stiffen. His head
jerked back and he turned with apparent difficulty to the row of
desks behind him. For at least three long seconds he seemed unable to
say anything. Then he gave a weak, hoarse shout. *"Martin Luther
King,"* he said. *"Shot."*

The word was cue for the greatest trial of television reporting
since the assassination of John F. Kennedy, with this time the
combined element of Negro rioting over half the country. Troops in
battle gear guarded the White House in the glare of flame that

spread from the capital to New York, to Chicago, Detroit, Baltimore, Boston, the long hot summer was reborn as the long weekend agony. Martin Luther King was murdered on Thursday, and not until Tuesday did the smoke begin to clear. Memphis, the fatal city, took the camera focus on that funeral day, and the face of the nation stared sadly from the endless cortege. The man in the white Mustang was still unfound, but tragedy was moving hand in hand with hope now. While the mourners marched the President met with his Vietnam counselors at Camp David in Maryland. Contact had been made with Hanoi. Negotiations over a site for a possible peace conference had begun.

For Lloyd Garner it was six straight days of broadcasting almost uninterrupted except for sandwiches and sleep during which he served as anchorman not only on his own regular program but a score of others flung together as events might dictate in the unfolding drama. It was throwing away the script, if there had been time to write one. It was riding the destiny of a people, if they had known where they were going, if anyone had known. And then, toward the end of it, in the last long hours of the Memphis story, his fatigue gave place to a strange new reservoir of confidence and power. For the first time, talking to those who watched and listened, he seemed to feel a kinship in their unseen presence, almost expected them to answer him, sometimes thought he heard them speak to him and touch him.

Queer, he hadn't really noticed them before, hadn't really thought of them as people, human as himself, with joys and troubles, yearnings, problems, even his fan mail seemed somehow unreal since now it was read and answered by others. He'd supposed these final hours of the funeral would be longest and hardest of all, trying to find new words to say it all again for the last time, ad-libbing freely without written copy, there had been no time for that and so much more air time than the press agency copy could fill. But now the words welled up out of that depth he hadn't known in himself, flowing like his returning strength, like second wind in this long marathon of sorrow, as the camera panned slowly across a line of watching children's faces, small and solemn and frightened and black. *"These are the faces of children I saw in Vietnam,"* Lloyd

Garner was saying, "*the innocent victims, the real victims, of hatred and bloodshed wherever it's found, this time, this week, not on some foreign battlefield but here in our own country, in America, our own homeland. This is what they will inherit, the tragedy of Martin Luther King, a gentle man who died by violence, the tragedy of fire and killing in our cities that followed in its wake, and this is what we will have to explain to them, someday, if we can.*" Now the camera pulled away and lingered in silence, one by one, on the faces of the leaders in the procession, close-up shots that filled the monitor screen. Lloyd Garner was speaking again. "*Every politician of national importance who has anything to gain by it in this election year is here today with grave and stately tread, and then there are the others, just stumbling along, the unknown, humble, anonymous thousands of others, mostly black, who are here by reason of real sorrow, of personal loss. And what do we say to them?*"

Coming off the air, feeling suddenly haggard under his make-up, he saw Walter Hacklin waiting for him and was not surprised. He was standing with Schonwald at the door to his office and they both looked grim, he thought he knew why. Then Hacklin summoned his easy false smile. "Want to talk to you a minute, Lloyd, if you're not too beat."

"I'm beat all right, but come in."

He collapsed into the chair behind his desk and looked up at them both, almost too tired to care what they said. "I've been listening, Lloyd. Buck doesn't entirely agree with me, but you went pretty strong those last few minutes of the funeral coverage, don't you agree?"

"Strong?"

The smile tightened. "Look, Lloyd, you know what I'm talking about. Something got into you, it didn't sound like you at all."

He managed a ghost of grin. "Like Hedley Johns maybe?"

"Now, now, Lloyd." It was his usual avuncular tone. "We can't just pass this off as a joke. My phone is ringing right now with calls from southern affiliates, they'll be saying you called Martin Luther King a gentleman, and so on. It just doesn't sit right, Lloyd. I've had complaints ever since you talked about the Memphis police."

Memphis police? He couldn't remember. That was days ago, a century ago. "What did I say about the Memphis police?"

"It wasn't what you said, not exactly. I've seen a transcript of that, it was okay. But you had a way of raising your eyebrow. You had a way of almost literally putting your tongue in cheek. Buck says it was unconscious."

"Thanks for defending me, Buck. It must have been that."

"But it won't do, you know," Walter Hacklin said. "People misunderstand. They think you're being sarcastic. Just the slightest change in your tone of voice will do it, you know that, even when it's unintentional. I'm presuming it was unintentional. You're supposed to be strictly impartial at all times. I'm sure Buck told you that long ago."

He nodded wearily but said nothing.

"And now this you said tonight about the politicians in the procession, Lloyd. It was terribly unfair. It was terribly dangerous for the network, do you realize that? Those Negro kids you were talking about, well, I guess we could overlook that. Buck supports you on that. But it was editorial, Lloyd, openly editorial. It just wasn't the *news*. Deliberately linking it up with Vietnam. That's not your job, boy, that's not the network's job unless we label it clearly and set it up as policy like on a local o-and-o station."

Schonwald said more gently, "Walter's right. We'll probably get kickbacks from people like Eastland. Thurmond. Kent Ward would never leave us open to them this way."

Kent Ward, his no-longer friend. He wondered if Ward had been listening today, and Hedley Johns. He hardly realized himself what he'd said, it just seemed to come. But for all his tiredness something in him felt good, felt clean. He had spoken out, he had been a part of what was happening. And he remembered the long ago night when Kent Ward had quoted Justice Holmes to him, today Lloyd Garner had shared the passion and action of his time.

Hacklin was saying, "I'm aware, of course, that this past week has been a terrible strain on you, Lloyd, on all of us. I'm sure that's why you went off the deep end on the air. When you're a little older, with more experience behind you, I know you wouldn't do what you did today. You're obviously exhausted and you need some rest. Except for these lapses I've mentioned you've done a superb job."

"Thanks." He wondered in the moment if the big boss had called.

"Things ought to quiet down for a bit now. I hope to God they do or we'll be so far in the red we'll never get out. We should be back on full commercial schedule tomorrow."

"How about that." He was beginning to sound like Bill Moran, the bitter battle veteran, but the effect was lost on the Hacklin smile.

"Take a few days off, boy. Go somewhere. Not too far."

"I may do that, Walter."

They left him, but at the doorway Schonwald turned back for a moment and winked. Good old Buck, he thought. He'd never expected to see that.

The studio lights were going down. He waved so-long to the camera crew he'd worked with practically nonstop for six days. They were all as exhausted as he was, but as usual he'd be the one to get public credit for the performance. "Tell the boys we'll have a drinking soon," he said to Greminger when the editor paused to say good night. He had the impression Greminger wanted to ask him about the conversation with Hacklin but was too timid. It was different with Harry Ferguson. The best news writer money could buy wasn't staying bought this time. He came in after Ferguson left, looked once over his shoulder into the studio, and then gripped Lloyd's hand with tears starting to his eyes. "You were absolutely great," he said in a low voice.

"What's the matter, Harry?" Lloyd grinned. "You afraid somebody's going to hear you?"

They laughed together and Ferguson left. Alone, Lloyd picked up the phone and dialed Alix Weddern's number. "It's me," he said. "I think."

"You sound so done-in, darling, I can hardly hear you."

"Tell me something, what's that place your family has with the kooky name in Georgia?"

"Quince Barony?"

"That's it. I was wondering if maybe we could go down there for a little while."

"*Darling,* of course we could."

"That's what I wanted you to say. I'll call you in the morning and we'll plan it, shall we?"

"We don't have to plan anything." She sounded suddenly very happy. "We'll just go as soon as you can get away."

He'd take a long weekend, no more. He'd be back in time to do the Wednesday program. That way he'd miss only two shows; it was safe enough. He didn't care if Jack Milhouse did them, he didn't care who did them. He was tired.

III: LIKING IT

14

They went the old-fashioned way, by train. Alix had been taking the same train to Quince Barony since she was a child, of course in those days traveling by rail wasn't as quaint. Being out of season, the Florida-bound limited was half empty and they had a leisurely, uncrowded dinner in the dining car adjoining their Pullman while the spring night fell outside the windows. He felt like a kid again, the thrill of going to New York on the Midnight from Back Bay station with Phil. His mother was taking them on a weekend to stay with friends, as she told them. The friends turned out to be a man's apartment near Central Park, a man he didn't like because of the intimate way he spoke to his mother. They played in the Park the next day and the man gave them money to go to Childs for lunch and then a movie. Lloyd was all of ten years old then and Phil thirteen. When they came back his mother and the man were drunk and holding each other up. The two boys were sent out to dinner and when they came back again their mother called to them from behind a locked bedroom door to go to their room and go to sleep.

But Lloyd didn't sleep. Lying there in the big double bed beside Phil, who was already snoring, he realized they were sleeping in a woman's room, probably the man's wife who was away somewhere or just gone, like his own father. He wanted to talk to Phil about how bad he felt seeing this man with his mother, so intimately, but Phil either didn't care or didn't notice, anyway he went to sleep right away. But Lloyd lay awake listening for telltale sounds that he'd learned to recognize in Boston, little laughs or moans, a man's grunting words, the creaking bed, and water running like anguish in the bathroom. The buried sadness rose in him for a moment, remembering. Why had she taken them to New York when she knew what she was going to do and they were going to see her do?

Probably because she had no one to leave them with at home. Then did she have to go at all? He had hated her, too, as well as the man, by the time they got back on the train again. It went *clackety-rook-clack-clack,* just like this one, the heavy wheels on the rails, a pounding rhythm in the night of his memory, and Alix said, laughing at him, "You haven't heard a word I've said."

"Every word."

"I don't believe you but it doesn't matter, you were sweet to indulge me in this old chug-chug, trains must be such a bore to you fast-moving people."

"I love it. I was just thinking about how happy I used to feel on trains when I was a kid." But not after the trip to New York.

"You see? I knew you'd gone off and left me. But I feel the same way about trains, darling. So secure and easygoing, so unresponsible again. Let's just be that way while we're together these next few days, shall we?"

"I want to."

"We'll just eat and drink and sleep and fuck, shall we?"

Now he was laughing at her. "I can't help it, the way you say it sounds so proper."

"It *is* proper, what could be more proper? The trouble is people make it so secret and naughty and it shouldn't be at all."

"Are you recommending public fornication, in say the new Madison Square Garden?"

"They'll have duller nights there, believe me."

They were the last ones in the dining car, having a second brandy and more railroad coffee. "They want to get rid of us and clean up," Lloyd said.

"They do not. Look at those happy, grinning black faces just kowtowing."

"You just don't leave the right tip and watch the grins vanish."

"Lloyd, they're not like that at all, not on this train. I ought to know."

"You mean we-all are bound for you-all land, where little Sambo and old black Joe are just awaitin' to do our pleasure?"

"Something like that. Why, I've seen that big bald one every winter for years, don't tell me he's not basically a happy man."

"Not any more he isn't. Not after Memphis."

"Martin Luther King seems to have left quite an impression on you."

"He has, as a matter of fact."

"That's why I'm glad I'm getting you out of that madhouse for a little while, your nerves are absolutely shot, darling."

"My nerves are fine." But he knew she was right, he'd have to watch what he ad-libbed from now on. Walter Hacklin might overlook it once, on grounds of fatigue and inexperience, but only once. Those words that got into his head, where did they come from? Wherever it was, that was dangerous territory. Let other people do the gambling, he hadn't come this far to jeopardize it now.

Alix was saying, "You need to get your perspective back, and I'm here to see you do."

He smiled and stood up. "Never mind my perspective. Right now I want to close my eyes and sleep." He was swaying in the unsteady car, the white steward careened forward with the check. Lloyd paid it and turned around to where the waiter stood smiling behind them. He gave him a ten-dollar tip and the man followed them all the way back to their stateroom, opening doors and summoning their porter to take over where he left off. "We just don't want to be disturbed," Lloyd said to the porter. When the door closed he said to Alix, "Did you hear him say yassuh boss?"

"He did not say yassuh boss. He said, yes, sir, good night. And was that a ten-dollar bill you gave the waiter? You'll spoil them to death."

"By way of tribute to Martin Luther King," he said, feeling quite drunk and very, very sleepy.

Alix was standing on one shoeless foot stripping off the other shoe. "This train is rocking along, Lloyd Garner."

"So are we. How many drinks did we have before dinner, five, six?"

"Whatever we had, you needed it for your nerves. You were ghastly pale when we came aboard, now you look more of a semblance of yourself."

"I bet you couldn't repeat that last phrase in a hundred years."

"I don't have to. You're the expert, not me."

"Go ahead, it's easy. More of a selfless of yourself."

She laughed and he dropped forward on the bunk. The train gave back its steady rhythm, *clackety-rook-clack-clack,* all the way from Back Bay station.

In soft hazy sunshine, sweet mildness in the air, already the breath of summer, a buggy was waiting for them at the whistle stop, a single platform in the pinewoods. This was how the rich came to their hideaways, their own railway station, their own woods. The driver, old black Joe himself, bowed low and took off his hat, his whip in his hand, the one Simon Legree used to borrow when there was trouble at the cabins. "Pompey, this is Mr. Garner, I'll bet you've seen him on the television, now haven't you, don't be shy."

By God his name really was Pompey, what else? He certainly had seen Mr. Garner on the television, yes, sir. It was a two-horse buggy and in spanking trim. Away they went, side by side in the rear seat, Pompey flicking his whip up front with their bags, along a road as soft as sand between the endless tall trees filled with bird song. Lloyd closed his eyes and leaned back, his head still ached with hangover, and Alix briefed him on the people. "Of course we came so suddenly we couldn't pick our company, it's just our luck to find a group, but I think Lawson said they'd be leaving on the weekend so we may be alone by Monday." Lawson was Uncle Lawson, head of Ansel Brothers, it was his plantation. "Of course everybody in the family adores Quince Barony and brings their friends, so often people just want to stay on," raising her voice slightly, "how many are there, Pompey?" the old man cocked his head, having heard every word of course, and said he reckoned five or six, Miss Alix. "Pompey, I was eleven years old when I first saw you, how old are you now?" And chuckling, pausing again to think, he said he didn't rightly know how old he was, he never had. The sun was hotter, off in the woods somewhere distant Lloyd heard a dog begin barking and others took it up musically. Yes, he was going to like it here.

At breakfast in the dining car, the rural Carolinas rushing past the windows, women looking at Alix's clothes from other tables, she had talked to him in a low voice with no Pompey to overhear. "You nearly killed me last night, what was wrong with you? I never saw you that way."

"If I hurt you I'm sorry, I was drunk, that's all."

"You were something, I was really afraid of you."

"I'm sorry, darling, I don't remember last night much, just being very, very tired, that's all."

"You don't remember the new thing you did? The way you kissed me?"

"I remember that, yes."

"I liked that. Nobody ever did that with me."

"I sometimes wonder what those two husbands of yours did do, if anything."

"They never did what you did last night. Of course I know about it. Of course it's in every movie now, remember the girl in *Charlie Bubbles?* She was just starting to do it to Albert Finney when they moved the camera away."

He studied her in the morning light, all sophistication on the surface, mostly child underneath. "I'm going to teach you to do it to me."

"That? No thank you. But I liked you doing it to me, are you going to do it again?"

"If you order me to do it, yes."

"Don't worry, I will."

Lloyd Garner, your obedient servant. What Alix Weddern wanted was an obedient servant, he knew that now. What she wanted was to be laid and love it, but only the part of it that was her pleasure, not his. His part was the Thing, frightening in erection, repulsive in repose, born to do a job, not to be loved for itself as part of him. "I am your obedient servant," he said, "okay?"

"Now you're more of a semblance of yourself again," she said, and they laughed, remembering. The sandy road became a broad avenue of tanbark, narrowing again a little later to a gravel drive. A lake glittered off to their left, green lawns went down from the house to the water, and what a house. He looked at it again, three rambling wings on either side of it, probably built successively onto the central manor in the same colonial style. A manservant, black face shining above the immaculate white coat, waited in front of the farthest wing. He separated their luggage and installed them in two huge bedchambers facing across a glistening parquet hall, each room with its dressing room and bath, each with broad windows looking out at the lake. "They off shootin', Miss Alix, I do believe nobody here in the house jus' now."

Not even Miss Scarlett? To Alix when they were alone in her room he said, putting his arms around her, "All this sure am heavenly, but remember I go back on the air Wednesday night and that's final, no matter what I might say in a drunken moment."

"I'm going to drug you."

He smiled down at her. "Do I take a shower in your room or mine?"

"In yours. Mine is for sleeping together tonight."

"Okay." He kissed her and she clung hard, then broke away from him with a small breathless laugh. "Go on and take your shower or you'll get me started again, you lovely man."

Lounging with their juleps in full-length chairs on the manor terrace, they watched the others drive up after their day in the field. Two servants were removing the guns from the back of the long, luxurious station wagon, a bronzed young man slipped out of the driver's seat and turned the car over to another servant, looking as he did toward the terrace, squinting, then waving in recognition, "Hi, Alix!" the voice assured and dry. An older man climbed more stiffly out of the middle door, backing cautiously onto the gravel, laughing and saying something to the others in the car. These were two women and yet another man, this one young like the first one. The women got out last in hunting khakis and low boots, wearing open shirts with little scarves at their throats, one older, the other about Alix's age. All turned and waved to the terrace, then headed for their own wings. The two older ones became a couple, passing below the terrace where Lloyd and Alix sat while the two young men and the girl moved off to the wing nearest the car. "Don't drink it all up," the man remarked with a smile at Alix and a nod to Lloyd, the woman said cheerfully, "Galt, can you make two more of those and bring them to us right away? I can smell the mint."

The young negro hovering at the back of the terrace said, "Yes, ma'am," and went to work at his bar against the wall. Lloyd looked after the two who had spoken. "His face is familiar."

"His name is Tom Hollis and his face ought to be familiar, he's the biggest tobacco tycoon around. That's his wife, they're friends of Lawson's, both awfully nice. You're going to like the Burnleys too."

"Who was that driving?"

"Mills Aspenwall." She giggled. "He's been trying to make me since I was sixteen."

"I've heard of him, isn't he a big polo player?"

"He's a big ass. Yes, he plays polo."

The Burnleys came to the terrace first. She had changed into a short dinner dress like Alix and he was wearing a jacket like Lloyd, both stooped and kissed Alix on the cheek and shook hands with Lloyd. He liked the girl's fresh, snub-nosed face, all tan and freckles, and her happy smile. "Old friends from Washington," Alix said, "I can't remember whether you were at Kent Ward's the night Lloyd and I met."

"I don't think so," Burnley said to Lloyd, "but I feel I know you anyway, along with a few million other people."

"We watch your program every night, guests or not," his wife said. "It's required of all State wives, you know. Even the Secretary's wife."

"Well, I guess I can't help being a bore," said Lloyd, "but I can't say I like being a chore." Everybody laughed at that. Declining sunshine slanted across the lawns, Galt's second potent julep probably made it look even more beautiful than it was. He was beginning to feel a little more at home with people like this, lately he'd had a lot of practice.

"I'm trying to remember what it is you're doing, Wade." Alix lay back lazily in the long chair. "Whatever it is, I bet you'd rather be back in Paris."

"European desk," he said. Lloyd watched his clean profile against the light. "But they've given me a hint I'll be going back with the team for the Vietnam talks. Hank's dying to go, of course. We've kept the apartment."

"Come visit us, Alix," Hank said.

"Then it's going to be Paris?" Lloyd asked Wade Burnley.

"Between ourselves, yes. Officially, the other people are still hold-ing out for Warsaw."

"Wherever we go," drawled Alix, "we'll end up giving them every-thing they demand."

"Not with Averell heading up the team. Oh dear." He turned to Lloyd and smiled. "It just slipped out, but that has to be between ourselves too."

"Fear not. I'm not planning to phone any hot news tips to New York. In fact I've been sitting here debating whether to retire from broadcasting and ask for a job at Quince Barony."

"I think it could be arranged," Alix said. The Hollises appeared and Galt got busy with his bar. "Gillian and Tommy, this is Lloyd Garner, as if you couldn't tell."

"I could but Gillian couldn't. Hello, Lloyd."

"Only because I'm half blind, darling, but I can see him perfectly well now, I can see everything if I'm close enough."

"How do you do at last, Mrs. Hollis?"

"To be frank, Mr. Garner, I thought I was going to miss Hedley Johns, I was so used to him, but I must say I'm quite satisfied with his successor. By the way, what's he up to? Isn't he doing something on educational TV?"

"He's about to become director of the Voice of America," Wade Burnley said, "as Lloyd probably knows."

Lloyd didn't know but smiled and nodded as if he did. The things you learned on a shooting weekend in Georgia.

"Another fella from your network is going in as his right-hand man," Burnley went on. "Drew Stimson. It'll be announced next week."

"Oh, I know Drew," Alix said. She would, of course.

"I'm sorry you couldn't have made it a few days earlier," Hollis was saying to him. The pale eyes in the flat, shrewd face were friendly but appraising. "We're all off tomorrow, unfortunately."

"Speak for yourself, Tommy. Not all of us." They turned at the new voice, Mills Aspenwall's. He was wearing a dark blazer with faultless cavalry twills. "Don't bother to introduce me to Lloyd

Garner, I recognize him." There was something unpleasant in the way he said it, even with the smile.

"Didn't you say today you were coming back with us?" Hank Burnley said.

"I did. But I've changed my mind, dearie. I didn't know Alix was going to be here. Galt, a rum collins."

"Won't it be ducky," Alix said with open displeasure, "just the three of us."

"You shoot, of course, Mr. Garner."

"I'm sorry to say I don't."

"Well, you can follow us around. Alix is a very good shot, I taught her myself." He perched on the edge of her chair. "Budge a little, that's a good girl. It's been rather a long time, hasn't it?" He laughed and said to the others, not including Lloyd, "Alix doesn't ask me to her parties any more."

"You wouldn't fit, Mills dear," Alix said.

"That's what I mean. All her friends are intellectuals now. And Jews." He turned suddenly to Lloyd. "Can't you wangle an invitation for me, Mr. Garner?"

"Not being a Jew, Mr. Aspenwall, I don't know how much I can help you, but I'll see what I can do when I'm alone with her."

Alix led the laughter and Aspenwall colored slightly under his tan. He tasted his drink and then said, "Galt, I've told you at least three times you put too much sugar in this drink."

"I'm sorry, Mr. Mills, can I make another one?"

"Never mind this time. Next time try to remember, if it isn't too much for you."

"Yes, sir, Mr. Mills."

"And add a pinch of cyanide," Alix Weddern said.

At dinner in the white, high-ceilinged dining room the talk was about the day's shooting. Lloyd sat back and observed the gentry in their natural habitat. Later it was about visits to Quince Barony in the past, much laughter over remembered midnight coon hunts, and other places where shooting had been done. Under the circumstances it was a little difficult to include Lloyd in the conversation but everybody made him feel a valued member of the group except

Aspenwall, who concentrated his attention on Alix despite repeated rebuffs. They were all more or less drunk by this time, it was obviously the correct thing. At Quince Barony you killed birds in the daytime and got drunk at night and the language spoken at all times was small talk. Having coffee on the terrace afterward Lloyd noticed, however, that Tom Hollis's small talk was more a matter of manner than topic.

"How near are we to civil war?" he asked casually. He was standing alone with Lloyd out of earshot of the others, looking out across the moonlit lake.

"Civil war?" Lloyd looked at him.

"With the colored. It will have to come, of course. There's no other solution."

"Oh?"

"The only question now is when the fighting starts. Do we let them begin it, or do we begin it?"

"If it comes to civil war," Lloyd said, "it won't be fighting, it'll be a massacre."

Tom Hollis nodded thoughtfully. "A necessary massacre. From what you understand, from what you know of their stockpiles and strategy and so on, would you say they could keep going more than a few days?"

He wanted to joke about it but said instead, "Certainly not much longer, if it happens."

"I agree. I suppose the first thing they'll do is try to seize control of communications. I guess you fellows are ready."

"We're not worrying about that," Lloyd said, truthfully.

Hollis gave a short, pleased grunt that sounded like Sidney Greenstreet and extracted a cigarette case from his pocket. "Smoke?"

"Too much, I'm afraid." But he accepted it.

"Don't say that. I'd be disappointed to think you've been taken in by all this hysterical talk. You get the Tobacco Institute's releases, of course."

"Of course."

"That's the truth of it, the scientific truth, no more, no less. But the government's after us anyway, especially on TV advertising. They won't get far in Congress, though, my North Carolina friends assure me of that." Tom Hollis offered the flame of an oddly shaped gold lighter. "Seen one of these yet? Swiss. Amazing little thing. I'll send you one."

"Well, thanks."

The biggest tobacco tycoon around was looking thoughtfully at the lake. "A couple of years ago," he said, "I was standing right where we are now with your boss, Lloyd," and he didn't mean Buck Schonwald or Walter Hacklin either. "He's a wonderful man despite his age, he certainly has got all his marbles, and a few to spare."

"He certainly has."

"Ever visited him at Sea Island?"

"I'm sorry to say, not yet," Lloyd said.

"You'll like it there."

"I'm sure I will." And he wondered again when he would meet the big boss, if ever. Tom Hollis was chuckling reminiscently beside him.

"Know a fellow named Milo Wilson in your network?"

"Very well."

"We gave him a hard time once. We were talking contract with your Sales people and Wilson had the conference table all prettied up with cigarettes in little silver jugs. They were the wrong brand."

"Oh boy," Lloyd said.

"My people kept picking them up and shredding them in their fingers sort of absent-mindedly while they were talking."

"I can believe it."

He laughed. "Just a boo-boo, of course. It didn't matter. But I still remember Wilson's face when he realized."

"I can see him."

"And this antismoking campaign doesn't matter either. People are going to keep right on smoking, don't you think?"

"I suppose so."

"Of course we've got to keep plugging. We're not so proud we couldn't always do with another friend."

Lloyd, watching the moonlight on the lake, felt the other man's eyes on him but didn't turn his head. Down the terrace a little way Mills Aspenwall was entertaining the ladies. Lloyd knew Alix

would want to be rescued. Now Tom Hollis looked at his cigarette
lighter and said, in the casual, almost negligent tone, "Ever think of
setting up a Swiss bank account, Lloyd?"

"Why, no, I can't say I have."

"If you decide to look into it, call me, will you?"

"Why, sure."

He turned to look at Hollis. The small, hard mouth was curving
in a smile. "How does the slogan go? You'll be *so* glad you did."

Alix was saying, her voice a little higher, "I'm not going to let
Lloyd stay up another minute after what he's been through this week
and I'm tired too, dears, so we'll just say good night and good-by right
now, I doubt if we'll see you before you leave in the morning."

"You'll see me," Mills Aspenwall said. "We have a shooting date,
remember?"

"We have no date of any kind," Alix said. "Lloyd and I came
down here to rest."

Aspenwall smirked and glanced out toward the lake. "You've got
a fine night for it," he said.

Talking in bed: "Why do they call her Hank, Alix?"

"Her name's Henrietta, that's why."

"I kind of like Frank Merriwell too."

"You mean Wade, I guess. He's nice, very nice, but if we're
going over the guest list I prefer the Hollises."

"I didn't have much chance to talk to her."

"She's a Bostonian, as you probably know."

"How would I know? All you people sound the same whether
you're from Boston or New York or Philadelphia."

"I thought you might know her family, she's a Saltonstall."

"Now you're teasing. I never knew a Saltonstall except at a
distance. Or any of their friends. They might as well be some odd
species of hornbilled duck."

She giggled. "You're not too far off, at that."

"I can't say I like Tom Hollis, exactly. But he's interesting. He
offered me a bribe to be a friend of smoking."

She giggled again. "He didn't."

"He did. We didn't talk figures, but he said he'd put it in a Swiss bank account. I was sort of amazed, in a way. Well, that leaves Mills Aspenwall."

"I told you. Anyway, you could see for yourself."

"That he's a shit? If he carries on much the way he did with me he must get a lot of smacking down."

"He resents you, darling, I knew he would. And I wish you wouldn't use that word. I can take most words but I have difficulty with that one."

"Why should he resent me? I haven't got anything he wants."

"You've got me. That should have been obvious to everybody at that table."

"Does he need a piece of tail that bad? I mean apparently he doesn't see you from one year to the next."

"Darling, I am not a piece of tail and I certainly hope you don't think of me that way. Mills is always possessive about girls he's known all his life and he can't stand strangers where they're involved."

"Especially if the strangers aren't gentlemen."

"There's something of that in it too. You know how people like Mills Aspenwall think." She stirred and moved closer to him in the bed. "Actually you're a gentleman and he's not, but he has a very narrow view of the word."

"His father's view, no doubt."

"And his grandfather's, who went to school with my grandfather."

"Don't tell me, let me guess. St. Paul's."

"Middlesex. Why are we having this silly conversation, darling? I can think of much better things to do."

"Not with Aspenwall hanging around. He's probably listening at the door right now, trying to peek through the keyhole. I think my control was pretty good with him tonight, don't you?"

"Admirable. Everybody thought so."

"How do you know everybody thought so?"

"I could tell."

"But nobody spoke up."

"Darling, it would just make more of a scene."

"And one must at all costs avoid making more of a scene."

"But don't you agree?"

He laughed softly and pulled her still closer to him, turning to taste her warm and scented shoulder. He was thinking Alix's men, her bits of tooled masculinity with their dark silk breast pocket handkerchiefs from Sulka's, their contrasting shirts and collars, their rebuilt English shoes, their automatic cordiality and essentially false politeness, adaptable by well-worn usage for any occasion, and their smug ignorance of what was going on everywhere in the world except the State Department and Wall Street. At one end of the spectrum was Mills Aspenwall, at the other the kind of rich young liberal who supports socialist causes but has no intention whatever of yielding any of the prerogatives of his own wealth. "Lloyd," Alix whispered at his ear.

"Yes, darling."

"Are you too tired? Are you falling asleep?"

"Just thinking."

"Perhaps I ought to let you go back to your own bed tonight, I'm being selfish."

"I don't want to go back to my own bed tonight or any night. I hate to sleep alone."

"Oh. And I was going to take that as a compliment."

He brushed her cheek with his nose. "Don't be sensitive."

"Lloyd, do you know what I'd like? For you to take me quietly, just for a little while, not the fierce angry way you did on the train, I'll never understand what happened to you last night on the train. Then you'll come and I'll come with with you, so quietly, and we'll sleep like babies till noon." When he didn't answer she said again, softly insistent in the silent room, "Lloyd, have you fallen asleep?"

He smiled, his breath against her cheek. "No, just reviewing the day's events. This place, those people at dinner. They're not my kind, of course."

"Darling, don't be snotty. So what if they're not the brightest people around? They have taste and the leisure to indulge it, they have the houses and clothes, the good looks and good manners, if they want to use them. They follow the sun. They support the colleges and the arts and the hospitals with their surplus money, and they help pay for the poor with their taxes. Is it a crime to be lucky enough to live well and be able to afford it?"

He was smiling. "I couldn't agree more. I don't consider myself superior, it's the other way around. There's probably nothing more fun than being a gentleman. And caring about a lady. If I had the chance I'd retire and take a shot at it."

"Are you serious, darling?"

"Sure, only I couldn't afford it."

"If you married a rich woman you could afford it."

"I'd have to care about her, that's the snag."

"You worry me when you talk like this. Are you telling me there's another girl?"

"Yes and no," he said.

"Yes and no?" He could feel her body stiffen almost imperceptibly.

"I mean no other girl in particular. Nobody I know now. Maybe somebody I will know, later. Somebody I may be better suited to."

"I thought we were well suited."

"You know we are, in many ways. But I'm not part of the world you live in, look at me with those people in there tonight. And I guess I have no world at all of my own to offer somebody like you."

"Lloyd. What are you saying to me? Are you saying you've decided to stay married?"

"Definitely not that. I haven't told you, my wife is in analysis, Alix. She's a very sick woman."

"Her mind?"

"Alcoholism."

She spoke out of the new silence. "You could have told me this. Why did you think it would make any difference?"

"I don't know why I didn't tell you. It just wasn't necessary in the beginning, I guess. You were not involved."

"And now you feel I'm involved?"

"Alix, I care about you, you know that."

Her voice, half a whisper, sounded husky and troubled. "Not enough to want to marry me, I gather."

"How do you feel about it?" he said.

"Marry me, Lloyd. That's how I feel about it."

15

They flew back to New York in plenty of time for him to do the Wednesday show. Mills Aspenwall, defeated, had decided to leave with the others, so they had Quince Barony to themselves for three days of laziness under the sun, of picnics in the woods and firelit dinners, and three nights of long, restoring sleep. Only once, laughing, had Alix mentioned what she called her drunken proposal on that first night in bed, but she didn't withdraw it, and he joked back that he had the deal under consideration and would let her know. She seemed content to leave it at that and was perhaps a little embarrassed that she had been so unconventionally direct. She took care of his comfort like a devoted wife and forbade him to talk about his job or the news. He couldn't even watch Jack Milhouse on the evening program. By command of Uncle Lawson there was no TV at Quince Barony, not even radio except in the slave quarters. Lloyd caught up with the headlines on his way back in the plane, then sat back to think while Alix napped at his side.

She wanted to marry him. They had laughed about it but she meant it, he knew he had only to say the word. She probably looked at marriage as a gamble anyway, judging from her two previous experiences, and what was easier for her than a divorce and eventually trying again? Yet she could give Lloyd Garner everything he didn't already have, her position, her friends, an established social future. He sat there remembering the days and nights at Quince Barony and wishing this had happened ten years ago, when they were both ten years younger. How old was Alix now? Probably older than she would admit, possibly five or six years older than he was. He had seen it sometimes for a moment in the tired skin around her eyes, no wrinkles yet, she was too exquisitely cared for, but she was no kid any longer, and how lovely, how desirable they were, the kids. That girl who haunted his memory at odd moments, right in the middle of his work, a girl he'd seen and admired at Seward Pratt's at a cocktail party, when Alix had said, "You like the sweet young things," the faint tinge of woman's bitterness in her look as she said it, another sign.

Not that girl actually, not that particular girl, he didn't even remember her name and had no special desire to look her up, but girls *like* that one, and it wasn't just because they were twenty or twenty-two. He'd seen farm girls in New England who had the same physical perfection, the same untouched freshness and that filly's wildness of innocence, ready to kick up their heels and race. But those country kids had only part of it, the rest was in the training, the poise that was like birthright, the finishing school sheen, the scent of money. It was a way they had of walking the world as if they owned it, and they did, like the girl at Seward Pratt's. They were bred in the bone and eventually they were Alix Weddern, a perfectly turned out product equal to every demand that life could make of them, eventually passing the riding glove along to their children and moving on to the next easy, pleasant stage; it was what life was all about.

Alix had had two marriages and no children. He hadn't asked her why. They had been intimate enough for him to observe she used no diaphragm for her lovemaking and didn't believe in the pill, maybe she'd learned in her first marriage it was unnecessary for her. Did it mean she couldn't have children? But he wanted children, he knew now how much he had always wanted children, and they would have everything he had never had as a child, because he would give it to them. He remembered the day at Alix's Long Island club. There were children all around them that day but she had shown no interest in them. But Lloyd Garner's wife would have children and would love them as he did. In the moment he had a brief, dreamy vision of a country place, Connecticut maybe, the kids on the summer lawn, the swimming pool, he would willingly spend the rest of his life living it that way.

With the right girl, of course, and who was the right girl? Like a dream, like a smile, she hovered just beyond his consciousness, she had always been there, he knew it but he hadn't caught her yet. Would she ever be flesh within his grasp?

There was plenty going on in the days after his return. Bobby Kennedy beat McCarthy in the Indiana primary. Students were rioting at Columbia and protesting at the Sorbonne. And the Red Sox, Lloyd noted in private dismay, were not doing well. He decided that the Red Sox were the one thing in Boston he really missed, and determined to get up there for a weekend game when possible. Not with Alix, he couldn't quite see Alix in Fenway Park. Maybe with Bev Hambleton, maybe he'd drive up in the gleaming silver Jaguar XKE he acquired soon after he got back from Quince Barony. Bev grinned with admiration and envy the day Lloyd showed it off to him.

"You borrow that, Uncle?"

"It's mine, like it?"

"Wasn't it kind of extravagant?"

"Sime Sussman says extravagance is a phase I'm in. I'll come out of it after I've had to pay taxes a couple of times."

Today Bev Hambleton wasn't grinning. He'd come in from the newsroom with his lips set tight and he looked angry. "Can I talk to you, Lloyd?"

"Go ahead, talk."

"Privately."

"Gaby's just going out to lunch. I think."

The secretary was putting things in her purse. Bev waited, not looking at her. "All right, all *right*," Gaby said and threw them a mocking smile as she left.

Lloyd leaned back at his desk. "Sit down, young man."

"I'll stand, thanks."

"What's wrong?"

"Buck promised me the next reporter opening. Now he's giving it to somebody else."

"To somebody else? Who else?"

He shrugged. "Does it matter? Somebody from the outside."

"That doesn't sound like Buck, if he promised it to you."

"I'm goddamn mad, Lloyd. I've been working hard, you know I have. I'm ready for the job, Buck knows I am."

"Have you talked to him?"

"I don't have to, Bonnie tipped me this morning."

"And you're taking it secondhand from a secretary?"

"If he wants to see me he knows where he can find me. I'm not going to him."

"You're an idiot. You want something in this place you've got to hustle it, you know that."

"Screw him. Screw them all, Lloyd. I'm going to quit."

There was a silence. Gaby came back to collect something from her desk. "Sor-ry!" she trilled. Neither man looked at her. "All right," Lloyd said, "I'll speak to him myself. Right now."

He walked through the studio and crossed the hall into Schonwald's outer office. Bonnie said, "He's got somebody in there."

"So?"

He opened the inner door and walked in. Schonwald was just getting up from behind his desk and standing beside it was a tall young light-skinned Negro. The producer was smiling. "Meet the newest member of the staff," he said. "Cliff Miller, this is Lloyd Garner, I guess you recognized him anyway."

The young man said, "Yes, I sure did," and they shook hands, the hand was sweating a little, the smile calm and shy.

"You'll be seeing Cliff around, Lloyd. I have a feeling he's going to do a good job for us."

"Good luck," Lloyd said. "Good luck, Cliff."

He waited until Schonwald took Miller out to Bonnie and came back to his desk. "You want to see me about something, fellow?"

"About Bev Hambleton, yes."

"I want to talk to Hambleton, he's in for a temporary disappointment."

"He already knows, Buck. He's sitting in my office getting ready to quit."

He blinked. "Come on, is it that bad?"

"He didn't ask me to talk to you but I am anyway."

"Sure. Sit down, Lloyd." He was loading a fresh pipe.

"He says you promised him the next opening. Is it the job you're giving to Cliff Miller?"

Schonwald sighed. "I never promise anything, you're aware of that, but I suppose I did indicate something of the sort."

"Is it because Miller's black, Buck?"

He glanced toward the closed door and back again. "Look, you've been here long enough to know I don't make final decisions on anybody."

"But they told you to hire somebody black, is that it?"

He lit the pipe carefully and leaned across the desk. "Look," he said again, "what's all this getting at? And since when have you decided to take a hand in hiring around here? It seems to me you're doing all right, Garner, why don't you just leave it at that? Of course I know Hambleton's a pet of yours, a young man of fashion who makes all the big parties—"

"The question isn't whether he's a pet of mine or whether he's a young man of fashion, Buck. You told him he could have this job and you're giving it to the Negro kid."

He grinned. "You against Negroes on the staff, Lloyd?"

"You know me better than that. But now you've got your token black man who looks like a white man the problem's solved, right?"

He didn't like it. "You have any idea how tough it is to find Negroes capable of doing our job, light or dark? There's a dozen white boys for every one of them, and able to do the work better too. You don't believe me just come and sit in on the interviews, I spend half my life these days interviewing Negro prospects. I'm for them, Lloyd, I'm for them, but try and find one that can help us. Even this kid I took on today is a gamble, but they pressure us all the way down from the White House to do something about it. And then when I pick one I can go with, Sales is on my back about he's not pretty enough or the affiliates start beefing. Christ, where's my responsibility? Is it race relations or getting out the best news program on the air? And you come around crying because Bev Hambleton's upset."

"Listen, Buck. Bev Hambleton was brought up to be a playboy, everybody knows that. He doesn't have to work but he finally chose to try to make something of himself, by himself, before it was too late. He could have gone on playing and become a good-for-nothing drunk like his father, and he still could if somebody doesn't give him a little practical encouragement, like a promotion. From the work he's done I think he deserves it and so do you, or you wouldn't have told him so. I also appreciate the color thing. The black kid who was in here just now is good, or he can learn to be good, you can see that just by meeting him, and he has the right to encouragement too. But tell me something, isn't there enough money in that overflowing till to take on both of them? You know there is."

The man behind the desk looked at him in silence. Then he said, "Miller gets the job and Hambleton will have to wait for the next one."

Bev Hambleton got up from the chair beside Lloyd's desk and stood there waiting. "I talked to him," Lloyd said. "He's sorry to disappoint you. The next opening is yours."

"Thanks," Bev Hambleton said. He held out his hand and Lloyd shook it. "I won't be back."

"Bev, don't do it."

"I'll call you, Lloyd, you've been a friend."

"Don't do it, boy. Look, we'll go have a drink right now and some lunch, how about it?"

"Thanks, no." He turned to go.

"I'll come with you Bev. We'll talk about it, okay?"

"Thanks, no," he said again and went out through the newsroom. Lloyd watched the tall figure retreating, graceful and elegant as always, the head held high. He was bound for the nearest bar, of course. What did you do, run after him? Not Bev Hambleton. Maybe something could be done about Bev after Paris. Right now it would have to wait.

For the Vietnam talks were about to begin and the evening news shows of all the networks would be moving to Paris for the opening of negotiations. Not that they expected a quick peace agreement. They'd only originate in Paris for a few days, but each had to show the competition it was on the ball, and the competition would have to show *it* was on the ball, and among them they would spend another fortune, and for what? For a couple of shots of Averell Harriman getting out of a car, as Milhouse put it.

Lloyd looked at him and enjoyed it. "You mean *you're* not coming, Jack?"

The black eyes smoldered. "What do I care about a lousy junket? It's only they're always talking about economy around here and I can't even get an extra writer for my show."

"I thought you liked to write yourself."

"I could do it better any day than those jerks in the newsroom."

Alix Weddern wanted to go too; the Burnleys were already in Paris and she could stay with them. But her mother wasn't feeling well and didn't want her to leave the country, and reluctantly she would have to pass up the chance.

"Going to be faithful to me?" she said with a little mock grimace, twisting his lapel.

"Alix, don't clown. I'll be back in a week."

Seat belt buckled while the big Boeing reached for cruising altitude, Lloyd surveyed the first-class section and noticed there were only four other passengers in it besides himself. It was an extra flight because the traffic to Paris was so heavy for the Vietnam talks, and Gaby figured he'd have a chance for privacy on this one. She'd been right. He was glad to avoid a night of shoptalk with Ferguson and Greminger after a busy week of broadcasting; there would be time enough for that in Paris. He chuckled to himself. In complicity with Gaby he had eluded Jay Weiss. The PR man had already left on an earlier flight with the rest of the staff and probably was worrying right now about whether Lloyd had missed his plane.

He had noticed on boarding that the tourist section behind him was crowded, every seat occupied by the time the first-class types were escorted to the forward area. Here, all was spacious luxury. The dapper steward was at his elbow again. Another Old Forester, sir? And why not? At the airport he'd been given the privileged treatment before boarding and plied with drinks and canapés in the Clipper Club. Now he settled back content and listened to the steward explaining to the man up the aisle about the dinner menu. "It says the dinner is prepared by Maxim's," the man was saying in an evident French accent. "Is there a Maxim's restaurant in New York?"

"Oh no, sir, it's Maxim's of Paris, of course."

"Then I don't understand how Maxim's could prepare my dinner tonight."

The steward laughed politely and glanced at Lloyd Garner. "Perhaps I can explain, sir. The dinner was prepared in Paris and then frozen. Right now it's being thawed out and will be served to you piping hot."

It was the Frenchman's turn to laugh. He looked up at the steward and said, "My wife often tells me Americans are crazy. I think I begin to understand what she means."

The steward bustled off to the front of the section to look after the middle-aged couple who had held most of his attention since take-off. The man kept a sealed dispatch case close to him and Lloyd decided he was Government and important. The only other passenger in first class was a woman sitting halfway forward on the right. She had not been in the Clipper Club and Lloyd hadn't seen her face. Almost imperceptible movement under them indicated the pilot was leveling off. The captain came on the speaker a moment later, brisk and homey, to say they were at thirty-three thousand, the flight would be smooth, the weather in Paris tonight was rainy but there would be bright intervals during the day to come. Lloyd unbuckled his seat belt, dropped his head back against the luxury of the broad seat and closed his eyes.

His arm was being very gently jogged by the steward, this time with a stewardess in attendance behind him. Trays on wheels and bottles on wheels were moving along the aisle with them. "Another drink, sir? Champagne, sir?" The stewardess was smiling with wonderful teeth. A plate of hot hors d'oeuvres was set down in front of him and he nodded to the champagne. His nap had made him thirsty, the wine was glorious. He drank it all immediately and on the return journey the stewardess refilled his glass from the big bottle with the French label. The teeth were smiling professionally. "Like that, Mr. Garner? I'll be back." Behind him beyond the closed door the tourist passengers were doubtless tying into their humble repast, drinking coke or coffee and elbowing one another

in their narrow seats. The murmur of their talk rose distantly above
the rushing, soothing sound of flight. Ah, well, he smiled to himself,
the serfs deserve roast pig once a year, after all, and he thought
of his brother Phil who would fit perfectly in economy class.

He reached to pull aside the window shade, nothing out there
but jet stream and blackness, and suddenly felt very alone. Lately
he'd gone farther than he'd ever been to places he'd never expected
to see; for a moment the feeling of unreality returned, he was
dreaming it all. But he had that feeling less and less often now, and
another glass of champagne with the flambéed duck passed him
back into his normal state of calm. There was music somewhere in
the background; up here at thirty-three thousand over the black
Atlantic it made a comforting sound. But wasn't the cabin getting
a little too chilly? He pulled his jacket closer around him and accepted
the brandy, leaving most of the elaborate iced dessert. "Would you
care to come up forward, sir, and enjoy a cigar?"

Excellent idea, wasn't that what you said? And he strolled up
the spacious aisle, glanced at the Frenchman at work on his dessert,
glanced at the open magazine of the woman sitting alone. She was
reading a fashion thing like *Vogue*. He noted as he went by that
the Diplomatic couple had finished dinner and were dozing, the
dispatch case still on his lap. In the little lounge behind the cockpit
he stretched his legs luxuriously and watched the two stewardesses
stowing away the dinner stuff in their galley. They smiled their
practiced smiles at him; he wondered if they had any brothers in
Vietnam.

The label on the cigar said it came from the Canary Islands.
He wasn't used to cigars but found this one pretty good. The
steward passed, rather hurriedly this time, and went into the
cockpit, emerging shortly behind a crewman who held a screwdriver
in his hand, they went down the aisle and into economy class. The
two stewardesses were saying something with lowered heads; one
glanced at him and giggled a little. "What's the matter, we losing
an engine?" he called over to them.

She straightened up. "Oh, no, Mr. Garner, just a little trouble with
the heating system, they'll fix it right away."

He grinned. "I've got enough heat inside me right now to last the whole trip."

"Yes, *sir!*" she said. "Can we get you some more to drink?"

He shook his head. It was definitely colder. He stood up, discovering that he was a little tight, and made his way back toward his seat. For the first time he got a good look at the woman traveling alone. She had moved in from the aisle seat and was sitting by the window, her head back against the rest and her eyes open. Their glances met and he smiled at her. It was a young, nice face under a mass of tawny hair that gave a tousled effect, and her answering smile was as open as his own. He stopped beside her and looked down. "Are you as chilly as I am? Can I get you a blanket or something?"

"Please," she said. Her voice was boyish and clear.

He found a blanket in the rack over the seat and one for himself, dropping into the empty seat beside her and spreading one of the blankets over her lap. "How's that?"

"Oh, much better. Have they turned off the heat?"

"They're having trouble with it. We can survive, though, if we can get them to bring us another drink."

"That's a lovely idea," she said.

One of the stewardesses in the lounge saw him holding up the brandy glass and gesturing with two fingers of the other hand. She smiled and nodded. Next to him, the girl in the window seat unfolded his blanket and dropped it over his knees, bending forward to drape it around his legs. The gesture was so warm and spontaneous that he turned in surprise to look at her.

"Isn't that better?" she said. She had a sweet smile.

"Thanks, little mother."

They both laughed and she pushed back the hair that had fallen forward over one eye. "If I'd known about you," he said, "I wouldn't have sat back there while we ate dinner all alone."

"Wouldn't it have been nice?" she said.

"I didn't see you in the Clipper Club."

"I barely made the flight. My boss kept me late going over some designs, it's always that way."

The stewardess brought the brandies on a little tray. "Then you make this trip often?" he was saying.

"Twice a year. And my name is Lee Maxton."

"Lloyd Garner." As if she didn't know. He touched her glass with his glass and they drank. The cold in the cabin was refreshing and his head felt clearer. "We're lucky it was only the heat that went wrong," he said. "When you think there's only an inch or two of wall between us and the great outdoors."

"I never think about that when I'm flying."

It was good advice. For a time they sat in silence, like two old friends, sipping their brandies and facing straight ahead, and he wondered why this girl gave him such a feeling of ease and pleasure, or was it just the liquor talking to him? Looking solicitous, the captain came out of the cockpit and bent deferentially over the Diplomatic couple, probably apologizing for the cold air. The Frenchman, snug under his blanket, appeared to be sound asleep. Lloyd said to Lee Maxton, "You're traveling on business, I suppose."

She nodded. "Paris and Rome."

"Fashions?"

"Indirectly, yes, I design for a textile firm." She turned and smiled at him and for the first time he saw the color of her eyes, a glowing deep green. "Naturally I don't have to ask what Lloyd Garner does. Or why he's going to Paris." For a moment urgency gripped her voice. "Isn't it the most wonderful thing? The end of this war, in sight!"

"I wouldn't be too hopeful, but it's a start."

"But we *must* be hopeful. We've resigned ourselves to it for too long."

He had the impression she was disappointed that he didn't reply. She leaned back again with a weary little sigh. "Tired?" he said then.

"Terribly. I guess you are too. I guess you always are."

"Sometimes, when the news runs heavy." He put his empty brandy glass beside her empty glass on the stewardess's tray and settled back again. "Warm now?" he asked her.

"Deliciously warm."

"You know, I think I'm kind of drunk."

She giggled faintly. "Me too."

The main cabin lights dimmed out, leaving only a few lights burning along the row of seats, and almost immediately the captain's voice was with them, the measured tones professionally soothing and friendly. "We'll have the heat up again soon. Meanwhile, I hope you're all cozy under your blankets. Just ask the stewardess if you need more."

"I can't help it," said Lee Maxton, "he reminds me of that Shelley Berman record. *Coffee, tea or milk . . .*"

"Berman almost killed the airline industry with that record."

She stretched and snuggled under her blanket. The Diplomatic couple switched off their seat lights and a stewardess drew a curtain to shut away the light in the lounge. Lloyd said, "Are you a New Yorker, Lee?"

"No, and you'd never guess where. Missoula, Montana. Admit you've never heard of it."

"Of course I've heard of it, I've read the name of every town in this country on the air, but I've never been to most of them." He pushed her seat back to reclining position. "There you are."

"Thanks," she whispered.

"I'll let you sleep," said Lloyd.

She murmured something he didn't catch, and he pushed back his own seat, smiling at the tousled head that turned toward him a little. Soon she was breathing deeply and steadily. He tried to remember the color of the soft cashmere sweater she was wearing over her brief dark skirt. He couldn't remember the color of the skirt either, but he remembered his glimpse of the knees under the textured stockings, they were extremely well-shaped knees, small-boned and dainty. Through the glass of an uncovered window up the aisle he saw pale moonlight and a trace of mist in the vastness of sky. Somebody, probably the steward, moved past him down the aisle, barely visible in the dimness. He had acted on impulse almost before he was aware of the impulse, and turned and kissed the soft hair so near him. He was drunk, all right. She stirred, not away from him but closer. Her hand moved as in sleep to rest on his thigh. For a long time, he had lost the feeling of minutes, he sat beside her with his mouth against her hair, inhaling a faint fragrance, part perfume, part her body. He was beginning to feel acutely excited by the touch of her sleeping hand. This was what night flying and alcohol could do to you. He hardly dared move now, her trusting body was so close, and he was aware of all of it. Her breast under the soft sweater lay against his wrist. Her breath was warm and fresh on his cheek. A desire rose in him suddenly so strong that he tensed and turned toward her, moving his body against her. Was she awake? Surely she was aware of him, surely her hand could feel his pulsing hardness, now. Then helplessly he lost all control, his hand pulled her shoulder to him under the blanket and he buried his face in her hair, all at once feeling her breathing quicken and her limp hand come alive and tighten on him and hold him hard while he clung to her in his fierce shooting pain and joy. "*Lee,*" he said into her hair. "It's all right," he heard her saying in a small voice muffled deep in his shoulder, "is it all right now?" "My God," he blurted, astonished, gasping, still gripping her with all his strength, "I haven't done that since I was a kid, can you ever forgive me?"

16

He stirred in sleep, he was dreaming a baseball game in a stadium he'd never seen before and he was batting and striking out. The face under the pitcher's cap, high up on the mound and staring down at him, was Buck Schonwald and then Jack Milhouse. Crowd cheers echoed weirdly from the empty stands, somehow like voices from the control room heard in the studio, there was feedback on the amplifiers, the flags of all the teams fluttered in the night game lights above them. Then he woke with a bar of sunlight across his eyes, he was sitting upright, his head back, and a girl named Lee Maxton was sitting next to him in the window seat of a plane, watching him and smiling a little. "Look," she said and drew him by the arm.

They were circling over Paris. He had expected to see Paris in the rain, but it wasn't raining this morning, it was travel-poster sunshine, and that was the way Lloyd Garner saw it for the first time, the river gleaming, winding among the turrets and towers. The cathedral down there on its little island, after a thousand years, and that other church all white and perfect on its hill. They were starting the long slow glide into Orly airport. He said to Lee Maxton, "I can't remember anything after you forgave me."

"You went to sleep," she said, "and then so did I." She was wearing a little green jade ring on her right hand, the color of her eyes.

"Why were you so sweet to me?"

"I don't know. It just happened."

"Was it because you were drunk? I was drunk."

"No."

"Can I see you again?"

"Of course."

He took one of her hands in his hand, long-fingered and light as lace. "I'm glad I met you, Lee."

"So am I."

"Will you drive into Paris with me?"

She shook her head a little sadly. "They'll be waiting for me in a car at Orly, our Paris boss has a place near Fontainebleau and I'll be spending the weekend there."

"Is he married?"

Her fresh and clear laugh, like a small boy's. "To a very attractive French girl." Suddenly she looked at him differently. "Are you married?"

"Technically, yes. But it's been over for a while."

"Over, or just suspended?"

"Over. Can I see you Monday?"

"I go to Beauvais Monday. I won't really be free till Wednesday."

"Not Tuesday?"

She laughed again. "Wednesday."

The no smoking signs went on and a stewardess opened the door to tourist class behind them. "I'm at something called the Meurice," he said. "Will you leave a message there?"

"I will," she said.

"Will you kiss me now?"

"I will."

They faced each other and she put her arms very far around him and he drew her slenderness close. Kissing her was a feeling so pure, so new, it was like the innocence of forgotten first experience. She trembled briefly in his arms and murmured without words; suddenly the cold delicious dark of last night was around them again and he hoped she was taking back the orgasm she had given him. The aircraft was jolting along the runway when they opened their eyes.

The network operation was on the fifth floor of an old building near the Palais Royal. Paris brushed past as they drove into the narrow street, everybody in a hurry, the taxi horns beeping, a truck driver standing up at his wheel and shouting, an unbelievably long loaf of bread stuck in the arm of a boy on a bicycle. Did everything

have to be so goddamn continental? Lloyd laughed in a kind of high
exuberance; something in the giddy air made him feel that way. Jay
Weiss, who sure enough had been waiting in the car that took them
from the airport, growled and complained about his stomach.

They went up in a crowded rickety elevator, the faces around
them reflecting a curious blend of tension and despair, as though
life had been more leisurely here once upon a time and they
resented the change. The outside hall was cluttered with pieces
of television equipment guarded by an old man in a faded uniform.
Lloyd felt like stopping to kiss him on both cheeks. Within, voices
and an explosion of laughter. "It's that Jacques Roul again," muttered
Weiss.

They walked in on a young man standing on a chair and per-
forming some sort of pantomime to illustrate his speech, in French.
The young man had his back to the door but turned around at the
new burst of laughter that greeted the visitors. He was laughing with
the others when he jumped down, a jaunty type with a mustache.

"Ah, Meester Garner! I am Jacques Roul." The others melted
away into the next office and Roul led the way into a little
studio crowded with French technicians, all talking. "Where's
Gibson?" said Weiss.

"At the Crillon seeing Harriman. So also is Kent Ward," said
Jacques Roul, pronouncing the name like one word. "This is my
work of art, Meester Garner." Roul had filled the studio with
equipment from New York and carpenters had built a simple set
for the occasion. Next to it a newly installed teleprinter was grinding
out UPI copy for Earl Greminger, who would script the news and
lead-ins for the show as usual while Russell Gibson, the Paris
correspondent, and Ward would both do daily pieces on camera and
possibly, as Schonwald suggested, discuss the issues with each other,
time permitting. The show would go live from this studio.

Weiss pulled out his notebook and began taking notes on the
equipment. Jacques Roul watched Greminger bending over the teleprinter and laughed. "They don't waste any time, your colleagues
from New York."

"They're very conscientious, Jacques, just like me."

"Of course. Even I am working, for a change. A riot every

night." The Frenchman cocked an ear. "Meester Kentward has arrived," and Ward came into the studio with Russell Gibson. What was the word for Gibson? Relaxed, friendly. Lloyd liked him at once. But it was different with Ward, he could see immediately his attitude hadn't changed. It was the first time Lloyd had been in the same room with the Washington correspondent since his cocktail party in Georgetown, but while Gibson smiled and shook hands warmly, Ward nodded without smiling.

"It's a nice setup," Lloyd said to Gibson.

"You can thank Jacques for that, he said we must make Lloyd Garner feel happy."

"Lloyd Garner always feels happy, but thank you, Jacques."

Roul bowed. "I leave you, gentlemen, it is time to prepare for my evening riot." He passed Greminger in the doorway and winked at him in such a way that Greminger looked puzzled.

"Buck's on the phone, Kent, he wants to ask you something."

"You mean he wants to tell me what not to say tonight. I'll be in your office, Russ." He left them and followed Greminger.

Gibson said, nodding after them, "What's wrong, Lloyd, is he mad at you?"

"I didn't know you'd noticed. Yes, he hasn't forgiven me for ignoring that strike."

"Is that all? I thought that was forgiven by now."

"By just about everybody but him, I guess."

"I wondered if he resents you for taking over from Hedley Johns. He said one or two slightly bitter things about you after he arrived yesterday."

"Such as?"

"Oh, you're just a ventriloquist's dummy mouthing the stuff they write for you."

"And?"

"And you don't fight the system, and Hedley did."

It was as though they'd known each other for years. "Russ, Hedley Johns is Hedley Johns, and Lloyd Garner is Lloyd Garner."

The dark unillusioned eyes were amused. "Will you be free enough to have some dinner with me tomorrow?"

"Nobody's as free as I am on an operation like this."

"Isn't it the truth?" Russ Gibson murmured, smiling. Jay Weiss came importantly up to them. "Sorry to interrupt, Russ, but we got to take a lot of pictures of Lloyd right away."

"Pictures?" Lloyd said.

"Around town. Key man of the team against historic backdrops— the Arch, Napoleon's Tomb, like that. We're lucky, we get them to New York in time for Monday's morningers."

"See what I mean?" Lloyd said to Russell Gibson. "Busy busy."

The hotel elevator looked like a throne room. "You're closer than you think," Jay Weiss told him, "Russ Gibson says it's the hotel for royalty."

It felt pretty good being royalty, but of course he was used to it by now. Luxurious adjoining rooms looked out over the Tuileries gardens, stately and splendid in the failing light. "I wish we could stay a month," Weiss said. His stomach was feeling better now that a courier was on his way to Orly with the negatives.

"Out," Lloyd said. He took a shower and a nap and had just finished dressing when Matt Ferlin knocked on his door. The bureau Number Two was young and morose. "Feel like I know you, Lloyd," he said shaking hands, "but then I guess you get that from everybody being on the air every day, they even pick you up sometimes on the French TV."

"Yeah? I didn't know that."

"What do you feel like eating? Russ says it's on the bureau so we can go anywhere."

"You decide, Matt."

Ferlin hadn't been in Paris for a year without learning the restaurants. They walked up the Champs-Elysées and had dinner outdoors at Laurent under an incomparable night sky, he let Ferlin do the talking, Ferlin seemed to have a lot to say. For one thing he was resentful that New York didn't use more of his stuff. He said he'd about given up digging for exclusives. "Like I get something good, really worth a spot on your show, but perishable, you know, and they tell me just ship the film because they won't pay the expense of the satellite, so by the time it gets there they don't want it any more, and they don't even bother to pass the film

along to Milhouse for the morning news. Most of the time they
don't use our cables, either. Or they grab a line from the AP or
UP guy who covered the same story with me and hand it to you
and you read it, right?" He sighed heavily and ordered a second
bottle of wine. "You get this feeling here like not existing, you know?
Like everybody's forgotten you."

"But you've got a big story now, Matt."

"It's Russ Gibson's story, it's diplomatic."

"How about radio? I've heard you on that morning news."

"Only when Gibson doesn't want to do it. You know something?
I'm instructed to do a piece for radio for *you* to read tomorrow, how
about that?"

"First I've heard of it."

"If radio can get a TV name to do their spots they turn down their
own men every time."

"What do you care?" Lloyd said. "Don't you like living in Paris?
I think I would."

Well, he did like being in Paris but he'd had it long enough
now and wanted to get back to New York so he wouldn't be left
in the backwash, you know what I mean. It was a bad idea to stay
away from the center of things too long. He wanted to go to
Washington next and maybe get in line for the White House job,
then he'd really be on the air and start getting a name. He didn't
have to tell Lloyd that was the way you played it. Satisfied by a
superb meal and getting sleepy again, with time all turned around
by his trip, Lloyd listened patiently and realized how much what
Ferlin was saying was like what he heard from the reporters in New
York, only they all wanted to get overseas. Ferlin was burbling on
about Paul McIntosh. "I suppose he's sucking up to Schonwald all
the time."

"Don't they all?"

"Any idea if Buck's considering McIntosh for Washington?"

"None."

"You do something in New York for me, Lloyd?"

"If I can, sure, what?"

"I want you to have a little heart-to-heart with Buck, that's all,
just catch him alone for a minute, right?"

"The Washington job?"

"Just get me out of Europe, anything in New York, right?"

"I'll do that, Matt."

"You can if you want to, I know, don't think I don't know."

"Russ seems to be one hell of a nice guy," he said to change the subject. "Does he want to go home too?"

"Look, Russ *likes* it here. I don't think he's done a job back home for fifteen years, he's worked *everywhere* but New York."

"Sounds like a nice life."

"He can have it."

Over the brandy Ferlin confided that he'd been banging his French secretary recently, though with some misgivings. Oh, Claudine wasn't a bad piece of ass as French girls went, and French girls went very well as pieces of ass, but she was beginning to talk marriage and marriage was the last idea Matt Ferlin had in his mind, to anybody. Better for a reporter not to be married, especially in TV where your working hours were worse than a newspaper's, right?

"Right."

He sighed. Jacques Roul knew what he was doing, never touch the office stuff, he knew now he never should have started with Claudine.

"Jacques seems like quite a character."

"He's okay, for a Frenchman."

"I like Russ."

"Tell you something not generally known." He leaned forward. "He's queer. Oh, you'd never know. He's very discreet." But Matt wasn't especially interested in the subject. "Speaking of my secretary," he said, "how's Rita Valenti?"

"She's not my secretary any more, she quit to live in Rome." He leered. "But you got to it before she left, didn't you?"

"Why do you say that, Matt?"

"Come on, everybody's had that. I'd have had it myself by now if I didn't have to come over here."

"I guess I'm the exception," Lloyd said. "My relations with Rita were strictly business."

"Sure," said Matt Ferlin.

He did the radio broadcast in a booth adjoining Jacques Roul's improvised TV studio. A microphone and one technician, period. Lloyd grinned at the Frenchman. "Life used to be so simple, eh, Jacques? Now it costs ten times as much money and you need twenty times as many people to put that little image on the screen."

"Meester Garner, you remember the great days. So do I."

"And how was last night's riot?"

"Nothing much, but they will come. The Communists are showing interest. The labor chiefs don't like the students taking the leadership." The mustache quivered with his smile. "But I enjoy to cover the Sorbonne. I am renewing old acquaintance with the jeunesse universitaire. Many pretty girls, Meester Garner."

Outside the booth the technician was warming up New York, then the voice came in jovially, somebody he didn't know. "How's Paris, Lloyd?"

"I like it. What happening there today?"

"Never anything happening here, you know that. Get me a job over there, will you?"

"Glad to." Their voices bumped cheerfully across the void.

"Signal good. Any time, we're taping."

Lloyd could hear himself in the earphones, he sounded good. Matt Ferlin had written a routine color piece. Paris never so beautiful, sunny weather, all leading U.S. journalists are here, Vietnamese group very elusive but we'll get a good look at them when talks open tomorrow, and as to what the results of all this will be, who knows? Lloyd signed off. "You get that okay?"

"Very okay. Any messages?"

"No, thanks, just give my regards to Buck Schonwald if you see him around."

"Sure will," the voice said with respect. "Good night, Paris."

"Good night, New York," the French technician said.

It was his first transatlantic broadcast and he would receive a fee for doing it. Matt Ferlin would receive nothing, he must remember to give Matt a bottle before he left.

He was meeting Russ Gibson at Lucas Carton. Blue dusk lay over the city as he found his way to the Opéra and along the boulevard toward the Madeleine, following Jacques Roul's direc-

tions until he saw the restaurant just across the square. He was a
little early but Gibson was already there, sitting at a corner table
and surrounded by respectful service, sipping a champagne cocktail
and offering Lloyd the same.

"Does everybody drink all day here? They seem to."

"It's something you get used to, Lloyd. They don't drink much of
the hard stuff, though."

"I've always been a bourbon man myself."

"We keep bourbon in the office for homesick congressmen," Gibson said. "Jacques doesn't care enough about bourbon to steal it."

Lloyd laughed. "That Jacques."

"He's invaluable. If he were American, New York would pay him
decently, but he's not, so one of these days we're going to lose
Jacques. Then nobody will be more surprised and indignant than
New York."

"He knows his way around, that's obvious."

"It isn't easy to find and train people like Roul. Naturally New
York takes it all for granted."

"How about yourself, Russ? Will you stay in Paris much longer?"

He shrugged slightly, the man who'd worked all over the world,
who'd covered six wars since 1940, the habitual foreign correspondent, weathered by all climates, travel-beaten, as much at home
in Beirut or Hong Kong as London or Moscow. "I've been here three
years now and it could easily be another three before they make up
their minds to make up their minds, you know how they are."

Lloyd grinned. "Meantime you're learning a lot."

"Only that the living is different everywhere, but the dying is
always the same."

He ordered dinner then, and what a dinner! Hot pâté in a crust
served with tiny flavored French pickles, then on to something
called gratin de homard, complete with delicate pieces of lobster
meat, mushrooms and truffles, all this taken with a golden wine. Next
came a skewer of little game birds, eaten with fresh string beans
glazed with a rich yellow sauce and accompanied by a red burgundy
called Clos des Ducs, and there was more of the burgundy with the
tray of cheeses before they brought the champagne with wood straw-

berries and Normandy cream so thick you could cut it with a knife. It was the best meal Lloyd had ever eaten. "My God," he said.

Gibson was watching him, amused. "I'm almost never disappointed here, they ought to have three stars in the Michelin. I like Lucas Carton and Lucas Carton likes me, but of course the visiting firemen go by the stars, so I have to take them to the Tour d'Argent or the Grand Véfour and so on and then arrange for them to get laid afterward, it's one of the major functions of the Paris bureau." He smiled. "By the way, do you want us to get you laid?"

He thought of Lee Maxton and said, "Thanks very much but no thanks, Russ. A meal like this is enough for me."

"That's the way the French look at it. Eating, just eating, is an end in itself, you can make a career of it. Not selling it, not writing about it, just doing it. And cafe-sitting is another career, not even reading a book or drinking anything, just watching the people go by, just watching the colors of the day."

"How long are the Vietnam talks going to last?"

Again the shrug. "Years, maybe. They're grim little fellows, these men from Hanoi, even when they smile their grim little smiles, which isn't often. And everything they think, if you can tell what they think, and everything they say, is upside down and a world away from what we live by. Of course you have to remember that's the way we sound to them."

"But we're logical, and they just lie."

"Never the twain and all that, Lloyd."

"But they ask for everything and give up nothing."

"That's what they'll do here too."

"At this rate, how will we ever get together?"

"Something's got to give sometime."

"But how long do we give them?"

"We wait and hope."

"And keep on killing each other."

"What else can we do?"

"Stop shooting while we talk."

"They just build up again."

"We can bomb Haiphong."

"And bring in the Russians?"

"Then the hell with it and let's get out of their country."

"But it isn't their country, it belongs to the little brothers down south."

"Let's get out anyway."

"We promised to hold back the Red Horde, remember?"

"So let the Red Horde in already, isn't it inevitable?"

"Then the rest of Asia goes Communist."

"Who needs the rest of Asia? Aren't the British pulling out?"

"The British are realists, they know how to admit defeat."

"Then why can't we admit defeat?"

The older man smiled. "To admit defeat would be to admit we made a mistake."

"Can't we make a mistake?"

"No, because we're perfect. If we abandoned that standard our whole political morality would collapse. Besides, we've got the good old M.I.C. They'd like to see the war go on forever."

"So just because a bunch of natives are willing to keep on dying like flies we're stuck with them on the flypaper."

"Natives get to be Communists, so we have to take them seriously."

"Why? We've got the weapons and they haven't."

"For now, yes, but they're getting them, and they'll have them all eventually, along with frigidaires. They own the future, Lloyd, whether we like the idea or not, because they've got the people, the West is just a minority. It's just a matter of a couple of generations before Asia and Africa dominate the world."

"Russ, you depress me."

"Aren't you permanently depressed? I thought everybody was."

Lloyd looked around him at the potential minority, the restaurant was full now, full of the laughing, gossiping, eating and drinking American press contingent. He saw Kent Ward with some people at a nearby table and recognized Wade Burnley, of the Quince Barony group. Half the world might be starving, like they say, but the diplomats always live well. "How long is Ward staying on, Russ?"

"He says he's going back with you people Saturday."

"With a crisis for De Gaulle cooking here?"

"He's leaving that to me. You've got an election coming up, remember?"

"I like Kent, Russ. In the beginning he was a friend."

For the first time he saw an almost feminine softness come into his eyes. "It really bothers you, doesn't it? Why don't you talk to him on the plane? He'll be relaxing then."

"It's an idea, I'll see what I can do." And he looked back toward Kent Ward's table. Wade Burnley saw him and raised a hand in salute, and he remembered then he'd meant to send Alix Weddern a gag postcard. But he didn't want to think about Alix Weddern, he wanted to think about Lee Maxton. In the moment he almost told Russ Gibson about Lee, but decided he wouldn't be very interested.

Earl Greminger was standing by the studio teleprinter when they stopped in after dinner. He was holding a piece of wire copy in his hand and looked somber. "What now?" Lloyd said cheerfully, "we got troubles?"

The editor handed him the copy without saying anything. It was a UPI dispatch from Saigon. It began: *Burt Staley, a veteran television correspondent, was killed early today when a Viet Cong terrorist rocket penetrated the wall of his apartment and exploded. He was thirty-six.*

Across three continents and two oceans, live, film, and tape, the Lloyd Garner show was anchored that night from the cramped little studio in Paris. Greminger had kept the headlines to a minimum and Kent Ward came on almost immediately, gloomily surveying prospects for the Vietnam talks. He was followed by Russell Gibson on the spreading student rioting and its political import for De Gaulle, then Paris switched back to New York for satellite tape of Saigon's night and day of terrorism, seen as Communist pressure on the peace negotiations, Bill Moran reporting. The correspondent concluded with a terse report of Burt Staley's death and a brief biography of the bureau chief, then returned it to Paris without further comment. But Lloyd Garner said, ad-libbing: *"A very few days ago I was with Burt Staley in Saigon. He was the finest type of American newsman. He had the best years of his life still ahead of him. Like so many others who have lost their lives in the Vietnam War, or who will lose them, his death at thirty-six can only seem a tragic waste."*

He was aware that Earl Greminger had begun to signal frantically from behind the camera. "More news in a moment," he said, and with the cue the New York commercial came up on the monitor. Nobody in the Paris studio spoke, and he sat there watching the rest of the program, the Kennedy and McCarthy campaign teams wrapping it up along the road to Oregon. Then Jay Weiss came to the studio door. "Buck on the line for you, Lloyd." It figured.

"Yes, Buck?"

"I wish you'd told us you were going to speak about Burt Staley. Earl could have scripted it."

"Does every damn word on this show have to be scripted? It was only a few seconds."

"It's a matter of principle, fellow. It screws up the timing."

"Look, Buck, it just came out. Do I have to apologize? Something had to be said. Moran didn't say it, so I did."

"I think Moran felt too bad about it to say any more, Lloyd."

"Okay, so I'm sorry, okay?" He waited for more censure but it didn't come, the voice was just a little hurt and reproachful.

"Try to remember what I said, will you?"

"Okay, Buck." He turned the phone back to Jay Weiss.

It was after one o'clock. Gibson and Ward had left together before the show ended. Lloyd joined Greminger at the elevator. "Let's stretch our legs and find a drink," he said, and they walked into the misty Paris night.

"Was Buck upset?" the editor said.

"About what you'd expect." They walked on in silence awhile and Lloyd spoke again. "Did you know Burt well?"

"We started out together on the *Trib*, as copyreaders. I didn't see much of him after he came to the network because he wanted to get into the field and they sent him overseas."

"He was a decent guy."

"As good as we had." He seemed to hesitate. "You know, Lloyd, Vietnam's an awful touchy subject, it might be better to stay away from the political side unless it's scripted, I guess Buck told you that."

"No, he didn't say anything about the political side."

"But don't you agree? I mean." He hesitated again.

"Burt Staley's dead. I liked him. I don't want to talk about it any more, do you mind?"

"Oh, sure, you're right, Lloyd. I feel the same way myself."

"Let's go across to the Left Bank and get a beer at Lipp's."

"I think there's still trouble over that way."

"Suit yourself, Earl. That's where I'm going."

"I'm with you," the editor said, and they crossed into the Place du Carrousel. Mist clung to the casements of the Louvre above them, beyond the dark emptiness of the Tuileries the Champs-Elysées glimmered in shadow until the sudden illuminated brilliance of the Arch at its far end. This part of Paris was all but asleep, but not the Left Bank. "Listen," Greminger said, and they could hear a distant muffled clamor from the Latin Quarter, saw a column of colored smoke rising into the opaque sky. Two police reinforcement trucks hurtled suddenly past them across the vast square bound for the river. Greminger's voice had an edge of nervousness, "This thing is getting serious, all the unions will be in it tomorrow."

Helmeted riot units blocked this end of the automobile bridge but they were able to cross the river on the Pont des Arts. The red glare was above their heads now and the clamor was very near, confused shouts and cries sounding along the Boulevard Saint-Michel, a crashing like shattered glass, then the eerie *eek-onk, eek-onk* of fire apparatus somewhere up near the Luxembourg. "Let's take a look," Lloyd said and quickened his pace. The quai was as busy as daytime, ahead of them a solid mass of police had cordoned off the entrance to the square and was holding back an eddying crowd that pressed toward the barrier. Greminger was having trouble staying close to him, in the babble of French around them he gripped Lloyd's arm, "We've come far enough, we can't see anything anyway."

"We'll get through, come on." He pressed forward, *this was excitement, this was fun.*

"Jay said to keep you out of it, Lloyd."

"What?" He stopped abruptly, breathless in the jostling mob. "Say again?"

"I promised Jay not to let you fool around with this, it's dangerous."

He heard his own incredulous laughter. "So you're the substitute bodyguard."

"Seriously, Lloyd."

The men and women around them turned at their English with grinning, curious faces just as the line of black steel helmets parted up ahead and they could see the square, a chaos under floodlights, littered with broken barricades, torn-up paving blocks, splintered traffic stanchions, cadavers of trees. Along its far side the cafe terraces were deserted, their tables and chairs scattered in the gutters, their glass fronts staved in, children stared speechless from upper windows. The action had come this way but now it was farther on or in retreat toward the Luxembourg. The crowd heard howling sirens and the stamp and surge of a cheering, singing multitude, nearer, receding, then nearer and receding again. There was a crack like a carbine shot and a great burst of shouting full of defiance and joy. The police line closed again and faced this way. "Come on!" Greminger was saying, pulling at his arm, "let's get out of here, fast."

He let himself be led back down the quai. On the river bank opposite, lights were on in all the windows of the Préfecture, Inspector Maigret was working late tonight. But wasn't Maigret retired now, living down there on the Loire, or had they called him back for special duty in this mess? What was it all about anyway, students raising hell in Paris, in New York, the Berkeley campus thing all over again? But Russ had said on the air tonight it was a lot more than that, now the Communists were in it officially and the strikes had spread all over the country. These French, did they want De Gaulle or didn't they? Why couldn't they make up their silly minds, or was it just vacation fever, just time for a change and a few days off the job?

Greminger, still sweating in the damp air, stopped and wiped his forehead with a handkerchief. "I'm glad we're out of that," he said.

"Who does Schonwald think I am, a babe in arms?"

"Suppose one of these tough Paris cops knocked you on the head tonight, Lloyd, where would we be for tomorrow's show?"

"You'd think this was Saigon. One of these days I'm going to surprise the hell out of all of you. I'm going to cover a story on my own."

The idea obviously amused Earl Greminger. "I don't see how you could," he said, "you're too busy."

17

Lloyd Garner, key man of the network team, attended the opening of the Vietnam talks and was photographed with the conference hotel in the background. He also dropped in at the American briefings but didn't have to cover the story himself since Greminger was writing his news copy, since Ward and Gibson were doing the commentary, and since Weiss was dramatizing the network's Paris operation with feature pieces for New York release. So mostly there was nothing for Lloyd Garner to do until about nine at night, when he appeared in the studio to be made up by a Frenchman who looked like Buster Keaton and to go over the headlines and lead-ins with his editor. And this, he reflected, was just the way Schonwald wanted it; this was part of the deal.

He used his free time to check out Russ Gibson's view of the French philosophy, basically cafe-sitting followed by meals, and since the Paris public didn't know him from Adam and it was too early in the year for the American tourist invasion he was able to pass unnoticed most places he went. For the first time it was an agreeable sensation; he found he had lost his desire for security in recognition. He rose late each day, lunching in expense account splendor with Jacques Roul and dining in the undesired company of Jay Weiss. On these evening occasions Jay showed him the latest stories he'd written about Lloyd Garner's activities and prints of the pictures taken of Lloyd Garner in front of Paris landmarks. The stories included quotations from invented observations by Lloyd Garner on the international situation.

"It's only an idle suggestion, of course," Lloyd said, "but did you ever think of asking me first before you write this stuff?"

The little man shrugged. "Why bother you? Relax and enjoy."

"But for instance how do you know I'm optimistic for a Vietnam settlement before the election?"

"Funny, I thought Earl said you'd told him that."

"I told him nothing of the kind."

What did you do? You laughed and forgot about it. It was one more aspect of the unreality he lived with.

Accompanied by Jay Weiss he ate sole glazed with vermouth at Maxim's and, of course, numbered duck at the Tour d'Argent, which turned out to be less restaurant than view, but Notre Dame and the Seine from that angle looked incontestably glamorous. With Jacques Roul as guest adviser he tasted the best pea soup in the world at Lapérouse, sampled the chichi ambience with the Seventh Avenue buyers at Lasserre, and drank a Romanée-Conti at the Grand Véfour which he knew he would never forget. Now, watching the mellow light falling over the fountains on the square, he sat on the terrace of the Régence making the acquaintance of Mandarin-Curaçao and listening to Jacques analyze the properties of this particular apéritif.

"I like the taste but it doesn't seem to be very strong," said Lloyd.

"You think so? Three or four more and you will go out of here on your knees."

"I'll take your word for that."

It was also, how you say, aphrodisiac. It was like certain burgundies, good for women when men drink it. A proper knowledge of Mandarin-Curaçao and you could pace yourself exactly for whatever you wanted to do, that is if you made love before dinner. If you intended to make love after dinner, that was a different prescription. For instance, Jacques Roul was making love tonight before dinner, so he would have to leave pretty soon. The girl he was going to meet had to be home by seven to cook dinner for her husband and there wasn't much time to do what they were going to do, particularly because she required two vermouth-cassis first.

"Jacques, you kill me."

"Lloyd, is that good or bad?"

"Definitely good."

"Perhaps you too are making love before dinner tonight?"

"Alas, I'm having dinner with Matt Ferlin."

"The discontented one," said Roul. "Will Claudine be present?"

"I doubt it. He seeks to discourage Claudine." When you talked with Jacques Roul for a while you began to speak like him. "He's homesick, Jacques."

"No, he would be discontented there too."

"Tell me something, do you remember kisses?"

"Kisses who?"

"I kissed a girl on a plane the other day. I can still taste it."

"Ah."

"I think I may be falling in love, Jacques. For the first time in my life. I can't be sure that's what it is because I never felt this way before. But I suspect."

"She is in New York?"

"She's in Paris, at least she will be tomorrow. We have a lunch date."

"Ah."

"There was a message from her at the hotel today. That's when I began to suspect."

"Get a good night's sleep, Lloyd. Have breakfast of champagne only. Be sure there is burgundy for the lunch. Then you will both be in form."

He stood up to leave and shook hands. All the French always shook hands.

"Jacques, you kill me."

"I am glad."

The sun was shining gloriously, foolishly, the air was singing, when they came out of the restaurant hand in hand. What had they said at lunch? In the taxi they sat close together without speaking, as if waiting, and he tried to remember. He had been standing in the entrance hall when she came in. It was the first time he had seen her at any distance, seen her walk, a swinging, loping walk. He thought he had never seen any girl walk that way, not even the actresses, her head riding high, her knees seeming to open a little when she moved, the most sexual walk he had ever seen on a woman and she seemed entirely unconscious of it. How old was she? Twenty-five? Thirty? Her body was eighteen. He had watched her recognize him and come toward him with a glad little smile, wearing a dark blue dress, no hat, she wasn't a hat girl. "Lloyd, I'm late." Wasn't that what she had said? After that he couldn't remember anything except the joy of being close to her. It was all the fault of that breakfast of champagne only and that bottle of burgundy they had emptied together. He knew now what wine was for, and Lee Maxton seemed to know too.

The taxi crossed a Seine bridge and a few streets farther along the quai drew up before a small hotel that looked right down on the river. This was where she always stayed in Paris, a walk-up, a winding old carpeted staircase to the third floor. The windows of her room opened onto a tiny balcony, a balcony for two, and you could see the Louvre on the opposite bank. For a moment after the door closed behind them they were still silent, there was a vague scent of her perfume in the room, the scent that had haunted him ever since the plane. Then she moved to him and put her hands on his shoulders. "It's been a long time," she said.

No one had ever stood so close to him, no one had ever looked at him before. And she spoke again, simply, like a child. "I want you," she said.

"I don't deserve you." His voice was trembling and his body trembled when he took her in his arms. They didn't speak any more. The kiss was timeless, like oblivion. Afterward she drew away from him and loosened the back of her dress, letting it fall to her feet and dropping her half-slip with it. Her arms went back to release the band of white that held her breasts and as she bent her head her hair fell forward over her eyes. With a beautiful urgent movement, solemn as the silence between them, she stepped out of her shoes and lay down on the bed, looking up at him, and he went to her and pulled off the white clinging girdle and stockings. Very slowly she lifted her legs and her knees went back almost to her breasts. She was open and waiting for him.

What made it so exquisitely different from any other time he had known? Not her body only, though it was all perfection, slim and white and gold, more the quality of her feeling, more what she changed and made perfect in him, more the thing they were together, by accident, by the trick of fate. Near the end he needed her as he had never needed anyone, then he had known nothing except a distant sound of music, heard but not real.

Gradually he became aware of real sounds again, of cars going by along the quai below, the hoarse little whistle of a barge passing on the river, a voice on the stairs that came near and receded. He opened his eyes and looked up at the ceiling, aware as if for the first time that she was really still beside him, her right hand clasped in his left. He tightened his fingers and felt her answering pressure. "You're unbelievable," he whispered, turning to her. "I stopped thinking. You had no protection. I didn't even—"

"I don't care." They lay facing each other, she put her fingers over his mouth. "Don't regret anything. We didn't want it any other way."

He took her hand and kissed it, and felt a shiver run through her body. "Cold, little mother?"

She smiled. "A rabbit just jumped over my grave." She kissed his hand and slowly drew away from him, sitting up. "While I'm in the john pull the covers up and let's get underneath, I don't want *you* to catch cold."

He lay between the sheets listening to the water running in the bathroom, so perfectly still and satisfied that it was like sleep. "What are you thinking?" She startled him slipping in beside him fresh and cool and he opened his eyes again.

"You, what else?"

"Darling. Have you had lots of girls?"

"My share, I guess."

Her fingers were twisting in his hand. "Do you know, Lloyd Garner, I know practically nothing about you."

"You know everything about me, now."

"I know the best about you. We started with the best."

He drew her closer with his arm. "We haven't wasted any time, have we?"

"It's not my fault if it happened so quickly. I just couldn't help myself. You must have thought I was very bold."

"I'll never forget today, never."

She shivered again. "I have a feeling all this is a dream and I'll suddenly wake up in a train somewhere. I dreamt about you in Beauvais last night and woke up and wanted your arms around me."

"This is no dream," he said. "Not from now on." He turned and kissed her, a long kiss that left them both breathless, then dropped back on the pillow and let himself go slack again. Her answering movement was swift and sudden. She was kneeling at his side and pulling down the covers, her mouth hot and moist on his thighs, her hands gripping his waist. He reached to take her in his arms. "Lee . . ."

"Let me . . ." The words dim and fierce at his body. "I want to . . ."

He gave himself up to it, letting the long waves of feeling sweep upward over him, letting his arms fall away from her to his sides, lying there until it was unbearable, until he struggled up to pull her down beside him. Now it was he who knelt over her, looking down at her, the touseled hair half concealing her face but not the tears in her eyes. "You're crying . . ."

"I can't help it." The words were like a gasp and she twisted her head from side to side. "I'm so happy . . ."

His plunging body was hurting her but she took him without uttering a sound. His eyes were closed, his hands under her shoulders stung her yielded flesh, but she watched him with adoration, aware of everything that was happening to them both. Suddenly he cried out and her hands slid down the wetness of his back to draw him closer still. Then she too was lost. The room revolved slowly, like a carrousel.

He reached for his watch on the bed table and stared at its faintly glowing dial, they had slept until nearly eight. Jay Weiss would be frantic, they all would, he'd have to get to the studio right away. Beside him he was aware she was awake too. "Is it late?" she said softly.

"Do you realize we've slept four hours? Now we can't have dinner, and I was going to give you a big one."

She stirred and he knew she was smiling in the dark. "You did give me a big one. I'm beginning to lose count. You're quite a man, Lloyd Garner."

"Anything I was was you."

"Sweetheart."

"I'm hungry. Can we get something from room service while we're dressing?"

"There isn't any room service in a place like this."

"We'll get something on the way."

"Kiss me first."

They had a sandwich and beer at the corner cafe and hurried to the office. Jay Weiss was pacing in the hall outside the elevator.

"For Christ's sweet sake," he began, and Lloyd said, "Ah-ah, Jay, language. This is my nurse, Jay Weiss, Lee Maxton."

He ignored her. "We were just about to call Schonwald and tell him you disappeared, where the hell have you been?"

"Mr. Weiss has no manners, Miss Maxton. That's why he's in public relations." He took her arm and they left Weiss standing in the hall. Jacques Roul was grinning in the studio doorway.

"Your friends have worried, mon cher Lloyd, how they have worried! I told them if this is the way they live in New York I am sorry for them."

"Do something for me, mon cher Jacques. Get me on the same plane as Miss Maxton Saturday, she'll show you her ticket." To Earl Greminger, standing by the teleprinter and smiling nervously, he said, "Any probs, Earl?"

"Russ and Kent are on their way over. Everything's under control."

"Of course it is. Tell that madman out in the hall to cool it, will you? He was waiting for me at the elevator." He took the script from the editor's hands and sat down to read it. Jacques and Lee had vanished into the outer office and Lloyd could hear him on the phone to the airline. It had been a routine news day and, as usual, the Paris negotiations had gotten nowhere. Russ Gibson said when he came in, "Who's that pretty girl out there?" and Lloyd said, "She's the reason I'm flying to Rome on the way home, I guess my attempted love-in with Kent will have to wait for another time."

"You're pale," Gibson said, "you've been being bad."

"It's just your Paris food, Russ." But he didn't believe him, of course.

Lee watched the show perched on a stool just inside the studio door. She was hidden from his view by the camera but her presence filled the room, he had never felt as sure of himself or as proud. Just before sign-off Greminger handed him a last bulletin. *"Matt Ferlin reports just now from the scene that the worst street-fighting of the week has broken out in the center of Paris, where police are battling thousands of students and strikers."*

Jay Weiss was standing in the office, waiting, when they came out of the studio. Gibson and Ward had already left. "Mind if I join you two people?" he said.

"We certainly do. I'll take care of myself tonight, Jay."

The PR man appealed to Lee Maxton. "Look, young lady, he ought to go right back to his hotel where it's safe, New York doesn't want him wandering around town tonight. Why don't you both just come along with me, we'll all have a nightcap at the Meurice, okay?"

Lloyd was laughing. "It's all right, Jay, we're heading away from the action, you don't have to worry about a thing." He took Lee's arm and they left him standing there.

In the elevator Lee said, "If there's something you ought to do I don't want to be in the way, Lloyd."

"I want to take you to dinner, period."

She looked surprised. "But the bulletin said there's more trouble, shouldn't you be covering it? That little man can't stop you, can he?"

"We've had two camera teams over there all evening, what could I do? My job's done for the day."

"But don't you *want* to see what's happening?" She sounded puzzled and somehow dismayed. "I can get back to my hotel by myself."

He smiled down at her. "When you've seen one riot you've seen them all. We're getting out of this part of town and fast, we're going up the Hill."

The taxi driver seemed as glad to get them away from midtown as Jay Weiss. He was also drunk or crazy or both. He talked to himself all the way to Montmartre at high speed and landed them on the Place du Tertre feeling lucky to be still alive. Once Lee said, "Jesus!" softly and clutched Lloyd's arm and he shouted, "Hey, slow down to sixty, man!" but without visible effect. They were both laughing uncontrollably getting out of the cab.

"Well, we made it, love."

"I thought it was our last ride together," she said.

Up here it was business and pleasure as usual, the rioting could have been a hundred miles away. It was just like the picture post-cards, the lanterns, the strolling crowd, the artists peddling portraits, a little band wheezing away at one end of the square. They didn't try to talk in the noise, heading for a cafe that would keep them out of the traffic. People were eating inside and talking to strangers from table to table while an old man hammered at a rickety piano. "What do they call applejack again?" he said.

"They call it Calvados."

They were sitting there drinking it, watching the crowd pass by, when Lee said suddenly, "But don't you feel out of things, up here tonight?"

"I feel *in* things, I'm with you. But the noise is awful, let's try to find something quieter." He signaled the harassed waiter and paid, and they walked out into the milling mob again and down a sloping street past Sacré-Coeur. They followed the railing of a ter-race that looked out over the city. Behind them the din of the Place du Tertre faded and was gone. Other couples were drifting slowly across the terrace, stopping to look or kiss. Lee slowed her step and stopped, silent. A vault of misty darkness arched high above the scattered lights so far below. It was chilly and she tightened her fingers on his arm. "Somewhere down there," she said softly, "is the revolution, and just like all revolutions most people don't even know it's happening, or don't care."

"It's no revolution, it's men on strike and kids raising hell, what's revolutionary about that?"

She looked up at him, her face indistinct in the pale dark. "They're doing it because they want to change things."

"And they will, a little. Violence won't help."

"But don't you see? They *have* to use violence or nobody will pay any attention."

He laughed, indulgently. "Okay, okay." They were passing a bench set back in the shadows along the terrace and he drew her

over to it and sat down, his arm around her. "Can't we just talk
about us? There's so much we don't know about each other."

"We need a little time," she whispered and dropped her head
against his shoulder.

"Like today in the hotel, you asked me about other girls. What
about your men? Have you had a lot of them?"

"Not a lot of men. A very few men." She was smiling faintly.
"After all, I'm twenty-nine years old, and I'm not a nun."

"Just one-night stands, you mean?"

"No. If I went to bed it was the beginning of, I suppose it's
called an affair."

"And they didn't stick?"

She seemed to hesitate. "There's one man. I guess he's the
nearest I ever came to falling in love."

"He's still around?"

"I've been seeing him in New York, yes."

"He's in love with you?"

"I suppose it would be called that."

"Somebody in your business?"

"He's a lawyer. Just now he's very active politically, working for
Bobby Kennedy's campaign, that's how I met him."

"How is he in bed?"

She laughed. "Really, Lloyd, you sound like the district attorney.
Did I ask you a question like that? I haven't even asked you about
your wife."

"It's a simple story, Lee. She was a drunk."

"Was?"

"Oh, she's alive and strong. She's under treatment. We've decided
on divorce."

In the long silence between them he felt content and complete.
Suddenly his life was settled. He knew where he was going and he
knew who was going with him. Then Lee spoke again, slowly, softly.
"Lloyd, I do want to ask you a question. It's been bothering me since
before I met you."

He laughed. "If it's about politics, no comment."

"It's about you. Why didn't you go out on strike that time, with
the others?"

For a moment he couldn't answer, the memory troubled his heart. He tightened his arm around her shoulder and drew her closer, hearing his own voice husky and low. "I've thought about it a lot since then. It was wrong. I'm sorry I did it. I was just scared and selfish, it all came too fast, and too soon. I wouldn't do it again, I couldn't. I know that now."

She was gripping his hand hard with both her hands. "I like you most of all," she said, "when you tell the truth, to yourself." Abruptly she stood up, smiling down at him. "Do you think we can find a taxi? There's something I want you to see."

"At this hour?"

"The markets. Next year they're moving them out of the city. Les Halles will be gone, Lloyd."

"You sound as if you can't bear the thought."

"I can't."

He took her arm. "Let's go."

And he began to see how she felt when, a little later, another maniac driver set them down on the edge of it. If the revolution had passed this way tonight no echo was left. Night was dissolving slowly toward day, the sky was lighter above the great black iron framework of sheds and alleys, above the incredible confusion of color and smell and sound. "It's a world," Lee said, "it's dying."

"I've never seen anything like this," he said.

"You never will again."

For an hour they wandered through the heart of it, happy and speechless in the soft spring air, then Lee said suddenly, "I'm tired and I'm sad, I've had enough, darling."

It was dawn and the cafes were still going strong. They sat on a balcony and ate onion soup and cold sliced eggs in mustard sauce and ham from the Ardennes and drank hard white wine out of thick glasses, surrounded by laughing, leering faces, jostled and stepped on, saluted by drunks. In the taxi she slept all the way to her hotel. He woke her gently and guided her up the stairs to her room.

He undressed her and she was asleep again before he pulled the covers over her body.

18

Paris was springtime, but Rome was the incoming tide of summer. Huge flowers blazed along the Appia Antica as they drove into the city along a route suggested to the cabdriver by Lee. They had escaped from Paris just in time, the strike was paralyzing the whole country. The airports were closing down, trains stopped moving wherever they happened to be, tourists were stranded with their baggage in open fields. De Gaulle, returning early from Bucharest, made his remark about the dirty bed and girded for a showdown with his enemies. Lloyd and Lee were aboard one of the last flights cleared from Orly. Now they laughed in the joy of sun and sky they felt all around them. "I'm going to show you *my* Rome," she said, and she did.

The hotel was a former palazzo, opening onto a narrow side street somewhere near the Piazza Venezia. Ocher and cinnamon walls looked down on the cobbles of an inner courtyard that shut away the clamor of the traffic, in the quiet of high noon a woman's voice was chanting snatches of a song without words, absent-mindedly, from one of the upper stories. Here in a place like this, among the ancient stones, the ancient smells, you could forget New York and Paris, they just never were. They stayed in their room only long enough to hang up some clothes and then, again guided by Lee, had lunch on the terrace of the Casina Valadier, the city at their feet. They drank a chiaretto with their antipasto and more of it with a risotto of tiny shellfish. Rome lay somnolent in a broiling sun. There was no more pressure of place or purpose, this was the golden weekend of his life. He looked away from it all and back to her, dazzled. "I didn't know it could be so beautiful, and you've been here so many times."

"Not so many times, it would take a lifetime to begin to know it really well."

"A girl in the New York office, she was my secretary very briefly, she lives here now, the lucky kid. I think you'd like each other, or do women ever?"

"In their own way, if the coast is clear," she said.

"Now I can really see the color of your eyes, they're Montana green."

She laughed. "I'll make a note of that, it's a good name for a fabric."

"The other night," he said, "my God it's a thousand years ago, you saw me working, but I still have no idea the kind of thing you do."

"It would bore you to death. Or do you want to hear about polyester doubleknit and nylon in textured and tricot styles, a current project? Of course you don't."

"I can't even pronounce it. Let's agree we never talk each other's shop."

Her face went serious. "Don't deny me that, darling. What I do doesn't matter, but what you do is important to everybody, I'll always want to hear you talk about it."

"Not today."

They finished lunch and went down the curved stone staircase into the Pincio. In the gardens of the Villa Medici the birds in the still afternoon sounded like nightingales. They were lovers in a book, walking in the classic shade, hands entwined, he could feel her slender thigh through the thin dress moving against him. "But where *is* everybody?" he said.

"Sleeping. Rome is where they invented the siesta."

They stopped at the edge of a little lake where swans glided around a marble pergola. "We had so much catching up to do," she said softly, "how wonderful we have this time in Europe to do it, life's going to be so different for both of us in New York."

"Not so different, we'll be together every day."

"I wish," she said.

"You'll see."

They walked on slowly under the trees. Suddenly he stopped and put his arms around her, feeling her respond with her whole body, he could taste the tiny delicious beads of sweat above her lips. "You darling," he said, "you went all out with that."

"I love you." She was looking at him gravely. "I think it began the first time I saw you on that little screen. And heard that lovely voice. Somehow you seemed, I don't know, as if you needed love. Of course I never expected to meet you, that was too much. And then by heavenly luck I did. And that first afternoon in Paris I wanted to have all of you to myself, always, and to give you everything."

"You did give me everything. You do have me all to yourself."

It was true, he knew it now. For a moment he thought of Fran, how easy it had been to forget Fran, and the past he never wanted to think about again. A month ago, less, he would have been eager for the chance to see Rita Valenti in Rome. She was here somewhere, today, he could find her right now if he tried, but suddenly it didn't matter if he never found her. Or Alix Weddern either. Alix was waiting for him in New York. Like Rita she had been a lover and a friend, he would have to see her once more. He would tell her before Lee came back to New York and she would take it hard. He would see her pain but he wouldn't feel it. There was only Lee.

And Lee said, almost as if divining his thoughts, half whispering the words, "Darling, just be sure."

"I'm sure."

Evening. Purple shadows lay across the courtyard and the air was cool. He turned from the window and saw her smiling at him from the bed. "Awake long?" she said.

"Just a few minutes. This is quite a room, especially that canopy thing over the bed."

"Have you noticed the bidet?" she said. "It goes back to Michelangelo at least."

He looked at his watch. "We take the longest naps, it's eight o'clock again."

"But what day is it?"

"Saturday, I think, does it matter?" Time had become meaningless.

"Can't we just live here forever and just make love and sleep and make love and eat and make love again?"

They made the street after a successful effort to resist making love, but it was close. At the Corso there was a taxi stand and they drove through the blue Roman night across the river into Trastevere to Lee's favorite outdoor restaurant. He looked around him in delight, "Why haven't the tourists found a place like this?"

"You got to know the ropes, pardner."

She knew them, too, from the minestra di foratini to the piccione con arancini, served with a noble red wine called Grignolino to the accompaniment of violin, mandolin and guitar under a rising moon. He ate like a starved man and she watched him, smiling. "In the morning," she said, "remember we must wake up in time to go to church. Nothing grand, just a church I want to show you."

"I'm not a Catholic."

"Neither am I, just a sort of vague Protestant, but I always go to church on Sunday, what are you?"

"I'm a sort of vague nothing," and he thought of his father, a nonpracticing Catholic, and his Lutheran-born mother who didn't bother about church for herself or her sons. He changed the subject, "Do you go home to Missoula much?"

"Always at Christmas. The whole family tries to make it but we're getting pretty scattered. I have four brothers, all older, and they live all over the country."

"*Four* brothers."

"Why do you think I'm named Lee? I was expected to be a boy. So they taught me football, baseball, basketball, hockey, shooting, fishing, and I hated all of it, no, I take some of that back, they taught me to ride and ski, and I like riding and skiing, what are your sports, Lloyd?"

"Eating and drinking, anything wrong with that?"

"I guess not. In Ecclesiastes they're all for it, you know, along with making merry."

"Who's Mary?" he said. "Never mind, strike that. You and your books. Ecclesiastes is in the Bible, isn't it? The only Bible I ever cracked was a Gideon in a New Hampshire hotel room, I couldn't seem to get into it."

"Someday you will."

He looked at her. "That's another thing, Lee, I've begun to think about someday. I never did that before, I guess I'm not a very thoughtful guy."

"What else do you think about?"

He grinned. "The Boston Red Sox and whether there's a new movie in town. Of course not all the movies came to Boston."

"Will you take me to a movie in New York? Something good?"

He kissed her hands. "You can count on it."

"I'll read to you in exchange, your education's obviously been neglected."

"It's a deal."

A church bell rang eleven across the little square when they got up from the table and walked to an open carriage with a straw-hatted horse. "Where now?"

"We did only one hill in Paris," she said, "I'm going to show you all seven here."

"No coins in the fountain?"

"This is Lee Maxton's tour, not Cook's."

He sat back in the carriage with his arm around her and listened to her unfaltering Italian directions. The driver seemed to be game if they were, at times Lloyd wasn't sure about the horse. But they did them all, the Palatino, the Capitolino, the Aventino, then the Celio, the Esquilino, the Viminale, the Quirinale and so back to the hotel. The churches of Rome were sounding three o'clock as they drove into the courtyard and Lee was asleep again.

She went to the airport with him to see him off on the late evening plane and after he'd checked in they sat side by side in the bar of the great glass terminal looking out across the fields of Ostia Antica and saying nothing. He was remembering Lee's little church by the Porta Latina where they'd arrived too late for the service but knelt together in the back pew, the first time he'd knelt in a church since he could remember, the worn wooden rest was hard on the knees. In the hotel before dinner they'd made love for the last time, and he wondered if it was a virginal quality about her that made each time seem like the first. Just innocently undressing she turned

him into a maniac, just tonguing her breasts started her coming in
bursts like a machine gun. She could come all by herself just sitting
at the same table with him in a restaurant, not touching at all.
He would see her give a little shudder and go a little pale and close
her eyes and bite her lip, then open her eyes again and laugh a
little with a sigh like a groan and say, "I just came," as if he
didn't know, but he would say "Why?" and she would say, "I can
smell the back of your neck from here, that's why." And when
they came together, and it was always together, to the split second,
every inch of her was vibrating, from her lips down to her toes, and
kept on vibrating, helplessly, long after he was quiet and soft again,
while her little girl hands strayed over his back with the touch of
feathers. The total adoration she gave him was part of it too. He was
the only man in the world. He was the only man who had ever made
love to her.

He said now, "What are you going to tell the fellow in New
York?"

"I'm going to call him and tell him I can't see him any more, it
wouldn't be fair to either of us to be together again."

"Will you tell him about me?"

"If he asks me, yes."

"But won't you be seeing him when you work for Kennedy?"

"Probably. But there'll be people around, I'll make sure of that."

He smiled. "Well, I wish you both luck. I mean you and
Kennedy."

"Who are *you* going to vote for?" she said.

"Will it matter? Either way we'll get a hack politician and things
will go on as before, it's always the way."

He saw the tears come suddenly to her eyes. "Oh, Lloyd."

"But isn't it?"

"Things can be changed if people work for them. *You* can change
things, more than almost anybody."

He put his arm around her and kissed her hair. "We're back to
shoptalk again. Can't we just smoke a cigarette and digest that
glorious dinner peacefully? Aren't you happy when I make love to
you?"

She stirred closer to him. "It's heaven, it always is. It's stronger all the time, you know that." She gave a little troubled laugh. "But I exist from the neck up, too, you know."

"Sweetheart, you're the brainiest girl I ever met."

"And so do you, even after you've finished your day's work. And there are things that are more important than either of us, than both of us."

"No."

"But Lloyd, you don't seem to realize that millions of people depend on you to tell them the truth of what's happening, every day, everywhere. If you're not going to care, who is? If you're not going to *do* something about it, who is?"

"Look, I have my uses. Like when I go to Saigon, or Paris, Walter Hacklin sets up a round of meetings with the clients because that makes me an authority on the situation, get it? So I'm supposed to tell it like it is, even if I don't really know that much about it. But I tell it anyway, and the affiliate owners and the agency executives and the network brass all listen and nod their heads and think, that's Lloyd Garner, he's been there, for three days, or a week, so he has the poop, he has the real inside. And then everybody has another drink on the network. Including me."

"You make it sound so futile."

"It *is* futile for one man to try to know what people think I know. A newsman is a guy who knows a little about everything but not very much about anything, and I'm only a mouthpiece for a lot of reporters who find out a little about one subject every day and a writer puts it all together every night and I speak it like an oracle from the magic box and the listener can take it from there, if he wants to. Nobody expects any of us to solve the problems of the whole world, baby. The world's not getting smaller, like we used to think, it's getting bigger and faster and more complicated and harder to understand than it ever was before. It takes computers now to make sense of it, and even when they do most people don't pay much attention, it's just the way humans are. So what's left? The problems that are still simple enough and close enough to handle, like the problem of Lloyd and Lee, and we're lucky enough to love each other and be together and to make the most of it while we can, and if other people aren't as lucky as we are that's their problem, not ours." He laughed. "Whew! Now can I have that cigarette?"

"That was quite a speech, darling." She sounded sad.

"I shouldn't sound off like that, it only depresses you."

"No, I want you to. I want so much to know what you're really thinking."

"Me, thinking? Who has time to think? Maybe in the good old days, whenever they were, not now, it's all going by too fast."

She sighed again. "I guess nobody tells anybody, not very often. But I want us to."

"We're pretty good the way we are, if you want my opinion."

"Lloyd," she said, "I know more about your opinions than you think I do. I've been putting them together, bit by bit, because I want to know who you really are."

He kissed her lightly. "My little psychiatrist. But I don't want to hear it, I know it already."

"You've got everything figured, is that it?"

"Just about."

"Then you know we don't think alike about some pretty big things."

"Do we have to? Isn't it more fun this way?"

"You see everything in terms of fun, don't you?"

"That's not quite fair. I've got a job, I work at it, hard, it isn't all fun. But when the job is done for the day, yes, I may turn it off and turn on the fun. Like right now I'm inviting Lee Maxton to spend her next New York weekend with me and my Jag somewhere in the country."

"It sounds wonderful, darling, a weekend in the country! But I can't go."

He stared at her. "Of course you can go, why can't you?"

"I'm assigned to canvass in a slum area weekends as soon as I get back."

There was a silence.

"I'm sorry," she said softly, "but I can't let them down."

He tried to keep the surge of anger out of his voice. "What's this thing you have for Bobby Kennedy?"

"Darling, we've just been talking about it. It isn't Bobby Kennedy. It's the whole situation."

"You can put it off once, for God's sake."

"I've put everything off too long, Lloyd. You may not feel what I feel, but I can't sit by and watch what's going on any longer. Doing something like this is little enough, but it's something."

He took her hands in his hands and saw her ready to cry. "I love you," he said, "isn't that something too?"

Somewhere above their heads a loudspeaker began an announcement. "They're calling your flight," Lee said. "It's time to say good-by, for now."

In his seat, waiting for take-off, he thought about their last conversation, it made him impatient and uneasy. He'd found his woman, the woman every man wanted, why did there have to be these complications between them? What was a woman for, anyway? To be helpmate and playmate, to love and share and approve. So why did Lee have to add an extra dimension to their relationship with her feelings about his work. Was Lloyd Garner's job essentially different, after all, from the work of a technician? Wasn't that what Schonwald had called him, with admiration, a damn good technician? He was a tongue for the camera, no more. They wanted impartiality in the network news and that's what he gave them, right? And it was easy, because that was the kind of man he was, wasn't he? Hell, he *felt* impartial, didn't he? You do your thing and leave me alone to do mine, wasn't that democracy in action? So students were tearing up the pea patch and blacks were fighting for a bigger share of the buck, so okay, I report it that way, factually, soberly, just keep it out of *my* back yard, that's all. Mine and Lee Maxton's, because we're together, from now on. Let her fool around on the edge of politics, this Bobby thing, if it meets some hang-up in her, she'll settle down, she'll settle back into the New York routine. He smiled, remembering everything and looking ahead, and suddenly he was very tired. Now that this first phase was over he'd have a few days to recover from the excitement before she finished her work in Italy and came home and it all began again. My God, that wonderful girl.

He was asleep five minutes after take-off.

19

Buck Schonwald said, "Looks like you got out of France just in time, fellow, all hell broke loose there over the weekend."

"So I've been hearing. On the radio."

The producer ignored the crack, but Lloyd knew how it irritated him to be reminded of the network's Sunday lapse in its news schedule. "Smart of you to catch that flight to Rome, the rest of the team had to drive to Brussels and wait a day."

"You know me, Buck. Brisk." He felt that way, too, ever since Lee Maxton. Happy, snotty, a man.

"Things are happening in New York, Lloyd. See what went on up at Columbia during the night?"

"Yeah. What's the matter with these kids? The troublemakers are the ones that have everything they need."

The big man shrugged. "Next year it'll be something else. Greminger's getting a raft of stuff on it together for tonight, he brought back some good film from Ferlin, it's a perfect tie-in. You can give us your own impression of the Paris students."

"You mean you want me to write my own piece?"

"No, Earl's already got it written for you, he was in here most of last night." He grinned. "While you were chasing ass in Rome."

That would be Jay Weiss, of course. "How do you know what I do on my days off?"

He grinned. "You sure as hell weren't interviewing the Pope."

"I couldn't. I didn't have anybody to write the interview for me."

That made him laugh outright. "Lloyd, as long as you sit down in front of that camera in there every time we want you nobody around here cares what you do."

"How about if I told you Jay Weiss shot up a whorehouse in Paris and damn near got shot himself by a gendarme."

Now they were both laughing. "I wouldn't believe it. Not Jay."

"You tell Jay Weiss I can match his pipe dreams about me any time."

"How's Rita?" Schonwald said.

"Rita Valenti? I didn't see her."

He probably didn't believe that, either, and who cared whether he did or not. Lloyd changed the subject. "Speaking of Matt Ferlin, I have a message from him for you. He wants to come home."

Buck nodded. "I'm aware of it. Maybe if things quiet down over there. I think Matt's been doing a pretty fair job in Paris, what's your opinion?"

"That'll be the day," Lloyd said.

"What'll be the day?"

"When Schonwald is interested in Garner's opinion."

"Come on, fellow, you know I always value your advice."

"What would you say if I advised you to send me up to Columbia and let me write my own copy for it?"

A pause. Then looking at him through half-closed eyes, "You're teasing. You've got all you can do in the studio, all anybody can do." He added after a moment, "It's the first time I've heard you suggest anything like that, Lloyd. What happened on the weekend in Rome?"

"Travel is so broadening, Buck."

"Yeah. Now let's be serious. About that ad-lib on Burt Staley, I don't want you to forget the little understanding we had when I gave you this job."

"*You* gave me this job?"

"All right, when *we* gave you this job. You take care of the broadcasting, and we put the words in your mouth, right?"

In the silence they looked at each other without smiling. Then the producer laughed and spoke again. "What's wrong, kiddo, ain't you happy? You know we want you to be happy. So I'm sorry if I needled you about Rome, no offense meant, okay?"

"Okay," Lloyd said and grinned back at him.

Schonwald was right, of course. Crossing the studio to his office, Lloyd remembered it had all been decided before his first broadcast. You took it or you left it, and he had taken it because that was the way to win. If you wanted the job you did it their way. Lee Maxton notwithstanding, he wasn't about to change it now.

Gaby threw her arms around him and kissed his cheek, the first edition of the *Post* and hot coffee were on his desk, the rat race resumed. "What's the scandal, Gaby?"

"The Red Sox lost four games while you were away."

"Don't remind me, I read about it in Paris every day."

"Yaz is way off his pace."

He looked at her and laughed. "You're turning into a real fan, has somebody been teaching you?"

"Nobody teaches me anything except my boss."

"Then you've got a lot to learn, little girl. Has anything been heard from Bev Hambleton?"

"Not a word, as far as I know."

Alix Weddern might know. But he wasn't ready to talk to Alix Weddern, not yet. He hadn't even sent that gag postcard from Paris. He could see her right now, pacing the polished floor of her apartment like a racing filly, in a rage because she hadn't heard from him, knowing he must be back by now. He could see her little private sitting room, the sunlight on yellow brocade, the Social Register by the phone that rang all morning as usual, but not with the right call.

He let it cool for two days, hoping Alix would call him first, that would force the issue and they would make a date and he would tell her. But Alix didn't call, and he realized then that of course she wouldn't, it would be up to him. Meanwhile he had been trying to locate Bev Hambleton. Gaby kept calling his mother's apartment, his usual sleeping address, but there was no answer at all. None of Bev's colleagues in the newsroom had heard from him. The Racquet & Tennis was holding his mail and would be obliged to learn his whereabouts. Buck Schonwald was mildly mystified and mildly indignant; Bev had failed to make his resignation official and hadn't even collected the week's salary he still had coming. This had upset the cashier and the business department and they were bothering Schonwald with calls. "I've put him on emergency leave," he told Lloyd, "which is more than he deserves. What does he want from me, apologies?"

Buck was too busy for apologies, but then wasn't he always? Except, of course, when his star broadcaster got a little tough with him. But Lloyd still remembered those half-closed eyes and didn't think he'd try it again, even for kicks.

Gaby had been awaiting Lloyd's return from Europe to start her vacation, and now the substitute secretary fell behind in her mail chores, so Lloyd took on part of the job himself at night after the show to keep Lee Maxton out of his mind and help reduce the mounting backlog of praise, challenge or vituperation for the way the show was covering the presidential hopefuls. In addition, the usual extensive correspondence had to be maintained with all the regulars, with the nuts on Cuba, Russia, China, with the rabid racists in the South and, now, the North as well, with job seekers, with amateur inventors and designers and sloganeers who were sure the network needed their ideas, with anguished liberals and menacing leftists or rightists who deplored the program's imagined bias on the old issues, civil rights, crime, Vietnam, students. There were also occasional warnings that Lloyd Garner was marked for assassination.

He kept the answers brief and noncommittal but invariably polite. The really wild letters were thrown away without response or turned over to the network legal department, in a few extreme cases forwarded to the police or the FBI. And, of course, there were the letters from female admirers to which he no longer paid any real attention, not even to the hot ones. Lee Maxton had changed all that, Lee Maxton seemed to be changing a lot of things. After the precious anonymity of Paris and Rome with Lee he felt an accumulating distaste for people in the mass, for the way he was stared at when he went out to lunch, for the whole public side of his life which in the beginning had pleased and excited him, even for those unseen, the millions, who watched him out of the void for half an hour a night. Sometimes, for a moment, the image crossed his mind of the faces in the Martin Luther King funeral procession that so deeply had moved him the night of that strange broadcast when something inside himself had taken over, had seemed to dictate the words he was speaking, but it was a memory that made him feel uneasy and he dismissed it, only to see it return when least expected. Who were they, after all, the silent people looking out of the monitor, and who were those millions watching them with him? The surveys showed the viewers were nobody much, didn't they? Most of the people who "mattered" hardly looked at TV anyway, and that included the News. Kent Ward had said something like that in their long-ago talk in Washington, when the miracle of Lloyd Garner's future lay still unsuspected. Even those who watched compulsively retained little or no impression of what they saw and heard, but was it because, perhaps, the policy of balance and blandness kept their vision blurred? It was another uneasy thought, this was not for Lloyd Garner to decide. On the third night after his return from Europe, however, he found himself on the scene of a bitter policy fight in Buck Schonwald's office.

The producer had summoned him immediately after the show. He stood facing Milo Wilson across his desk as Lloyd came in, both men white-lipped and furious. "We won't do it," Schonwald was barking, "we're already carrying four and a half minutes over my dead body."

"You look pretty lively to me, Buck." Wilson glanced at Lloyd with an effort at a smile.

"Never mind the sarcasm, Milo, and try to understand, for once. You can load this show with your crap just so far and no farther before you sink it. Your audience is going to take just so much and no more, then they'll reach over and switch to the competition."

"You're exaggerating, Buck, they'll take a lot more than you think they will."

Lloyd said, standing there, "You said you wanted to see me, Buck?"

"Sales," Schonwald snarled to Lloyd, "is trying to lay in another thirty seconds of commercial in front of your headline sign-off."

"Not trying," Milo Wilson interrupted, "it's already been okayed by Walter and the time is already sold to the client."

"I told him," Schonwald went on to Lloyd, ignoring it, "we've made our last concession to Sales on this show and we'd both quit before we'd accept it."

Wilson gestured in exasperation. "For Christ's sake, Buck, lay off the dramatics. You're not going to quit and neither is Lloyd. If Hacklin was in this room right now you wouldn't even suggest such a thing."

"I'd like to know why Walter *isn't* here. I'd like to know why he didn't consult me on it first."

"Walter's a busy man, he can't be bothered consulting with you on every decision he makes."

"In fact," Schonwald went on, "I'd like to know whether he actually gave his okay to this, it doesn't sound like him."

Wilson was paler. "You calling me a liar, Schonwald? Okay, pick up your phone and check it out."

"It's not up to me to check out anything. Walter wants me to change the format of this show he can tell me himself and we'll take it from there."

"You'll take it from there all right when you get it in writing." Milo Wilson headed for the door.

"Just remember to tell Walter he'll get something from *me* in writing," Schonwald called after him. "*And* Lloyd Garner. *And* Bob Lentz and a few others."

The other man slammed the door to the outer office. For a moment Schonwald stood there in silence, then his face broke into a grin. "It's an old technique, Lloyd. First he goes to Hacklin and says I agree. Then he comes to me and says Hacklin agrees. He figures we're both softened up then and he starts trying to persuade us. And you know? He sometimes gets away with it."

"Is he going to get away with it this time?"

The producer shrugged. "Probably. But I did my best."

"Of course if we quit," Lloyd said, "there's always Jack Milhouse to take over."

Schonwald laughed and put an arm around his shoulders. "Nobody's going to quit. I just called you in for psychological support. And believe me, nothing would bug Wilson like Jack Milhouse doing the show."

"Why's that?"

"He's too independent. He was famous in Chicago for sneering

at commercials on his show if he didn't like them. He'd only have
to do that once in New York."

"But you'd admire him for it, right?"

"I might admire him," the big man said, "but I'd be saying
good-by to him in the same breath."

The two Buck Schonwalds. Lloyd thought about them going
down in the elevator and walking east through the city summer
night, going nowhere in particular. He also thought about Alix
Weddern. He'd have to phone her, he couldn't put it off any
longer. He felt lonely, but only for Lee Maxton, it would be
only a few more days now. He glanced up and saw he was passing
Sardi's East. The dinner crowd would be gone by now and Gino
would be there, he was always grateful for Gino. Rita Valenti
had taken him to Sardi's East in his first days at the network. Of
course Alix thought the place was a bore.

Gino guided him to a corner table. "We saw you from Paris, Mr.
Garner."

"Never mind Paris. I was in Rome, too, Gino."

The suave and lovely smile was all Italian. "Now you are talking,
Mr. Garner."

"And that's where you belong, not in this crazy town."

"Are the horses running in Rome? That's what I want to know."

"Everything's running, believe me."

They laughed together, Gino made this place feel like home.
He also had some news, the house was having a caricature made
of Lloyd Garner from a publicity photo Jay Weiss had brought in
and would hang it at the end of the bar with the gallery, if that
was all right.

"All right? That's fame, Gino."

The maître d' brought him his drink. "Gino, you follow a good
profession."

"You think so, Mr. Garner? You can have it."

"I mean it. You help people be themselves."

"I'm the one who needs help, not the customers."

"You listen to them, they tell you their secrets, and they're as
safe with you as a priest hearing confession. Like if I was to tell you

I'm in love with a lady and I have to tell another lady I can't see her any more."

The Italian smile. "It happens all the time."

"It's not easy to do, Gino."

"But it has to be done, Mr. Garner."

"How would *you* do it?"

"Gently, Mr. Garner."

He had suggested the Carlyle for cocktails because it was only a short walk for Alix from her apartment. She came in wearing a brief black coat over a black sheath and looking, as always, extremely expensive. He stood up and kissed her cheek and saw her appraising him. "It must have been a late night," she said.

"Do I look that bad? I'm sorry."

"You sounded tight when you called me. Finally."

"I don't know why," he lied, "I'd had nothing but coffee. But I was dead tired, we were working on film from France."

"You still could have come up, I didn't care how late it was."

"Alix." He took her gloved hand. "You just don't understand the pressures in this job. It's been one of the busiest periods we've ever had, there wasn't a second free to call you till last night. Now sit down and be sensible like a good girl."

"You want me to be a good girl, but you're a bad boy."

He laughed. "Honest, you can ask anybody."

Her little smile was still suspicious. "I had a definite impression you were avoiding me."

"Now why in the world would I want to do that?"

"I had Houghton standing by for dinner tonight."

"I *am* sorry. I'm always sponging on you at home, I thought you'd be pleased if I took you out for a change."

She was a little less chilly after her first drink but the sparring went on. "I watched you in Paris every night and I almost called you at the Meurice a couple of times. But I was stubborn, I wasn't going to call till you called me first."

"I know I told you I would, but it was the damndest treadmill, Alix, I never seemed to have a moment and by the time I was through working I just sacked out."

"With some galloping girl, I bet."

"Please, don't talk foolishness."

"I wish you'd looked up the Burnleys, Lloyd."

"I was much too busy and I'm sure he was too."

"Not Wade. Hank did say he'd seen you from afar in a restaurant."

He laughed. "So you did call Paris."

"Just for chitchat with Hank."

Just to check up on Lloyd Garner, of course. "And which galloping girl was I with that time?" he said.

"As a matter of fact Wade said you were with another man."

"That is correct." He called for two more drinks, this was going to be tougher than it seemed last night on the phone. And he remembered Gino's advice, "gently." "Have you any thoughts about dinner, my dear?"

"None whatever, I leave it to you."

"How about right here, they have a dining room, don't they?"

"I don't like it here, I never have since the Kennedys began coming."

He grinned. "I didn't know you were violent about the Kennedys."

"I'm violent about most Democrats, but especially the Kennedys. I've told Kent Ward he ought to give up going to Hickory Hill. And now that that little rat Bobby's in the race, who knows what will become of us all? Murdered in our beds, probably, if he ever gets to be President."

"Who do you like on your side?"

"For President? We all like Nelson, of course, after all we *know* him, but I suppose one's about the same as the next, even that awful Reagan, as long as he's a Republican."

He was amused by her vehemence. "You kids stick together, don't you?"

"But that's the secret, dearie. Look what happened last time. We didn't stick together and we lost out."

"You really think Goldwater would have made it if you had?"

"Of course, and he would have made an excellent President. So sensible."

"So sensible? That's why he didn't get in, he's a kook."

She ignored it. "What are they saying about Nixon?"

"He'd sell his own grandmother to make it."

"If that's what he needs to win," she said, "more power to him."

"I've just realized, Alix, you'd make quite a politician yourself."

"Thanks." She was relaxed now, sipping her drink.

"Like for instance Pat could use a good social secretary."

"Please, I can't bear the woman."

"You know the Nixons? Of course you would."

"I did meet them once, at Wiley Buchanan's, but they're not my dish of tea, I'm afraid. Anyway, you know much more about all these people than I do."

"I'll keep you informed." He smiled and asked for the check.

They decided to dine at the Lafayette, a favorite of Alix's, and he said as they looked at the menus, "Doesn't Jackie come here? How can you *stand* the place?"

"Jackie's not a Kennedy," she said, and laughed and took his hand. "I've missed you, darling, I thought you'd never come home."

She was herself again, they were together like old times, which made it harder than ever. A week ago, little more, he had thought it probably inevitable that Alix Weddern would be his wife. Now as he looked at her the image of a girl in Rome stood at her shoulder; he tried to keep Lee Maxton out of his eyes. With his new French background he ordered like a gourmet, choosing a classic émincé de volaille and a classic Haut Brion, and with the drinks before dinner and the green chartreuse afterward, he managed to get them both fairly drunk by the time they were ready to leave, the second time in two nights for him, but he still hadn't said what he had to say to her, not even a hint. Last night he had almost said something on the phone. He had been drinking to bolster his courage to call her, but just his tone was enough to put her hackles up; damn women, they could almost read your mind. Now she was calm and reassured again, or was she, and expecting the evening to end as usual in her bed, with the future unquestioned.

From the Lafayette he wanted to go on for a nightcap, anywhere, but Alix said they'd have it at home. All the way up Park in the taxi he talked hard about the way things were in Paris, about Kent Ward, Russ Gibson, Jay Weiss, anybody except Lee Maxton, holding her hand but no more than that, and then they had arrived and the doorman hurried up to open the taxi door and Lloyd said, hugging her a moment and then letting go, "Alix, I'm suddenly dead again, I'd better not come up tonight."

In the half light of the cab she was looking at him. He saw her eyes grow bitter and waited for the bitter torrent of her words. Then just as suddenly her face softened, the eyes went alert and comprehending, and he knew in the moment it wasn't necessary to say it, Alix knew too. "That's probably wise," he heard her say, her voice quiet, even calculating. She would never break it off herself. He felt her lips against his cheek. "Good night, dear Lloyd," and she had left him, walking quickly across the sidewalk and into the building, the old doorman following like a dog. The street was empty.

He sat there looking at a closed door and knew he was giving up a world. Then he let it go, he had made the passionate choice. "Where to, mister?" the driver was saying, and he gave him his address. It was the middle of the night in Rome but he would call Lee the minute he got back to the apartment; she would be waiting to hear his voice.

IV: KEEPING IT

20

He didn't wait for Lee to call, he picked up the phone on his desk as soon as he came out of the studio and dialed her number. It rang once and a half and then she said, "Yes?"

"You know," he said, "it's amazing what you do to me, just the sound of your voice."

"Can you hear the joy in it, is that it?"

"When did you get there? I wanted to meet the plane but of course it was impossible."

"About an hour ago, the traffic coming in was awful but I didn't mind, I knew you were too busy to talk to me till now."

"Did you see the show?"

"Do you have to ask me that?"

"Lee, listen sweetheart, *damn* it, do you know what this is doing to me, just talking to you?"

He heard the low, familiar giggle. "I'm afraid I do."

"What's the matter, don't you want to do it to me?"

"I'm afraid I do."

"You believe me, don't you? Do I have to show you?"

"When you get here, yes," she said.

He laughed and felt the heat rising through his body. "I could hardly do the show tonight. I was *nervous*. I'm never nervous. I couldn't wait to talk to you. I was supposed to be reading the news and I was saying to myself the plane's landing about now, she's coming down the ramp about now, she's getting into the taxi about now, what's she wearing?" He could hear her low laughter. "Well, what *are* you wearing?"

"Nothing. I'm about to take a shower."

"*Nothing.*"

"I'll be pretty when you come, I promise."

"Pretty."

"I mean decent. Dressed."

"Can I come right now?"

"As quick as you can."

"Do you still love me?"

Her laugh cascaded. "Lloyd, you nut."

"I mean I haven't seen you for over a week, and in the meantime some guy—"

"Please, just come."

"You could have met somebody on the plane."

"You're torturing me, you're deliberately torturing me."

"You mean you want to see me as much as I want to see you?"

"You'll find out."

"Okay, while you're under the shower think about a restaurant, it'll be our first dinner in New York."

"I will. But come here first."

"Why?" he said.

"You know why."

"Maybe we won't get out to eat at all."

"There's a delicatessen."

"Shall I pick up some wine?"

"Got wine. Lloyd—"

"What, sweetheart?"

"You looked so lovely on the air tonight, better than I've ever seen you."

"I was thinking about you, I told you that."

"I knew you were, I could tell."

"I want to know something. How do you feel?"

"You know how I feel, how do *you* feel?"

"I feel alone," he said.

"You don't have to, not any more, not ever again."

"I know I don't. I'm coming down there now."

"I'm waiting for you," Lee Maxton said.

It was a brownstone on Murray Hill, he'd seen it before, he'd driven past twice while she was in Rome, just to look at it. A two-room apartment on the second floor looking out on a garden at the back, a carpeted walk-up with an old-fashioned bannister. In the open doorway she was outlined in soft lamplight, all slenderness and yielding. He almost ran down the hall. Afterward, breaking away from him with a little half-smothered laugh, she said, "You squeezed the breath out of me."

"You did that to me on the phone."

She was wearing a simple green dress open at the throat and a strand of pearls. She stood looking at him with her back to the lamplight. "Well?" she said.

"I'm just looking at you. You don't know what it does to me."

"I can see what it does to you."

"I warn you."

"I'm warned," she murmured and put her arms around him and kissed him, moving all of her body close against him, bringing back everything he remembered of her body.

"I said cut it out, you don't know what it does to me."

"I can feel what it does to you." She took his hand and led him into the dimness of the bedroom beyond and he knelt before the living column of her flesh, his face pressed against her thighs. She was naked under her dress and her skin was hot to his hands. He knew then that loving her was giving, not taking, she needed him beyond cost or count as he needed purely to give himself without reason, he knew only that he was fulfilled.

He could feel the precious passing days like holding them in his hands, one by one. Since celebrating their reunion they dined out nearly every night in an orgy of gourmandise. Together they checked out Craig Claiborne's daily tips and agreed on the restaurant where they would meet after the broadcast. Late mornings on his way to the office he would pick out a new cookbook for Lee's collection. Most places they tried only once, but a few were special and noted down for return visits, jealously preserved for when they could be together, quiet and close, as inconspicuous as possible. The famous places were disappointments either because the cuisine fell far short of the prices or the atmosphere of self-conscious chic was oppressive. They preferred discovering their own, Fornos and other Spanish and Mexican haunts, Chinatown, the little Middle East restaurants in the Twenties that were handy to Lee's apartment. In effect they were living there together like a man and wife with demanding jobs. They met for dinner when both were free, went to the theater and bed together when they could. In the morning because she had to leave earlier he stayed out of her way and read the papers while she bathed and dressed, then prepared his own breakfast in her kitchenette.

She was trying to get him off his habitual reading diet of newspapers and news magazines and occasionally a Simenon mystery, trying to entice him instead with Camus or Arnold Toynbee or the Churchill war memoirs. Some evenings, when she cooked for them and they stayed in, or came home early from a movie like *Elvira Madigan*, she read to him from, of all things, the Bible. These were the times he loved best of all, the hour nursing a brandy while she trimmed his hair with an expert's skill, while the talk smoldered toward the ultimate closeness. And sometimes, before they made love at last, after watching night baseball or an old Humphrey Bogart on TV, he would read aloud from her dog-eared paperbacks of American and English verse the poems she loved and wanted him to know, *Dover Beach*, some Dylan Thomas, some T. S. Eliot. Their love-making was less impromptu, less violent than the first times but as rich, as exciting, as it had ever been. No one, not Fran in the beginning years, not Alix, no one had ever been as satisfying sexually. Jo Ellison in the office, who rarely found fault with his speech these days, said, "You sound happy, Lloyd, it's good for your broadcasting," and Buck Schonwald growled, "You're putting on weight, fellow, watch it, your collar's getting tight."

He told Lee about it in bed, lying with his arm around her naked shoulders, breathing the faint fragrant scent of her hair in the darkness. "I'll never get *that* fat, I work off most of it on you."

"I never knew anyone who loved to eat the way you do."

"I've discovered why," he said. "I never had anything good to eat when I was a kid."

"My poor baby."

"Yes. What did your brother give you tonight?"

"Steak at the Brass Rail, what else?"

"The Brass Rail!"

"He loves it, we always go there. He watches you in Minneapolis, by the way."

"God bless him, then."

"Joe's a big family man, there's always a new set of pictures in his wallet."

"So what's wrong with that?"

Her fingers closed over his hand. "You want a lot of kids, don't you?"

"A boy, from you."

"I've wondered," she said, "why you and Fran didn't have a child."

"I married her because she was pregnant, Lee, but it never happened."

She was silent. Somewhere far down in the bay a ship's whistle sounded. Then she said, "I could never marry for that reason, not even you."

He smiled beside her. "Are you trying to tell me something?"

"Only that I refuse to trust the pill."

"Mrs. Lloyd Garner is going to Reno to shed me as soon as she can get away from her job. Sime Sussman got the word yesterday."

She lay there as if daydreaming in the dark. "I wish I could see a baby picture of you. Mother's favorite."

"My mother was her own favorite."

"You never told me anything about her, Lloyd."

"I tried to. A couple of times. When my father left she found a lot of new friends, that's all. I'll never forget how I felt, I was all of nine years old. I saw—" He stopped, painfully, and heard his own voice harsh. "I hated it, do I have to talk about it?"

"Of course not." The words came low and soft.

"I'll say this for my mother, she *spoke* well. Maybe I just inherited a knack. You're glib, a teacher of mine used to say in high school, you make it *sound* good."

"Did your father, didn't he ever come back?"

"A few weeks ago, yes. After twenty-eight years. I didn't know whether he was dead or alive, and there he was standing in my office. All of a sudden I remembered him, and I couldn't remember I'd ever seen him smile. I had no memory of that at all, just a household tyrant, very quick with a slap, very harsh with his wife.

I remembered things I'd forgotten years ago, like hearing my mother crying after he'd been tough with her over some little unimportant mistake, of course he never admitted a mistake himself."

"Twenty-eight years," she said.

"And even that day, Lee, after all that time, he had no excuses, no apologies for anything. He flatly refused to give me any reason for what he'd done. No,"—he shook his head—"No, he's not my father, he never was. I told him so. I gave him some money and he left. I watched him walk out of my office," he said, "and I knew I'd never know any more about him than I do now. And I thought, if I ever have a son I hope he'll feel, a little, what I wanted to feel that day and couldn't, a little love, or a little respect, something, something to be remembered for."

She didn't say anything, her hand still holding his hand.

"And that's the news till now," he said. "No, I forgot, you wanted me to tell you about my mother." They were lying face to face. "The first time was when I came into the parlor where they were all drinking and a man had his hand inside the front of her dress and she was laughing, and another time I woke up in the middle of the night with my brother sleeping beside me and I heard her in bed with a man in the next room and she was saying, You can have it, dear, but not that way, and another time I came home from school early and the door wasn't locked and all the shades were down and she was in her room with another woman and some men, I stood outside the door listening to them talk and move on the bed and I heard my mother say Try Jack now, Helen, he's good, you're good, Jack, I know, I'm married—"

"Please, no, darling, no," Lee was saying. Her hand came up to cover his mouth and he felt her tears wet against his shoulder.

The French crisis had died down, the back to work movement began after De Gaulle dissolved parliament, called a new election and reshuffled the government. Now the news spotlight could concentrate again on the politics at home, Kennedy and McCarthy seesawing through the primaries, Humphrey toiling along under the weight of the Johnson albatross, Nixon staying out of trouble. The evening news program added a commercial just before Lloyd

Garner's sign-off headline summary, and nothing further was said about it between Buck Schonwald and his anchorman, nor did the viewing public appear to object, at least no letters were received on the subject, which seemed to vindicate Milo Wilson's thesis. Lloyd resisted the temptation to kid Schonwald, deciding it was better to let sleeping commercials lie.

It was not so easy to ignore Matt Ferlin, back from Paris on general assignment to the Garner show and accompanied by his bride, that same Claudine of the Paris secretarial staff he had vowed to Lloyd he would certainly not marry. It was Claudine, Matt said, who kept insisting that Lloyd come to dinner with the Ferlins in their Queens apartment, but Lloyd repeatedly eluded the invitation so as to keep his free evenings for Lee. He finally took the Ferlins to lunch at Leone's, Matt said Claudine was crazy about Italian food.

Now she sat feeding her face on the mounds of pasta and cheese that covered the table, looking heavy and married and settled, Matt looked merely despondent. Lloyd remembered her as a cute little Parisienne in her own setting, but the charm was gone. "And how's Jacques Roul?" he was saying to keep up his end of the conversation.

Claudine shrugged her shoulders, it was obvious that Roul had never been eligible. "I thought we would meet your wife today," she said.

"I'm afraid not."

"Matt says there is rumor of divorce," and she giggled.

"That's his business," her husband said, "so why don't you just shut up about it." He sounded surly after several drinks and just as discontented as he was in Paris. Lloyd wondered if maybe pregnancy had something to do with this marriage too. He changed the subject. "What happened to that Wall Street spot of yours, Matt? I thought we were using it this week."

The other man glowered. "I put in ten days digging that out and today Greminger told me they may not even use it. What do they hire reporters for if they don't use their stuff?"

"I know what you mean." He tried to sound sympathetic.

"You do? I broke my ass on that story, and even if they use it, what'll I get, a lousy fifty bucks. Down in Washington the guys scrape up a fast spot four or five times a week and haul in a fee for every one of them."

Claudine said, giggling again, "I think Matt works much more hard than you do, Lloyd, for much less money. Of course, we don't know how much money they pay you."

"Will you shut up?" her husband said.

"I do what they tell me to do, Claudine."

"And who would not, for so much money? Ask them to give Matt more money, a raise, Lloyd, we are going to need it." She laughed good-humoredly and patted her stomach.

"I didn't know. Congratulations!"

Ferlin ignored the reference. "She's discovered the high cost of living in New York," he said. "I'm beginning to wish I was back in Paris."

"Not I, I love New York, don't I, Matt?" She had consumed most of a bottle of wine with her lunch and her French accent had become more pronounced.

"She sure does. She spends her days in Bohack's," Matt explained, "there's so many new things to want."

"Of course I miss Paris," she said. "Paris is cozy. But my God I am glad to get away from that tapette Russ Gibson. Matt is too."

Lloyd laughed politely. There was no more discussion of his income and things were easier. But Matt had a pearl of information. "I hear Bill Moran's finally coming home, Lloyd, they're going to use him at the conventions."

"I met him in Saigon, you know."

"Don't I know. You know what he called you in a letter he wrote McIntosh? Little Lloyd Fauntleroy and his governess, Jay Weiss."

He hadn't heard that and he flushed. Claudine was watching him delightedly. Little Lloyd Fauntleroy. He wondered if it was general gossip by now, they were probably all snickering about it behind his back, Milhouse especially. He could hear Ferlin explaining the nickname to his wife.

"Poor Jay," Lloyd said, turning it away, "I wouldn't want his job."

"I wish I had his expense account," said Matt Ferlin.

"Little Lloyd Fauntleroy," he said again. He shook his head. "How about that?"

"But it's the kind of thing that's always said about somebody in your position," Lee said, "they can't resist it. I don't see why you're letting it annoy you."

She was wearing green slacks and a paler green transparent shirt with nothing underneath, looking groomed for summer, looking handsome as a handsome boy with shorter summer hair. She had given him Bombay gin and tonic and then a madrilene with hot bread, cold chicken with a mustard sauce and a salad. The rosé wine was decanted into a frosty earthen pitcher. It was a typical Lee Maxton menu and he should have been relaxed and happy by now. Instead he had related and related again his feelings about Claudine Ferlin and her husband and Bill Moran's letter to Paul McIntosh. "Oh, come on, darling," she said finally, smiling at him across the table, "it's only a petty little joke, forget about it." She got up and switched on the TV in the corner of the room.

"What are you doing now?" he said.

"Channel Thirteen's doing a special on black power, don't you want to watch?"

In answer he walked over and switched it off again. "I'm sick of black power. *And* student demonstrators. *And* Vietnam. I've had it up to here, all of it, I have it every day. When I finish work I want to forget about it. I want to eat, drink and make Lee. Period."

She was not smiling. "Don't you *ever* think of anything else?"

"Not at night. Not with you. When I walk out of that studio I leave it all behind me."

Her eyes were part pleading, part perplexed. "But it isn't something you can turn off, the way you just turned off the TV. Don't you ever think about the news on your own time?"

"No. Do you mind?"

"Don't *you* mind what's going on all around us, like who gets nominated for President, for instance?"

"It doesn't matter. The same kind of people will still run the country."

"Oh, Lloyd!" She bit her lip in open exasperation.

He did consent to watch the Kennedy-McCarthy debate with her, perched on the arm of Lee's big chair, Lee curled up in the chair beside him, sitting on her bare legs and intently leaning toward the screen. He was smoking a light cigar she had given him after dinner as an inducement to cut down on cigarettes. Another delightful dinner, he was proud of her French-style cooking. She had served him minute steaks thin as paper barely cooked at all, an endive salad and a slightly chilled Beaujolais, with fresh strawberries for dessert. Now, watching the broadcast from Los Angeles, there was no conversation. It was very apparent soon that Bobby Kennedy was campaigning while Gene McCarthy was discussing the issues, that Bobby was talking to the camera, his rival at a point on the studio wall or eyes half closed, that Kennedy was in California, McCarthy might have been anywhere. One was dealing in people, these people in these districts in this election, the other in ideas. And Lloyd knew, then, that McCarthy was going to lose this primary. He leaned and kissed Lee's hair. "You'll have something to boast about when you ring those doorbells tomorrow, your boy's winning tonight."

"Do you really think that?" There was joy in her voice.

"I like the other fellow."

"I didn't think it mattered to you."

"It doesn't. Neither one's going to get the nomination."

"Bobby's going to get it," she said.

"Why do you have so much faith in Bobby?"

"He's the only one of them all who really cares."

"Doesn't Nelson Rockefeller care?"

"Nelson Rockefeller just wants to be President because he's had everything else."

"Nixon's going to be President."

"Shush, let me listen."

He dropped his hand to the back of her neck and began touching her softly, running his fingers up and down her spine, and suddenly she jerked away from him, it was the first time she'd ever done anything like that. "What's the matter with *you?*" he said, startled.

"I told you, I'm trying to listen. Don't you care about what they're saying?"

"I care about you. And I want you to turn that damn thing off."

"Darling, will you be quiet, *please.*"

"I want you to turn it off and come into the bedroom and let me make love to you."

"Not now, later."

He laughed and got up and poured two snifters of brandy, putting one in her hands when he came back to the chair. He had to close her fingers around it, she was lost in what she was hearing. So he sipped and waited half listening, remembering his perfect dinner, breathing the brandy fumes deep and enjoying his cigar. If Schonwald had his way the show would move to L.A. for the primary next week but Hacklin had vetoed the project as unnecessary expense. They would anchor the election special in New York and Lloyd would have Monday and Wednesday nights with Lee. Not Tuesday, though, she would be with Bobby's friends at his New York headquarters watching the returns. He inhaled the cigar lovingly and looked back at the screen, the debate was ending. The announcer's close came with time to spare and the camera held a wide, lingering studio shot, McCarthy smiling and impassive and somehow a little smug, Kennedy on his feet and moving around nervously center front until he realized they were still on the air, then pausing, reluctant to leave until the last photographed second was squeezed out, you could see him sense this instinctively. Lloyd murmured, "The politician to the end."

It made her angry. She twisted to look up at him. "Of course he's a politician, he has to be. If Adlai Stevenson had been a politician he would have made it, you know he would. Bobby knows you have to have it all."

"Plus a little help from Daddy."

Her eyes were bright with sudden tears. "You hate people who were born rich."

"No, just envy them."

"Bobby's the only real hope this country has."

"But does the country know it?"

She stood up suddenly and faced him. "Why don't you help a little and tell them?" The words were almost a cry, he had never seen her as upset. She shook her head, turning her back to him, and when he moved a step toward her to take her shoulders in his hands she eluded him with a swift motion and almost ran into the other room. He heard the bathroom door click shut and lock and the sound of rushing water in the washbasin. Slowly he walked after her and tried the knob of the door. "Lee, I'm sorry," he said. "To fight about *politics*, honest!"

"Go away." She was sobbing.

The dinner, the wine, the brandy, the being together, all ruined. He walked back into the living room and switched off the blatant pitch for a hair cream now holding the screen. How could you take anything seriously when it always ended in a commercial? And which was the reality? In the silence he stood there a moment, hurt and irresolute, it was their first quarrel. He could hear the water running in the bathroom and almost went back to speak to her again. Instead he put the cigar butt in the nearest ash tray and opened the door into the hall. If she could play temperamental he could too. He went down the stairs and into the street and found a taxi and went to his own apartment, it was the first time he had slept there since Lee came back from Rome.

21

It was clear halfway through the evening that Bobby was going to win in California. All the networks, on the basis of their key voter deductions, gave him the victory in advance of the official returns, one of them by a possible ten percentage points. Sitting in the New York studio on stand-by, watching the monitor screens with Schonwald, Lloyd peered at shots of the local Kennedy headquarters in hope of catching a glimpse of Lee. She must be hoarse with excitement somewhere in that crowd.

For nearly four days now he hadn't seen her or talked to her, not since the night he walked out of her apartment and left her weeping over that nonsense about politics. He shouldn't have left her, he knew that now. But what was done was done. Lloyd Garner didn't sit and wait for anybody, not even Lee Maxton crying on the other side of a door. She had been building to a scene like that ever since the night in the Rome airport, maybe even since the night in Montmartre when they'd looked out over the city and the street-fighting was down there and he'd ignored it. They had to have this thing out sometime and reach a mutual respect, she would have to understand the way it was. Somehow he'd got through the long, lonely weekend resisting the impulse to call her, to go to her, knowing that each of them was too proud and too stubborn to make the first move. Now, when all this Primary hoopla was over, she would be herself once more and they would be back together. In a way maybe it was good they had endured this separation. They had been together too much, too close, for too long, but it was teaching them how much they needed each other, they wouldn't be foolish again.

Gene McCarthy was on the screen. He felt a passing twinge of sympathy for the Democrat who had started it all, who had fought hard, alone, from the beginning and now was seeing it slip away, yet you had the feeling that winning or losing was not what mattered the most to him. A man with so little of the phony in him couldn't ever have really expected to win the nomination, let alone the presidency, not these days, not any more. Kent Ward, in the L.A. studio, had been talking tonight about how Wendell Willkie did it, but that was back in the mists of history, it was a different country every four years. What the hell was America anyway, growing by the millions, moving like lightning, shifting with each new electorate? The politicians were riding a whirlwind and of all the states they knew least what California would do. America was only a guess.

The special from Los Angeles wrapped it up at midnight and went off the air, the news teams on the coast were exhausted after the climax of the campaign, after months of unending crisis and surprise, a crescendo that was still gathering power. The Tet offensive, the battle for the dollar, Johnson's decision not to run, the murder of Martin Luther King and the nationwide rioting, the Paris Vietnam talks and the upheaval in France, now Bobby's bid to restore the Kennedy dynasty and the threatened war in the streets, what was coming next? Wearily Buck Schonwald walked through the studio in shirt sleeves to where Lloyd still sat before the cameras, dark now but still ready. "That should do it from here for tonight, fellow, but let us know if you're not sleeping home, okay?"

"Why, Buck, I never sleep anywhere else!" Lloyd said, and Harry Ferguson, who had been undecided whether to laugh at Lloyd's reply, decided he wouldn't laugh. Lloyd winked at him and said, "Coming down for a drink, Harry?"

"I'd like to, I really would, but I've got a lot to do before I can get out of here tonight."

So he was alone when he walked into the pub across the street and sat at the end of the bar and asked for bourbon and soda. The place was almost deserted at this hour but the TV over the bar was still on and the station was covering Bobby Kennedy's goodnight speech to his cheering followers in the hotel, half a dozen viewers squatted on their stools and watched it over their drinks like people with nothing better to do or they would be doing it.

The bartender, Jack Milhouse's friend, set down the bourbon with the extra care that was supposed to mean special treatment for a celebrity and gave him his half-sneering smile. "Quite a night for the news, eh, Lloyd?"

"Lloyd" was part of the treatment, of course, this guy was the kind that made everything he said sound confidential and knew the Broadway gossip and resented all success, who called you a cheapskate behind your back if you didn't leave at least a dollar tip and remarked to the other customers that a few months ago you were a nobody and now look at you. New York was full of bitter night servants who knew they could do your job better than you could, whatever the job, if they'd had your chance. It was all luck and the breaks. "Quite a night," Lloyd agreed. He wanted to watch the screen but the man's looming shoulders were hiding it.

He leaned closer. "Winchell was in here tonight."

"Is that so."

"The only reason he comes is I'm here. I know Walter for twenty-six years, Lloyd, from where I worked near the *Mirror* over on the East Side, that's all gone now."

"Is that so." Bobby Kennedy's speech faded into the cheering and clapping and whistling. The reporter on the scene was saying something, trying to make himself heard, and the bartender, still blocking the view, ran on about the old *Journal American*.

"The best paper this town ever had, Lloyd. The columns, you know? Slocum, Kilgallen, them. The Telly went too. Norton Mockridge used to come in here every day, every day. Like Jack Milhouse does now." He gave Lloyd a look meant to be withering reproach. "I give Jack stuff all the time."

"Yeah."

"Drink up, this one's on the house, Lloyd." He was giving him another chance. "The boss went home, if there's a drink on the house he wants to be the one to say it, know what I mean? Not that he pours very often, not him." There was confusion on the hidden screen, a different kind of sound not noticeable at once. Past the bartender's shoulder Lloyd saw the somnolent viewers straighten one by one, stiffening as they watched. A sharp cry of pure alarm came off the screen, was it some hysterical Bobby Girl,

jostled in the crowd that had said good night to the winner? A
voice along the bar said suddenly, as if astonished, *"Hey, Joe!"* and
the bartender turned away at last, grudgingly ready to fill a glass.

But it wasn't that. Something was happening in the hotel in
Los Angeles, something unexpected was happening on the TV.

Toward dawn on the Thursday, a few hours after Bobby Kennedy
died, Lloyd left the studio for the first time since the shooting and
took a taxi to Lee Maxton's apartment. He was fumbling with his
keys in the hall, so tired he could hardly stand, when he heard the
soft groping movement beyond the door and she opened it. Without
speaking he took her naked body in his arms. They stood there in
the doorway a long time, motionless and silent, then he closed the
door behind them and half carried her back to her bed. "I didn't
want to wake you," he said, so hoarse it was almost a whisper.

"I knew you'd come as soon as you could."

He was pulling off his clothes and dropping them on the floor.
"Go back to sleep," he said.

Her eyes were huge and gray in the pale light, she looked as if
she had cried until she cried herself out. "I wasn't asleep, but I can
sleep now."

"So can I."

It was all they said to each other. When he woke it was late
morning and she was gone. A little penciled note on the bed table
pad said, *I'll be watching,* and no more. She was back on her job
and it was time for him to resume the long vigil that had begun
thirty hours ago at Good Samaritan Hospital and would end at last
four days later in Arlington Cemetery under the night flares of
farewell. Not since the assassination of the young President, maybe
not even then, in the cathedral scenes, in the dragging journey of
the funeral train, in the massed suffering of Resurrection City, had
television so revealed the face of grief.

On Sunday the nation stood still. For Lloyd the day was release
from his longest continuous broadcasting effort since he came to
the network, relief, too, from a burden of mourning on Lee Maxton so heavy that every moment with her lay in its shadow. They
were together from late each night until morning, they slept in

each other's arms, and not once did they talk about it. Twice he awakened to hear her softly weeping and held her closer to him without words, not once had they kissed or touched sexually.

They woke in the Sunday high noon stillness and looked at each other.

"You're smiling," she said. "You're really smiling."

"Only because you look so much better, darling."

"You've been so patient with me, I love you for that."

"Only for that?"

"For that and everything else I love you for."

"I had to be away from you so much. There was nothing in the world I wanted to do when it happened but get into a taxi and come right here to be with you."

"No, you had to be where you were."

"I never should have left you that night you were crying."

"It's forgotten," she said. "But I'm glad you're here now."

"Where you want me to be is where I want to be."

Outside the day was clear and bright, she was looking wistfully at the window. "For the first time," she said, "I feel like moving and being alive again."

"Shall we take a drive in the country?"

"Oh, Lloyd, could we?"

"Now *you're* smiling," he said. "Almost."

He had the car brought around and they drove up the West Side Highway and across the bridge into New Jersey, then north along the Palisades and into the Harriman Park. The pines stood high and cool above their heads, the little lakes glimmered in early summer sunlight. Driving homeward in the Sunday traffic he turned off anywhere to escape it. They found themselves on a narrow country road and suddenly alone. "What are you thinking, Lee?"

"Almost nothing. Just content."

"Really content?"

"Why? Don't I seem to be?" She stared ahead at the road.

"I just want to be sure. You've hardly said a word all day."

"Do we have to talk? I thought it was nice."

"It was nice. I just wanted to be sure."

There was a sign a little ahead, *La Provence, French Restaurant*. "Hungry?" he said.

"Starved, aren't you?"

"Let's try it, for better or worse." He slowed and entered the driveway. It was for better, decidedly. The house looked down on a pond from among its fir trees, at that hour they were the only people in the place. The décor had taste and charm, the linen and glass were impeccable. The woman who made their vermouth-cassis behind the tiny bar recognized him without talking about it, the chef came out with the menu, they might have been in some little place on the road outside Paris. Leaving after a superb dinner he kissed Simone on both cheeks, she had a lovely, lively Provençal face, and he went into the kitchen to salute Paul personally. People were beginning to come in, for an hour the dining room had been theirs alone, he was glad to get away before the crowd but sorry to go.

"We'll be back, Simone."

"Be sure to bring her," said Simone.

Driving in, switching on the radio for the first time, they listened in silence to a London report on James Earl Ray, the man just arrested there for the murder of Martin Luther King, and heard comment by a New York panel on the theme of violence in a country whose citizens owned a hundred million firearms without federal restriction on their purchase or possession. Would Congress now, at last, act to share the nation's collective guilt, and could that guilt be charged further to the movie makers, to TV, with their daily spate of terror and hatred? What new tragedy would the summer bring in this year of our shame before the world? And what could each of us, as individuals, do now to avert disaster?

Lloyd Garner, full of good food and wine and gliding effortless through space in a Jaguar, leaned forward and with a finger flicked the talk to silence. He didn't want to hear about it, it was tragedy but not his tragedy. Martin Luther King and Bobby Kennedy were dead. He was alive. He wanted to stay that way, for himself and for the girl beside him. He glanced from the road ahead at Lee sitting deep in the low seat at his arm. In the dim light from the dashboard her face was expressionless, she looked as if she didn't care whether he turned it off or not. Yet something in her look had troubled him; he had felt it vaguely in the back of his mind all day, a thing so subtle it had eluded him since he woke beside her this morning. Something had changed in her, for the first time something was withheld. Something that had been his, and theirs, was gone.

He tried to recapture it in all the ways he knew, the ways they had known in the beginning together, not by talking about it, not by evoking their special memories, but by wooing her as if they were starting again, carefully, watchfully. They slept together without sex. He could wait until she was ready.

It looked like another period of calm in the news and his evenings were nearly always free. The long hot summer was underway but so far the streets were quiet except for an occasional night or two of sporadic racial trouble in widely separate parts of the country. For the second time since April, Kent Ward remarked in a Washington commentary, the nation had weathered the shock of assassination and seemed now again to be settling back into its mood of apathetic resignation. Congress, under intense pressure from the lobbyists, was balking at the drive for stricter gun controls and seemed more interested in the motives of Earl Warren in stepping down as Chief Justice. Only the political campaign showed signs of fresh vitality. George Wallace was emerging in the South as a threat to both parties in the election.

Providing no new major disaster occurred, and so far this had been the year of the tragic unexpected, the next big network effort would be the national conventions. That was just the home front, of course, there was always Vietnam and the Middle East, but no surprises could be foreseen for the immediate future. The President was talking to his friends about further rapprochement with Russia and progress on a missile treaty appeared possible. And the French, confounding the prophets, had given Charles de Gaulle a resounding vote of confidence; the electorate had turned its back on disorder and unrest. From which, Kent Ward suggested in another of his Washington spots, Richard Nixon could perhaps take a hint about the way a majority of Americans might now be feeling about their own country. Rockefeller and Reagan would have to show some movement soon or it would be too late to catch him. The uneasy Democrats, Ward pointed out, could look forward to losing the election unless they could shore up their declining prospects and forge some kind of unity. As it appeared now, Bobby Kennedy's death had left them a choice of McCarthy or Humphrey, and a lot of them wanted neither.

Lee Maxton said there had been hope among her political friends that Ted would take up the fallen gauntlet and try for the nomination as his brother's heir, but the senator from Massachusetts had withdrawn into emotional coma, he gave no sign, and Lee had transferred her allegiance to McCarthy. She was working at his New York headquarters two nights a week.

"I'd like to meet some of these politician friends of yours," Lloyd said. They were dining at the Coach House, a recent discovery in the Village.

She smiled in her new, subdued fashion. "I don't think they'd interest you, not really."

"Why not?" he demanded.

"They'd bore you. They talk politics."

"I can talk politics."

"I know you can, but as you say you work with it all day, and these are the kinds of people who work with it all night too."

"Including your ex-Kennedy lawyer friend?"

"He's one of them, yes."

He laughed. "As long as they haven't got time to make passes at you I guess I can't complain."

"I wouldn't go so far as to say that," she said, "but politics comes first."

"So *they* make passes, do they? And who are *they*?"

"Please," she said. "Eat your dinner."

It was the best Bordeaux he had tasted in America and one of the best meals they had eaten together. She had been quiet, almost distant, through most of it but after the dessert, a cunningly prepared melon with a mixed fruit glaze, they made the acquaintance of Château d'Yquem. "My God," she said, "how do you describe something like the taste of this?"

"You can say it tastes like summer. You can say it tastes like Lee Maxton's mouth on a rainy night. You can't really put it into words and you're not supposed to. You're supposed to sit back and let it enchant you."

"It's doing that, all right."

She looked at the check when it came, the first time she had ever done that, and he glanced at her in surprise. "Something wrong?" he said.

"That's a lot of money, Lloyd."

"It's the going rate for a dinner like this."

"Don't you feel odd spending it?"

"Not in the least, why should I?"

"It would buy so much for people who have nothing."

"Like who, for instance?"

"Like the children in Biafra, to name a few."

There was a pause. "That's true," he said. "But are you going to let it spoil a wonderful meal?"

She didn't seem to hear the question, she was looking at the Cartier watch he had given her when she came back from Europe. "I wonder," she said, "how much money you've spent on our meals, just our meals and drinks, since Paris."

He laughed. "A lot, I guess, I didn't keep count."

"A thousand dollars?"

"Possibly, and it was worth it, don't you think?"

"I don't think anyone has the right to spend money that way."

He looked at her, she was still staring at her watch. "Now tell me I shouldn't have bought you that, either."

"It's so beautiful," she said, "and you shouldn't have."

"Lee." He took both her hands. "It's not *us*, it's not *you*. Where's the girl I was with in Europe such a little while ago? She didn't talk like this, she wasn't the way you've been since, well, you know how long. And now we're sitting here after a glorious dinner I hoped would make you happy, and instead—" He heard the desperation in his voice. "What is it, darling? Why have you changed? What can I do to find you again? What can we do to find each other? Stop eating and drinking? It can't be just that. It can't be just the way you feel about the man who died. Not permanently."

He saw her eyes full of tears. "Believe me, I'm not trying to make
you unhappy."

"I know that. I just want us to be back together the way we
belong, and we're not. Is it another man? If it is, tell me, and we'll
take it from there."

She shook her head. "No, it isn't another man."

"You know I want to marry you. I thought that was our understanding. As soon as my wife can get to Reno and get it over with
we'll be in the clear. Lee," he said, "don't you want to marry me any
more?"

"I don't want us to make a mistake," she added. "It would be so
much harder afterward."

He was gripping her hands. "Mistake? How can you even say it?
I never felt as sure of anything in my whole life. Ever since
that first day in Paris. And I thought you felt the same way."

"I did," she said slowly, "at first. Now I know you, Lloyd.
Now I know how very different we are, fundamentally, deep down."

"Of course we're different. You're a woman and I'm a man.
But can't a man and a woman adjust to each other? Can't they
learn to change for each other's sake? I want to give you everything I am. I want to be what you want me to be."

"Can you learn to care about the world?" she said softly. "I guess
it's as simple as that."

They were looking at each other, her hands still in his hands.
Her eyes had cleared, they held him, watchful, steady, but he
knew how far away she was. Then she said, "I start my vacation
at the end of the month."

He stared at her. "You haven't even mentioned it."

"Because I hadn't decided what to do, go home, or what."

"I could have told you, you're spending your vacation with me,
naturally."

She smiled a little, still fingering the spoon. "Wouldn't it be nice
to go to Europe together."

"Nothing in this world would make me happier."

"Oh, Lloyd, you *can?*" The joy leaped in her voice and as sud-

denly fell away when she lifted her eyes and saw his face. "You
can't."

"It's impossible. Schonwald's put the whole staff on alert till
after the conventions. But couldn't we go then?"

Barely perceptibly she shrugged and looked down again. "July
is the only time I can get away. I guess we can just forget it."

"Darling," he said, "there'll be other vacations."

"No." She was shaking her head and speaking almost as if to
herself. "It was only, I thought if we could only do that, just take off
and go back where we began, be the way we were in the beginning,
then maybe everything—" She stopped, struggling against tears.
"Could you ask them to bring some coffee?" she said.

Walter Hacklin, accompanied by his wife, departed for Europe
on his annual visit to the network bureaus the same day Lee Maxton flew home to Montana on her vacation. Fortunately there was
no conflict in schedules, the *France* sailed at noon and Lee's plane
didn't take off until two-thirty, so Lloyd would drive her to Kennedy and could still get back to the studio in time for his afternoon's
work. He wanted to skip the Hacklins' bon voyage party but it was
a traditional must for the news stars and he had to make it along
with Jack Milhouse and Weldon Duff, both of whom were already
in evidence when Lloyd arrived with Buck Schonwald. The pre-
vailing drink was champagne, the cabin as luxurious as a Plaza
suite and the news department brass abounded. "Does the big boss
come to this?" Lloyd wanted to know, and Schonwald laughed at
him.

"For your information the big boss is in Canada at the moment.
Unofficially."

"Prospecting for uranium, no doubt?"

"Don't even joke about it, not to these people."

Joyce Hacklin swam up to him in the crowd almost immediately.
She was as smooth and hard as the man she was married to and
might have been a pretty girl a long time back; he had met her
briefly at 21 a couple of times. "What I want to know," she said,
glass in hand, "is what you do with your weekends, Lloyd Garner,
I've just about given up on you in Greenwich."

"Please don't, Mrs. Hacklin, will you invite me just once more when you come back?"

"Joyce to you." The predatory smile. "And where do you hide your wife? Walter doesn't know."

"She's about to move to Reno for a while."

"Oh. Then you're on the loose."

"Well. If you want to put it that way."

"I'll have to find somebody glamorous for you, or is there someone you'd like to bring?"

He didn't have to answer the question. Weldon Duff joined them, looking like Captain Video. "Am I intruding?" he boomed, on as usual.

"Go away, Weldon," Joyce Hacklin said, "I want this man to myself."

"I guess I know when to drop dead." He moved along, nursing his vacuous grin.

"You've hurt his feelings," Lloyd said.

"He doesn't have any feelings and you know it." A steward was refilling their glasses, Lloyd noticed Jack Milhouse big-shotting it with the parting host and Milo Wilson. As usual he was making the most of his opportunities. All at once the man from Chicago seemed aware he was observed and threw Lloyd a half-mocking smile. Joyce Hacklin saw it too. "How do you two boys get along?"

"Who, Jack? We don't see too much of each other because of working hours."

The husky chuckle echoed ten thousand martinis. "You're a diplomat, that's obvious. Personally I think he's a creep, but he's managed to push the rating up."

He smiled. "I didn't know you watched the business that closely."

"Sweetie, where do you suppose I was working when I met Walter? I can see a knife out through three layers of soundproof studio wall. But I guess you know Walter likes you, and more important so does the big man upstairs."

"It's always good to know that, Joyce. I haven't even met him yet."

"Not necessary. It's performance that counts with him. So keep your nose clean and you'll be around as long as you like, Lloyd

Garner." She drained her glass, gave him one more quizzical glance and went to greet some people coming in from the corridor.

He looked at his watch, the sooner he got away from here the more time he'd have with Lee. But he had a chore to do first. Milhouse had joined Schonwald for a heads-together on the other side of the cabin and Hacklin and Wilson were alone again. "How long you be gone, Walter?" Lloyd said.

"I'll be with you in Miami, my boy. And keep your fingers crossed, we may still be able to switch the Chicago convention down there, I hope to God we can. But I was just saying to Milo, Daley's as stubborn as anything he's got in those stockyards and Humphrey's scared to death of him, he needs him so bad."

"Give my best to Paris."

They shook hands. As he left he waved a good-by to Joyce Hacklin, he had an idea Joyce Hacklin would be a tough ally in a fight.

Walking back to the street along the pier he saw warships tied up at the Hudson waterfront and more at anchor in the river. Taxis were disgorging passengers for the *France* and he had no trouble finding a cab right away. They drove south and then east to Murray Hill. Lee came to the door barefooted wearing a bra and a half slip, her skin smooth and honey-colored in the soft light. "I just finished packing, is it that late?"

He kissed her tousled hair. "Relax, lots of time. I got away sooner than I expected."

"And was it terribly gay?"

"It was Madison Avenue on A deck, but the champagne helped."

"I almost forgot." She scurried into the kitchenette and came back with a half bottle of Veuve Clicquot and a small white towel. "Here, open this, I was pretty sure you wouldn't want to change horses."

"You darling, it's like the old days."

"Can't I have a bon voyage party too?" She smiled up at him. "Just don't let me miss that plane." But it was her politeness smile, not her real one. The manner, the whole mood, was charm, nothing more, and he dreaded what it meant as he had dreaded it these past days and nights it had stood between them.

"Quick, the glasses," he said, unloosening the cork, and she ran into the kitchenette again. He held his glass up to the light from the window, marveling. "Look at it, full of life."

"Two hours in the bottom of the icebox, right?"

"Just right." He put his arm around her shoulders and pulled her close a moment, feeling her body respond affectionately, no more than that. "You and I should be on the *France* today, Lee, not them."

"People like us haven't time to go anywhere by *boat*," she said. She dodged prettily out of his arm and sat down on the nearest chair, reaching for the shoes on the floor beside it.

"Someday we'll have time," he said, but she didn't answer. "Well," he went on, "aren't you going to tell me what you're going to do in Missoula?"

"Sleep, then read, then sleep again, every day."

"And aren't you going to ask me what *I'm* going to do while you're gone?"

The shoes were on, she tossed her hair back and looked up at him. "What are *you* going to do while I'm gone, how's that?"

"Work all day and get drunk at night because I miss you."

She glanced at the little clock on the mantel. "If that's right I ought to wash my face and start dressing right now." She stood up.

"Not till I've loved you good-by," he said.

She laughed the oddly formal little laugh. "Are you out of your mind? I'd never be able to get up."

"Then I'll carry you to the plane, okay?" He put his empty glass down on the window sill, then put his arm around her, holding her close, and began unclasping her bra at the back. "Do you realize how long it's been?"

"Lloyd, you mad fool, we haven't time," her voice muffled against his chest.

"Be quiet, did you think I was going to let you go without giving you something to remember me by?" He held her at arm's length, the bra fell away and he bent to kiss her breasts.

"No, it's not fair, I can't resist that." Her shoulders yielded, trembling in his hands.

"Now you sound like the Lee I used to know and I want her back." He pulled her close again and ran his hand down inside the front of her half slip, she wore nothing underneath it. "Lloyd, Lloyd," she was whispering in little gasps, "when you take me in your hand like that you take everything."

"Almost everything." He picked her up, her body heavy and warm in his arms, not struggling any more, and carried her to the bed in the other room. Now she lay perfectly still on her back, looking up at him with troubled eyes. They were saying this was the last time.

22

The big heat closed down. Thermometers pushed into the high nineties along the eastern seaboard the day Johnson and Kosygin signed copies of the nuclear limitation treaty, and Kent Ward followed the Moscow spot from steaming Washington with expressions of hope for a new Soviet-American détente. But he noted the Russians were making menacing noises about Czechoslovakia's relations with the West, not the most encouraging of omens. At home the spotlight brightened on George Wallace. During today's line-up meeting Greminger and Ferguson had disagreed over a Wallace film spot on which a congressman from Virginia and a spokesman for the SNCC exchanged opposing views. The writer wanted the congressman heard first and the editor thought he should be heard last. Schonwald was called in for a decision, saw both film clips and said, "Run the colored man first."

"But, Buck," Ferguson pleaded, "the congressman's a rabble-rousing punk, anyone can see that. The Negro has dignity and decency sticking out all over him. *He's* the defense and he should speak last."

"Run the Negro first," Schonwald said. "We're not about to take on the Congress."

Lloyd Garner had his mind on other political matters. He was flying down to Washington after the show as a guest of the President and the First Lady at a White House dinner dance, for the first time he wore a tuxedo on the air. Schonwald grinned at him as he left. "If you get to huddle with Lyndon tie him up for an exclusive."

"Consider it done, Buck."

It was much less pompous than he had expected, the White House almost homelike under softly lighted chandeliers, flowers everywhere, and he remembered the first time he had been under this roof, humble and tense and new, to be thrilled at his meeting with the great Kent Ward. But Ward wasn't there tonight, Lloyd seemed to be the only broadcaster among a scattering of news people and a random crowd of military, cabinet members, senators and representatives, ambassadors. They sat at small round tables serenaded by a string orchestra in scarlet jackets and Lloyd found himself between the wives of a Chilean diplomat and an admiral on sea duty. Afterward they moved to the East Room for dancing to the strains of another orchestra, the President first on the floor and changing partners indefatigably. Lloyd danced with both his table neighbors, then made his way back to where the drinks were, smiling and nodding answer to smiles and nods from strangers. In a way tonight was culmination of everything he had become, and in his hour of pride and triumph he wished above all that Lee Maxton were here to share it.

Thinking of her now brought the dazed feeling again, the sudden sickened emptiness, the memory of their silent drive to the airport and their silent good-by. That day she had surrendered her body but that was all. No words were necessary, she had left him. In their last hour together he was already alone. And since then, nothing, not a note, not a call, while his loneliness hardened into impotent anger.

A voice, suave, familiar, startled him. Drew Stimson said, "Having fun?"

Lloyd turned and laughed. "Almost spilled this whisky. I didn't know you were here, Drew."

"Just invited for the dancing. It's obvious I don't rate at your level." The smile was warm and friendly and this time the elusive Drew Stimson was in no hurry to move on. "I don't think you know how much you're admired around here."

"I don't think I do, no."

"But you are. Take it from a government employee."

"Haven't you always been?"

Lightly and warily, "Where in the world would you get that idea?"

"I mean don't we all work for the government?"

"Oh, I see." The easy laugh. "I guess your taxes must be pretty

high by now. Maybe one of these days you'll get tired giving it all to
Uncle Sam and do what I did."

"I might at that. Could you get me a job with the Voice,
Drew?"

"Oh, you wouldn't need me. And you could do better than the
Voice." Stimson took his arm and guided him to a quieter corner.
"Seriously, I have reason to believe you could run for Congress,
and win, if you said the word."

"Me?" He stared at him. "Now you're really putting me on."

"You don't have to believe me. Ask somebody else."

He grinned. "Like the President?"

"Not directly, no. He happens to be well disposed, however."

"Come on, I've only barely shaken hands with the man. He
never laid eyes on me before tonight."

"He lays eyes on you every night, Lloyd. He has three TV
sets upstairs going continuously for his personal use."

There was a pause. Music rose again above the babble of talk
and dancing resumed. Lloyd said, "Level with me, Drew, just what's
it all about?"

"Let me say this much. If you're interested for 1970 you could
have the nomination. There are people who would very much like
to see you take it."

"And just who are they?"

He laughed. "Let's leave it this way, they're the people who
could arrange it."

"And you're speaking for them?"

"I was asked to broach it, yes. In a completely informal way,
of course. Since you were going to be here tonight."

"You'll be telling me next you got me invited."

"Not at all, nonsense. That was a White House thing, this is a
party matter."

"I never knew you were so big with the party, Drew."

"I'm not, but they know I know you."

He was smiling and remembering. "Drew Stimson," he said,
"always in the know."

Stimson waved a deprecating hand.

"The man who always knows about me before I know about myself," Lloyd went on. "Take the case of me and Hedley Johns."

"How do you mean, Lloyd?" The smile was pleasantly puzzled but the eyes were guarded now.

"The only part of it I haven't figured out yet is whether you were working for Johns or working for the network. Or maybe both at the same time?"

The smile had faded. "If you're interested in the nomination," Drew Stimson said, "give me a ring at the Voice one day. I'll put you in touch with them."

So we were back with Them again. It was where you always ended up, like Buck Schonwald who was still trying to find out who They were, to hear him tell it, but always lost the trail outside Walter Hacklin's door. Lloyd stood there watching Drew Stimson disappear into the crowd, remembering the first day they'd gone out to lunch together in New York, when he'd called Lloyd Garner a mystery man. But Drew Stimson was the mystery man. Of all the surprises he'd experienced since Milo Wilson came to Boston to offer him a job, this was the most fantastic. But then maybe nothing was fantastic in Washington. He wondered if the network people knew, and decided not to speak of it unless Hacklin or somebody else brought it up, but he'd mention it to Sime Sussman and get his reaction. *Representative Lloyd Garner, Democrat, New York,* or was it some other state they had in mind, and for which safe district? Not that he'd do it, at least the way he felt at this elated moment, but the idea was exciting, something he'd never even thought of. TV news could lead anywhere, he had again the feeling that his future was illimitable. And suddenly he thought of Lee Maxton again, forgetting his anger, forgetting his pride. Mightn't this be what she needed to hear, to put them back on the track together?

He called her from the airport on his way back, a little drunk after the White House party, still exhilarated, reckless. An older man's voice answered, her father he supposed, to say politely that Lee had gone to bed, was there any emergency? No, not exactly, he just left his name.

But already he knew that when they told her in the morning she wouldn't call him back.

He told Sime Sussman about the message from Drew Stimson and watched the little eyes darken and dance. "Yeah," the agent said, listening. "Yeah. Yeah."

"What do I do about it?"

"You do nothing. You keep your mind on your work. We play the cards right, we get a few more years like this one, and you're set for life, you can do anything. Congress? Politics? Right now you got all the politics you need with this Milhouse. He called me, Lloyd. He wants me to take him on. I told him, sorry, I don't take clients in competition for the same work."

"Milhouse makes me feel uneasy."

"Sure. In this business everybody's looking over his shoulder all the time, it's part of the game. But this guy's no threat. Keep an eye on him, that's all. And don't show worry. Ever. To anybody. You got your contract, you're solid in this spot, and even if you weren't they're not going to change horses, not for a long time." The harsh chuckle. "You know something? They never expected you'd be so good at it. They figured they could tame Hedley Johns when they put this Stimson up to warning him about you, but they had to be ready in the crunch. And when Johns crunched out they had to make good, they had to put you in there. Well, you really came through for them, Lloyd, it's been like a pleasant surprise all around."

"Nobody was more surprised than I was."

"And ever since, they've been saying see, just one more case where the big boss had the instinct."

"How do I meet him, Sime?"

"So do you have to meet him? You should pray for him at night, that's enough." He looked down at a memo on his desk. "Another thing. The lady hasn't left for Nevada yet, from what my Boston man tells me."

Lloyd shrugged, she could wait a year for all it mattered now. "There's no hurry. Not any more."

"I thought there was somebody in the wings."

"So did I, but I was wrong."

The little man leaned forward. "You're better married again, it's better every way. But don't rush it. Take your time. Make the right choice." He cackled. "That's one I can't help you on."

"I made the right choice, Sime, but she didn't choose back."

"Yeah?" The eyes were softer. "That's the way it goes."

Take your time. He had nothing but time right now. "Sea Probe," the weekly documentary, went off the air for the summer. "Come On Along" followed its custom and replaced Lloyd Garner with a new regular guest, none other than Jack Milhouse. Sime had signed him up with a lecture bureau but the first dates were set in November, after the election. Meanwhile, provided with a visitor's card, Lloyd dropped in at the Players several times after the show, but if the company had to be male he preferred to eat with Dobie Dobrinoff and drink until he was sleepy enough to go back to his apartment and the phone that never rang.

He'd met Dobie Dobrinoff on "Come On Along" during one of the actor's periodic guest spots on the panel and Dobie suggested a drink. The grinning, bull-like face peered at him, eyes narrowed. "Hey, Lloyd, you look different on the tube, you know? Like older, stern. But they cream with the smile."

"That's part of the gimmick, Dobie."

"You're just a kid." The grin spread again, lighting up the whole bar. "I dig you, Lloyd, I do. I watch that show. For years. I'll never forget what's his name but I like you better, honest."

"What's his name went to NET for a while, didn't you catch him?"

"I didn't catch NET yet." The laugh was half a bellow. "And Hedley never came on the talk shows, not Hedley, so we never got to be soul brothers."

He remembered Kent Ward's words about TV and show biz. "We're all soul brothers on 'Come On Along.'"

"Yeah! How about that nun was on with us today?"

"Ever meet Kent Ward, Dobie?"

"Naw, but I listen at him. Tell me something, wouldn't it be kind of nice to know what *he* thinks sometimes?"

They laughed together. Dobie Dobrinoff wasn't stupid.

Three days later the actor turned up again in his office wearing an old corduroy jacket and a fake beard and chewing an apple. Lloyd looked at him. "Where the hell did *you* come from?"

"Well, I'm doing a soap this week and we broke after rehearsal, so I thought I'd step into the lift and rap a little with my buddy."

"That's a costume?"

"I'm old Uncle Ed, wiseacre of Happy Valley and adviser of young girls. They wrote me in because I needed the tax money, you mean you haven't been *watching?*"

Gaby Berman began to laugh. "I see your secretary knows my true identity," Dobie said. "Okay, so I'm really president of Face Men of America Incorporated, most exclusive club in the country. You don't even get to be a member till you can tongue a silver dollar out of a full highball glass without spilling a drop." He leered at Gaby. "Want to join the women's auxiliary?"

"What have I got to lose?" she said.

"I like this girl, Lloyd. We take her to lunch?"

"Isn't that lunch you're eating?"

He tossed the apple core into a wastebasket and put his beard in his pocket. "How about Romeo Salta?" He threw an arm around Gaby. "Ready, luv?"

"I've already got a lunch date," she said.

"I'll call you. Come on, Lloyd."

They had drink in the bar across the street and the actor asked about Gaby Berman. "I could eat that. You had it?"

"I never thought about it."

"Don't jive your mother."

"So help me, I never noticed it. I liked my first secretary but she went to Rome."

"Rita Valenti?"

"You would know Rita."

"A great broad." He smacked his lips. "But she's in Rome and Gaby's here. Look into it, baby, she'd be wild."

"Dobie, this is a conventional little Jewish girl who lives with her parents in the Bronx, she's a good secretary and I want to keep it that way."

"With an ass like that she needs more exercise than she'll get at a typewriter. Investigate it."

"I don't want to investigate anybody, not any more."

And over two bourbons and lunch he told him about Fran, and about Alix Weddern, and then about Lee Maxton.

Dobie Dobrinoff picked up his hand and kissed it. "I'm sorry for your trouble, Lloyd."

"I know it and I love you for it because you mean it. You're the first guy I can talk to since I left Boston." And he thought of Harvey Lewin who couldn't take his best friend's success.

They sat in silence until Dobie said, "I know it's like hard to look at it, right now, but later you better pick up with the society dolly. You got yourself something there, you know? I mean like rich and a dish and a swinger, all wrapped up in one neat little bundle. She might even make it on the long haul."

"I can't picture it with Alix, Dobie, not since Lee."

"Alix? Alix Weddern?"

"Now tell me you know her. You know everybody."

The actor grinned and shook his head. "She's in the columns a lot and she was pointed out to me in the spots, that's as near as I went. Don't lose it, Lloyd, what else you gonna do in your spare time?"

"Watch baseball, I guess. You like baseball, Dobie?"

The laugh exploded over the room. "I'm a Yankee-hater from way back."

"You're my man. Let's go see the Red Sox kill the Yankees."

The weekends without Lee were the hardest to bear, but Dobie was making up for some of it. The game was just getting underway when they reached their seats behind the visitors' dugout, comfortably full of whisky and lunch.

"When I was a kid, Dobie, I used to beg, borrow and steal my way into the ballpark. And God oh God how I wanted to be that batboy, just for once."

The sharp pang of memory was sudden at his heart. And could Dobie feel as he did the excitement of this moment, almost to tears? The sky clear and vast above the green field, the uniforms

flashing brilliant across the diamond, the restless, yammering crowd?
Then the standing in silence for "The Star-Spangled Banner," and
that hush before the first pitch. Here for a couple of timeless
hours the world was confined to a total sweetness, there was nothing
else, it was his own joyous wartime with all the enemies of the Red
Sox. Why couldn't they just substitute baseball for *all* their wars,
wouldn't that fill the need for combat? Could any man be happier
than these guys out there on the field? They had their battle every
day, their chance, their trial, and took their hero's rest each night to
start again tomorrow.

Dobie said, grinning at the upper stands between innings, "They
know we're here, baby, that camera's right on us."

"It's a Jay Weiss stunt, wouldn't you know, he got us the
tickets."

"Well, you gonna wave back?"

"The hell I am, and neither are you."

But how much it would have meant to him if this was Fenway
Park instead of the Stadium! To come home like this, a hero of
sorts like those men in uniform out there, Lloyd Garner, a Boston
boy, sought out by the TV camera in the stands, sitting there with
another famous television face, Harvey and Stan and the whole
crowd over at the station looking at him, talking about him. Suddenly
nostalgia filled him, and Dobie, watching, touched his arm. "Where
are you now, soul brother?"

"Boston, if you have to know. I put in nine years there, Dobie,
and I'll never get it back. Sometimes 6 A.M. to midnight, ripping
and reading. Giving weather and baseball scores and traffic con-
ditions. Coming in at dawn to open the station and filling with
farm bureau reports. Doing police missing persons at seven, diet
hints at eight-thirty, grabbing the UPI hourly roundup in between.
Maybe some days I'd pick up a couple of four-dollar fees for commercials, if I was lucky." He laughed, remembering. "The things
that could happen, you wouldn't believe the lousy amateur operation.
Once our sports reporter was getting ready to call a Boston College
game and the technician on the field got his wires crossed. He told
Skelly, 'Get the lead out of your ass, here comes "The Star-Spangled
Banner," ' and by mistake his voice boomed out of the amplifiers."

"What happened?"

"Nothing. Thirty thousand people stood up."

"I used to be a man in the street reporter myself, sponsored by Timberlake's Drugstore," Dobie said. "That's how I got my start in radio, on a two-fifty-watter in McKeesport. If they hadn't of fired me I'd be there still."

"Why did they fire you?"

"I asked a farmer how crops looked and he said they looked goddamn lousy and I told him he shouldn't use bad language on the air and he said then why the fuck did I ask him? The studio threw the key on us and played 'Nearer My God to Thee' on the organ."

"The great days of radio," Lloyd said, and settled back to some more beer with a hot dog in the other hand. Sparky Lyle's slider was working well, Yaz got a triple in the fifth. But it wasn't to last, the visitors ran into trouble in the seventh and still more trouble in the eighth. *Pepitone and White, those murderers.* Final score: Yankees 7, Red Sox 3, another one lost.

"Never mind, the season's young yet," Lloyd was hoarse from his shouting, "they can still win the pennant again."

"Yeah, and this way you can still lose your voice."

"My day to yowl, Dobie. Let's climb out of here, I'm thirsty."

They taxied back downtown and drank and ate at Christ Cella's, dutifully signing autographs whenever anybody came up to the table. It felt strange being on the town without Lee but the bourbon softened the sadness. Dobie was telling him he should have known Cella's as it once was, when the regulars sat across from the stove, and Lloyd said, "Pietro's is still like that."

"You know Pete? You know Nat?" The hairy paws drummed happily on the table.

"Lee loves it," he said, as naturally as if they'd been there together last night, but they wouldn't be together there, or anywhere, again. He stood up abruptly. "Let's crawl, Dobie."

He hadn't crawled since the night he made Third Avenue with Harvey Lewin, poor old Harvey, he could see him sitting in some shabby saloon off Scollay Square staring at the TV. He probably caught the Lloyd Garner show every night and nursed what it did to him.

Dobie led the way tonight, they walked up Second to Fifty-fifth, and Lloyd took some deep breaths and felt a little better. "The fresh air's what I needed, Dobie."

"This is air?"

In Clarke's they had a couple with Jimmy Glennon. Dobie introduced him across the bar. "He'll bullshit you, Jimmy, but he's all heart underneath."

"So are you," Jimmy Glennon said with his short, sharp laugh, "and God knows you're the biggest bullshitter of them all."

Afterward they backtracked to Lembo's for two more, then moved slowly northward on First, stopping now and then for a single in the crowded places where the just-beginners in buttondown shirts were making it with minis from the model agencies. "Dobrinoff, why you no get married and settle down like these kids will?"

"I've had it, twice, master. Any cat still wants to get married after twice is out of his tree."

"I want to marry Lee Maxton."

"You told me, remember?"

"That's Lloyd Garner," he heard the voice at his left say, and he wheeled at the bar and stared at the group. "I was just telling them who you are," the kid laughed, "they don't believe me. Now you know," he said to his friends, "that's Lloyd Garner."

"You want to make something of it?" He raised an arm.

This time the laugh was stricken. "What's that, Mr. Garner?"

"And that's Dobie What'shisname," one of the girls said. "Hi, Dobie, I've seen you lots." She was an edible nineteen in a beret, striped fisherman's sweater and very short skirt.

"Come with us, little doll, you want to grow up very fast?" said Dobie What'shisname. She was giggling and the boy next to her put down his beer and took her arm firmly. Lloyd turned his back on them and finished his drink. "Dobie, your mouth is watering, it's time to move." They steered each other out and up the block.

"Where now, master?"

"Home to bed, Dobie."

"Listen." He was teetering at the curb. "I thought of something, this house over on Lex, most gorgeous hookers in New York, a swimming pool yet, everything. We go as many as we can, all included for a C apiece. They got mirrors, electricity, the works, how about it?"

"Not if there's electricity."

"Man, you're insane, they do wonderful things to you."

"Yeah, but I don't know whether I'm AC or DC." He was signaling a cab. "Good night, Yogi Bear, you're all heart."

The phone was ringing as he opened the apartment door, for a wild half-drunken moment he thought it might be Lee. Then Earl Greminger said, "Lloyd? We've been trying to reach you. Buck says you better get over here. There's trouble in Cleveland, it looks like the worst yet."

23

Ten dead in Cleveland's night, three of them policemen and seven Negroes. Eighteen wounded, fifty arrested, looting and burning losses still not estimated. Bill Moran, back from Vietnam with his unfailing capacity to find the bloodshed, had been in the midst of it. "This is it," Buck Schonwald said, "now watch the chain reaction."

The country had been waiting for it, the papers filled up with reports of a timed series of black uprisings and a snipers' war. Police mobilized in the cities, Washington issued appeals, the law-and-order issue rode high toward the Republican National Convention soon to convene in Miami Beach.

In New York Lloyd Garner anchored a series of prime-time specials with spots from Cleveland, Detroit, Chicago, Baltimore, Atlanta, Memphis and Los Angeles. The networks marshaled their news forces from coast to coast, the red alert was on. Among the telegrams from viewers was one from Tom Hollis, the tobacco tycoon, recalling a conversation at Quince Barony. Walter Hacklin, just returned from Europe, said, "I want a copy of that, Lloyd. Better send a copy to Milo's office too." He was looking at Lloyd with respect. "Didn't know you knew Hollis."

"Just a chance meeting at a house party. We talked a little."

"And you'll be sure to write him a very cordial response to his wire."

"Rest assured, Walter."

But Tom Hollis's forecast failed to materialize. Gradually, day by day, the story faded, the latest surprise in this unpredictable year. It was now no longer sure there ever was a plot for co-ordinated Negro rebellion, or had it misfired after Cleveland? Or had the plotters lost heart or changed their plan because of troop mobilization and preventive arrests? Or would it all come later in the year?

For now, the long hot summer had cooled off again and there was time for a breather before moving the show to Miami Beach. Lloyd had a drink with Dobie Dobrinoff at the King Cole bar. "You're wearing that beard again."

"I left it on for you, little darling, and to annoy Salvador over there." Dali was sitting at a nearby table. "Uncle Ed did the soap this week."

"Still advising young girls in Wiseacre Valley?"

"Something like that. Any news from Montana?"

"Don't even talk about it."

"Take heart. They all come back if you wait, you'll see how it comes out."

"All the others, maybe, but not this one."

"How you know, master?"

"I know."

"So you're going to let it bug you? Che sará, sará, as our old buddy Rita would say."

"I miss Rita. I guess."

"Yeah. Did you know she's living with some guy in Rome that worked for TV news here?"

Lloyd stared at him. Of course, that would explain all of it. "Bev Hambleton by name?"

"I didn't ask the name. He's rich and social."

"Who told you, Dobie?"

"English actor chap just back from making a picture. Does a great take-off on Burton."

Rita and Bev, together in Rome. He smiled. For a change, something made him feel better. He wished them well, he wished them very well. He stood up, "Got to pack my duds, Dobie. Miami in the morning."

"Tricky Dicky got it all sewed up?"

"So they tell me. Anyway, the show must go on."

But there was other big news before the Convention show went on. The Pope startled the world by reaffirming traditional doctrine on birth control. The Russians suddenly renewed their pressure on Czechoslovakia. Once more a round of quick specials anchored by Lloyd Garner, this time from Miami Beach, on international reaction to the papal ruling and protests from aroused American priests and Catholic laymen, never forgetting equal time for rebuttal by their bishops. Watching and listening to the monitor screen sunk in his broadcast desk, Lloyd marveled at the seeming certainty of these old men who must know as well as everybody else that overpopulation was the root of the world's problems. And in central Europe the crisis boiling over again, Russell Gibson reporting from Prague, Kent Ward from Washington. It gave the Republicans a brand new campaign brickbat, see what comes of trusting the Soviets' peaceful assurances. The hassle seesawed, the Czechs agreed to fire their recalcitrant general, then defied the Politburo at Cierna while the pendulum swung back.

Troops were on the move the night before the Convention opened but Lloyd Garner, voice over film, told his audience, "This is Bratislava. The Czech leaders sit opposite the Russians at the conference table. The story is in the faces. *You are not our masters.* The Czechs have won."

In Miami Beach, sun-scorched and rain-splattered by turns, only the resident one-time refugees from Hitler seemed to be paying much attention to what went on in Europe. They had heard news like that before and probably thought it was too good to last. They and the refugees from Castro were the only people to whom this carnival midway by the ocean had any more than a transient reality. Looking the place over in a Hertz convertible while Jay Weiss collected color beside him, Lloyd had seen them emerging from the sleazy small hotels at the southern end of Collins Avenue to buy The New York *Times* from their later Cuban compatriots, then disappearing into the lox and bagel joints on every corner for breakfast. Northward along the strip, a planet away, in the huge plastic palaces with private beaches, the delegates were engrossed in preparations for their dullest national convention in history. It was a fact accepted in advance and nobody expected it to be anything else. Ronald Reagan's hopes and Nelson Rockefeller's assertions to the contrary, it would be Nixon on the first ballot, the rest was window-dressing. And this time there would be no unsettled world outside to crowd the ceremony with its doubts or misgivings, Miami

Beach was not Miami. Police units held the bridges against any possible invasion by disruptive elements from the American mainland. It was a nice Republican feeling to know all this, as Kent Ward had pointed out on opening day, and factions like the Poor People's Campaign which turned loose a bunch of rowdy pickaninnies in the palace lobbies were not to be taken seriously, they were just out of place. Such ineffectual noise as they were able to raise was easily drowned out by the Eureka Marching Band of New Orleans, pro-Nixon. Southern delegates noted with satisfaction there were still some good darkies around. Additional moral reassurance was provided by the genial presence of the Reverend Billy Graham, who aced the fourth hole on a pitch-and-putt links at Key Biscayne and said he liked to think the Apostle Paul was the first golfer, "He fought the good fight and finished the course."

Inside the convention hall, spearheading the flow of information from a total network staff of six hundred and an array of equipment in trucks and trailers spread across an acre around the hall, Lloyd Garner watched the desultory rituals move toward climax on the floor below, Kent Ward at his side, Hal Thorpe off camera to their right and Earl Greminger to their left. Behind the broadcast booth in Main Control, where Bob Lentz called the camera shots from a bank of stand-by monitors, Buck Schonwald presided over the intercom system and issued the coverage orders to separate control areas in touch with the reporters inside and outside the hall in the streets beyond. For two days now this elaborate establishment had functioned through presentations of the colors, pledges of allegiance, national anthems, calls to order, invocations, speeches, benedictions and everything that went with them except news. Each night Lloyd Garner went to bed in his room at the Fontainebleau after boning up with Earl Greminger on the next day's boredom in his vast data book. The Dade County public works department had chosen this week to paint the traffic-light pole near the hotel driveway, creating an impossible bottleneck to add to the indescribable confusion of movement, with the result that the only way to beat the jam and get to work under an hour's travel time was to go by boat.

It turned out to be the pleasantest experience of the day. Out here

on the water at least he wasn't recognized, pursued by the autograph
pack, shouted to across the crowded lobbies, surrounded at the
candidates' mammoth cocktail parties where he attracted more attention than most of the delegates. In Miami Beach there was no
escape but to the quiet of his hotel room, a quiet only relative
because weary as he was he could still awake at the tramping
footsteps in the corridors when they came back loaded at two or
three or four from the night clubs, the noisy celebrating wives,
the drinking that went on twenty-four hours a day in the oil
company public relations headquarters down the hall. Already, with
the convention only two days old, he was too tense and tired
from lack of sleep. And the Democrats would be even worse, they
always were, Jay Weiss warned him, with the added troubles this
year of the Chicago telephone strike and crippled communications,
the networks had failed to get the convention transferred to Miami.
Weiss, as usual, occupied the room next to his and escorted him
everywhere outside the hotel.

Now, coming down the hall from the elevator, resigned to another
turbulent night, he noticed the light through the crack under his
door but didn't think about it until he turned the key and went in.
The girl was sitting in the big chair near the window, facing the
door as if waiting for him.

"Good evening," she said, not moving. She looked very calm. "You
can close the door, I'm not going to shoot you."

He was standing staring at her. "I'm afraid you're in the wrong
room," he said after a moment.

"I'm in the right room. Will you please shut the door?"

She was coming into better focus in the light of the big floor
lamp, a tall girl, young, with something about her that vaguely
reminded him of Rita Valenti. He heard his own brief laugh.
"Will you kindly tell me how you got in here?"

"The door was unlocked. Either you or the maid must have left
it that way." Her voice was not unpleasantly husky. She still
hadn't moved her hands from her lap.

"That's possible," he said and tried to remember whether he'd
locked it. "But it doesn't explain what you're doing here."

She smiled a little. "I wanted to talk to you. Can you think of a better place?"

"Look, young lady." He took the key out and swung the door shut behind him. "Look, this is my room and I happen to be very tired. I want to go to bed. If it's an autograph then tell me your name and let me sign something and be a nice person and just leave, will you?"

"My name is Jan Moreno but I want more than an autograph. And if you're tired and you want to go to bed don't let me stop you, go right ahead."

He laughed again. "With you sitting here?"

"Why not?"

In the silence he sat down on the edge of the bed and looked at her, seeing her look back at him with a glimmer of amusement in her almond eyes, still perfectly self-possessed. She had clasped her hands, strong and long-fingered, and sat there as if waiting for him to speak again. Finally he said, "Tell me something, Miss Moreno, do they let you wander around this hotel just trying doors to see if they're unlocked? I thought the place was full of security guards."

"It is, but by now they think I'm a delegate's daughter or something like that. I've been waiting for a week for a chance to see you alone."

"A week?"

"I was sure I could do it Saturday or Sunday but you started staying out somewhere very late. Whose party was it?"

The tone of cool interrogation made him chuckle. "Why should I tell you where I was? Suppose you tell me how you get into this hotel every day, or do you live here?"

"I come in through the kitchen. I almost had you last night. Who's that man living next door to you?"

"What's he got to do with it?"

"He got to your room ahead of me."

"That's too bad, Miss Moreno. But I'm surprised somebody with your gall didn't just come in anyway."

She smiled. "Not with two men here."

"You had a feeling we might rape you, something like that?"

"Maybe."

"It's just as easy for one man to rape you as two, have you considered that?"

"Lloyd," she said, "let's not waste time talking nonsense."

"Then would you mind just saying whatever you have to say and let me turn in? I've had a long day, several long days in fact."

She nodded at the bottle of bourbon on the table and said, "Aren't you going to have a nightcap? And can I have one too?"

"Not if I'm going to find myself in some police court charged with corrupting a minor."

"I'm not a minor. I'm twenty years old."

He appraised her. "Miss Moreno, we'll have a drink on condition you'll agree to go away after we finish it."

"If you want me to, yes."

He shrugged and stood up. "Soda or plain water?"

"Whichever you take," she said.

He poured her a modest highball and made a strong one for himself, then sat down on the bed again. "Now. Who *is* Jan Moreno and why is she sitting in my room at one o'clock in the morning?"

"Jan Moreno is a secretary who lives in Miami."

"I'm sorry, I don't need a secretary."

"She doesn't need a job, she already has one."

He was beginning to like her impudence somehow, now that the oddness of the encounter was wearing off. "Then what does she need?"

She laughed. "Not what you're thinking, not necessarily. But I guess you get a lot of offers like that."

"I'm not thinking anything, I'm merely asking."

"She needed to meet Lloyd Garner and she did."

"Is that all?"

"She knew that if she wrote him a note he'd throw it in the basket, so she tried something else and she was lucky."

"But why Lloyd Garner?"

"Because he's important."

"Come on, Miss Moreno, there're a lot more important people than Lloyd Garner around here right now."

She shook her head. "Not to me they aren't."

"In other words," he said, "you're a loyal viewer."

"Every time you're on the air, since the first night, I'm watching."

"It must be a bore for the rest of the family."

"No family. My mother, that's all."

He drained his drink, he was relaxing. "And your mother works in the kitchen here, is that it?"

Suddenly her laughter pealed. "No, that isn't it."

"You'll have to keep your voice down, I've got a duenna in the next room."

"I thought so. Sometimes he gives me the eye in the hall."

"I wouldn't blame him for that."

She smiled. "I don't see you giving me the eye."

"I may just do that," he said, "if you don't finish your drink and go home."

"I've finished it and I want another one. Aren't you going to have another one?"

"I am, yes." He stood up again. "But you're not."

"I'm not attractive enough to get the eye from Lloyd Garner, right?"

"You're very attractive. Remember your promise. Go."

"When you're all tucked in for the night, yes."

They were both laughing like friends. He went back to the table. "This is positively the last drink, for both of us."

"Then make me a decent one, please? Not that little thing you gave me the first time."

He did. She sat back contented with it and seemed to have no more to say, and he wondered how many others like Jan Moreno were prowling the convention hotels tonight. A troop of delegates and wives thundered past the door on their way to the oil company suite down the hall. "Don't they ever sleep?" he said. For a moment his eyes blurred and he put his hand up, he was getting drowsy.

"Poor boy," she said softly. "Poor, tired boy."

"I'm tired all right."

"Get undressed and get into bed, I'm going to rub your back till you go to sleep."

That was the last step before sex. But he felt no need for sex, from this girl or from anybody, not since Lee. "You're going home, Jan Moreno."

As if in reply she switched off the lamp. "You're going to bed," he heard her say in the darkness, "and then I'll leave."

Suddenly he was so weary he didn't care whether she stayed or went, and she was standing beside him, helping him off with his jacket. She didn't surprise him any more, he only knew he felt like a child in the secret dark. Now he was sitting on the bed again and he could see her dimly outlined. She was kneeling in front of him, slipping off his shoes while his fingers groped to unbutton his shirt. "Poor, tired boy," she said again, the soothing voice no longer the voice of a stranger. He stood up to drop his trousers and she pulled down the bedcovers and put her hands on his shoulders, gently guiding him to lie face down on the sheets. "Now isn't that better?" she whispered. He felt her pulling up his undershirt and touching his bare back, her hands were cool and tender and firm.

She was reaching all his nerves. "My God that's good, you're sweet." He heard his own muffled words. He felt nothing sexual at all, only the relief of this searching, kneading pressure on his body, only the kindness of her hands. The sounds from the hall receded, the darkness was deeper, the room was slipping away from him. He closed his eyes and gave himself gratefully to sleep.

Jay Weiss woke him with the usual signal, knocking repeatedly on their connecting door until Lloyd acknowledged it. His watch said nearly eleven, he must have slept a long time. Only when he realized he was still in his shorts did he remember the girl. She had gone while he was sleeping and without leaving a trace of her presence, almost as if he'd imagined it all. Lloyd smiled at his desk as he adjusted his earpiece and faced the camera, thanks to a girl named Jan Moreno he felt rested and refreshed.

Jack Milhouse, down there below him on the convention floor, was asking Hall Control for the mike again. He had prevailed on Walter Hacklin to bring his morning news show from New York, contrary to Schonwald's plans, and had further pleaded for interview assignments during the sessions, in which he had emerged as the most persistent questioner of delegates on the network staff. The questions were usually longer than the answers. "Jack's offering Romney with new angles," repeated Hall Control, and Buck Schonwald said from Main Control, "We'll take Milhouse now."

Lloyd sighed and sat back, looking across the convention hall at Tom Hardwick and Graham Gordon in the other network booths. There were no new angles in the interview but Jack Milhouse was on the air, which was what mattered to Jack Milhouse. "That dead horse again," said Ward. He smiled, but not at Lloyd. He was professionally cordial when they were on camera together, but that was it. He was still as distant as their last shows together in Paris.

Greminger was taking advantage of the break to lean over and put a piece of copy in front of him, a list of those expected to be nominated tonight for the presidency, Nixon, Reagan, Romney, Rockefeller, wait a minute, *two* Rockefellers, Nelson and Winthrop, also Thurmond, Case, Rhodes, Fong, Carlson, Hickel and, of course, Stassen. Lloyd would read the list during the first reasonably long stretch of time available and then turn it over to Ward, who could have himself a minor field day with the hopeless cases and the perennial Stassen. Lloyd didn't care how much spotlight Kent Ward got, he always enjoyed Ward. It was Milhouse, down on the floor, who annoyed him. He was making a name for himself with a lot of people who never saw the morning news and between sessions he was ingratiating himself with Hacklin and Milo Wilson in the network's hospitality suite at the hotel. He was also using his morning program to interview a steady stream of controversial delegates, something the convention anchorman couldn't do in the booth, and he was attending caucuses on his own wherever he could get in, even when they'd been assigned to other reporters, then phoning tips to Ferguson in the newsroom adjoining the floor.

Lloyd tapped his foot, listening. "He's going over a lot of stale ground."

"What else is there to talk about?" Kent Ward said.

"How about this?" Greminger said, and thrust another sheet of copy at Lloyd. He could hear Hal Thorpe's voice on the intercom, "Buck, Buck . . . There's a newsroom bulletin on a Negro violence threat across the bay, better go with it right away."

"Tell Milhouse to wrap it up, *now*," Schonwald barked to Hall Control, and in a moment Lloyd had the air again.

"It's just been learned that Florida's Governor Kirk and Negro leader Ralph Abernathy have left the convention and headed for the Liberty City district of Miami in an effort to calm local residents agitating for better housing, education and jobs. Negroes there called a vote-power rally and are charging the police with interference with their legal right of assembly, resulting in some bottle-throwing to which the police responded with a tear gas barrage. The governor and the Reverend Abernathy intend to hear their protests and make a personal appeal to the Negro leaders to restore order among their people before the situation develops into a major racial disturbance." Lloyd paused and added, *"We have our own team of reporters at the scene and we'll bring you a direct report shortly."*

He could hear Schonwald barking to Street Control, "Get Moran, get Moran for a remote," while on the stand-by monitor he could see Jack Milhouse looking up at the booth again and talking excitedly into his mike. Hall Control broke in, "Milhouse ready to go again with comment on the Negro trouble, Buck. Buck, can you hear me?"

The hell with Milhouse, Lloyd Garner could do it any day as well as Milhouse. Lloyd Garner had air now and he was keeping it.

"It's to be doubted," he said, *"whether most of the Republican Party delegates here in the convention hall are paying much attention right now to these developments across the bay in Liberty City, they're too busy getting ready to whoop it up for their favorites as the race for the nomination enters its last hours. The simple fact seems to be that in all the speeches made so far at this convention, in all the assurances given by the candidates for the nomination, in public and private, none of them have seemed to come to grips with the real problem of poverty, resentment and bitterness among Negroes that right now is boiling up on the other side of Biscayne Bay as it has boiled up this summer at sorespots all over the nation. For all these delegates seem to be thinking about that problem, what's happening in Liberty City at this moment might as well be happening in some foreign country."*

He paused. He was aware that Kent Ward had leaned forward and was listening intently. *"Was it by design,"* he went on, his thought racing ahead of him, *"that Miami Beach was chosen so as to insulate this convention carefully from the real happenings of the real world? Are these Republicans, in their comfortable optimism, in the luxury of their hotel rooms on this safe little island off the mainland, in their well-heeled security at home, are they so sure of an election victory this year that they can afford to ignore the real threat to the nation's unity we've seen burst out so recently in Cleveland, in the other big cities of our country? It's to be hoped it isn't so,"* said Lloyd Garner. *"It's to be feared it may be so."*

He saw the commercial break signal suddenly warning him. *"We'll be back in a moment,"* he smiled at the camera, and the message rose at once on the monitor to soothing music, it was springtime in living color, it was brookside, a man and a girl were trying each other's cigarettes, everything was going to be all right. In the moment he thought of Tom Hollis and wondered if he'd been listening to what Lloyd Garner had just said. Hal Thorpe was grinning at him. There was an expression like surprise, like friendliness, on Kent Ward's face.

Buck Schonwald said, appearing abruptly, angrily, in the doorway behind him, "Lloyd, for Christ's sweet sake, are you out of your skull? You keep that up and we won't have a friend left around here." He slammed the booth door shut again and went back to Main Control, Lloyd didn't look back. He was looking down at the convention floor, where Jack Milhouse was staring up at the booth and snarling something to Hall Control into his mike. "Moran standing by," Street Control said on the intercom, and Schonwald's voice said, "We'll go to him right after this commercial."

It was too bad about Milhouse. They would switch next to Bill Moran in Liberty City and then it would be time to start talking about tonight's candidates for the nomination.

He was standing in the rain-sodden crowd at the foot of the marble staircase, so long its upper reaches were lost in the black clouds billowing in off the Atlantic. The shouting was splitting his eardrums, but where was it coming from? All the faces were silent, thousands of them, watching the stairway and waiting, and nobody was looking at him, that was what hurt. Then the shouting was nearer, the mist up there was breaking into rainbow. Suddenly, triumphantly, the sun burst through in a shower of golden balloons and he could hear the band playing "Happy Days Are Here Again." That was Nixon dancing soft-shoe down the marble steps, his arms linked with John Lindsay and Jack Milhouse, all three in top hats and tails, all three singing and waving to the crowd, knees dipping, feet kicking in perfect unison, white carnations in their lapels, white teeth gleaming with the big smile. Applause like thunder rolled up at them from below and a man standing behind him almost knocked him off his feet. *"You blind or something? Clap, you fag!"* It was Schonwald. Fearfully he clapped his hands, he tried to shout with all the others but no sound came from his stricken throat. A phone was ringing. His eyes still closed, he rolled over and answered it, "Yeah?"

"Earl Greminger, Lloyd. You won't believe it but I thought you'd like to know. He's just announced his running mate. Spiro Agnew."

He was suddenly awake. "You've got to be kidding me." Then he laughed. "And I was just dreaming Lindsay was in." He didn't mention Jack Milhouse.

"A cold-blooded deal with Thurmond. It's going to hurt him."

"Nothing hurts him. Not any more."

"We're putting together a lot more stuff on Agnew, I'll be around when it's ready. I suggest you go over the Agnew stuff in the folder, right? He's the story tonight."

"Floor fight?"

"I wouldn't be surprised from the way the boys were talking after the announcement. I'll bring all that."

His eyes were getting used to the light of day. Even the heavy drapes over the windows couldn't keep out that crazy sun altogether. Slowly he sat up and swung his legs over the side of the bed. His head ached and he had a hangover, the first of the Convention. He shouldn't have let Jay Weiss lure him off to that Italian place, what was it called? Too many bourbons and too much red wine, he was tired, tired, tired, thank God this would be the last heavy day. Tottering erect he went into the bathroom and turned on the shower, in a little while he'd have to start thinking again. That was the trouble with the anchor booth at a Convention, you had to think, and when you started thinking things came out of you ad-lib you didn't suspect were in you, and it was the Martin Luther King broadcast all over again. You said what you felt and the bosses came down on you like a landslide. This time, though, Hacklin hadn't said anything, not yet, anyway. And Lloyd had ducked out with Weiss right after sign-off before Schonwald could get back to him. But not before Kent Ward, still at his desk, had looked across at him and said quietly, "Good night, Lloyd, good show." He'd even smiled a little, for the first time since Washington!

How long ago it seemed, could he even remember what Lloyd Garner was then? Only that he was not the same Lloyd Garner who sat before that microphone in Miami Beach last night. He sighed and stepped under the warm, soothing douche. He felt glad and relieved and uneasy, all at once. Had he really meant to say what he said on the air? Every time he said what he thought, there were headaches; he'd be glad to be back in the New York routine. In New York it was all done for you, all right there on Teleprompter, predigested and condensed to bulletin length, you didn't have to think about a thing. That's all the viewers wanted anyway, bulletins and commercials, they were itching to get it over with and get on with the movie. Buck Schonwald was right, they wouldn't stay tuned to anybody longer than a minute and a half unless you had the pictures, preferably violent, and already they'd seen so much violence overseas and at home it had to be damn bloody to make air. He'd bet Milo Wilson was shuddering at this Convention's ratings, the stale hoopla, the empty speeches, no matter how you tried to jazz it up for them nobody believed it any more. Then what did they believe? Even that was no longer mysterious. The computers knew, from now on the People Machine would be picking the candidates and arranging the elections. As Kent Ward said last night in his closing, it was the last year for the Conventions as the country knew them. Somebody would have to invent some other way to hold the TV audience.

A floor fight, Earl Greminger had said. Well maybe, in a manner of speaking. Now, looking down from the booth at the final session, Lloyd saw most of it being promoted by the reporters on the floor, and the delegates were responding as if they knew it was hail and farewell. But it wasn't up to them, not really. Lloyd Garner, sitting omniscient, omnipotent, high above, saw them as puppets on the television string. It was Lloyd Garner, fount from which all knowledge flowed, the wisdom fed to him in capsules as occasion required from Greminger's vast file, the political record and personal history of every man and woman of interest on that floor, it was Lloyd Garner who told the only truth of what was happening down there. For it wasn't so until television told it, unless television wanted it, and, if it wasn't good enough, until television made it better.

Last chance to get yourselves on the magic screen, ladies and gentlemen, last chance to tell the world, if we decide to let you, last chance to pretend it wasn't all settled before you came into this hall tonight and that you as individuals had some choice, had some say. The anchorman smiled as he looked down through the bulletproof glass, watched Milhouse move from delegation to delegation. Let him scramble, it was his final appearance. There was a flurry in Rhode Island, New York was restive, dead horse George Romney emerged for the last time as the liberal hope. But the steamroller had already started on its way from the Hilton Plaza and there was no stopping it now, the theme was Republican unity and the symbol was Richard Nixon, who would be all things to all men.

Listening to the acceptance speech, Lloyd glanced at a report just phoned by Bill Moran from the riot area in Liberty City. A pitched battle developing between Negroes and police, Vietnam in the streets of Miami. But that was another story, you couldn't hear the shooting in the convention hall. These were politicians, across the bay they were only people. They could wait until after the ovation, the people would have to wait.

24

Earl Greminger came in from the studio holding a sheaf of wire copy and looking worried. "The Czecho thing is heating up again, Lloyd. More troop movements near the borders. We should have known it wasn't going to be as easy as that."

"You think they'll move in this time?"

"If they do it'll be Hungary all over again. Buck just told Gibson to go back to Prague."

The new crisis developed with co-ordinated deliberation. One by one, taking their cues from the Kremlin, the Warsaw Pact satellites lined up against their sister regime. Only Romania dared this time to stay out and speak up, with open support from the Communist parties in France and Italy, while Tito encouraged the rebels from the side lines. Lights burned all night in the Vienna embassies, the Prague-Moscow air shuttle went back into daily operation. As far as the Russians were concerned the Bratislava agreement had failed to do the job. But the Czechs, Russ Gibson reported now from their capital, were closing ranks behind the adamant Dubcek. "This far," they declared, "and no farther."

From Washington Kent Ward doubted that the Russians were going to bluff twice. Nato was worried, and so was the White House, the President was understood to be privately urging Kosygin and Brezhnev to take it easy. In New York Lloyd Garner said, "*Attention has been diverted from the political campaign at home, the whole world is watching Central Europe.*" Suddenly he found himself anchoring a fifteen-minute crisis special each night after the eleven o'clock news. Just back from Miami Beach, he was working fifteen hours a day again and for once he was glad to think of nothing else.

Tuesday, Wednesday, Thursday merged into unbroken waiting for the climax. The pressure mounted and waned, solutions and settlements were rumored and dissipated in reports of new military moves. One effect was already certain, as Ward observed on the Friday evening show, the bitterness engendered within the Communist alliance would not die out in this generation. A fateful weekend was beginning in Europe, and the domestic spotlight would now shift to Chicago, where delegates to the Democratic National Convention were gathering a week in advance of the opening session for the battle over the platform. *"We'll be reporting all next week from the convention hall,"* Lloyd said in his closing summary, *"and we hope you'll be with us then."* He smiled his best smile, and he wondered, as he always did now, if Lee Maxton was watching.

All during this week back in New York, knowing she must be back too by now, he had fought his need to call her just once more, to say, to say anything, to hear her voice. But being without her wasn't as hard now as it had been in the first days, he was becoming used to his defeat at last. The unendurable had eased, now it was only this dull, nagging pain at heart that took the spirit out of him. Sometimes, alone at night, the image of Lee naked returned to bring him almost to orgasm, he clenched his hands and pounded the wall to try to shut away the memory of her body. Clearly he had done his best to hold her. It wasn't good enough, and he was tired trying to remember where, how, they had at last gone wrong. If this was the way she wanted it, this was the way it had to be. Maybe, eventually, there would be something to replace her, a thought he couldn't face for now. Boarding the flight for Chicago he felt a sudden sense of relief. At least she wouldn't be in the same city, at least he wouldn't be driving past her apartment late at night, alone in his car, just to look up at the house she lived in, just to look at the door that was closed against him. Was she alone in there? All he had to do was to pick up a phone. No, he couldn't take the bitterness of refusal again. If ever there was another call it would have to come from her.

He felt it as soon as he got off the plane at O'Hare and walked through the airport to the waiting limousine, an electric tension in the air. He saw it in the hostile eyes of police and

obvious plainclothesmen, sizing you up as you went past. He
heard it in the worried briefing Milo Wilson gave Hacklin and
Schonwald on the drive downtown to the Conrad Hilton. Wilson
had been working with the network vanguard on the Chicago ar-
rangements. And Lloyd didn't need to know, as he did already,
that the excuse for all restrictions on TV was the public safety, that
rumors of an assassination plot were sweeping the city, "Daley's
rumors," Schonwald called them, or that today National Guard
units had started moving in to help control antiwar demonstrations
in the streets expected to provide setting for the most tumultuous
political convention in modern American history. Even this week
before the convention began it was going to be tumultuous enough
inside the committee rooms where the Democratic platform would
be hammered out between factions already at war over credentials
and the unit rule, between Humphreyites and McCarthyites, hawks
and doves. And once the big show got underway it was going to be
tough enough to handle with the communications strike, the short-
age of phones, and Daley's crippling limitations on TV news coverage. The networks had been fighting it for weeks, from the White
House to City Hall, but it was a losing battle. Lyndon Johnson and
the party establishment held the reins and were not about to drop
them.

"We're doing everything possible," Milo Wilson was saying as
the car swept into the city, "but we still can't find out how many
cameras they're allowing on the floor and they're still stalling on
the number of passes for the reporters."

"The bastards," Schonwald muttered. "What about remotes?"

"The union's still refusing to allow microwave coverage, so no
mobile units. Walter, we can't even get permission to park outside
the Hilton or the Blackstone, and the parking lots won't give us any
space."

"They'll give it to you if you offer them enough money, they're
just using the situation to jack you up."

"They won't do it at any price, Walter, we tried that."

There was a pause. "So. The fix is in."

"It looks that way. The union says absolutely no live facilities except for the amphitheater, which means we're cut off from all hotel headquarters for the duration."

"What about the police?"

"We've assured headquarters our cameramen won't use lights to attract a crowd, and we'll cap the lenses if anybody tries to use us for the action."

Wilson sat back and sighed. "I've got a bad feeling," he said.

"You've got a bad feeling!" said Schonwald.

The Conrad Hilton stood massive and somehow grim amid the newer buildings along the lake front as the flashy Fontainebleau had also faced the water, but there the resemblance ended. The suave good humors of Miami Beach had been replaced by a tangible hardness of purpose in the atmosphere incomparably different from what had gone before. This was a hard town and something else was going to happen here. Lloyd felt its pervading imminence as they drove up Michigan Avenue and debarked under the scrutiny of more police at the door. Cops were all over the lobby, too, watchful and wary. "Two o'clock in the amphitheater," Schonwald said in the groaning elevator, "and we'll see if anything works."

Jay Weiss, of course, had been assigned the room adjoining Lloyd's. He could hear the little PR man cursing at the phone five minutes after they unpacked their bags. "I can't even get the operator!" he shouted through the connecting door, "the goddamn thing's out of order." But it wasn't any more out of order than Lloyd's phone. They gave up waiting for room service and drank Lloyd's emergency bourbon tempered slightly with water from the bathroom tap. "I got treated better in the Saigon Caravelle," Weiss whined. "Let's get out of this flea bag and eat a Chicago steak."

There was certainly nothing in Miami Beach to compare with that steak, discounting the stockyard stench that pervaded everything in the amphitheater area. Schonwald and most of the network news team were already there eating when Lloyd and Jay arrived at the big, noisy restaurant. Walter Hacklin, naturally, could be reached with the upper echelon at something called the Standard Club, Buck said, where he was mingling with his own rank and maintaining personal contact with the kingmakers. Lloyd said, out of

Weiss's earshot, "I see I've got Jay on my back again," and the producer growled cheerfully, "Yeah, with strict orders from me not to let you out of his sight."

"That's nice, you afraid I'll be kidnapped maybe?"

"With this town the way it is now, fellow, anything could happen."

But it wasn't Chicago that took the spotlight as the new week began, not yet. The Communist armies of eastern Europe made their move. Russians, Poles, East Germans, Hungarians and Bulgarians coldly invaded and methodically occupied Czechoslovakia, seized its liberal leaders and canceled all previous deals. This time the nightly news specials were anchored from Chicago, where Kent Ward noted the inevitable repercussions, the peace candidates for the Democratic nomination had been hurt.

Not that anybody really expected McCarthy to win it, but forlorn hope remained among the faithful that Ted Kennedy might somehow ride in on a draft and give the antiwar forces their miracle. Lloyd, lying numb with fatigue on his bed after the latest special, listened to the delegates tramp and chatter along the hotel corridor. They'd been getting noisier and more numerous night by night. Convention eve traffic was heaviest of all. Some damn fool among them stopped at the door just then and began rapping insistently, he had the wrong address. "Lloyd, baby, you inside?" Dobie Dobrinoff said finally, "it's only me."

It couldn't be, but it was. The wild grin awaited him in the hall. "How come, Dobie?" He was suddenly awake and glad.

"On my way back from the Coast and the flight made a Chicago stop, that's how come."

"But you've got no place to stay, there isn't a hotel room in town."

"Hugh's always got a bed for me, you been over there yet?"

The invitation was in a pile of mail on his bureau. "Isn't this for later?"

"Honey, that party started years ago."

Lloyd put his ear to the connecting door, not a sound from Jay Weiss's room. "Just checking my night nurse, Dobie, he's either asleep or dead."

The lobby was even more of a madhouse than when he came in

from the amphitheater today, they ran the gauntlet from the elevator. Some McCarthy kids near the door were singing a campaign song, one of them grabbed at Dobie's suitcase as they went through and slapped a sticker on it. "Ooh-ooh!" trilled a voice, "that's Lloyd Garner with him!" But they were safely past and in a taxi.

"I caught you a lot on the Coast, Lloyd, you been working."

"Yeah, haven't you?"

"A nothing, a quick bit, but it was bread."

"Would I like it out there?"

"Man, it's your kind of country. The girls taste burnt orange."

"I wish I could look at women the way you do, like a piece of filet mignon."

The actor turned and kissed his cheek. "It's the only way."

"You nut, you slobbered all over me."

"Try Kleenex. You glad we're back together?"

"More than you know, Dobie."

"Listen, how's Lee Babe?"

"That's why I'm glad you're here."

Dobie Dobrinoff put his arm around him. "So what's gonna be?"

"Forget it. This is a permanent boycott."

"What's that, some new perversion?" His laugh blew out to the front seat and the man at the wheel gave them a wizened smile from the rearview mirror. "Chicago," Dobie said. "Crazy."

"That's right," the driver said.

"What's with all these police?"

"You heard about it. The Yippies."

"Yippies wouldn't hurt you. I'm a Yippie."

"You're no Yippie," the driver said. "I think I drove you before."

"You know it, sonny, I was doing radio out of here when you were in knee pants."

He cackled. "Not me, I'm sixty-three Tuesday."

"I'm seventy-one Wednesday," Dobie said, "happy birthday." He gave him a five-dollar bill getting out. "Buy some extra candles for me."

"Tell your friend to be careful," said the driver, "we wouldn't want no harm to come to him."

The people at the door knew Dobie and recognized Lloyd Garner.

Music and voices drifted through the big house, room gave upon room. Dobie took him on a tour of the place, pausing to observe various sports in progress in the swimming pool, the billiards, the Ping-pong and pinball corners, before they found the center of intellectual activity and met the host and saw the automatic waterfall. The bunnies, of course, were conspicuous among the guests, who seemed about equally divided between political types from the Democratic power centers and refugees from New York and Hollywood night spots. Dobie said, pulling him down beside him on a plushy divan and calling for drinks, "You like my friend's little pad?"

"I think I'll just move in."

A woman's voice startled him. "I thought I might run into you here," Joyce Hacklin said, "but hardly in such bad company." Before they could stand up she had slid in between them, a drink in her hand.

"Were you speaking to him or me?" Dobie said and kissed her.

"You know who I was speaking to, you bum."

They laughed together. Lloyd said, "I didn't know you knew Dobie."

"This one broke me in, Lloyd. I was only a slip of a girl."

The actor was grinning. "Oh, was that you?"

Lloyd looked around them. "Where's Walter?"

"You won't find Walter here, sweetie, this place is for the swingers."

She looked as if she belonged. A waiter brought their drinks and Joyce Hacklin drained her brandy and told him to bring another. "No," she went on, "the real reason Walter's not here is he's afraid somebody might take a picture of him."

"Somebody just took a picture of us." Dobie motioned toward a smiling girl photographer a few feet away.

"And about time too. I've always wanted a picture with Lloyd Garner for my scrapbook."

"How about a picture with me?" Dobie Dobrinoff said.

"Come on, Dobie, *you* remember those pictures of us, and they weren't for any scrapbook." She turned to Lloyd. "How come your bodyguard isn't with you?"

"I ran away from him tonight."

The shrewd and candid eyes were slightly glazed. "I ran away too. I think Walter's asleep. He better be."

"Good old Walter," Dobie said.

"You threw another scare into him in Miami, Lloyd." The husky giggle. "He hasn't been so surprised since you called Martin Luther King a gentleman."

"Oh, that. He hasn't mentioned it."

"Too busy, I guess. He's been half crazy with Chicago problems." Her brandy arrived. "I told him I kind of admired your guts for the Miami speech, but with Walter that's beside the point, of course. The Republicans were anything but flattered, naturally, but then you can't tell a Republican what a Republican is, they don't believe you."

"Yeah." He was smiling.

"If I were you, though, I'd save that kind of stuff for your radio shows. You can say anything on radio and nobody cares."

"So I've noticed."

"George Sowerby does your scripts, right? He's quite a man, Sowerby. That's why he's not writing for TV."

"And you're quite a woman," Lloyd said.

"Look, I know what's going on, anything else you want to know?"

"How do I meet the big boss?"

She threw back her head and laughed. "Don't say I said so, but he's coming out for the nominations."

He was distracted suddenly by a kind of flurry at the other side of the room, a man with a shocked and sheet-white face and a freshly bandaged head was the center of a gathering group near the doorway, seemed to be answering questions, accepted a drink with a shaking hand. "What's that all about?" Lloyd said, standing up. Joyce Hacklin was still talking.

So it was that Lloyd Garner, easy among peers under a special pleasure dome, learned of the first battle of Lincoln Park. The survivor had given the details to the room. It had been a day of peaceful mobilization of the anti-Vietnam forces, of speeches, singing, clowning, which had ended with a show of defiance of the park closing order and a savage police charge aimed as much at the reporters as the demonstrators. The scene was to be repeated with intensified brutality on the Monday and Tuesday nights, but since portable facilities were forbidden, no live pickups were possible from the amphitheater and Lloyd had to report the story verbally during the credentials fight on the floor. One of the short takes rushed to him in the booth said network correspondent Matthew Ferlin had been injured and taken to Wesley Memorial.

Jay Weiss woke him at eight-thirty after four hours' sleep. "Walter wants us to go see Ferlin, Lloyd."

"You go." He rolled over.

"Seriously, Buck called me, he had Hacklin on the phone."

He was trying to open his eyes now. "Is he hurt that bad?"

"Pretty bad, you can come back and sleep some more after, okay? And you better shave."

Lloyd had talked to Ferlin only once since the news team arrived in Chicago. Matt was following the Yippie mobilization with a camera unit and bitching about delays in getting his film on the air. A network still photographer was waiting for them in the lobby when they came out of the elevator. "They going to let me shoot in the hospital?" he said to Weiss in the taxi.

"They better. Matt's our boy."

"Hacklin thinks of everything," Lloyd said.

"That's why he's where he is."

Ferlin's head was bandaged all the way around and he was sitting up sullenly in bed. Lloyd summoned a cheerful grin. "How's my old pal from Paris?"

"I'll live." He looked resentful of more than his injury.

"Anything we can do, Matt boy?" Jay Weiss said and turned immediately to the photographer. "You got enough room?"

"Just move a little closer to the bed and face me," the photographer said to Lloyd. "Now kind of look down at him sympathetically, you know."

"What the hell's going on?" said Ferlin.

"Walter Hacklin wants a picture. He heard Lloyd and me were coming over to see you."

"That was mighty thoughtful of Walter Hacklin."

"Yeah," Weiss said. "Okay, Hurley?"

"Hold it like that." He took several quick shots from two angles. Lloyd said, "How did it happen, Matt?"

"The sons of bitches switched direction all of a sudden and came right at us, we never had a chance to run. One of them grabbed Werner's camera and stomped on it. I had my arms over my head against this cop in front of me, I was holding my badge, but another one hit me from the side. When I came to I was in the ambulance."

"Where was Moran?"

"Lucky, as usual." He glared at him under the bandage. "They shaved off some of my hair, how am I supposed to work without any hair?"

Weiss laughed. "You got your purple heart, man, all you do now is rest up and draw your pay. You want to change places with me?"

"Balls," Ferlin said.

"Can I phone Claudine for you or something?" Lloyd said.

"I talked to her."

The nurse who bustled in from the hall was middle-aged and authoritative. "No more visiting for this patient," she said sharply. "And no pictures." Suddenly she smiled. "Oh. Hello, Mr. Lloyd Garner."

"We're just leaving," Lloyd said.

"Oh, that'll be all right, certainly, Mr. Garner, seeing it's you."

"We got to go," Jay Weiss said.

The nurse turned to Hurley. "There's police downstairs, you better not let them see you with that camera."

"You got a lot of wounded in here this morning?" Hurley said. They were all standing with their backs to Matt Ferlin.

"Quite a few." She was still smiling at Lloyd. "Wait till I tell my sister who came visiting."

"Give her my best," Lloyd said.

"Well, thank you, I certainly will."

"And take good care of this young man for us."

They all turned as if they had forgotten the man in the bed. "He'll be all right, he'll be fine," the nurse said.

"I want a glass of water," Matt Ferlin said.

"I'll be right with you." The nurse looked back at Lloyd. "Did you visit your colored boy?"

"Oh yeah," Jay Weiss said, "I forgot, Lloyd, Cliff Miller got hurt a little too."

"He's right down the hall, Mr. Garner." The nurse led the way. Weiss said, "You can wait, Hurley, Hacklin didn't say anything about a picture."

"He's in here, Mr. Garner."

It was a smaller, darker room. Another Negro, an old man, was sitting up in the bed nearest the window, he didn't speak or smile. All that was visible of Cliff Miller's bandaged face was two puffed and cracked lips. "You asleep?" The nurse leaned over him. "You have visitors. Mr. Lloyd Garner."

Cliff Miller moved his head slightly toward the door and spoke with an effort. "Lloyd. Thanks for coming."

"You need anything, Cliff?"

"I'm okay."

"How did it happen, Cliff?"

It was almost a whisper. "The usual way." Then the cracked lips tried to smile. "Only difference, the cop called *me* the mother-fucker."

Jay Weiss said behind him in the doorway, "Walter knows about this, he's taking care of everything. We got to go, Lloyd."

"We'll go when I'm ready to go." Lloyd leaned and touched Cliff Miller's hand. "I'll be back to see you, Cliff, take it easy." And to the nurse, "I'd appreciate it if you'd phone me at the Hilton if there's anything I can do for him."

"I certainly will, Mr. Garner. He can't talk very well but the doctor said he'll be all right."

"He looks to me like they tried to kill him."

A cop stopped them downstairs at the outside door. "The camera," he said to Hurley.

"What about the camera?"

"Who you taking pictures of?"

"He didn't take any, officer," Weiss said. "They wouldn't let him."

"You're goddamn right they wouldn't let him," the cop said. "Now get out of here before I take the camera."

"You guys did a pretty good job on those people upstairs," Lloyd said to the cop.

Weiss took him hastily by the arm. "The police were doing their duty. Come on, Lloyd."

Their taxi was waiting for them. "LaSalle Hotel," Weiss told the driver, and said to Lloyd, "What did you want to do, get us *all* thrown in the clink?"

"I wanted to kick the dirty bastard in the balls."

"Lloyd, for Christ sake, control yourself." He turned to Hurley. "You're assigned to us for the morning so you can grab a couple shots of Lloyd where we're going now, right?"

Where they were going now was to witness the spectacle Hubert Humphrey had avoided on scheduled television, impromptu confrontation with Eugene McCarthy on the issues of the day, the hour, with George McGovern added to the great debate for good measure and the California delegation crowding the big room along with reporters and anyone who cared to drop in. There was a wait before it began, and as always the delegates showed more interest in Lloyd Garner than anybody else until Humphrey got there. He didn't mind their inane questioning this time, it helped him get over the deep unreasoning anger aroused in him at the hospital. Cliff Miller, the nice kid who got the job promised to Bev Hambleton, lying there like a mummy. Only maybe they wouldn't have let Bev Hambleton have it quite so hard.

Hurley was busy snapping pictures of him when Jack Milhouse pushed his way through the crowd. "I didn't know you were assigned to this, I thought I was."

He forced a smile. "Just looking around, Jack. I mean if it's all right with you."

"Oh, sure, sure. For a minute I thought Buck had his signals mixed."

"No, my assignment was visiting last night's casualties in the hospital."

"Where were you, Wesley? I hear the boys messed up some of them pretty bad."

"You're not surprised, are you? It's your town."

Lloyd watched him turn abruptly and weave back toward the

front of the crowd. Hurley had his pictures now, and with Jay
Weiss sticking close Lloyd moved toward the door and lingered
just inside the room. McCarthy had started to speak, and what was
it about his manner that made you think again he didn't really care
whether he won or lost. McGovern was much warmer, everybody
liked McGovern, and then Humphrey came on and said all the
things he had been saying for weeks, nothing new, he was Lyndon
Johnson's boy right down to the wire.

The hard news came later in the day, and it was McCarthy who
made it. Lloyd had slept and was back in the booth at the
amphitheater when Greminger handed him the first bulletin on it
with the night session already underway. Stephen Smith, Ted
Kennedy's emissary, had paid a call on the senator from Minnesota
amid rumors that McCarthy had abandoned hope for the nomination
and was offering to switch his support to the senator from Massachusetts.

"Take the night off, Jay, Little Lloyd Fauntleroy's going straight
to the hotel and bed."

Waiting for him as usual outside the booth at the session's end,
the PR man grinned. "How do I know you're not sneaking away to
meet your friend Dobrinoff at that nonstop party?"

"Dobrinoff's gone. You don't believe me check me in the room,
I'll be out cold."

But it wasn't because he was tired or because Dobie had returned
to New York, he just had no desire to sit around and drink, not
with what was happening in Chicago, not since he'd started visiting
the hospital. This morning he'd gone back there alone to see Ferlin
and Cliff Miller again before leaving for the amphitheater, where
tonight the rebel Democrats had foiled the Johnson-Humphrey
scheme to stage the Vietnam plank debate after TV prime time had
run out and keep Daley's cynical tactics as quiet as possible. Daley
himself had finally been forced to call for the adjournment. Lloyd
fought to keep out the note of exultation as he reported the mayor's
defeat, it was the first time disgust and hatred had threatened his
voice on the air.

Traffic was crawling on the way back to the hotel, past the

bristling checkpoints, the patrols, past the screens the city had put
up to hide the slums along the route to the amphitheater. Twice
his taxi was stopped and the driver questioned. They were spot-
checking cars for no apparent reason. Coming into Michigan Avenue
he saw wooden barriers ranged along the curbs, sirens whined somewhere in the Loop. From up ahead, where police floodlights went
on and off to scrutinize the park in front of the big hotels, came
a confused sound of shouting. Once again his taxi was stopped by a
cop, still blocks from the Hilton. "I'll get out here," he said abruptly
to the driver and handed him his money.

"Where you going, mister?" the cop said softly.

Lloyd stopped and looked back. "What's it to you?"

"Hold it." The voice was louder. The cop left the cab and came
up to him on the sidewalk; he was short and swarthy and compact,
eyes glinting under the helmet, heavy pistol in his belt. Lloyd
couldn't tell whether he'd recognized him. "I said where you going."

"Do I have to tell you where I'm going? What is this, Nazi
Germany?"

"Come again, mister?"

"I said what is this, Nazi Germany?"

"Identify yourself," the cop said.

Lloyd sighed and handed him his Convention pass, watched him
look deliberately at the picture on it, then hand it back with
something like contempt.

"Now tell me where you going."

"I'm going to the Conrad Hilton Hotel, for Christ's sake."

"Get off the streets," the cop said, "and don't give me no more
shit." He pushed him with one hand, a short, sharp shove, Lloyd
felt the blood surge to his head and spun half around, raising his
arm. But the cop was already moving away, indifference in his back,
and waving the cabdriver on. Lloyd stood a moment looking after
him, mastering a helpless rage, what did you do? What could you
do? Then he walked on toward the hotel.

The sounds ahead grew louder, more insistent, a nearer cacophony
of shouts and cries, a confused argument among unseen antagonists
in the summer night. He heard whistles and revving engines, police
cars moved nervously back and forth along the edge of the park.

Here the motor traffic was being stopped and turned into the side streets. Beyond, a line of helmeted police stood sullen before the hotels. For the first time he saw trucks and Jeeps and the shining tips of naked bayonets, the Guard was out in force. What the hell were they expecting, a tank attack? And where was the enemy?

But now he saw the enemy, closing ranks in the park across the street, shifting, fitfully visible in the green gloom of trees, swelling slowly into the thousands as they gathered to mock the Establishment and shout up at the Hilton windows in praise of McCarthy, in scorn of Humphrey. And half the hotel was watching appalled or amused from their rooms, some blinking their lights in sympathy, even cheering the protesters on. Coming up to the hotel, pushing his way through silent spectators standing motionless behind the police barriers, Lloyd heard the long and wavering, echoing cheer, somehow intoxicating, like a college football yell. He remembered now where he had heard this before, a night in Paris, but these were Americans, these were real, his own kind, his own blood, and he saw them plain at last, an army of kids, of girls and boys, here and there an older, harder face riveted by the floodlights but mostly just kids, fresh-faced, clean-bodied. There was laughter and derision in their cries, no fear, and a desperate kind of hope. As he turned in at the hotel entrance he stopped to look once more across the street, and every face was Lee Maxton's. Suddenly it all seemed so clear, so simple, the good against the evil, why was it like feeling this for the first time? Going up in the elevator he wiped the tears out of his eyes with a shaking hand and wondered if it was because he was so tired.

"You're a man of your word," Jay Weiss said to him over breakfast, "I checked you when I came in from the Hall and you were out cold like you said."

"I guess I slept pretty hard."

"You didn't miss anything. They kept on hollering outside till after four but there was no real fireworks, just a few scattered fights and a lot of tear gas."

"I could smell it in the lobby when I came down."

"Yeah." The real showdown in the streets could be expected

later today, Jay said with relish, when David Dellinger's antiwar mobilization forces and the army of Yippies attempted their forbidden march on the amphitheater. The authorities were just as determined to break up the march when it started, in fact Hurley had been warned privately by a friendly plainclothesman, a rare bird this week in Chicago, that reporters and especially cameramen were marked for the full treatment if they tried to get close to the action, wherever it broke. "Of course," Jay noted, "we'll be safe inside the Hall with the delegates." He was cozily amused at the thought.

Safe, behind the barbed wire, the lines of Jeeps with mounted machine guns, the Secret Service, the FBI, and you name it. Going in for the afternoon session through a doubled cordon of armed guards, Lloyd could feel tension as oppressive as the air before a thunderstorm. Just past the ridiculous electronic entrance mechanism that accepted credit cards as willingly as official passes, he saw two policewomen packing revolvers in holsters; they stared back at him coldly as he went by. Stalag 68, Kent Ward had called the place on opening day, no wonder the tag had stuck. And the faces of the delegates moving into the slowly filling hall showed they, too, could feel the undercurrents; they were up tight, or angry, or just scared, but they all looked ready to fight. Whatever happened outside this day, a decisive battle was looming in here even before the nominating session started. The Vietnam plank debate was finally to begin before an audience of millions, and its outcome would seal the fate of the party revolt.

Hale Boggs didn't look too happy down there calling the Convention to order. "Stay with the podium," Buck Schonwald snapped over the intercom, "that's where the story is now." No shots today of bored delegates reading newspapers, and it wasn't because Daley had ordered all papers confiscated at the door. The delegates were listening as they hadn't listened so far. For nearly three hours it went on with a mounting bitterness. Hawk and dove, dove and hawk, the speakers came forward to attack or defend. Zablocki of Wisconsin, obviously out of step with his delegation, announced that Humphrey supported the majority plank and was answered by hostile shouts from the floor. The governor of Missouri got the same reception when he spoke against the minority version. Efforts by Muskie of Maine to mediate were unavailing, and when the Kennedy team began taking the stand for the doves, Salinger, Sorensen, O'Donnell in their turns, the "stop the war" chant swelled into the galleries.

Scanning the floor from the broadcast booth, Lloyd watched the protest banners unfurling, the bitterness spread from New York and California to nearby Massachusetts and South Dakota, across the hall to Wisconsin and Oregon. That was Gore of Tennessee speaking now, scoring Lyndon Johnson by name, the first time that name had been taken in vain, for a war policy of disaster. *"Meanwhile, back at the ranch,"* Kent Ward told the camera between speeches, *"there is still no sign that the President will come to this convention, shall we say venture to come to this convention? although he has dominated it from the beginning as he has dominated the drawing of the Vietnam plank and appears to be having his way to the end. Eugene McCarthy confirmed today that he has offered to withdraw in favor of Edward Kennedy, the last hope for an early peace in the rebel view, but again there is no word from Hyannis that the senator will come to Chicago either. Nobody else is waiting in the wings, and if the Administration wins endorsement of its Vietnam policy when this debate is concluded, it will be too late to stop Hubert Humphrey."* Now it was Hale Boggs again, rebutting for the White House, pointing to Russia's new threat in Europe, warning of other dangers in the Middle East, linking both with the necessity for a strong stand in Asia. And then the surprise, the clincher, read by Boggs from the rostrum to an almost silent hall, a message from the U. S. Commander in Vietnam predicting that an end to the bombing of the North would bring a new Communist build-up in the South to five times the enemy's current strength.

The roll call followed. As the Administration victory tally was announced to triumphant cheers led by Texas and the session was recessed, Lloyd Garner sat back and let the camera tell the rest of it while New York's delegation mourned with "We Shall Overcome" and Bob Lentz in Main Control switched back and forth from the singers to the Convention band doing its best to drown them out and finally succeeding. It was all over. Lyndon Johnson had indeed had his way. Only the crowning of his faithful servant remained to be consummated, and there was no doubt left about that.

On his way back to the booth for the nomination session Lloyd ran into Bill Moran for the first time since Miami Beach. The young correspondent looked pale and tired but he threw him a taunting grin and stopped. They faced each other alone a moment over a tangle of cables in the narrow hall. "Still on the firing line, I see."

"That's for the troops, Bill. I have to stay at HQ."

"I hear you visited the wounded."

"Isn't that what generals do?"

"But you didn't say anything about it on the air."

"I leave that kind of comment to my chief of staff, Colonel Ward. Delegation of authority, don't they call it?"

The grin hardened. "Staley said you were going to show me the home front, Garner. Personally."

"Glad to, Moran, when I'm not anchoring."

The grin faded. "I'll hold you to that."

"I look forward to it. Good luck." Lloyd stood aside, still keeping his smile, and let him go by.

In the booth Harry Ferguson confirmed Joyce Hacklin's tip that the big boss would be in the VIP observation room tonight. Lloyd looked across at Kent Ward as they settled into their chairs. "Maybe I'll get to meet him at last, Kent."

"I'm afraid not. He was coming and changed his mind."

Ah, well.

This time the clincher came first, at the beginning of the session. Carl Albert, getting the jump on the opposition, read from the rostrum two telegrams from the President and Senator Kennedy finally and irrevocably taking them out of contention. There would be no stampede to either in the desperation of these last hours. That settled it, but the mood of the hall was far from settled; a ground swell of resentment rolled and eddied through the amphitheater, heard as a menacing hum under the surface of familiar sound. From his olympian station high above the tumult Lloyd Garner pointed out that New York and California again appeared to be storm centers. Restless delegates spilled into the aisles, the sergeants at arms were getting tougher about moving them back to their seats, almost as if they had a new set of orders from the pudgy man who sat smiling or glowering with Illinois. Jack Milhouse, headphones on, crouched near him, champing for action.

The voice of Hall Control broke suddenly into the intercom during the speechmaking. "Some kind of a fight over near New York, Buck. McIntosh is trying to get over there," and immediately Bob Lentz zoomed in on the scene. "Here we go!" Schonwald was saying, he sounded gleeful. "Take Mac the second he's ready."

Looking down from the anchor booth, Lloyd could see the vortex of struggling bodies in the aisle, a man was being half dragged, half carried by security guards out of the hall, a New York delegate, it looked like Paul O'Dwyer, had left his seat and was following, shouting, remonstrating, while McIntosh battled his way through the crush trying to reach the scene, his words coming up cut in the midst of the speech from the podium. ". . . *attempting to find out what's happening here but getting no co-operation from these officers . . . ah!*" He sounded as if his wind had been knocked out by a blow or collision. A police squad, clubs held high, was pushing forward in the jammed aisle, then the struggle passed out of camera-shot and Schonwald said, "Back to the podium while we find out what this was, tell McIntosh to stay with them and give us a report."

And the nominations went on, sandblasting their sentiment into the smoke fumes, fighting the rising tumult of sound. The hall shook with dutiful applause as Hubert Humphrey's name was put in. Nobody doubted it would be Humphrey now. This rough stuff on the floor was just a dying gasp. The machine was moving, inexorable, toward a first-ballot triumph, Illinois in the vanguard, New Jersey close behind, the Southerners swinging into line, Pennsylvania getting ready to clamp the lid down. The battle was over in the Convention hall, but not outside. Outside, in the streets, they had just begun to fight.

First word of it came through while the governor of Iowa was nominating Eugene McCarthy. Beyond Schonwald's words on the intercom Lloyd could hear Bob Lentz cursing close to tears at his crippled remotes. Violence had erupted in front of the Conrad Hilton and there was no way to get it on the air until the videotapes were edited and rushed to the amphitheater by courier. Even then there was fear they would be confiscated or held up at the door. No, a batch was here, had got through okay, would be ready at the end of this endless series of commercials. Lloyd, listening intently, heard Schonwald's voice at last on the intercom, low and urgent, *"Run it, get it on, fast!"* and a moment later Greminger thrust a sheet of paper in front of him, the camera's red light blinked on, he tensed and read.

"We've just received a videotaped report of rioting in downtown Chicago in the wake of today's attempt by anti-Vietnam War pro-testers to march on the amphitheater. The scene is Michigan Avenue outside Democratic Party headquarters in the Conrad Hilton Hotel an hour ago." Then voice-over, watching the monitor, witnessing it himself for the first time: *"It certainly doesn't look like an organized demonstration at this point, the police are charging into groups of young people, both men and women, apparently without provoca-tion, at least immediate provocation, and attacking mercilessly with their clubs, arresting them, yanking them over to the paddy wagons as you see there."* Shouts and boos went up off camera in the back-ground, a sudden close-up caught the contorted face of a cop, flailing a defenseless back, then a series of short, dull explosions sounded. *"Probably tear gas,"* Lloyd Garner said, trying to keep his voice con-trolled. *"And there . . . here comes the National Guard, moving in, pushing the crowd back, clearing the area in front of the Hilton."* Greminger slipped more copy in front of him and Lloyd glanced at it, still following the action on his monitor. The troops advanced slowly, grimly, bayonets glinting in the flickering light, machine guns mounted on screened Jeeps. *"We're told by our news team on the scene that this violence in front of the Hilton was indeed entirely unprovoked, so far as anyone could tell, just indiscriminate police attacks, and sometimes by guardsmen, on any civilian trapped there, including women, as you saw yourselves a moment ago. At one point a group of screaming spectators were pushed right through a plate-glass window in the Hilton, we're told there were serious casualties. As you know, earlier this week television and other re-porters wearing prominent identification were singled out and*

beaten during the violence in Lincoln Park, so far tonight no word on whether any more have been attacked, but as you have seen reporters have been roughed up here on the Convention floor in at least three incidents witnessed by the camera."

Still talking, he could hear Hall Control come in, "Buck, can you hear me, Buck? We've lined up Daley, Milhouse ready to go with interview on violence," and Schonwald's voice, "Lloyd, as soon as tape ends call in Milhouse, we'll rerun it during the interview and Lentz can intercut, everybody get that?"

Lloyd watched him come up on the monitor, the mayor of Chicago sat there in the turmoil, unruffled and bland, submitting to questions. Yes, he knew about the trouble downtown, of course he knew about it. No, the situation had been dealt with, and was now under control. What was that, brutality? No, there was no brutality, of course not, the Chicago police, the finest police force in the country, simply responded to violations of the law and took normal action to restore order, that was all there was to it. Any other reports were propaganda devised to slander the pure name of the great city of Chicago. . . . As he spoke Bob Lentz was intercutting Daley's words with shots of staggering, bleeding demonstrators, a boy lying by the curb, a clubbed girl being led off by police, guardsmen in gas masks firing tear gas at a car and a guardsman shoving his gun at a woman inside the car. Then back once more to Richard J. Daley, filling the screen, the jowls moving blandly, controlled fury in his eyes.

Lloyd Garner said quietly, as the interview ended and Milhouse returned it to the booth, *"You have seen the face of fascism in the United States."*

25

"Messages, Gaby?"

She stood up at her desk and laughed. "Aren't you going to give me time to say welcome home?"

"Come over here and let me hug you." And she came over to stand beside his chair. He threw his arm around her outsized middle section and pulled her closer. "Like my friend the actor says, Gaby, the girdle hasn't been designed that can hold this steady."

She giggled and leaned to kiss him lightly on the head. "You did a great job, especially on Daley, aren't you proud of yourself?"

"Messages, please."

"Mr. Hacklin wants you in his office as soon as you come in." The vice-president was the only member of the news department she called by his last name. "Buck wants to see you. So does Jay Weiss. Sime Sussman called twice and said call him back." She grinned at him. "Everybody's looking for you, did you disappear in Chicago or something?"

"Just went off by myself for a while after the last show, I couldn't stand the sight of anybody any more."

It was true. He'd had a Hertz standing by after the final session and driven it all night, stopping in the morning at some little place in Wisconsin and sleeping most of the day, then driving back to Chicago. He made one last visit to Cliff Miller in the hospital before taking a late night flight to New York.

Gaby was fingering the two piles of unopened mail on the table beside his desk. "This stuff is mostly personal and ads. There's another letter from that general in the Pentagon. I sent listener mail into Helen's office while you were away, like about a thousand, Chicago's got a lot more than that, they're forwarding. The only immediate thing is the Overseas Press wants you to be on a panel tomorrow night, you want to accept?"

"You know I'm too busy for that."

"Whatever it is you do with your free time."

The phone rang and he picked it up before she could. "So you're back, baby buddy!" The voice was high and infectiously gay. "You just made it."

"Hello, Dobie. I just made it for what?"

"I'm down the street in the Gotham with something wild. Come over after the show tonight and roll a joint with us."

"I can't make it, Dobie."

"Wait a minute, listen to this." A girl's voice came in. "Are you all ready to go?" she said, "I am." She sounded as if she was already up there. Dobie came back. "How about that, sweets? We'll be waiting for you."

"I'll try." He hung up. Gaby was signaling from her desk and he picked up another phone. The voice like incipient cancer belonged to Sime Sussman. "I'm glad I caught you. You talked to anybody yet? If not, don't. Not till you see me first."

"What's up, Sime?"

"Things have been happening upstairs while you were in Chi. Big things. They've got plans over there, didn't you know?"

"Hacklin's waiting for me right now."

"That'll be it. He's going to tell you the show is expanding to an hour, how about that? No commitments, Lloyd, not even verbal."

"Okay."

"We'll go into it tomorrow. My office at eleven, right? And keep lunch clear too."

"What's the big conference?"

The hollow rasping was something like a laugh. "We're going to scrap your contract and renegotiate, that's all. Don't say *anything* to Schonwald or anybody else."

"Whatever you say, Sime." Everything was happening at once, as usual. Another phone rang and Gaby was answering it. She held her hand over the mouthpiece and said, "Jay Weiss."

"I've had him on my back for two weeks, what's he want now?" He turned a thumb down.

"He called and said he's on his way over, Jay, but he's not here yet. Well, you know where he lives." She hung up smartly. "That sonofabitch is a nusiance."

"Every flack is a nuisance. Gaby you can go to lunch."

She swung her bag as she walked to the door, then turned and looked back at him. "You all right?" she said.

"Why shouldn't I be?"

"I don't know. Something about you. You worry me a little."

He laughed. "Go," he said. "You're a sweet girl."

He had to wait a few minutes in Walter Hacklin's outer office before the secretary said, "Mr. Hacklin will see you now, Mr. Garner," opening the door for him.

"Hello, Walter."

The man behind the big empty desk, sitting there with the silent soap opera running on the screen above his head, didn't get up as he usually did and didn't smile either. He motioned to the chair in front of his desk and Lloyd sat down in it. Then he said, still not smiling, the bleak gray eyes not looking at him directly, "I'm sorry to call you away from your office the very first day back, I know you have a lot to do."

It was Lloyd who smiled. "No sweat, Walter. I thought you knew everything I do in that office is done for me by somebody else."

"And I'm sorry we didn't have a chance to talk in Chicago, I had to come back right after the nomination."

"You were lucky."

There was a silence. The imperturbable moonface looked somber. Finally Walter Hacklin said, "I probably don't need to tell you we're in serious trouble."

"We?"

"The network. All the networks."

"What's wrong, Walter?"

For the first time he faced him fully. "Chicago. It's Daley, mainly. The Washington reaction isn't very positive, so far, but we'll be getting it from them later. The mayor, however, is very, very unhappy with the riot coverage."

"So what?" Lloyd said.

An expression like pain flickered across Hacklin's forehead. "Taking a jaunty attitude won't solve anything at all," he said. "We have a major problem affecting our relations with the Democratic administration and we have to do something about it, fast."

"If I were you, Walter, I'd start thinking about relations with a Republican administration."

The eyes hardened. "We'll deal with that when it happens. If it does," he added, "I can't say your recent unfortunate remarks in Miami Beach will help us much."

Another pause. Lloyd waited.

"But that was Miami Beach," Hacklin said after a moment. "I'm talking now about Chicago. And as long as I live I'll never understand why you took it into your head to make that crack about fascism right after the Daley interview." He paused again. "I asked Schonwald about it. He couldn't enlighten me. Maybe you can."

He shrugged. "It was a conviction. I guess I couldn't resist it."

"But it's your *job* to resist everything of the kind." He spread his hands. "Conviction! Everybody has convictions, but in your business they're a private matter. You're not being paid for making your convictions public. Nobody gives a damn what you say privately, as long as you don't let it get picked up by the papers, but when you're on the air you're expected to restrain yourself."

"I do. As much as humanly possible."

"Have you seen any of the mail that's been pouring in since you made that remark?"

"I hear there's a lot of it."

"Most of it in favor. But we don't want that kind of mail, not for your program. We don't *need* it. It's controversial. It's upsetting to the people on both sides. What you said isn't news, it's comment. Not that comment isn't all right, but it has to come at the right time, in the right kind of show."

"I think you're fretting too much about it, Walter."

"Lloyd." The thin lips tried to part, patiently, in a smile. "I didn't ask you to come here today to argue with you, that's just wasting my time and yours. What's done can't be undone. If it was just that one remark of yours it might be explained away somehow, an unintentional error, anything, a little apology would cover it. But it's part of something much bigger. The tape coverage of the riots, the trouble with Daley, the involvement with leftwingers in the party and those goddamned Yippies. It's started a whole chain of events that could well end up in a Congressional investigation of television news, and that's the *last* thing we want."

"Why, Walter? Why shouldn't we welcome it?"

Again the pause. The eyes across the desk were saying more plainly than words it was none of Lloyd Garner's business even to ask such a question. "Lloyd," he said again, and this time the patience was almost pleading, "I was sitting here this morning remembering a morning in the Statler in Washington when a young fellow, a *nice* guy, came downstairs from his room to talk to me and I offered him a job. I never thought, looking at that boy that day, he could ever let any of us down in any way. Or, if he did make a mistake, a serious mistake, I was sure then, and I'm sure now, he'd do everything he could to make amends."

He stopped as though waiting. "Go on, Walter."

"I've been trying to figure out what would best help our position in this situation and I've come to the conclusion we should do a special giving Daley's side of the picture. We'd want you to anchor, of course. It would help restore the balance. We could work out the questions with the mayor and have everything scripted satisfactorily. What think, Lloyd?"

"Remember, Walter? I'm not paid to think."

The little corporate laugh ignored it. The look of charm was returning. "You're probably too tired to think right now. I know I am. God, what a week that was! But I've discussed the whole project with Buck and you two can take it from here." He stood up, dismissing him. "Well, I have a call in to Chicago and whatever's finally set up you'll hear about from Schonwald."

It was left at that. Walking down the hall he knew the Daley special would never have been set until after the word from the big boss. Sussman had been wrong, there had been no mention of the show going to an hour. Maybe that was what Schonwald wanted to tell him.

But he didn't see Schonwald until after the evening show, they'd both been busy all afternoon. He was waiting for him in the studio doorway as he came off the air. "Stop in before you leave, Lloyd, I'll stick around." The producer patted him thoughtfully on the rump, like a baseball manager on the mound, and let him pass.

Gaby was standing at her desk with a phone in her hand. "A lady on Outside, Private," she said, his heart jumped suddenly and he picked up his extension. "Lloyd Garner."

Alix Weddern said, "Lloyd darling, how nice to see you back in New York."

"How nice to talk to *you*," he said. It was not the voice he had hoped against hope to hear.

"Do you really mean that?" Her brief laugh sounded bitchy cool.

"Why wouldn't I?"

"Do you realize how long it's been since we were in the same room together?"

"Alix"—and he forced a smile into it, at the same time nodding good night to Gaby as she left—"do *you* realize what's been happening this summer? First Bobby Kennedy, then Miami, then Chicago? Frankly, I don't know how I survived Chicago on my feet."

"You looked pretty stable at Hugh Hefner's."

He laughed, keeping it light. "You've been reading the *Daily News* again."

"And just who was the lady in the picture?"

"My boss's wife."

"I watched you in Chicago. Thought you were a little stiff on the police."

"They were only doing their duty, right?"

"Lloyd Garner, are you putting me on, just a bit?"

"Maybe I am, just a bit." For a moment, for just a moment, he felt a kind of nostalgia for their times together.

"But I didn't swallow my pride and call you tonight to talk about the Chicago police," she was saying. "I only wanted to talk about you and me, fair enough?"

"It's not the best time, Alix. The office is full of people waiting to—"

"I can't hear a sound except your voice, darling. But of course I never do. When am I going to see you in person?"

"Why," he said, "why, sure, can I call you tomorrow?"

"Tonight," she said, "when you get away from all those silent people, come up and have a drink. There's nobody here but me." She laughed again, the little bitter laugh he didn't like. "I'll be waiting."

"Alix—" She was gone. He hung up, frowning, and reached for a cigarette. Then he walked down the hall toward Buck Schonwald's office. The young fag from the art department was hurrying past and flashed him a big smile. "Don't we look gorgeous with that make-up still on!"

"You're looking pretty good yourself, Teddy."

"Oh, *come on,*" Teddy said from behind him.

He'd forgotten the damn make-up. Just one more sign he wasn't with it. Schonwald was hanging up his phone. "Draw up a chair, fellow."

"What did you want to talk about, Buck?"

"The show's expanding to an hour next month."

"So I understand."

He looked startled, then angry. "So you understand! That's secret information, or did Hacklin tell you?"

"Hacklin didn't mention it. Sime Sussman told me this morning."

"Sussman! Who told *him?*"

"He didn't say. And look, Buck, don't take your feud with Sussman out on me. I've never given him any information about what this company does. Nobody ever tells me anything anyway, till it's ready for public knowledge. Including you."

"I just told you the show's going to an hour, didn't I? I would have told you sooner, in Chicago, but you lammed on me." His eyes narrowed slightly. "Where to, by the way?"

"Nowhere in particular."

"And what were you doing nowhere in particular?"

"Not that it's any of your business. I was thinking, Buck."

It made the big man laugh suddenly. He picked up a pipe and began to fill it. "Thinking!"

"Yeah. It's what I do now on my free time, didn't you know? Since I don't get to do it on the job much."

"*Too* much, lately," the producer said.

"So Walter tells me."

"Did he tell you Daley's demanding an hour's prime time to defend himself against TV?"

"He told me we were offering the time to Daley."

"Six of one," Schonwald shrugged. "It looks like we'll have to do it anyhow. Did Walter tell you he wants you to feed the questions to Daley?"

"All approved by the mayor in advance, right? And we stick to the script, right?"

He sighed and lit his pipe. "We'll have to go easy with him, Lloyd. We'll have to let him have his say. And we expect you to co-operate. No more speeches off the cuff."

"I wonder," Lloyd said, "what Hedley Johns would have said about that."

"You think he would have been in there like you with the bleeding hearts, is that it?" He leaned forward. "Listen, fellow, there happens to be something to be said for Daley's side of it. Was he supposed to let those animals walk all over him? That's what they are, they're animals."

"Some of them."

"You think the police had no provocation? You should hear my cameramen! They'd rather have a Chicago cop any day than a Yippie. You ask them, the wrong people were getting called pigs out there. They've already signed statements for the FBI." He leaned back again. "Anyway, where were you to know what went on? Sitting on your ass inside the Convention hall."

"I had a monitor in front of me. So did you. It was your director calling the shots."

"Yeah. And they won't let me forget it. Like I've got the government on *my* back, too. They want to know did we stage any violence this time. In *Chicago!* And they want all the Chicago outtakes."

"Which you don't have to give them, do you?"

"Of course I do."

"Why?"

"National security."

Lloyd smiled. "It covers a lot, doesn't it?"

He left the subject. "You don't seem too damn excited about the show going to an hour," the producer said.

"What do you want me to do, jump up and down? I've heard you talk about it for a long time. For your sake, I'm glad."

"For *my* sake? You realize what this will mean for *everybody* around here? The biggest challenge in the history of TV news. A hell of a lot more work."

"And a hell of a lot more money for the people who do it."

His eyes flashed anger again. "Is that all you think about?"

Lloyd shook his head. "It's all I used to think about."

"Anyway, the money's not my department."

"You should be happy. You won't have to talk to Sime Sussman."

"Fuck Sime Sussman, I didn't call you in here tonight to talk about Sime Sussman. I want to talk about a one-hour evening news strip anchored by Lloyd Garner."

"Fair enough. And we'll do just that tomorrow, after Lloyd Garner talks to his agent."

He put the pipe down. "This is where you work, fellow, have you forgotten that?"

In the pause they looked at each other, motionless. Lloyd laughed and said, "What's the matter, Buck? Unhappy about something?"

"Not exactly." He sighed again and looked down at the top of his desk. "I was just remembering the first day you walked into my office, less than a year ago. It didn't take you long, did it?"

He sat at his desk with only a lamp burning over it and thought about what Schonwald had said. The studio was dark by now, the night shift in the newsroom was the only sign of activity, the cameras stood shrouded in shadow. The clock above the control room, its tyranny suspended for the night, looked back at him stoically from the gloom. Not long, Schonwald had said, less than a year, and already the Lloyd Garner he had known was dead, forgotten by Lloyd Garner himself. And that young fellow in the Statler Hotel, summoned one morning by Walter Hacklin and offered the sun and the moon, where was he? They wouldn't forgive him for it, Hacklin or Schonwald either, but was it his fault or theirs that he had changed from the image they had created for him? That was the unpardonable error, to change, to grow, to *become*. You were all right only as long as you didn't let it happen.

The air-conditioned room was cold and stale. He shivered, looking around him, and thought he felt the presence of ghosts that wouldn't stay dead. Not long, a little year, and already there were so many ghosts, among them the Lloyd Garner who sat at this desk the night the strike was called and faced a decision, among them the man who called himself Lloyd Garner's father, who came seeking his son and was turned away like a panhandler in the street. My father, the failure. But Richard Garner had another son, a better son, who wouldn't turn him away. And Fran, alone in her struggle, Phil would be standing by there too. A memory of the early days with 'Fran swept over him in a surge of sudden tenderness, a morning at the beach, Phil standing in the surf watching them shyly, wistfully, Fran laughing like a child, clinging to him in the water like a child.

He felt the tears well into his eyes and stood up, as if to retreat from the shadows closing around his desk, from the voices that still echoed in these phones. If Alix Weddern really expected him to come to her apartment tonight, she would be waiting in vain, that was no way out. So would Dobie Dobrinoff wait in vain, doing his thing with his chick in the Gotham and offering him a soul brother's total welcome to their bed. Thanks but no thanks, Dobie. Right now he would join the ghost of Bev Hambleton at that shabby little saloon down the street, and think, and decide again.

Like that night, the strike night, the place was almost empty, like that night the same face was behind the bar; the radio made muffled noises, there was nobody to stare or try to start a conversation. He sat alone over his bourbon and looked once at his watch without seeing what time it was, like the clock he had abandoned in the studio, the red hand spinning slow and meaningless until morning. He had no appetite for dinner and no one to have it with, later he would think about eating something. Would Gino be working tonight? Gino always made it feel like home. Right now, come to think of it, that was about the only kind of home he

had, Primo at the Bistro, Emil at Costello's, Céline and André at
the Argenteuil, Tony and Tony's Wife, near him but not too near
him. He would have two or three more drinks here and some dinner
on his way back to the apartment, all he had to do was choose the
place.

26

It was starting like any other broadcast, preceded by the customary two commercials and a station break for two more, then the announcer's familiar intro to Lloyd Garner and "The News Tonight." *"A very good evening to you all!"* he said, as he always said, his voice calm and deep, his smile flashing briefly as it always did. No viewer could surmise from face or voice that today had been other than normal in the life of Lloyd Garner. If anything he might have seemed even more self-assured than usual.

Nothing unexpected in the opening headlines either. Humphrey conferring with aides on campaign strategy, Nixon confident of victory now his opponent had been chosen. There will be a satellite report from Vietnam on new enemy infiltration via the Ho Chi Minh Trail, we'll hear from correspondents on both sides in the Middle East on the smoldering crisis along Israel's borders. The cost of living is up again, so is the stock market. And we'll have a country-wide survey: what the man in the street is saying about election prospects. The headlines ended, the face on the screen dissolved into another commercial. Lloyd Garner, momentarily off the air, shifted to an easier posture in his swivel seat and licked the dry makeup on his lips.

(Schonwald's look of utter incredulity. "You won't do the interview? You refuse?" The tormented laugh. "You're teasing, Sussman put you up to this.")

"The Democratic candidate for President talked about his campaign plans today," Lloyd Garner was back on the air and reading from Teleprompter. *"Roy Jarvis has the story."* It was the reporter's turn. Lloyd watched and listened, curious how despite all the tired

jargon, the platitudes, the easy optimism, the man's decency came
through, he'd take him over the other fellow any time, but would
he beat him? The switch again, this time to Dave Billings with
the Nixon party, and Mr. Republican took it from there. The winner's gleam was in his eye, he'd done it in Miami and he'd do it
again, they'd put him in all right, the forgotten Americans, the non-
shouters, the non-demonstrators, the decent people of this country
who work hard and save their money and pay their taxes and care.
Could you beat a line like that in 1968? Possibly, only possibly.

Commercial time, gay music, nostalgia for travel, for the far
countries, the great jets cruising the air ocean. And Lloyd Garner,
oblivious to monitor, to studio, heard him again.

("Listen, fellow, listen carefully. I'm your friend, I'm warning you as a
friend. You want to see Jack Milhouse doing the new hour show?")

Fred Harrity now, from Saigon, voice-over with shots of the
B-52s roaring in on the mountain trail, explosion number three
million and six, the blast of flame, the smoke pillars bursting from
the mountain green. And back at the camp, just waiting out his
time, the American foot soldier, shooting at an enemy he can't see,
capturing hills with nobody on them, ambushed by an army of
vanishing zombies, coming home, if he makes it home, to what?

(Gaby, a little breathless, "Mr. Hacklin on the exec line." And the cool
immediate voice, all suavity regained: "What's this Buck tells me about
the Daley interview, Lloyd? You can't be serious, I thought we talked
that out together yesterday. I've just been on the horn with Chicago and
it's all set, he's in a magnanimous frame of mind, thank God.")

Gordon Kimball with the Cairo spot, the desert, new emplace-
ments along the Canal. New Soviet MIGs arriving, welcomed, a
shot of Nasser and the listening, trustless Arab crowd. Over to Tel
Aviv and Arch Gavagan next, brisk consolidation of the conquered
areas, an eye on Lebanon, patrols, patrols, and the wretched in their
fleabags on the Gaza Strip, waiting without hope.

The pause that refreshes, thirty seconds of that, followed by thirty more of girls in bras and girdles, the lift that upholds. Lloyd Garner adjusted his tie unconsciously, saw nothing on the monitor, heard only Walter Hacklin's voice again,

("No, Lloyd, you can't do this to me. You can't do this to us. Too much is at stake for the network, and that includes your future, my boy, your career, you understand me? I'm speaking now for authority even higher than this office, it's the final word.")

Time now for the feature, the swing around the country for the man in the street. The reporters find him in Newark, in Atlanta, in Minneapolis and San Francisco, a little town in Kansas, a village in the Ozarks. Well, he doesn't know. Maybe, he scratches his head. Look, we've had enough of this violence, I won't let my wife go out at night, not even down the street to the drugstore. Youth will have its say, these kids are talking a lot of sense, if we'd only listen. It's time for a change, that's the way I'm going to vote it. Ah, what choice do they give us, a political hack, a man who promises everything to everybody, or a redneck, why bother to vote at all?

Lloyd grinned. The guy had something there, then the smile faded, his eyes wandered off the monitor to the studio wall.

(Sussman, kind, hard, fatherly: "Don't do it, kid, don't throw everything away. Who you killing but yourself? I got them by the balls over there on a new contract, you'd be the king from now on, the king!")

More commercials, mouth wash, headache remedy. Washington came last tonight but it wouldn't be Kent Ward, he was taking a few days' breather after his Chicago labors. He hadn't said where, and Lloyd's efforts to reach him during the day had been futile. He wanted to talk to him, he wanted desperately to talk to him. He watched now, half listening, as Jerry Lacey closed out the show with the cost of living report. A good boy, Jerry Lacey, on his way, and it was the only way, going from the ground up.

The last thirty seconds of commercial followed Washington, the spot that came just before Lloyd Garner's headline summary and sign-off. In the moment, waiting for it to end, he remembered the day Milo Wilson fought with Schonwald over adding it to the show and Wilson won, Sales always won. He glanced down at the last sheet of copy lying in front of him, neatly typed by Greminger in the extra-size letters that made it easier to read. Greminger didn't know it, nobody knew it, but tonight Lloyd Garner wasn't going to sign off with headlines. He was making a headline of his own, and he needed no copy to say what he was going to say, the words burned in his mind.

The commercial ended, the tiny light on the camera glowed red, he was on the air again and he would tell them all now. *"A good-night word,"* he said, and thought he sensed the little shock in the control room at the unexpected phrase. He spoke slowly, hearing each word fall heavy and distinct through the suddenly intensified stillness in the studio. *"The anchorman of this program has a wonderful job,"* he was saying, *"and I am grateful, I will always be grateful, for the chance to talk to you every night, to be with you in your homes. But lately I have come to believe that I can serve best, not by sitting here in a studio reading words written by others, but by becoming a reporter in the real meaning of the word, by going out myself to cover the story, to find the truth, whatever and wherever it may be. In a particular sense I owe this to a man named Burt Staley, dead in Vietnam. I owe it to a man named Cliff Miller, lying on a hospital bed in Chicago. And I owe it to myself, as well as you. It seemed only right to me that you should be the first to know, and I will now notify my employers that Lloyd Garner is seeking reassignment as a correspondent in the field."*

He stopped. He had taken exactly the time allotted to the closing headlines but he was aware his image still filled the monitor, then the screen went to black and the plug for the next program came up immediately. The show was over.

He stood up, letting the script fall and scatter on the floor, walking swiftly across the studio, passing the startled, silent faces around him, speaking to no one. Behind him the door to the control room snapped suddenly open and he could hear the excited babble inside. Earl Greminger stood at the door to his office, staring at him as he passed with something like consternation. Buck Schonwald, looking stunned, was standing at Gaby's desk holding a phone to his ear and nodding dazedly. He didn't even see Lloyd walk past and into the hall toward the back elevator.

Alone in his bedroom, nursing a final bourbon, debating whether to start with a pill or wait to see if he woke up later and take it then, he faced the long night ahead. He had ended up walking aimlessly across town and eating a hamburger in the back room at Clarke's, where he didn't know anybody and wouldn't be bothered when recognized. The place was full of people as famous as he was and they let each other alone. His phone was ringing regularly every five or ten minutes after he got back to the apartment. He knew what that was all about, he would face it tomorrow. For tonight he switched off the phone and it rang no more.

A scrap of yellow caught his eye among the papers scattered over the bed table, the telegram Fran had sent Sussman from Reno, giving her address. Another ghost that wouldn't stay dead, he reached over and crumpled it in his hand, then dropped it on the floor.

What time was it? He stood up and walked into his little parlor to look at the clock, not even midnight yet. He had been drinking steadily since about nine but it had given him nothing, not even drowsiness, and he decided to take the pill before he undressed and went to bed. He was in the bathroom opening the little bottle when he heard a swift, light rapping on the door into the hall and Lee Maxton's voice, low and urgent.

"Lloyd," she said. "Lloyd, are you there?"

A choking joy was in his throat, he let the bottle fall from his hands and ran stumbling to throw open the door to her. "No," he was saying, dazed, "no, *no*."

"*Yes*," she said, "*yes, yes, yes*." Her words drowning in his mouth, her body drowning in his arms, and it was their first day, their afternoon in the Paris hotel and Rome and Murray Hill and all the lovely times before the bad times began.

He didn't know how long he had been holding her, still standing in the doorway, the door still open. "Why?" he said.

"Don't try to talk now, not now." They came into the room and he closed the door with one hand, holding her arm tight with the other. "I'm not letting go till I find out if you're real."

"I'm real, oh I'm real, just try me." Her voice smothered against his shoulder, and they kissed again, violent and close. "Yes," she was saying into his mouth, "yes, quickly. See, I'm ready, I'm ready, touch me, touch me."

"Sweet. My sweet."

"Oh, Lloyd, it's you again, there's no more nightmare."

"Sweet, sweet."

She closed her eyes. "It's Paris, and the river. Remember? Remember? And we're alive again. Don't wait, my darling, don't wait."

"I can't wait." They fell together on the couch.

"Yes," she was saying. "All of it. All of it. Oh, Lloyd, let it come, let it come. Now. *Now.*"

In silence they lay facing each other in the dark, two small, warm feet holding one of his feet, her breath so close to him that he could taste each word. She was speaking again, quietly and tenderly, and he listened, tranquil at last. "I guess I'd been coming to it gradually a year or so before I met you," she was saying, "the realization that I couldn't be decently happy without a political commitment in my life. I began to see it was the only way I could help keep the kind of America I want my children to grow up in."

"*Our* children," he said, and felt her smile in the dark.

"If you didn't give me a child a little while ago in this bed," she said, "I'll never have one."

"You'll have more than one."

She went on, softly, gravely, "Of course there were doubts in my mind from the beginning. I saw very soon there were points of strain, more serious than I wanted to believe, more serious than I wanted to let you know. But we never really faced them, because when we were together, when we could snatch that precious time to ourselves, we spent it doing the immediate joyous things without thinking about anything else. And we could have gone on indefinitely just the way we were if we had been only casual people sleeping with each other as a relief from boredom in little old sophisticated New York. But for me, it was terribly complicated by the fact that I was in love, really in love for the first time in my life.

That was why I wanted to be entirely honest with you and wanted you to know the truth of what I was."

"I wanted to be the same with you," he whispered. "For the first time with any woman I ever knew."

She kissed his shoulder. "We love each other. We always have. I know that. But I wanted it to be more. I wanted you so much to share my beliefs, it would make me frantic when you told me so calmly that you were impartial, that your work was impartial, like everything else in this year of indifference when most Americans don't seem to give a damn what happens about the political campaign or Vietnam or the Negro struggle or just about anything except their pay envelope and the kind of car they plan to buy with it. But I couldn't seem to make you see what I was feeling, and I knew we were beginning to break up, even before Bobby's death."

She drew a long breath and he felt the tips of her breasts touch him for a moment. "You were so kind with me. I tried to come out of it, during those awful days before they buried him, to be the way we were in the beginning, to believe that our own private happiness was all that mattered. But it only made me see how wrong we were to think only of each other as we did in Paris, and Rome, and then in New York. Those wonderful, wonderful hours, and yet I knew I could never live that way again, I think it was Bobby Kennedy's dying that finally made me understand."

There was a silence. Afterward she said, "And I turned back to Barry. I loved his courage, I loved the way he started all over again, right away."

"So his name's Barry. You never told me his name."

"It couldn't matter less, now. Before I left for Missoula he asked me to marry him, but somehow I couldn't say yes, not yet." Her fingers curled along his arm. "And then when I got out there I deliberately forced myself not to watch you on the air, I wouldn't let myself look at your broadcast all that month, I was afraid to. I was trying, so hard, to forget you, because I knew no matter how much we loved each other it could only end the way you and Fran ended, in more unhappiness for both of us."

"Were you sleeping with him when you came back to New York?"

"Yes."

"In your apartment?"

"I couldn't," she whispered. "I had to be honest with myself, and with him. He knew what I was going through. He greatly admires Kent Ward but he faithfully stayed with the other networks all through the conventions because I told him I couldn't watch you. Naturally it worried him, he knew that as long as I felt that way I was still feeling something very strong. I didn't know myself how strong it was till tonight."

"Tonight?"

"I came in late from the office, he hadn't expected me at all, and he was watching your broadcast. He didn't hear me. I just stood there until it was over." Her voice trembled. "I don't think anyone could ever understand what it did to me. It was more than what you said at the end, it was just seeing you again, you were back, you were back in New York, you were near me."

"Sweetheart," he said into her hair.

"We went out later to a restaurant for dinner, I was trying not to let him see I was upset."

"One of our restaurants?"

"I couldn't, not since you, I've never been back to any of them. I just sat there not saying anything. I don't think I heard what he was saying. But I could see so clearly what would happen if I married him. One day, somehow, I would come back to you. And all of a sudden I just stood up and said, 'Barry, I have to go now.' I just left him standing there, bewildered, holding his napkin in his hand." She had begun to weep. "He's such a damn decent man, Lloyd."

He put his arm under her shoulders and pulled her closer to him. "I'll try," he said.

They were asleep when the phone rang, startling him out of his dream. It was France, an inn, the brook sang outside, people were making happy breakfast sounds in the kitchen below, and Lee was with him, naked under the rough blanket. He sat up in dense darkness and fumbled for the phone, remembering then he had switched it back on before they went to sleep. "Hello?" he said.

"Don't tell me you're already in bed." It was unmistakably Bill Moran.

"Moran? What time is it?"

A pause. "Three twenty-two, Tuesday, three September. Milhouse said you'd be in a night club but I gave it a try anyway, always give it a try, Garner." He sounded hostile as always and vaguely drunk.

"Fauntleroy to you. Where are you?"

"In the office, where else? You busy with a friend?"

"No."

"Sure?" The short, hard laugh.

"What do you want?"

"You know what I want. Just got word here there's a job. Little ruckus in Harlem. Mad sniper, they're calling it, but it looks to me like the same pattern as Cleveland. This could be just the beginning."

"So?" Lloyd said.

He laughed again. "You forgotten? Or did you just want to forget? You told Staley in Saigon, remember? You'd like to show me the home front, remember?"

He was fully awake now and felt Lee stir beside him, hearing the barking, challenging tone at the other end of the wire. "Where do you want me to meet you, Moran?"

"Where you are now. Stand by in the street, I'll pick you up in a cab." He clicked off.

Lee said sleepily, "Is it some drunk, darling?"

"I have to cut out for a little while on a story." He leaned in the dark to kiss her cheek. "Go back to sleep and I'll wake you for breakfast."

"Mmmm," she said.

He felt suddenly serene and glad. He dressed quickly in the front room so as not to wake her again. Downstairs he had to wait less than five minutes for the cab. The street was empty except for a garbage truck moving away slowly farther down the block, a light mist hung along the canyon of buildings. Bill Moran was sitting slumped in the back seat when he opened the door and got in. The driver started off again at once, heading north and into the park.

"They're trying to round up a camera crew," Moran said. "They'll follow us up there."

"What's going on?"

"I told you. Somebody, maybe more than one, opened up with automatic fire from a roof and got two people in the street, one killed. Just missed a couple of cops. Before they located the source it started again on the next block, they missed a prowl car but they hit three more people. When I left the office they had the area cordoned off and they were still trying to track him, or them." Lloyd saw the sardonic grin in the shadow. "I'm a Cincinnati boy, Garner, don't know the Harlem terrain. I figured with your knowledge of the sector we'd have a better grasp of the story, right? I mean now you're a reporter and all. I heard your speech tonight, what was that, some kind of a grandstand play?"

"I meant it."

"Yeah. You trying to jack up your pay or something like that?"

"I meant it."

He was shaking his head disbelievingly. "Anyway, you sure stirred them up. Milhouse says Hacklin's going out of his head. Lot of telegrams and phones coming in. But then there would be."

He let it go. The curving roadway was ghostly in this light, the driver had his wipers going against patches of fog. Off to their right the opaque line of apartment houses reared unbroken into the darker sky, then the silhouetted masses of the art museum as the road curved away again. Lloyd loosened his collar and Bill Moran said, "Warm, huh? I like it. Reminds me of Vietnam. I'm going back next week." He peered at him. "Any messages?"

A dank smell rose from the lake below. They were rounding a hill and coming out of the park at 110th. Moran said to the driver, "Keep on north till they stop you, it ought to be soon."

It was. Up ahead they could already see the red flashing lights on police cars filling the avenue and restless figures crossing and recrossing among them. A siren sounded suddenly behind the cab, Lloyd jerked around to see another patrol car sweep past, the sidewalks were alive with people hurrying toward the action, buzzing with talk and sharp, excited cries. Four blocks farther on the taxi pulled up abruptly, a cop was waving them into a side street.

"All right, we get out here," Moran said and gave a bill to the driver.

"Take it easy, Lloyd," the driver said, "and tell us all about it tonight."

"Don't you want his autograph?" Bill Moran said, almost snarling.

They had joined the crowd in the street that shuffled toward the floodlighted roadblock, Moran two steps ahead of him. Tension hung above the neighborhood like a cloud, it was hotter, the electric air was heavy with the odors of Harlem. The curb was lined solid with police emergency trucks, ambulances, fire equipment, then the crowd thinned, a line of police stood facing them. "You got a card or something?" Moran said, looking back.

It wasn't necessary, a lieutenant standing with the sergeant in front of the patrolmen looked at them and said, "Lloyd Garner."

"The great man himself," Moran said. "You spot your cowboys yet?"

The lieutenant shook his head. "All quiet right now."

"Any more victims?"

"Not so far."

Behind them the black, silent faces watched and listened. "This is Bill Moran," Lloyd said, "the best man we had in Vietnam."

"Where's the cameras, Lloyd?" the lieutenant said.

"Come on," Moran said to Lloyd, "are we going in there or not?"

"Where is it?" Lloyd said to the lieutenant, who waved an arm toward the side street just beyond.

"I wouldn't go down there if I was you," the sergeant said.

"Let them through," said the lieutenant.

Lloyd felt his belly tighten, his mouth was dry. He nodded. Moran led the way. All at once they were in the open, alone, exposed. The crowd noise behind them seemed to subside and draw far off. Two police cars stood at the entrance to the block, one at each curb, there were police under cover in the doorways of tenements both sides of the street but no one moved, they were waiting. A cop standing beside the nearest car motioned them back. "Press!" Bill Moran called to him, loudly, calmly. He stopped in the middle of the street and looked up at the dark shabby buildings, not a face at any window. Lloyd followed his stare to the roof and saw the faint blue haze of beginning dawn.

But dark still held the pitiless street around them, he felt a shiver go through him. He had thought it would all be easy but this was hard, this was bad. "Maybe we can draw their fire and get it over with," Moran was saying, to nobody, to himself, and Lloyd looked at his back in a kind of amazement. They were moving again, near the right-hand curb, Moran ahead of him with a slow, steady step, surveying the buildings as he went. Lloyd followed fatally on. The street was quiet with an eerie stillness, an hour ago Lloyd Garner had been safe and triumphant with everything he loved, secure at last, now he was walking with a madman asking for death. Panic stabbed him and sweat broke out all over his body, he was losing control. *What am I doing here?* he gasped in his mind, *How did I get here?* or was it nightmare with Lee beside him and he would wake to her arms and the world he knew? His hands were trembling, he fought to hold them stiff at his sides. Two more police cars stood impossibly distant at the other end of the block, and each step he took seemed longer and farther apart, the longest walk of his life. Suddenly he heard his own voice like a stranger's, echoing hollow off the house fronts, "Moran, for Christ's sake, how long are we going to keep this up?" And the war correspondent, cool, mocking, "You worried about something? Okay, take off." He didn't even turn his head, it was all he wanted, it was why they had come.

The sound shattered air at the next instant, a spitting, cracking sound, flat and horrible, Lloyd froze and stopped, hearing shouts and the splintering of glass somewhere near. All at once the street lit up like a movie set, the searchlights blazed and swept upward, crisscrossing the buildings. He could see the white faces of men in helmets crouched with their rifles in the doorways, aiming. The bursts began again, the answering fire crashed. *"Get down, get down!"* somebody was shouting, shouting at the two men in the street, shouting at Lloyd Garner and Bill Moran. But Moran just stood there, his head high, looking up at the roof across the street, and it was Lloyd who turned violently to plunge for safety. It was all he knew before he knew nothing.

V: HERO'S TRIBUTE

27

In accordance with the widow's wish, funeral services for Lloyd Garner were held in a Catholic church, and on advice of Walter Hacklin the services took place in New York, at St. Vincent Ferrer's, three days after his death. The network underwrote all expenses and Hacklin was in personal charge of statements to the press, in which there was no mention of the fact that Mrs. Garner had recently sued for divorce and was actually in residence in Nevada when her husband was killed. The *Daily News*, however, disclosed that angle of the story and some out-of-town papers picked it up from the press associations. The mourners who filled the church, in addition to friends and colleagues, included devoted viewers who had never met Lloyd Garner and the usual gathering of persons who attend such ceremonies simply to observe the celebrities present.

They were not disappointed. Paying due homage to a fellow broadcaster who died in the pursuit of his professional duty were the stars of the big news programs on the other networks, and among the pallbearers, who included Lloyd Garner's brother, Philip, of Boston, was his immediate and presumably permanent successor as anchorman, Jack Milhouse. Representatives of network sponsors were at the services, notably T. Shelby Hollis, a personal friend of the deceased, who flew from California to attend. Hacklin told reporters that Bill Moran, who witnessed the tragedy in Harlem just before the mad sniper was shot to death by police, was too upset to serve as a pallbearer and had asked for immediate reassignment to Vietnam. An unexpected mourner was the network's top executive and biggest stockholder, known in the industry as the Father of Television, who rarely appeared at public occasions of any kind. He slipped into a back pew after the service began and left before it ended, thus going unrecognized by the most of the people in the church.

The eulogy, delivered by Kent Ward, the network's distinguished Washington correspondent, was widely quoted for its moving tribute to his late colleague's bravery in carrying out a perilous assignment beyond the normal scope of his daily work. Among condolences culled by Hacklin and read by Ward, from the White House press office, journalistic societies and other organizations, was one from Hedley Johns, Lloyd Garner's predecessor at the network, calling his selfless action a high example to the new generation of American television reporters. Quoting from Lloyd Garner's surprise announcement in his last broadcast, Ward concluded the eulogy with disclosure that the network would establish an annual Lloyd Garner Memorial Award for outstanding TV reporting in the face of physical danger.

Heavily veiled but erect and calm, Mrs. Garner followed the coffin out of the church escorted by Harvey Lewin, described in the network statement as a lifelong friend of the late broadcaster. The executor of the estate, Sime Sussman, also prayed with the family during the service. A crowd of several hundred persons stood in the street outside, some of them asking others whose funeral it was. In the limousine directly behind the flower-banked hearse Mrs. Garner was joined by her close friend, Grace Cassidy, and by Philip Garner. At the express desire of the widow these were the only persons accompanying her to the graveside, a Catholic cemetery outside Boston, where former colleagues of the deceased in that city would attend the brief ceremony of interment.

As Walter Hacklin, with Milo Wilson and their wives, was leaving the church, Jay Weiss put his notebook in his pocket and drew the vice-president of News aside. "Did you know the big boss was here, Walter?"

"Where?" He looked quickly around.

"He was in the last pew, he left right after Kent finished talking."

"Alone?"

"Yeah. He must have walked. I followed him out, you know, discreetly, but he had no car waiting."

Walter Hacklin had a car waiting, the Wilsons were spending the weekend in Greenwich with him. He nodded to the deputy inspector in charge of the special police detail assigned by the commissioner's office, the hearse would have a motorcycle escort to the Westchester line. It had been a relief to the commissioner when the ballistics tests showed conclusively that Lloyd Garner died instantly of fatal wounds from the sniper's weapon and not from police cross fire, even more of a relief that no Harlem riot had resulted as Bill Moran had anticipated, but it was embarrassing that the killer was still unidentified. Hacklin said as they drove off, "Jay Weiss just told me the big boss stopped in for Kent's eulogy, Milo."

"Isn't that something?"

"Lloyd always wanted to meet him."

"Yeah. You remember the day Carl Orbach brought that tape in from Boston and the big boss flipped over it? Hard to realize it was only a year ago."

"And what a year, Milo."

Joyce Hacklin said, "I'll never know why Lloyd was fool enough to go up there that night with Moran."

"He'd never have gone if I'd found him first."

"No use crying now," Milo Wilson said. "Milhouse will have to do."

"Jack's given us his assurance he won't get out of line on the new hour show, Milo. That should comfort your people."

Joyce Hacklin spoke again. "You knew he was your man when he did that ass-kissing special on Mayor Daley, right?"

Her husband said indulgently, "You just don't like Jack Milhouse."

"That's no secret," she said.

"Never mind, dear, Jack was made for the kind of show we want now."

"Wasn't that what you told me about Lloyd Garner?" she said, and when there was no answer she added, "Walter, tell the driver to find a bar, I want a drink."

"I'm for that," said Alice Wilson.

The church was empty but people still lingered outside in a post-funeral mood. Friends greeted friends and smiled at acquaintances, at least me and thee are still around. The mighty and the humble mingled socially this once, the talk was cheerful, the subject was changed. But there was some avoiding too. Mr. and Mrs. Weldon

Duff made sure to keep their distance from Mr. and Mrs. Lon Carey. Weldon didn't want Buck Schonwald to think they were still buddies after Lon's disgraceful retirement speech. Gaby Berman, Lloyd Garner's secretary, who had wept openly through the service, unexpectedly found Dobie Dobrinoff at her side as she left the church. They walked together toward the nearby subway station, Gaby recognizing T. Shelby Hollis in the crowd and noticing the extremely smart and extremely expensive clothes worn by his woman companion. "I suppose that's Mr. Hollis's wife," she said.

"Not his wife," Dobie Dobrinoff said, looking at Alix Weddern, "but I think she knew Lloyd."

"Didn't everyone," said Gaby Berman. "The flowers were beautiful."

The staff of the Lloyd Garner news program, headed by Earl Greminger and Harry Ferguson, had attended the service in a body and now went back to the office together. They had a show to get out, but their new anchorman lingered on the sidewalk with Buck Schonwald. "How's chances of replacing him on 'Sea Probe'?" he was saying, and the producer said, "I haven't talked to them." He looked at his broadcaster. "He hasn't even been buried yet."

"One other thing, Buck, while we have a moment, am I going to get Jay Weiss for my personal use?"

"Do you want him?"

"Not unless I get to check his releases before they go out."

"I can't see any objection to that."

"I'm changing agents, Buck, I called Sime Sussman."

"Milhouse, you're a damn fool if you do."

He laughed. "Now I *know* I want Sussman."

Moving down Lexington they passed Matt and Claudine Ferlin. They were waiting for a taxi but Ferlin was looking back at the crowd in front of the church. His wife noticed. "Who is it now?" she said. "Your eyes are falling out from your head."

"Well, how do you like that?" he said to himself aloud. He had seen Rita Valenti with Bev Hambleton.

"How do I like what?" Claudine Ferlin said.

"Nothing." Rita seemed slimmer but the wonderful chest was still there. Bev Hambleton stood gravely and stiffly beside her, very tall and tanned and out of reach, and Matt Ferlin turned abruptly away.

"Lloyd Garner had many friends," his wife said.

"More than he let on, that's for sure."

Rita and Bev, after speaking briefly to people who spoke to them, walked uptown to get away from the crowd. "Nice of Kent Ward," he said. "Didn't like Lloyd, I believe."

"De mortuis," Rita said. "They all do it, when it's too late."

He smiled down at her. "You know I can't understand Italian."

She took his arm. "You're going to do a lot of things you think you can't do."

"If you say so," he said. They were silent until they came to a bar he knew called the Whiffenpoof and went in. "Kind of think it ought to be bourbon and soda, don't you?" he said. Then they sat there in silence again, one of her hands in his hand. "Tired?"

"Not a bit." She smiled. "But I know you are, you didn't sleep on the plane."

"Are we still flying back tonight or do you want to stay a few days?"

She shook her head. "Not unless you do."

"I thought seeing all your little pals might make you homesick for New York."

"I'm homesick for Piazza Farnese."

"So am I."

They had another bourbon and then another. The place was filling up for lunch. He had been drinking from his quart flask all night on the plane and she knew how drunk he was. She said, "What are you thinking about?"

"Him, aren't you?"

"He was sweet, Bev. He didn't know what time it was but he was sweet."

"No, he didn't want to know what time it was."

"Neither do you. I think that's why I love you both."

"You can't love him any more, Rita, he's dead."

"I can still love you, can't I?"

"I hope that never changes." He paid the bartender for the drinks. "You hungry?"

"If you are," she said.

"No. Think I ought to take a nap."

"So do I, but where?"

"My mother's place, she's in Newport." He had a little difficulty getting off the bar stool and outside in the street he said, "Think we better walk."

"Whatever you say," Rita Valenti said. She took his arm.

The two cars rolled swift and quiet through the Connecticut countryside, for a time they had been separated in traffic but now the limousine followed close on the hearse again. Grace Cassidy was saying, a paper cup full of whisky in her hand, "I just don't trust him, that's all. I think we ought to get a lawyer in Boston to check on him, Harvey'll know somebody."

Fran said, her veil pushed back and her shoes off, "You've heard of death taxes, right? For God's sake, Lloyd only had his job eleven months, Grace, you expect him to be a millionaire?" She held out her own cup and the other woman filled it again from the flat bottle lying between them on the seat.

"He's a smart New York Jew, Fran, he's bound to cheat some."

"He already told me the life insurance will be a very substantial item. That's what he said, a very substantial item, does that sound dishonest? I like Sime Sussman, I liked him the minute I talked to him. He's an honest man, don't you agree, Phil?"

The man sitting next to her, his eyes on the hearse ahead, said "I just can't believe he's gone, Fran. I mean we all accept death, yes, but when it happens to somebody close, like Lloyd, like my mother, you just can't adjust your mind that it's true. We could arrive in Boston and he'd be waiting for us when we get out of this car and I wouldn't be surprised at all."

"Oh shut up," Grace Cassidy said to him, "you've been going on like that for two days. Fran and me are talking business. It's the estate. It's something important to your sister-in-law."

He continued to stare at the hearse. "Lloyd did the right thing about Fran, you can be sure of that."

"We're not talking about Lloyd, we're talking about Sime Sussman. All I'm saying is there's always a lot of legal angles. We ought to get one to check on the other, it takes one to catch one, that's all I'm saying."

"All right, *all right*," Fran said, her hand shook holding the paper cup. "Leave him alone, Grace, can't you see he feels bad?"

"I feel real bad," Phil Garner said. Tears streaked his face. "Every time I think of him lying in there like helpless, shut away, shut away forever."

"He doesn't feel anything," Grace Cassidy said, "he doesn't know anything."

"Of course he knows," Fran said and began to cry. "He knows and he's watching us and listening to us right now."

Her brother-in-law awkwardly put his arm around her shoulders for a moment. "Cry if you want to, Fran, it's good to grieve, you'll feel better if you cry."

Grace took her hand. "He didn't suffer, Fran, they told you that. He never knew what hit him. We all have to go, sooner or later, think of it that way. It's God's will, we all have our time to go." She leaned and spoke more softly. "It'll all be over with soon, then I'll take you home to a nice hot bath and a massage, how's that sound? We just have to go through with these last few hours and it's all over with. You've been so brave, she's been so brave, hasn't she, Phil?"

He didn't answer and Grace Cassidy went on, "I want to warn you one thing, Phil, your father's going to show up again and try to get some of the money. I don't know why we didn't hear from him yet, he must know about Lloyd by now, the whole country knows. Maybe he's laying around drunk somewhere."

"My father doesn't drink," Phil Garner said.

"You just better take care he doesn't try anything. He's a leech, he'll try to get every cent out of us he can." She picked up the bottle again and refilled her cup. "Shall I give the driver one?"

Phil said, "No. And don't give Fran any more, Grace. You been drinking too much yourself too."

"I only said should I give the driver a drink. After all, it's a wake, isn't it?" She drew Fran's head down on her shoulder and both women settled more comfortably, leaning away from Phil. "Be quiet now," Grace said, "our girl's going to sleep a little."

Houghton served them daiquiris, the curtains drawn against the afternoon sun, the chairs and couches in the big room somber in their summer shrouds. "Wouldn't it have been less trouble to have lunch out somewhere?" Tommy Hollis said.

Her little laugh had a sharp edge of irritation, as if she suspected him of avoiding intimacy with her. "I'd prefer it here. Today. Besides, is anything open? Ordinarily I wouldn't even be in town at this time of year." Alix lit a cigarette and looked at him. "I thought Gillian might come East with you."

"Gillian wouldn't be separated from her golf."

She nodded. "All those people in that church this morning. It made me realize how many kinds he knew. Of course he had to know them, just as you do. You all try to sell things to each other, don't you? I never did see Fran Garner's face."

"She's a well-built woman, I thought."

"Tacky."

"Didn't I see Bev Hambleton?"

She stared. "How very odd, I missed him. In fact I haven't seen him since he gave up that job of his. His mother doesn't know where he is either."

"He was with a very handsome girl in black."

"A friend of Lloyd's, no doubt." Her eyes were brilliant with pride and hurt. "When we, when I was seeing him he must have had all sorts of things going he never told me a word about." She thought she saw him smile very faintly. "You find that situation amusing? Yes, I guess you would. I don't know what it was about Lloyd Garner, he was the most *elusive* man I've ever known."

"Maybe that's why you liked him."

"It wasn't so simple, I'm afraid. One day it seemed we were as intimate as two humans can be, the next he'd forgotten me. What is that, immaturity? It's immaturity."

"Perhaps he just wasn't used to his new life yet. Too much too soon. But I'm sure he treasured you, Alix, as long as he lived."

"Tommy, how touching of you." She leaned to brush his cheek with her lips and motioned to the big silver pitcher on the coffee table in front of them. "Pour us some more of that, will you?" She went on afterward, "Just how many girls of his did you count this morning?"

He laughed. "Please. I know nothing about the boy. Did he have that reputation?"

"You were going to say there was only one girl who mattered to him, weren't you?"

"I wasn't going to say anything. I haven't seen Lloyd Garner since the one time I met him in Georgia, with you."

"I don't believe you. She was there in that church," Alix Weddern said in a low voice, "she must have been."

"I'm sorry, I don't know who you're talking about."

"I mean the girl he gave me up for. Your television friends must have given you the gossip."

"Alix, I don't think he gave you up for anybody, I thought you gave *him* up."

"Is that what he said?" She looked at him, tormented with vexation. "Perhaps he did say that. He lied to everybody."

"Don't we all," Tommy Hollis said and shrugged.

"I certainly hope you lied to him about you and me."

"Alix, you're ridiculous. I never saw him after Quince Barony." He paused and went on, "I'll say this much, in some ways the network was glad this happened."

"What do you mean?"

"He was becoming too outspoken. They couldn't count on him."

She snuffed out her cigarette and stood up abruptly, going to the window. "I don't want to talk about him any more," she said.

They finished the pitcher of daiquiris and went to the dining room for chilled mussel soup and lobster and a bottle of Piesporter. They were both a little tight by the time they went to her own rooms, each carrying a snifter of brandy, and shut away the rest of the apartment. He looked around him and Alix said, "What are you thinking about?"

"Haven't you done it over?"

"You should have seen what I had planned for Lloyd and me," she said. "I had it all worked out." Suddenly she put her head against his shoulder and he put his arm around her and kissed her, feeling her tears on his face.

"I missed you very much this time," he said.

"Tommy, after all these years?"

"I was so relieved when Gillian decided not to come, it would have been difficult."

"Don't you have to run off somewhere now? I can see you tonight."

"No." He kissed her mouth and felt her arms go around him. "Are you in the mood?"

"I'm always in the mood with you, Tommy."

"You liked the last time?"

"It was desperately exciting, you know that."

"Shall we do it again?"

"I'd adore it, you know I would."

"I want some brandy first."

"So do I."

He raised his glass. "Well, to Lloyd Garner," he said.

She was crying unrestrainedly and holding him very close. "He could have had everything," she said.

The phone was ringing in Lee Maxton's apartment. She was sitting in the big chair facing the blank gray television screen and she didn't get up to answer it. She had used the phone just twice since she came back to Murray Hill from Lloyd Garner's apartment, once to tell her office she was ill and would not be in until Monday, the other time to tell the man who called that she didn't want to see him or anybody. Also, she had used the phone in Lloyd Garner's apartment just once, to call his office Tuesday morning at half-past nine, when she woke up and found he had not returned. Between that time and the present, Friday afternoon, she had not gone out, she had eaten virtually nothing, and she had slept hardly at all, but the morning and afternoon papers had been delivered as usual each day and she had spent her time either reading the newspapers or sitting in the big chair reading nothing. In the newspapers she read that Lloyd Garner had become a hero, and was informed that the funeral service was to be held today, but she knew, she had known since she talked to Lloyd Garner's office Tuesday morning, that if she went to the church she could not control her grief or face his friends. When she was not reading the newspapers she stared at the silent TV set and tried to remember over and over everything she had thought and done since she first met Lloyd Garner, beginning with the night on the plane to Paris and ending with the night, three days ago, when the phone rang in his apartment and he woke to answer Bill Moran.

Now the phone was ringing again, as it had several times a day since the call she answered Tuesday afternoon, but it no longer terrified her. Now it only sounded patient, methodical, humble, and persistent, like the man who was trying to talk to her again, and she wouldn't answer it. A letter had arrived from him yesterday morning and a telegram an hour ago, and she hadn't opened them. By tonight, despite what she had told him, she knew he would be outside in the hall, and she would sit in the chair listening to him talk to her from the other side of the door. She knew what he was going to say, she had always known what he was going to say before he said it. She also knew that eventually she would let him in, and eventually life would resume as it used to be, long ago. The funeral service was over, what remained of Lloyd Garner was now on the way to burial in Boston. The late edition of the *Post* would have the details, and soon afterward she could watch it on television, it would be on all the stations.